THE GREAT UNKNOWN

THE GREAT UNKNOWN

PEG KINGMAN

W. W. NORTON & COMPANY
Independent Publishers Since 1923

For information about permission to reproduce selections from this book, write to
Permissions, W. W. Norton & Company, Inc., 500 Fifth Avenue, New York, NY 10110

For information about special discounts for bulk purchases, please contact
W. W. Norton Special Sales at specialsales@wwnorton.com or 800-233-4830

Manufacturing by Lake Book
Book design by Brooke Koven
Production manager: Anna Oler

Library of Congress Cataloging-in-Publication Data

Names: Kingman, Peg, author.
Title: The great unknown / Peg Kingman.
Description: First edition. | New York : W. W. Norton & Company, [2020]
Identifiers: LCCN 2019027189 |
ISBN 9781324003366 (hardcover) | ISBN 9781324003373 (epub)
Classification: LCC PS3611.I62 G74 2020 | DDC 813/.6—dc23
LC record available at https://lccn.loc.gov/2019027189

W. W. Norton & Company, Inc., 500 Fifth Avenue, New York, N.Y. 10110
www.wwnorton.com

W. W. Norton & Company Ltd., 15 Carlisle Street, London W1D 3BS

1 2 3 4 5 6 7 8 9 0

THE GREAT UNKNOWN

Prologue

S TEVENSON PAUSED for a moment to catch his breath and ease his pounding heart, for these immense iron hoisting tongs were unwieldy, and very heavy. He was working by moonlight beside a gryke—a chasm in the limestone—at the north end of a little offshore island: Coquet Isle. The light dimmed suddenly, briefly, as clouds blew across the moon's face; then brightened again. The nearest man-made lights were at the southern tip of Coquet Isle, atop the lighthouse; and the next-nearest lights after that were in the town three-quarters of a mile to the west. Amble, on the Northumberland shore. As he desired above all to avoid the notice of the townspeople, he worked by moonlight.

He was sweat-drenched, despite the hard wind that came scouring across five hundred miles of North Sea. Why must everything worth doing be so exceedingly difficult and slow? He had hauled these hoisting tongs, hinged like colossal scissors, all the way from Paris; likewise, his winch, chains, cables, blocks, tackles. He had hauled even this mast and beam from France, lashed to the deck of a lugger out of Rouen. He had brought all these not because they couldn't be had here, along this English coast—for they could; but they couldn't be had here secretly, privately, and without attracting notice.

Having chosen a convenient stone ledge well down inside the gryke, so that nothing should be silhouetted against the sky, he resumed his task. The setting-up of a crane was so familiar to him that he could do it alone, in silence, at night.

1

T HE NEW WET NURSE'S uncovered breast was mottled blue
and red under taut translucent skin; the nipple was small,
neat, and pink. It was a satisfactory breast; a serviceable nipple.
Seated on a low chair under the library window, this young mother
endured the scrutiny of three women and a man, the doctor. Of the
two babies, one slept, sated; but the other was furiously hungry.

"Uncover both, if you please, Mrs MacAdam," said the doctor
loudly to the wet nurse; loudly enough to be heard above the angry
baby boy squalling in the arms of Hopey, the nursery maid. Constantia MacAdam opened her bodice to uncover both breasts. Dr Moir
had already conducted his examination; already reported to Mrs
Chambers that there were no symptoms of syphilis or consumption;
no sign in this young mother or her surviving baby of any dependence
upon laudanum; no medical reason why Mrs MacAdam should not
be able to nurse Mrs Chambers's baby as well as her own. She claimed
to have had plenty of milk for two, during the five weeks that both
her twins had lived. He had watched her feed her surviving baby
girl—now asleep in the arms of their friend Mrs MacDonald. It was
evidently thriving, and the same age as Mrs Chambers's hungry baby
boy. The misfortune of the twin's death several days ago was due not

to any communicable disease, nor to maternal malfeasance; but only to the Divine Will, inscrutable and mysterious (in the form, Dr Moir guessed privately, of a congenital kidney disorder).

Though Hopey rocked and joggled and crooned to Mrs Chambers's hungry baby, he would not be quiet. At a nod from the doctor, she transferred him, crimson-faced and raging, to Mrs MacAdam's arms.

Mrs MacAdam handled this precious infant well: hands slow, quiet, firm. Clean, too. She took him into the crook of her right arm; fitted him across her body, his belly to her own. With her left hand she lifted her right breast to his mouth. For a moment he quieted, and eagerly nuzzled, grazing the nipple with his lips—but then craned away. His face crumpled. As he opened his mouth, drawing breath to squawk, Mrs MacAdam deftly filled his open mouth with her nipple, pressing against his toothless gums. His eyes flew open, and for a moment he seemed about to close and suck—but then he twisted away once more, arching backward in her arms; furiously rejecting this unfamiliar nipple, this wrong-smelling breast. In his rage, he pulled one arm free of his wrappings to thrash the air.

Mrs MacAdam set thumb and forefinger on either side of her nipple and pressed; her milk came, greyish and watery. She caught a droplet on her smallest fingertip and dabbled it onto his lips. Then again. His lips parted; his tiny tongue curled. Once more she offered milk on her fingertip, and this time he sucked it. Swiftly she put him to the nipple once more. He closed upon it; drew upon it; sucked. They all could hear him.

In less than a minute, her milk let down. He coughed once, as the milk came too fast to swallow, then greedily resumed; and three fine sprays of milk arched from her other nipple, the one he was not suckling; soaked her linen.

"Plenty of milk for two," Dr Moir was saying. Mrs Chambers was smiling. Hopey was smiling. Mrs MacDonald was smiling.

But Constantia MacAdam did not smile. She was transfixed by the sight of the baby's tiny splayed hand, clamped now like a small rosy starfish against her breast: a thumb and five perfect fingers. Not four; five.

The commodious old house was called Spring Gardens. It lay in spacious private grounds outside Edinburgh between Newhailes and Musselburgh, just above the harbour and the cottages of Fisherrow, to the west of the River Esk. Here, the Robert Chambers family had spent the summer of 1845 as tenants, while their house in Doune Terrace in Edinburgh was undergoing repairs. Now, in September, though summer was past, the Doune Terrace repairs were not yet complete—and here at Spring Gardens, therefore, the family still remained.

Besides the two infants—Charles Edward Chambers and Livia MacAdam—eight other children were living in the house. The eldest, at fifteen, was Nina. Next was Mary; then Annie, named for her mother, and the twins Jenny and Lizzy, both nine and very pretty, but vacuous. Grave little Tuckie was seven; then came the two little boys, both still in frocks: James, called Jemmie, aged four; and two-year-old William, called Willie—much distressed at his recent ouster, upon the birth of Charlie, from the privileged position of Baby. There seemed to be others, too, somewhere—for where were the Janet, Eliza, and Amelia sometimes mentioned? It was some days before Constantia MacAdam understood that these were only the formal names of Jenny, Lizzy, and Tuckie. Polly, it emerged, was a recently-outgrown nickname of Mary's, sometimes still used by mistake, or to annoy. There seemed to be a Rob or Robbie, too, heard of but never seen; he, however, turned out to be a thirteen-year-old schoolboy, his father's namesake, who had already returned to his school for the Michaelmas term.

For the girls, the summer had been a long holiday from lessons. Their adored governess, Mam'selle, had gone to France to visit her ailing mother and was not expected to return before October. Until then, Hopey, the nursery maid, presided alone over most of the rooms on the top floor of the house: day nursery, night nursery, big girls' rooms, and little girls' room. Hopey had been with the Chambers family ever since coming as wet nurse to Lizzy and Jenny, nine years before. If she wished, she might have had another nursery maid under her for the summer, to help look after all these children: to bathe them, dress and undress them; induce them to eat their meals and get into and out of their beds at the proper times; take them out to run across the sands and play at the shore; teach them to say "if you please, ma'am" and "thank you, sir," and the game of checkers; and to adjudicate their near-constant quarrels, grudges, squabbles, contests, disputes, jealousies, and bickerings. But serene Hopey preferred to manage by herself, until Mam'selle should return. An untrained homesick young nursery maid, said Hopey, would be muckle bother and small use; and hadn't the house lasses enough in it already?

It was Hopey who had surprised the first wet nurse in the very act of administering Godfrey's Cordial to the five-week-old baby Charlie. Instantly that wet nurse had been sacked—but how, then, was the baby to be fed? Both cow's milk and mare's milk were tried; both sickened him. Mrs Chambers had sent express to every domestic agency in or near Edinburgh, to no avail. Were there no young mothers with milk to spare in all the Lothians? Well, of course there were; but if said young mother must also be of decent character and good repute; and unhabituated to gin or laudanum; and in robust health without venereal or consumptive taint; and willing to come upon the instant to live in the Chambers household; and not already engaged to suckle some other woman's baby? Mrs Chambers's unreasonable stipulations narrowed the field to . . . none. It so happened that not even one such young matron could be found just then, at the critical moment of need.

Mrs Chambers attempted, belatedly, to establish her own milk, but at five weeks after her confinement, it was far too late for that. All her friends told her it would be so.

But one of these friends—Mrs MacDonald—had another friend staying with her just then, in Edinburgh: a young married woman called Mrs MacAdam. She was a family connection of some years' standing, whose husband was necessarily at some distance just at present; and, for obscure reasons (obscure to Mrs Chambers, at least), this young wife had deemed it best to come to the MacDonalds in Edinburgh for her first lying-in. It was just as well that she had, for there she had been brought to bed of twins, a boy and a girl. Though Mrs MacAdam's infant girl thrived, her boy languished; and at thirty-four days of age (on the same day, as it happened, that Mrs Chambers was obliged to sack that first wicked wet nurse) he died, having never pissed in all his brief life.

"Charlie is our darling, our darling, our darling! Charlie is our darling, our young Chevalier!" Lizzy and Jenny would sing several times each day as they romped along the upstairs corridor, to honour their newest baby brother. Indeed, all the children sang old Jacobite songs: "Will ye No Come Back Again," or "Johnny Cope," or "Awa' Whigs Awa'," at the top of their lungs. They were a musical family, and they were practicing for a gala occasion: a party to be given by their mother a few weeks hence.

The general feeling among all these children was amicable enough, but with plenty of the warmth of friction; that warmth amounting, from time to time, to actual heatedness; followed by a natural cooling. Their alliances constantly shifted and then reformed, like the polities of Europe—except for the twins, who were always to be found ranged upon the same side, in any contest or debate.

In this houseful of merry children, Constantia MacAdam had to herself a small room with a bed, a carpet, a chair, a writing table, and a window. It was separated from the day nursery only by a thin wall of boards, so that at any time she might hear voices through the partition. What a talkative, playful, mirthful clan they were! They reminded Constantia of nothing so much as a litter of tumbling puppies, one scarcely distinguishable from the next—except for Nina, eldest; Tuckie, gravest; the twins, twins; and the little boys, unmistakably boyish, despite their frocks.

Constantia's room smelled of milk, both sweet and curdled; and sleep, and babies. Day and night, at intervals of an hour, or two—rarely as long as three hours—Hopey would bring her an infant to be suckled, either Livia or Charlie. The babies were brought in raging with hunger; but when they were taken away again, twenty minutes later, they were soft and sweet with milk.

Constantia felt the family enfold her, not as servant, but as cherished friend and guest. Whether en famille or in company, Mrs Chambers always welcomed her in drawing room or dining room; but so irregular were the babies' appetites, and so profoundly fatigued was Constantia that Mrs Chambers urged her to order her meals brought up to her room whenever she liked. The food was good, plain, abundant and nourishing: mutton or beef, squab or chicken, mussel stew or fish, porridge, eggs, custards, bread and butter. There was generally ale or stout too, for the sake of her milk. She had plenty of everything, except sleep.

Constantia could not stray far from her room and the hungry babies, but each morning and again each afternoon she would take a turn in the garden below the house, whether it rained or shone. This being Scotland, and September, it often rained. She would walk down to the dovecote—the "doocot," the Scots called it—at the bottom of the garden, where the pigeons, looked after by the gardener, strutted and cooed, and bred as they pleased, and enjoyed the freedom of the sky. Her own pigeon was housed here, too, in a small pen to itself; the sole pigeon which still remained to her of the four she had brought with her from the place where she had been before. It could not be allowed to fly free, lest it fly away home immediately.

Just beyond the garden wall to northward she could smell the whitecapped Firth of Forth, and sometimes hear the waves. From the attic windows, the beautiful busy water could be seen, between trees. And on clear days, the far shore: Fife.

It was an existence as placid, as dull, as a cow's. Her suffering was muffled here, too, as though swaddled in layers of flannel. How curious.

But her room was just above Mr and Mrs Chambers's rooms, it seemed. It was not a well-built house, and sometimes she could not help but hear them, in what should have been their private moments. That was deeply disturbing; it raised the nap of her suffering again.

The baby Charlie had not only an extra finger on each hand, but also an extra toe on each foot. All these supernumerary digits were well-formed and, unless one counted, this unusual abundance, this superfluity, this redundancy, this exuberance of digits might go unnoticed.

Constantia thought she could discern a puckered reddened place on the plump outside edge of four-year old Jemmie's right hand, just where an extra finger might have been removed by a surgeon. But there was no such mark on his left hand, nor on Willie's hands, nor on the hands of any of the girls.

"I told her this morning that you were expected, and she promised to come down, if she can. And if she cannot—why, we will go up to her instead," said Mrs Chambers to her friend Mary MacDonald, as they passed from the gusty garden into the bright still orangerie which opened off the drawing room. "Ah! Here is our tea laid ready for us. Is there a more agreeable sight, on a blustery afternoon? I feared that my bonnet had been turned quite inside-out," she added, untying it and laying it aside undamaged. "Poor Mrs MacAdam! Hopey does what she can to spare her, but I know she gets scant sleep. My young Chevalier does very well with her, and has already gained back the flesh he had lost, and more—though he remains somewhat fractious still. It is the lingering effect of the laudanum he had from that wicked nurse, Dr Moir says; but that, he assures me, should go off quite soon."

"You will forgive my saying, once more," called a woman's voice promptly, from the adjoining drawing room, "that entirely too much fuss has been made about laudanum."

To her friend Mrs MacDonald, Mrs Chambers raised one eyebrow very decidedly—while she called out, "Oh, Lady Janet! Are you there? I did not know. Will you come and drink a cup of tea with Mrs MacDonald and me?"

Lady Janet, a guest who had been staying with the Chambers family for quite long enough, now appeared in the doorway. "You know that I speak plainly, Mrs Chambers," said she, an elderly woman whose cap was of a pattern which had not been seen for ten years. The cairngorm brooch which fastened her pelerine was, though large, of regrettable shape and colour. "I have used Godfrey's Cordial myself, from time to time," she said, "and it has never done me anything but good. Anyone of good character—of a strongly-formed and well-regulated character—may take it without danger. I must say again, Mrs Chambers—it is no pleasure to me to say it, but it is my duty—that you ought not to have sacked that first nurse. You were wrong to act in such haste. I make it a principle, you know, to speak plainly: your family was certainly better off with that modest and sensible nurse in the house than this mysterious hussy, with her French clothes, and the face and figure of—of an actress! A French actress! Or worse!"

Said Mrs Chambers, "Your ladyship knows more than I of physiognomy, it would seem; for I had supposed that a person's distinguishing qualities are evidenced by her conduct—not by her face, figure, or dress. I am quite prepared to admit that I have been wrong. No one could pretend that Mrs MacAdam is not exceedingly lovely: the soft speaking eyes! the golden hair! the sweet dimple to her chin! But if these are the infallible signs of base propensities, I can only plead that I have never heard it before."

"Oh, but to go by a false name!" said Lady Janet. "If it is by conduct that we are to judge—why, there, surely, is indefensible conduct.

To style herself 'Mrs MacAdam'! Has she never yet told you her husband's true name?"

"No, my lady; and I shan't press her," said Mrs Chambers, serenely, as she poured out the tea. "This, it seems, must be one of those matters on which we think differently, you and I. You remember my friend Mrs MacDonald?—by whose kind agency Mrs MacAdam came to us, in our time of need."

"I trust I see you well, Mrs MacDonald," said Lady Janet, "and I hope that you do not suffer as I do from these September gales. I do not suppose that you have knowingly brought any wicked person to lodge in our midst; but can you feel quite certain that this 'Mrs MacAdam' is in truth an honest married woman?"

"She is as honest a married woman as I am," declared Mrs MacDonald stoutly.

"You will have seen that she wears a ring," said Mrs Chambers, with a glance at her own wedding ring. Her fingers were ink-smudged, for she had spent the morning as usual at her writing table in the library.

"Anyone may be clever enough to provide herself with a ring," said Lady Janet. "But to go by a false name!"

"Perhaps we might agree to refer to it as an assumed name, a pseudonym," said Mrs Chambers, "which, I fancy, has a more respectable sound. She makes it no secret that MacAdam is a name assumed out of discretion, for her husband's sake—a discretion which is required of her for reasons which she is not at liberty to divulge."

"A complete stranger, of whom nothing is known!"

"But she is by no means a stranger, Lady Janet," said Mrs MacDonald. "I have known her for years. She was Miss Constantia Babcock when I first met her four or five years ago, a well-brought-up girl of eighteen or so. My husband knew her mother and father aboard ship, oh! years ago, when they all sailed out to India together. And my niece vouches for her, too, for they were little girls together in India. I have met her stepmother as well—oh, aye! the Rani who brought her up in the Indies, after her parents both had died. A remarkable personage, and a sterner and more virtuous matron never lived."

"But to conceal her name!" said Lady Janet.

"Although we are not at present to know her husband's true name," said Mrs MacDonald patiently, "there is not the slightest ground for suspecting folly or vice; I should never have dreamt of bringing her along to Mrs Chambers else."

"And folk may have perfectly innocent reasons for preserving a discreet anonymity," added Mrs Chambers. "No one can charge her with guile or deceit; only with a quite determined reticence on this particular subject, for which she may—indeed, must—have excellent reasons of her own. Now, my dears, if you like my gingerbread at all, you had better have it at once, before the children come in. They will be famished, for they have been upon the sands all the afternoon, with only a very large picnic hamper bursting with refreshments to sustain them. I fancy I hear them now."

This was by no means one of those tranquil households where children are seen and not heard. The children came in hungry, wind-blown, and red-nosed, bearing trophies of shell, rock, and seaweed to add to the collections already decorating the chimneypiece and the window sills. While the presence of children at downstairs tea was another of those matters on which Lady Janet disagreed with her hostess (and often found it her duty to say so), her conscience permitted her on this occasion to keep her own counsel.

Instantly the remaining gingerbread disappeared. The Chambers children were accompanied by friends, including one Emily DeQuincey, just Mary's age, who lived nearby and had come for the day to play. Emily was the youngest daughter of the notorious English Opium Eater. She was a well-behaved and musical child who, brought up by her respectable elder sisters and not her disreputable and impe-cunious father, was thought to be a suitable companion for Mary; she and her sisters were often at Spring Gardens. Fortunately, Lady Janet had no more to say at present on the subject of laudanum.

Nina, the eldest of the Chambers girls, came in at last. She had not been on the sands with the little children; instead she had remained upstairs by herself to draw and to read, in luxurious solitude and rare quiet. Even now she carried her book downstairs with her finger marking her place in it.

"Is not Mrs MacAdam coming down for tea?" someone asked.

"I keeked in, as I passed her door," said Nina, "and she has just got both babies fed—and to sleep, for a miracle. She'll be down in a moment." Presently, Constantia did come in, thirsty and too warm. Mrs MacDonald rose to kiss her, and Mrs Chambers gave her tea. To make room for her on the sofa, Nina retired to a chair under the window, where she resumed reading while the others chatted happily.

"What is your book, Miss Nina?" called Lady Janet, after some time.

"*Vestiges*," replied Nina reluctantly, looking up. "*Vestiges of the Natural History of Creation*."

"Good heaven!" said Lady Janet. "Something about that red binding aroused my suspicion. Does your mother know? Were you aware, Mrs Chambers, that Miss Nina has somehow got hold of that pernicious book, the *Vestiges*?"

"Pernicious!" said Mrs Chambers. "No, whatever that book may be, Lady Janet, I'm sure it is not pernicious."

"Pernicious, and sensational, and wicked. And blasphemous," said Lady Janet. "I am surprised—indeed, grieved—at your permitting the entry of such a book as that into this houseful of innocent children."

"Oh! I cannot tell what *good* mothers may permit, Lady Janet— but I for my part am confident that Nina may read it, if she likes, without coming to any positive harm."

"I beg your pardon," said Lady Janet, offended; and then, "You will, I hope, excuse my leaving you and the children to yourselves for a time. Others do not suffer as I do from noise." She gathered up her skirts and stalked out.

An embarrassed silence ensued. Then Tuckie said, "Mamma, how long is she staying with us?"

"She won't be at our Day o'Treason, will she?" said Lizzy.

"No, hinney, we shall have to manage without her that day," said Mrs Chambers, "for she has told me that she is engaged elsewhere."

"Day o'Treason!" cried Mrs MacDonald, delighted. "Is that what you are calling your party?" Mrs Chambers had invited all her lively and clever friends to a gala day: the centennial of Bonnie Prince Charlie's first and last great victory, the battle at Prestonpans of 1745. The actual anniversary was the 21st of September which, in this centennial year of 1845, fell unfortunately upon a Sunday. As it was impossible to celebrate such an event on the Sabbath, Mrs Chambers had determined instead upon Saturday the 20th as her day for celebration and memorial of that great Jacobite victory. The invitations had all been sent; and now the acceptances and regrets were flooding in, swelling each day's mail.

"I do so hope that the Princes are coming," said Jenny fervently. She was often a beneficiary of the sweets brought by her father's old friends, those handsome, clever, good-natured frauds, the Sobieski Stuarts—otherwise the Allen brothers—whenever they paid a visit. "Are they?"

"Alas, they cannot, though," said Mrs Chambers. "I had a note this morning from their 'equerry'—posted from London, where there is some important business afoot, a very deep secret. It is a relief in some respects; a release from the grave responsibility of furnishing an adequate pomp for their Middling-Highnesses. But we shan't have the benefit of their piper, more's the pity. I shall have to hunt up another for the occasion—and time is getting short."

"Oh, but I can bring you a piper," said Mrs MacDonald. "His name is Dr John Sing—but there! I am forgetting that Mrs Mac-Adam knows him very well—don't you, my dear?"

"From childhood we have been as—as cousins, I suppose, if not quite brother and sister," said Constantia.

"He has just taken his medical degree at Glasgow," explained Mrs MacDonald to Mrs Chambers, "and is now preparing to return to the wilds of Assam, where he was born, to commence his practice among the people there. And, though you might not expect it to look at him—for he is quite as black as that celebrated Mr Frederick Douglass, from America—he is as accomplished a piper as he is anatomist; or so I am told by my husband, who is well qualified to pronounce. Pronounce as to his piping, I mean; not his anatomising."

"I shall be very happy," said Mrs Chambers, "to receive an accomplished piper-anatomist at my gala day—of any colour whatever. How fortunate I am in my friends, whose circle of acquaintance always seems to include precisely those talents I want! First, milk; and now, pipe music!"

What was that book in which Nina's finger kept her place? That book in its modest red cloth binding; that *Vestiges of the Natural History of Creation*? Brought out by a London medical publisher the previous December, it had by now, nine months later, sold out four large editions: the publishing sensation of the decade. Though ignored by the scientific press, it had been reviewed by all of the popular periodicals at great length and in minute detail. It had been reviled from countless pulpits. It had been passed from hand to eager hand. Readers stayed up all night to devour it. Never had there been such a book as this. It placed before the common reader all the latest knowledge in the fields of astronomy, geology, archaeology, physiology, language, biology, and probability. It claimed to be, and was, "the first attempt to connect the natural sciences into a history of creation." It asserted (perfunctory nod to a Divine Creator notwithstanding) that everything—all "creation"—from immense universe to microscopic animalcule—had come into existence through the uninterrupted operation of natural law.

It asserted, shockingly, that humankind was no exception.

Furthermore, the identity of its author was a mystery; its title page bore no name. And that was the delectable, tail-swallowing part of the puzzle: Who created this? How had it come into existence?

* * *

The honest town of Musselburgh on the east bank of the River Esk, not far from Spring Gardens, was a favourite afternoon destination of the Chambers family. Of the two bridges across the Esk, the children favoured the old Roman one. They delighted in treading the very stones trodden by Roman sandals; delighted in halting, as Romans surely had halted (Romans! think of it!) at the center to lean over the wide parapet, and peer down into the clear dark water passing below, very rapid and smooth now, only a few hundred yards from its destination: rushing to obliterate itself, exhaust itself, extinguish itself in the sea. They brought things (leaves; bark; feathers) to be dropped onto the water and watched out of sight.

Constantia paused to lean over the parapet when returning from Musselburgh one afternoon with the children and their mother. Downstream of the piers there always swirled little eddies and whirlpools, ever-changing, yet ever the same. Or no; only approximately the same. Ever similar.

"Aren't they marvelous?" said Mrs Chambers at her shoulder. "Those dimples; those whirlpools? I could watch them for hours." To the children, she said: "Do you know what we are seeing, my darlings? Do you? It is only the nebular hypothesis in action! Here, Professor Nichol would tell us—here, where opposite gentle currents of water meet and intermingle, we see in operation the same natural law by which the universe's vast currents of gaseous matter begin to rotate as they coalesce." She rotated her hands around each other, the better to demonstrate. "In the enormous dark expanses of the universe—just as in this homely familiar river—the whirlpool is to be expected where currents meet; and this, my bairns, my darlings, my natural-philosophers-in-embryo, is the genesis of all rotatory movement in all the galaxies, in the nebulae, in the planetary systems of our universe. Of all creation. Is it not marvelous, and wonderful? Mrs MacAdam is properly brimming over with awe, I see—but Annie thinks only of getting home to tea. Aye, so you are, hinney; I can hear you thinking it. And Lizzy is hoping that Cook has made diet-loaf. Well, I daresay that she has. Come on, then; last one home is a pointed egg—a guillemot's egg!"

Mr Robert Chambers was an affectionate father who thoroughly enjoyed the society of his children, the youngest as much as the eldest. Each morning he went by horse-drawn railway up to Edinburgh, where he and his brother William published every Saturday the wildly popular family newspaper *Chambers's Edinburgh Journal*. Upon his return each evening, as soon as he had taken off his boots and put on his slippers, he came upstairs to visit his children. An old armchair in the day nursery was particularly his. He would take as many of the little ones onto his lap as would fit; and ask the elder ones how they had profited from the day just spent. He sometimes read articles to them from *Chambers's Edinburgh Journal* or other popular papers, and made them tell him what they thought. He told them jokes; posed them riddles; and laughed uproariously at the jokes they themselves thought up to pose to him. And sometimes—generally on Saturday evenings, Constantia noticed—he would roll onto the floor with his arms full of children; would wrestle with them, and tickle them until they shrieked with laughter and finally "melted down," as his wife called it. In their excitement, the smaller children were apt to wet themselves, and dissolve into tears. Then Mrs Chambers would send her husband limping down the stairs in his slippers, while she and Hopey remained behind to restore sober order and make all the children go to bed, and stay in bed.

Poor man! His feet hurt him.

And Constantia had also noticed that he bore a small puckered scar on the outside edge of each hand.

Mr and Mrs Chambers generally dined at six, very late. Constantia had heard Mrs Chambers say that this was because her husband was a member not of the Leisure Classes, who could dine whenever they liked; but rather of the Industrious Classes—who did not take their daily bread until they had earned it. That daily bread was often shared with friends old and new, all welcome to fit themselves unceremoniously around the long table anyhow, with scant regard for precedence, place, or elbow room.

When the babies were unusually slumbrous one evening, Constantia was able to sit down with the dinner-party of ten or a dozen. Among the guests were Mrs MacDonald with her husband Mr Hector MacDonald, of Edinburgh; Dr Moir and his wife, who had only to cross the bridge from Musselburgh; a prodigiously bewhiskered Mr Anstruther, a loud new acquaintance of Mr Chambers's; and a couple of bluestockings, Mrs Crowe and Miss Toulmin, who both wrote frequently for *Chambers's Edinburgh Journal*. Even before the mussel stew was finished, the conversation turned to literary matters, and inevitably to the sensational book of the year. "Oh, but who has *not* read *Vestiges*?" young Miss Toulmin was saying. "Every Hottentot in Africa must have read it, by now."

"*I* have not read it; nor shall I," said Lady Janet impressively.

Constantia had not read it either. Indeed, she had not opened a book since the birth of her babies, on the 25th of July; but she resolved now to read it just as soon as she might.

Lady Janet went on, "Incalculable harm may be wrought by such a book. I have just been reading the *Edinburgh Review*'s article about it, and found my apprehensions fully justified."

Miss Toulmin, seated at Constantia's left, leaned over and murmured in her ear, "The '*Embryo Review*' I always think of it—I cannot help myself—and now, I daresay, I shall have made you think the same!"

"Nothing could be more dangerous," Lady Janet was saying, "than that unknown author's theory of transmutation and development. Nevertheless, he gives himself—as the reviewer so elegantly puts it—gives himself the airs of a legislator over the material world.

The entire book, it seems, is riddled with error, both moral and material. The unknown author knows only enough to feel shame, or he would not conceal his name."

"Oh, ma'am! In present company!" cried Mrs Crowe, whom nothing and no one could abash. "Half of us at this very table often lay our words before the public—our pearls before the swine—without signing our names; and it is not for shame, I assure you. Who wrote the *Edinburgh Review*'s article, do you know?"

Embryo Review, thought Constantia, without meaning to.

"I did not notice," said Lady Janet.

"It was unsigned," said Mrs Crowe. "The *Edinburgh*'s always are; it is a matter of editorial policy, not of shame. But Dr Sedgwick has made no secret about his authorship of that review. Oh yes, it is quite generally known, ma'am, I assure you; the *Edinburgh*'s review of *Vestiges* is from the pen of Dr Adam Sedgwick, who is the—the . . . well, what is he, exactly, that voice from on high?"

"He is the Woodwardian Professor of Geology at Cambridge," said Mr Chambers, "and has been for lo, these long ages; for fully the quarter of a century."

"A vast period in the history of geology," said Mrs Chambers. "Perhaps this will be called by geologists of the future 'the Sedgwickian Era.'"

"I found that review distasteful," said Dr Moir. He was, besides family friend and physician, also a regular contributor, Constantia had been told, to the immensely popular *Blackwood's Magazine* under the pen-name "Delta." "One is entitled to expect a soundly-constructed and well-reasoned argument," he declared. "Temperate, careful, modest; and abstaining from personalities. But that review was none of those. No; its tone was waspish, sarcastic, contemptuous—self-righteous—sanctimonious! If the *Vestiges* author gave himself the airs of a legislator, the *Edinburgh* reviewer took upon himself the airs of—of a Pharisee. Furthermore, he seems to have misunderstood—misconstrued—and misrepresented the arguments set forth in *Ves-*

tiges at every possible opportunity. As I cannot suppose Dr Sedgwick stupid, I can only conclude that his misrepresentations must be deliberate. And perhaps even malicious."

"Oh; malicious?" said Mrs Chambers. "But he is a theologian, too, you know. A canon at Norwich Cathedral; a man who stands as high in the moral realm as in the material."

"I am not in the least surprised," said Lady Janet. "His is the reverent attitude of one who well knows his proper relation to the Most High; one who has habitually trodden sacred precincts. But reading the *Vestiges*, he says, is like being conducted through the glory, the magnificence of a cathedral—by a stone-mason! A guide who can speak only of ladders and scaffolds, of hammers and chisels, of stones and mortar-hods!"

This was more provocation than Constantia could bear, and she said, "I beg your pardon, my lady—but who could be better qualified than a stone-mason? Surely no one imagines that cathedrals build themselves! If one is so fortunate as to be guided through a cathedral by the stone-mason who built it, one is led, after all, by its maker! Do we not agree that the maker of any glorious creation, no matter how humble his livelihood, no matter how modest his tools, cannot be contemptible?"

"Was not our Saviour trained up as a carpenter?" murmured Mrs Moir.

"Quite right; cathedrals do not build themselves; men build them," chimed in Mrs Crowe. "Whereas all creation—if the author of *Vestiges* is right—did indeed build itself! Did spin itself up out of the fire-mist, over untold millennia, in accordance with natural law—"

"—itself a creation of the Divine Will; how could it be otherwise?" said Mrs Moir.

Said Dr Moir, "Even if we revert to earthly matters—I refer, now, to geology—Dr Sedgwick is no Pope; he is by no means infallible. No, I remember when he had to recant quite publicly—before the entire Geological Society—upon quitting the camp of the diluvialists and going over to the fluvialists instead."

"He has had grace enough at least to admit and recant, however," said Mr Hector MacDonald, who was an engineer and had wide experience of trials, errors, and a few superb successes. "After all, as the author of *Vestiges* has it, 'The human faculties lead unavoidably to occasional error.' Aye, we have made quite a motto of it, at our house, have we not, my dear?" he added, to his wife. "It is a truth which is often—remarkably often!—recalled to my attention."

Miss Toulmin said, "I found the reviewer's analysis of the author's mind so very interesting, however—"

"Never mind the author's mind," said Mr Chambers, as the soup was taken away and the fish brought in: a codling with horseradish, in egg sauce. "Dr Sedgwick goes much astray there; let him attend to the book itself."

"But are they not inseparable, an author and his works?" said Mrs MacDonald, who was not herself an author.

"—or *her* works," said Mrs Crowe. "No, indeed; at least, they ought not to be. I agree with Mr Chambers. Look, here is the book; study and judge the book itself; leave aside all your notions and your speculations as to who made it. Dr Sedgwick goes quite wrong when he joins in the game of guessing who the author might be."

"The Spectator," said Dr Moir, "declared that readers of a book always want to know whether its writer be a dark man or a fair; mild or choleric in disposition; married or a bachelor—so as better to understand what is written."

"Yet the Spectator himself declined ever to assume any bodily shape whatsoever," said Mr Chambers.

"Yes, a great tease—and a clever feint, too, on the part of the authors," said Miss Toulmin.

"'Author'—such an odd word," said Mrs Chambers. "Though any word sounds odd, if repeated often enough. You are our Latin scholar, Dr Moir; what is its origin?"

"I believe it is from Latin *auctor*—which means, originator; creator," said Dr Moir.

"How puffing-up, for us scribblers!" cried Mrs Crowe. "A faint perfume of divinity wafts over us; over even us, lowly ink-stained wretches that we are!"

" 'Advanced thinkers' will ever mock," said Lady Janet, "but it is an established fact that all Creation, and every kind of creature, has come into existence in a perfect and permanent form, not as the result of any 'laws of nature' in operation during immense ages; no! but called into existence by a power above nature; by an act of the Creator—of a personal and superintending God, concentrating his will on every atom of the universe. No wonder, then, that the chastened author of *Vestiges* has fallen silent. No reply is possible."

"Oh, but his reply—"

"Or hers—"

"The reply may be on the press even now," said Mrs Chambers. "One might suppose."

"Here is our roast chicken. Who will have a wing?" said Mr Chambers. "Mrs MacDonald?"

"Look, and marvel: a *wing*!" cried Mrs Crowe. "Is it not a marvelous development, the wing?"

"It is a marvelous *creation*," said Lady Janet. She and Mrs Crowe would not look at each other, though they sat directly opposite across the table.

"Less marvelous than bread sauce, in my opinion," said Mr Mac-Donald, to end an awkward pause.

"Dr Sedgwick concludes that the author may be a woman," Miss Toulmin said, "on account of the foolishness of the reasoning. He cites in particular the hasty jumping to conclusions."

"He grossly insults the sex, then; and reveals his own ignorance. He cannot be a married man," said Mrs Crowe, who had lived apart from her husband for over a decade.

"Indeed he is a lifelong bachelor, I believe," said Mrs Chambers. "To whom certain common instances of development must remain unfamiliar—to whom babes, for example, are theoretical only; a mere fancy."

"Just hear us, though!" said Mr Chambers. "We at this table have fallen into the same fault as Dr Sedgwick: for we have strayed off the high road of pure fact and impersonal argument—and into the bog of personal speculation. Aye, but we have; we have sunk to commenting upon the personality of the author of the review, not upon the review itself. It is all but irresistible, you see, whenever the author's identity is known."

"And even when it is not," said Mrs Chambers.

"I happened to look into *Pride and Prejudice* again the other day," said Mrs MacDonald, "from the pen, as we all know, of 'A Lady'—and was much struck by the opening sentence: 'It is a truth universally acknowledged, that a single man in possession of a good fortune must be in want of a wife.' Compare that to the first sentence of *Vestiges*: 'It is familiar knowledge that the earth which we inhabit is a globe of somewhat less than 8000 miles in diameter.'"

"Ah! So you, too, suppose that the writer of *Vestiges* was 'A Lady'?" said Mr Anstruther.

"No, indeed," said Dr Moir. "Who can it be but Sir Richard Vyvyan?"

"He has denied it, unequivocally," said Mr Anstruther.

Said Mrs MacDonald playfully, "Perhaps it is the work of Mr Balderstone." The domestic doings of "Mr and Mrs Balderstone" were frequently reported in *Chambers's Edinburgh Journal*; the Balderstones were fictive versions of the Chambers family, written up by Mr Chambers himself whenever something charming, comfortable, and amusing was needed to fill out the sixteen weekly pages of that newspaper.

Mrs Crowe said, "A London correspondent of mine assures me that a bosom friend of hers has uncovered evidence—quite conclusive—that the author is Ada, Countess Lovelace."

"All that business about Mr Babbage's Analytical Engine would suggest so," said Miss Toulmin. "But on balance, I think it is far more likely to have been Mr Gilaroo."

"Or Mr Stukely," said Mrs MacDonald. "He seems more the type than Gilaroo, don't you agree?" Mr Stukely and Mr Gilaroo were also figments of Mr Chambers's fruitful imagination, another pair of imaginary characters whose fireside chit-chat on timely subjects often appeared in *Chambers's Edinburgh Journal*.

Mrs Crowe said, "It has actually been reported to me—never mind by whom—that *I* have been credited with the authorship of *Vestiges*! Which I consider a great compliment. If it were mine, I should be proud to own it, Dr Sedgwick and all his sarcasms notwithstanding."

"The author will soon come forward, I daresay," said Dr Moir. "Someone will claim it. The author will be unable to bear watching all that acclaim, all that éclat, going to waste; gang agley. Authors always do acknowledge their creations, eventually."

"Not always," said Mr Chambers. "Who knows who was 'Junius'?"

"Who *was* Junius?" Constantia whispered to Miss Toulmin.

"But that's just it; no one knows," Miss Toulmin whispered back. "It is a nom de plume."

"No; I mean, what did this unknown Mr Junius write?"

"Oh! furious political polemic, I think it was; back in the seventies, or so."

"It must become known, sooner or later," Dr Moir was saying. "Books do not spring, Athena-like, full-grown from the brows of their authors. There are typesetters, and press-men, and proof-readers, and so forth. Someone knows; and someone will tell. The publisher must know, certainly."

"He declares that he does not, " said Mr Anstruther loudly. "He claims that all was done through an intermediary."

"If we ask everyone, we must hit upon the right person," said Mrs Moir. "Someone must own it eventually."

"Perhaps not," said Mr Chambers. "Even when the King asked him—and very rude it was, too, of His Majesty—Sir Walter Scott did not admit that he was the celebrated Author of *Waverley*."

"No? what *did* Sir Walter say, then?"

"He simply denied it," said Mr Chambers.

"Lied to his king! Shocking!" said Lady Janet.

"He said to me, years later, that not even his king had a right to expect an answer to such a question."

"But everyone knew that he was the Great Unknown—the Author of *Waverley*, and of all the rest, too," said Mrs MacDonald. "It was the worst-kept secret of the world,"

The fowl had been cleared away, and a joint of lamb set before Mr Chambers. "It is no secret now," said he as he rose, the better to operate upon it. "But it was a close secret for quite a long time, until Sir Walter's financial dealings became a matter of public record. Even then, it wasn't talked about; who would be so ill-bred as to press a man as to the offspring he does not choose to acknowledge?"

"Do you know, Chambers, some people say you wrote that book, the *Vestiges*," said Mr Anstruther abruptly.

Mr Chambers—in the act of separating shoulder from ribs of the joint of lamb—said, without looking up, "I wonder how people can suppose I ever had time to write such a book." He applied a quick twist of the wrist, and the joint gave way under the knife. "What will you have, Lady Janet: fat or lean?"

"Horrid!" cried Lady Janet. "I shall instantly denounce any such rumour as a falsehood, and a slander, if ever I hear it repeated in *my* presence! Oh—I beg your pardon; lean, if you please. I shall not shrink for a moment, in any company, from delivering my testimony—for I know Mr Chambers to be incapable of writing so horrid, so atheistical, a book! No decent father of a family could bring himself to write anything of the kind."

"I am obliged to you, Lady Janet, for your good opinion. With caper sauce? Aye," said Mr Chambers, and passed her a slice of the lean, with sauce. "As it happens, I was just entering Baird's bookshop the other day when I heard a fellow there loudly declare to Mr Baird that 'Mr Robert Chambers was certainly incapable of writing the *Vestiges*'—but for quite another reason; which was, that, 'Mr Chambers was very much over-rated!' 'Good day to you, Mr Chambers!' sang out Mr Baird, upon catching sight of me as I crossed the threshold; and the aforesaid fellow of remarkably poor judgment clapped his hat onto his head and slunk out without meeting my fiery eye. I did not quite know whether to be amused, angered, or humbled. Fat or lean, Mrs MacDonald?"

"Just a little of each, pray; with sauce. Now, I have been puzzling over the meaning of 'upper' and 'lower,'" said Mrs MacDonald. "As in 'the upper Silurian,' for instance, or 'the lower Devonian.' Is it a term of—of altitude? Of latitude? Or what is it?"

"No, no," said Mrs Crowe, "'upper' and 'lower' refer simply to the physical arrangement of the rock strata. They indicate recency, you see; and sequence. What is oldest, having been laid down earliest, lies lowest, and is overlain by what is more recent; the most recent of all lies uppermost; that is to say, highest."

"Certain exceptions have been found," added Dr Moir. "There are places where the strata have buckled and folded, sometimes having toppled over completely, so as to reverse their proper sequence. Nevertheless, as a general rule, it can be said that 'upper' and 'lower' refer to time; and sequence."

"Oh . . . I see," said Mrs MacDonald; but then, after thinking for a moment, she said, "There is no question, then, of—of superiority? Not of any physical or moral superiority?"

"Oh, but it is that too, in a certain sense," said Miss Toulmin, "for those organic things which are more recent—higher—are also more fully developed; and advancing therefore nearer to perfection—"

"Now there is a leap of logic which would excite Dr Sedgwick to paroxysms of misogyny!" brayed Mr Anstruther.

"'Perfection,' is it? We have among us a believer in Progress—in perfectibility!" said Mrs Crowe.

"As to progress—" Constantia began to say, but broke off in confusion.

"Why, then, do we call ourselves the 'descendants' of our ancestors?" Mrs MacDonald said, cutting through them all. "Ought we not properly to say that we are 'ascended' from them, rather than 'descended' from them?"

"Indeed, I do not know, Mrs MacDonald," said Dr Moir courteously. "Unless it may be a habitual and respectful deference to our forbears, no matter how undeserving they—mine, at least—may have been."

"Well, I am still perplexed, but I daresay it is my own fault," said Mrs MacDonald. "Pray allow me another foolish question: Is it birds before frogs? Frogs before birds? Am I the only one who struggles to remember the order of appearance of the animated tribes in the strata?"

"Oh, but it's just the order of our dinner, isn't it?" said Miss Toulmin. "Out of the fire-mist there condenses first of all a primordial soup, in which there develops, during untold ages, a profusion of calcium-bodied creatures whose remains compose all the limestone and chalk, and culminating in such choice morsels as mussels—as in the musselkalk, don't you know—and mussel stew; developing next into fishes and frogs and such swimming delicious creatures as codlings; thence ascending still, to the flying creatures, represented at this table by the poulet; and now, now, the mammiferous climax: our shoulder of lamb!"

"Oh! And for pudding, Mrs Chambers, are we to regale ourselves upon a trifle of—of angel's wings, perhaps, or some such celestial thing?" asked Mrs Crowe.

"Alas, no angel's wings were to be had at Musselburgh today," said Mrs Chambers. "I fear we shall have to content ourselves with a charlotte."

"But a charlotte is just the thing! Named for a princess, is it not? And made with *lady*-fingers?"

"Aye, so it is, come to think of it . . . and flavoured with candied *angel*ica, too!"

After the charlotte, the entire company repaired at once to the drawing-room, where there was a pianoforte piled high with music.

Nearby stood Mrs Chambers's harp, a new Erard fully fitted out with everything desirable by way of pedals and fourchettes. From the piano, Mrs Chambers started everyone off in a rousing rehearsal for her rapidly approaching Day o'Treason: three hearty verses of "Johnny Cope"—finishing with a flourish of chords. "Anyone who wants tea," she said, "must give us a Something. A song, or a poem, or something amusing, in that line. You have had your dinner without singing for it—but as for tea—well, that is another matter altogether! Come, Dr Moir, I know you want your tea directly, if not sooner; I daresay you are willing to lead off?"

He was. He had come prepared, with the words of his song in his coat pocket to save himself the trouble of remembering them. Accompanied by Mrs Chambers at the piano, he rendered the company a creditable version of "The Pope He Leads a Happy Life."

Mrs Crowe and Miss Toulmin were ready, too, with a duet which, they declared, was all the rage in America: "Excelsior."

Constantia knew herself utterly incapable of singing aloud before them all. Did those babies not require her yet? Hopey would come fetch her when she was needed—but now she was thinking of just slipping away; of running upstairs to check on them.

"Now, Mr Balderstone," Mrs Chambers was saying to her husband, "what novelty have you brought from town for us?"

"I will claim my usual exemption, for the usual forfeit," said he. "No song, no tea. The hoodie-crow must not croak, in a houseful of canaries."

"Hm! We have not yet heard from you, Mrs MacAdam . . . will you favour us?"

"Oh, the same as Mr Chambers, if you please, ma'am," said Constantia, vastly relieved at being shown this way out of the ordeal. "I want no tea, so pray excuse me; in any case, I could not produce anything like a song."

"As you like. Lady Janet, what will you give us, this evening?"

Lady Janet read them a brief devotional verse, which was met with respectful and appreciative murmurs.

"Come now, Mrs Chambers, it is your turn at last," said Mrs Moir, after the MacDonalds had been heard, and Mr Anstruther forfeited. "Do let us hear your beautiful new harp."

"You must give us your own song, 'The Geologist's Wife,'" said Mrs MacDonald. "Indeed you must; I have told all my Edinburgh acquaintance about it. Oh, do! And pray explain, Mrs Chambers, the occasion for your song."

"Oh—here, among friends," said Mrs Chambers, flushing, "I may as well confess! I cannot tell what *good* wives may do, when their husbands set off for walking tours in the Highlands—I am given to understand that commonly they attend to shirts and bootlaces and the like—but I, for my part, composed for my husband this little song to carry with him." Moving to her harp, she leaned it tenderly against her right shoulder, and shut her eyes. Her inky fingertips skimmed the familiar landscape of its strings, awakening a whisper of chords, harmonics, arpeggios. Quickly she tuned, the improvements discernible to no one but herself; and then, having flashed a smile toward her husband, she sang:

> *Adieu then, my dear, to the Highlands you go,*
> *Geology calls you; you must not say no;*
> *Alone in your absence I cannot but mourn,*
> *And yet it were selfish to wish you return.*
>
> *No, come not until you search through the gneiss,*
> *And mark all the smoothings produced by the ice;*
> *O'er granite-filled chinks felt Huttonian joy;*
> *And measured the parallel roads of Glenroy.*
>
> *Yet still, as from mountain to mountain you stride,*
> *In visions I'll walk like a shade by your side.*
> *Your bag and your hammer I'll carry with glee,*
> *And climb the raised beaches, my own love, with thee.*

Let everything mind you of tender relations;
See, even the hard rocks have their "inclinations"!
Oh let me believe that wherever you roam,
The axis of yours can be nowhere but home.

And if in your wanderings you chance to be led
to Ross-shire or Moray to see the Old Red,
There still, as its mail-covered fishes you view,
Forget not the colour is "love's proper hue."

Such being your feelings, I'll care not although
You're gone from my side for a fortnight or so . . .
But know if much longer you leave me alone
You may find, coming back—a wife turned to stone!

Everyone laughed and applauded. Hopey appeared at the door, and Constantia had to go upstairs, to the warm hungry babies.

After the dinner guests had gone, Mr Chambers disappeared into the library to attend to some business—for no longer, he promised, than a quarter of an hour. He returned half an hour later to his wife's bedroom, which, as the house was so full, the two of them were obliged to share. Although they did not regard this sharing as a hardship, the continuing presence of Lady Janet, which occasioned it, decidedly was.

"Who is that Mr Anstruther?" asked Mrs Chambers, already abed, as her husband undressed.

"He is a paper-manufacturer, who is perfecting—he claims—a new process for making paper inexpensively, of wood fibre. My brother considers the manufacture feasible, but wants my opinion of the man."

"Ah," she said. They heard, briefly, one of the babies crying, above.

It might be their own Charlie. Light quick footsteps passed to and fro overhead, and the baby hushed almost immediately. "Do you know," Mrs Chambers added thoughtfully, "I should like to convince Mrs MacAdam to sing, one of these evenings."

"Why?"

"Because I should like to have a glimpse into her soul."

"How alarming! I daresay she will be prudent enough to keep silent," said he. "What do you make of the souls of those of us who decline to sing?"

"Not everyone is a singer. There are plenty whose music is of another sort—whose genius is of another sort. I mean only that . . . I still marvel, always, upon first hearing some new acquaintance sing, especially if it is someone whose measure I thought I had taken. How often have I been astonished at the voice which comes from a person I had dismissed as—uninteresting, or dull-witted, or mean-spirited, or simply unhandsome: sallow, or plain, or sadly chinless! How often I have found that I had judged wrong! And how marvelously, how instantly does the singer gain in beauty, in my eyes, upon giving utterance, upon revealing this hitherto hidden splendour! At once the veil falls from my eyes, and I am dazzled by the shining spirit which, until then, I had been too stupid to perceive, or even suspect."

"Never stupid, my dear."

"Oh, but I must be—for this has happened often enough that it ought not to catch me by surprise, still—but it often does. Often enough that I ought not to place much faith in my judgment of anyone, until I have heard her, or him, sing, or play. Now, I did not much like your bewhiskered Mr Anstruther, my dear—so ill-bred of him, at dinner—"

"Aye, rather."

"But I have not heard him sing. Occasionally it is borne in upon me that I must almost always go about my business blind to the inner beauties of nearly all those around me. For I have never heard the laundress sing, nor the conductor on the railway, nor the man at the tollbooth. I heard the gardener today, however, when he thought no one was about; and although I had hitherto mistaken him for a meager little bent body, I came at once to see him truly: a braw figure of a man!—just so soon as I heard the fine tenor voice of him."

2

THE GARDENER CAME with the house, and he did not much approve of children in his grounds. They were particularly hard on hedges. He was attached to his garden as a ewe to her hill; as a salmon to its stream; as a pigeon to its doocot. Owners and tenants will come, and will go; but Mr Gunn had tended Spring Gardens since boyhood, succeeding his father there. He drank rather too much, because his work left his mind (quite an active one) free to ponder the ways of Providence, and furnished a great deal of matter to ponder.

As he saw it, the fundamental problem was this: How could there be so much scope for improvement in the Almighty's creation? How was it that he himself, a mere gardener, had, in the course of a lifetime's sweaty and dirty labour, so improved upon the wasteland that had been here until his own father had commenced to cultivate it? In short, why hadn't God made a garden here in the first place? While Mr Gunn despised the horticultural ignorance of almost all mortal beings, he was obliged to grant that God was probably not ignorant; was probably capable of making quite a good garden, if only He chose (had indeed once done so; it was written). Why did He not so choose? And why—while he was at the business of lodging complaints—why did God so evidently grudge Mr Gunn's own poor efforts to remedy

His omission in this respect? Why the late frosts which blackened the tender young seedlings? Why the gale winds which disfigured the noble old trees, amputating their limbs, even ripping them out by the roots? Why the rabbits? the blights, the careless children, the birds? "Providence" indeed! To Mr Gunn, when in his cups, this seemed a bitter sarcasm; and "Heavenly Father" was still worse. Any earthly father who treated his offspring so cruelly, so carelessly, with such unjust, offhand callousness as did this Heavenly Father, would fall afoul of a Sheriff's censure at least, if not a prison sentence, or a term in the asylum for the unfit.

The unfit.

He had asked himself whether these merciless decimations might not be the divine method of weeding out the unfit; had examined this question strictly, and thoroughly; and continued to re-examine it periodically. He had concluded, however, that they were not. The garden's most promising sapling might fall victim to random death; might be decapitated in a moment by a falling branch. If the wind had been blowing from the west instead of the east, the branch would have fallen six inches away, thus sparing the best sapling ever bred; sparing it to glorify the world. But no; the best sapling ever bred was destroyed, a victim not of any unfitness in itself, but of gravity and chance; or else of Almighty wantonness.

Explaining this pervasive wantonness and waywardness in all things—the liability, nay, the irresistable *tendency* toward death, decay, and destruction—was the business of the clerics, but Mr Gunn did not have much faith in their tortured explanations. The more he thought about it, the more certain it appeared to him that he might as well attribute divine qualities to—oh, to choose at random—gravity. He might as well offer up his morning offices to Gravity; his prayers of petition, of praise, of thanks:

O Gravity, our heavenly Father, Almighty and everlasting Lord, which hast safely brought us to the beginning of this day, defend us in the same with thy mighty power, and grant that this day we fall into no sinne, nor off of thy planet Earth, neither runne into any kinde of danger: but that all our doings may be ordered by thy governance, to do alwayes that is righteous in thy sight, and to hold down fast upon thy Earth which hast made for us thy children; through Jesus Christ our Lord. Amen.

Nevertheless, Mr Gunn went out every morning, still reeking of last night's gin and blasphemy, to resume teaching the Almighty a lesson; to demonstrate to the All-Powerful what He ought to have done with this particular piece of land. Look: a well-grown allée here, symmetrical; and there, beech nodding to oak; now, isn't that pleasant? Wilt Thou taste the fruit of my orchard, my peach trees which I myself have bred, during my own lifetime, over twenty peach-generations; are these not incomparably sweeter and more fragrant than the bitter wee nubs which Thou hast vouchsafed unto us, Thy children? Regard my roses! (the only true claim of the French to culture—their only true contribution to humanity—is these roses, bred from the promising but undeveloped and undistinguished stock Thou sawest fit to furnish unto us, Thy cherished children, cherished just as the sow cherishes her naked helpless piglets when she rolls over them, when she crushes and smothers them in the filth of her stye; cherished just as the salmon cherishes its spawn which it deposits in the gravel of the streambed, and swims away)—I beseech thee, O Almighty, smell *my* roses, each offering up its own distinct and ravishing perfume!

The Almighty continued an inattentive student, however, and the gardener continued to drink gin each night. He would have preferred wholesome whisky, but gin was cheaper. His wife had died a decade earlier, and all that now remained of her was a collection of bird nests lined up on the bookshelf in his cottage. These beloved nests were lined with her hair, for she had always gone out to the garden to comb her long hair. Some of the nests were evidently from the summers of her youth, when her hair was still black; and others were from later years, after it had gone white. (Gone white within the period of a month; the month in which all three of their handsome strong sons had died, of the typhoid that raged through Scotland that year.) There were several nests lined with coarse russet horsehair, too, from the summers when a pair of horses had grazed the field beyond the wall. One of these nests held three small unhatched blue eggs— not because Mr Gunn had stolen the nest before they could hatch; not because some flighty mother had abandoned them—but because a late frost had frozen them under their diligent mother's breast, so that they never hatched though she continued to sit on them for six weeks afterward. O, Almighty east wind! Mr Gunn had not gathered the nest until the bird, despairing of her lifeless eggs, had abandoned them at last.

The noble beech tree that had dropped a branch upon—had destroyed—the most promising peach sapling ever germinated had not always been so fine. The beech in its youth had been inconspicuous. In middle age, ungainly; too slender. Only now, in its maturity, had it attained nobility. It seemed to Mr Gunn that trees became handsomer under the beams of human regard. Could this be? Could a tree feel those beams, and form itself according to those wishes? Was the tree truly handsomer now than ever before? Or did it only *appear* handsome, because it was by now so utterly familiar to him, and therefore pleasant to his sight?

Every tree inside the garden wall was deeply familiar. They were imbued with personalities, and associations. Mr Gunn adored puns, even Latin puns. For him, the medlar espaliered against the south side of the north wall represented that Lady Janet who lived with the Chambers family; she, the meddler! Whereas the fruitless peach which he kept for the sake of its glorious flowering represented Mrs Chambers: she, the unimpeachable!

Despite his frequent despairs, Mr Gunn often sang, and he knew a great many old songs well-suited to his various moods. What moved him to sing? Sometimes it was exhilaration, caused by a bird, or a blossom, or a breeze; but at other times he lifted up his voice in sorrow, or in fury. There were songs for anything.

From where he worked, strawing the rhubarb bed against coming frost, Mr Gunn could see the wet nurse seated on a garden bench under a drooping rhododendron, reading in the fickle September sunshine. Somewhere atop the beech tree a thrush practised its crunluaths. A gospel verse sprang into his mind: "But woe unto them that are with child, and to them that give suck, in those days!" Both babies napped on a blanket spread on the grass at the wet nurse's feet. He had tried speaking with her once or twice, about pigeons. Mr Gunn doted upon his pigeons. After a lifetime of observing them, he marveled still at their resemblance to humankind. He never tired of watching their courtship: their flirting, their coquetting—and even kissing. They "married," too, remaining faithful to the same mate as long as they both did live. And although they were birds and not mammifers, they fed their insatiable offspring on "milk" disgorged from their own crops. They were gratifying to breed, for they bred frequently, all the year around; their hatchlings matured to breeding age in a matter of weeks; and they manifested a remarkable disposition to sport. This did not mean that they were particularly frolicsome. "Disposition to sport" was a phrase from a book he knew well, written by Mr Patrick Matthew of Gourdiehill—and it had stuck in his mind. It meant that the offspring were apt to differ from their parents. He had mentioned this to the wet nurse, but evidently she was not much interested in pigeons or their breeding; and evasive when he asked whence she had her bird, and why. Is it a French bird, he had asked her—for the bird had a foreign look about it, and he had been told that she had lived in France. No, she had said, it is English. Oh; where in England? Just English, she said. I had it of my husband.

* * *

Constantia was reading, in fits and starts; hearing birdsong and the older children, playing nearby; and waiting for the babies to awaken and relieve again the increasing pressure in her breasts—nearly as hard now as the lichened breasts of the crumbling marble Demeter upon her plinth in a recess of the yew hedge.

Lizzy burst through the hedge, in tears. "Oh, Mrs MacAdam! Do bring it back!" she cried, cradling something in her hands. "It was just pecking in the grass near the corner of the house, when that six-toed cat leapt out at it, and it flew up all in a rush to get away, and hurtled against the window and fell down again, and the cat went for it, but I chased the wicked cat away, and picked it up myself. Do bring it back, Mrs MacAdam, do! Surely it cannot be dead, for it was alive, not a minute since, and the cat never touched it. Take it, here; cannot you bring it back?"

Sometimes birds were only stunned by crashing against windows, but this plump young pigeon was dead. Its head fell sideways as Constantia set down her book and received the still-warm body into her cupped hands. It was a Spring Gardens pigeon, not her own English bird. Its eyes and its beak were open; indeed, she could see its tongue. She turned it, smoothing the pearlescent feathers, and the head lolled back. Its clean fine-scaled feet were like pink coral; like curls of seaweed washed up on sand. The edges of the pinion feathers were both stiff and soft; the small feathers covering the breast yielding like fine chainmail over the exquisitely-made body beneath. Jeanne D'Arc, thought Constantia, and felt surprise at so odd and unbidden an idea.

"It cannot be dead," insisted Lizzy.

"It is, though," said Constantia. "I am sorry." And she was; an ocean of sorrow lay in her chest, leaden as the North Sea; lapping cold and salty against her heart.

"If I keep it warm and quiet, won't it come right again?"

"No," said Constantia, "it cannot come alive again. Dead is dead."

"I hate cats!" cried Lizzy hotly. "I wish God never made them!" And, taking back the dead pigeon, she ran off, cradling it.

Such a wish, Lady Janet would have said, was sinful. Who were you, to criticise His arrangements, for His creation?

The wind came up, and clouds blew in front of the sun. Constantia gathered up both babies and carried them indoors, leaving the blanket on the grass and the book on the bench.

Mr Gunn watched these for a while; then, when rain threatened, he went and picked up the blanket and folded it. Taking up the book, he recognized it: *Vestiges of the Natural History of Creation*. There was a bookmark, an orange thread. The wet nurse was reading the chapter about the Origin of the Animated Tribes.

Mr Gunn had, six months before, borrowed a copy of *Vestiges* from the Mechanics Institute library, read it overnight, and sent it back the next morning. Then, several weeks later, he had borrowed and read it again, taking time to copy out certain of the most striking passages. He had by now committed to memory those passages which most interested him, and he often mulled them over as he toiled over his spade or his fork. One such was this sentence from the unknown author's closing remarks: "It will occur to every one, that the system here unfolded does not imply the most perfect conceivable love or regard on the part of the Deity towards his creatures."

Mr Gunn had meditated so long and so closely upon this thought that it had suffused him entirely, as tea suffuses hot water. Indeed, as he labored, forking up the waterlogged soil, he sometimes found himself panting these words as though they were a song, to the tune of "The True Lover's Farewell":

> *It will occur to every one*
> *That the system here unfolded*
> *does not imply a perfect love*
> *on the part of our Almighty God*
> *Towards us, His suff'ring creatures.*

There was a second verse, too, also derived from the closing remarks of the unknown author of *Vestiges*: "It is necessary to suppose that the present system is but a part of a whole, a stage in a Great Progress, and that the Redress is in reserve"—which fell thus into verse:

> *To compensate for God's neglect,*
> *'Tis necessary to suppose*
> *the present system only part of a Whole*
> *—a stage in a Great Progress—*
> *with Redress lying in reserve!*

It is *necessary* to suppose.

Redress *must* lie in reserve. Surely?

Mr Gunn knew the book's concluding sentence: Let us wait the end with patience, and be of good cheer. Not so different from Luke 21:19: In your patience possess ye your souls.

Mr Gunn had concluded that time meant nothing to the Deity, just as it meant nothing to animals. During a summer of his boyhood, his father had lent him to a neighboring farmer, to follow the plow-horse from sunup to sundown, every day. The horse had one day conceived a profound aversion to a particular corner of a field and, in spite of any inducement or punishment that Mr Gunn (Johnny Gunn, then; plowboy) could contrive, had refused to set foot beyond a certain invisible line on the ground, only standing trembling wide-eyed staring at nothing, as terrified as Macbeth who look'd but on a stool. No whip, no encouragement, no example could make the horse stir so much as one step further. Yet that corner of the field was prime ground, and could not be left unplowed. What was to be done?

Johnny Gunn had felt fury rising in his breast. How dared this dumb beast to defy him! To delay him! And then he had calmed himself, reasoning: If you cannot master this horse, you do not deserve to call yourself his master. If you are not cleverer and more patient than a horse, you can claim no right to compel obedience from it. You are bent upon making this horse obey you Now—because you have a notion of time passing. But for this horse, *all* is Now; all is the present moment; it has no notion of future or past moments, only a continuous stream of present moments. Let us stop and stand here, at the invisible line. You can wait as long as this horse can, and a little longer, too. And you need not pay the slightest regard to how long it may take—for the horse will not consider any delay to be a victory on its own part—having no concept of delay, or the passage of time; precious fleeting commodity, time!

Johnny Gunn took his book out of his pocket (for he always had a book handy for the beguiling of spare moments, rare though they were) and, the reins looped across his shoulders, sat down upon the unplowed part of the ground before the horse, and read his book.

Robert Burns had walked behind a plow, with a book always in his pocket. Had composed songs behind the plow; behind a horse as stupid as this one.

Johnny Gunn sat and read. Under the influence of this unexpected calm and quiet, the horse gradually forgot to be alarmed by the alarming qualities of the unplowed corner of the field. After a while, it dozed, hipshot; roused, looked about, shifted its weight to the other hip, and dozed again, heavy lower lip falling away from the long teeth stained black and yellow, worse than any snuff-eating old dame's. A bell sounded, at some distance: a schoolbell, calling in the scholars. This marker of the passage of time meant nothing, nothing at all to the reader nor to the horse. A dog barked. A man whistled. The reader read on. The horse dozed on. Hunger stirred in the belly of the reader, but he read on. Hunger stirred in the belly of the horse, too. Its guts rumbled noisily, and it awakened from a doze, its head jerking up. The sun was more westerly than it had been, and cooler.

In the dusk, they finished plowing the terrifying corner of the field, calmly back and forth, as the moon rose. Johnny Gunn felt himself a god. Time was trivial, beneath his notice, the merest trickle. He had won: had prevailed: had imposed his will upon this stupid horse. Why should time mean anything more to him than it meant to God, or to this horse? A fine disregard.

But the farmer who owned the field and the horse—and Johnny Gunn for the summer—took a different view; Johnny Gunn had been thrashed and sent to bed supperless for his sloth.

Mr Gunn had been an ardent Chartist, for a while. Am I not a man? Have I not cultivated this garden all my life? Have I not paid taxes all my life? (Spontaneously the pun came: *Taxus*. That was yew; his cherished hedges.) He had attended Chartist meetings, when the Chartists had conducted them a few years ago; great well-attended meetings which drew working men from miles around. He had marched during the general election of 1841; had declared his fervent support at the hustings for the Chartist candidate—young Stevenson the stone merchant—who was standing against Macaulay; had actually dared to cherish a hope that Stevenson and the other Chartist candidates might actually win a few seats in Parliament! But the polling had concluded in dismal failure; despite spending a great deal of money, Stevenson had polled only 26 votes, against his opponent's 300 and some. And then under the heat and glare of Crown prosecutions, the Chartists had once again melted away like summer snow. Some hundreds of imprisonments, deaths, and transportations inflicted upon the unlucky were sufficient to disperse the rest; to silence them, to send them slinking into silent exile in such remote and insalubrious places as France and Holland. Had not poor Holberry died in prison, undone by the treadmill? Had not Frost, Williams, and Jones been convicted of treason and sentenced to death by drawing, hanging, and quartering? The subsequent commutation of their sentences to transportation for life to Botany Bay was not mercy; no, it was a display of princely puissance and caprice. Where was bold young Stevenson the stone merchant now? (And the book that Mr Gunn, regrettably, had lent him?) Melted away; not to be heard of, a bounty offered for his capture and delivery to the Sheriff of Edinburgh, to be bound over to answer on charges of conspiracy, sedition, and no one knew what else. Mr Gunn felt certain all this was falsehood and injustice, but so many had been convicted, transported, imprisoned, on charges equally unjust: Vincent, Peddie, Lovett, the great O'Connor himself—and hundreds more besides.

Were he and his fellow Chartists *not* men, after all? Had they hearts not of oak, but of willow, of whin? Had they proven themselves unworthy of the rights which, for a while, they had noisily demanded? Surely, any men worthy of the rights they demanded would have persisted in their cause. Opposition and even persecution should have strengthened their resolve, not dissolved it. What modest demands they were, after all, and how reasonable, those Six Points of the People's Charter!

In Scotland, nearly everyone learned to read. Every minister presided over not only his kirk, but a free school as well, so that everyone, rich and poor alike, learned to read and study Scripture for themselves.

But people who can read will do so; they will read and study not only Scripture, but anything, and everything.

Alongside the birds' nests, Mr Gunn's bookshelf held a row of books. There was a gap where one book was missing. He had lent it a few years ago to Stevenson the stone merchant about the time of that bitterly-contested election. When Stevenson had disappeared, the book had disappeared with him; Mr Gunn had resolved never to lend a book again. The lost book was called *On Naval Timber and Arboriculture*, and had been written by a Mr Patrick Matthew of Gourdiehill, an uncommonly prosperous farmer, long before, in 1831 (the year when all of Mr Gunn's sons had died; all, within that terrible month). It treated mostly of how best to grow trees suitable for shipbuilding. Mr Gunn had bought this book because he had met Mr Matthew, another Chartist, and respected him; and because sylviculture interested him. But tucked into the back matter of this book was a curious little essay, an appendix which Mr Gunn had reread many times over the years. He thought that other people should read it, too. In it, the author declared that

> it is only the hardier, more robust, better suited to circumstance individuals, who are able to struggle forward to maturity, these inhabiting only the situations to which they have superior adaptation and greater power of occupancy than any other kind; the weaker, less circumstance-suited, being prematurely destroyed. This principle is in constant action, it regulates the colour, the figure, the capacities, and instincts; those individuals of each species, whose colour and covering are best suited to concealment or protection from enemies, or defence from vicissitude and inclemencies of climate, whose figure is best accommodated to health, strength, defence, and support; whose capacities and instincts can best regulate the physical energies to self-advantage according to circumstances—in such immense waste of primary and youthful life, *those* only come forward to maturity from the strict ordeal by which Nature tests their adaptation to her standard of perfection and fitness to continue their kind by reproduction.

It was, as the author remarked, an immensely wasteful design. Stupefying in its wastefulness. Insulting, in its wastefulness. How absurd, the husbandry Mr Gunn practised, in the face of such a principle! How futile.

But it seemed to Mr Gunn that there was yet another important aspect of Nature's harsh winnowings which went unmentioned by Mr Matthew—and by the unknown author of *Vestiges*, too—and that was Chance; Luck. It was not only the "weaker" or "less circumstance-suited" who were prematurely destroyed; for even the hardiest, most robust individuals, those best suited to circumstance (his sons!) might be felled nevertheless, by bad luck (surely, not by Malice!), without ever having met any opportunity to continue their kind by reproduction. (Surely it could not be Malice? It ought not to be Malice. *Malus*, he thought, his glance falling across the crabapple tree in the corner, where its stunted crabbed fruit was now turning red. How unbearable, to inhabit a Nature which operated upon a principle of Malice! Even Caprice, Indifference, or Ridiculousness was better than Malice.)

Unlike the nameless author of *Vestiges*, Mr Matthew did not lard his remarks on this subject with any sanctimonious references to a Divine Creator, and His Mysterious Ways—and, unlike *Vestiges*, Mr Matthew's book had escaped the notice of readers, and the criticism of reviewers.

Why had the very interesting little appendix in this book attracted neither audience nor attention? Could so important, so manifestly true an idea as this fall to the ground unnoticed? Could so valuable a seed fail to germinate, take root, flourish, and bear fruit?

Was he, Gunn, the only person who thought about such matters? What was everyone else thinking about instead?

"Don't speak to us of God Almighty! There isn't any, or He wouldn't let us suffer so!" It was at a strike, a rising of the unemployed weavers in 1832, that Mr Gunn had heard this blasphemy shouted by a miserable starving weaver; and it had stuck with him ever since, echoing through his mind. As time went on, these words had somehow transformed themselves in his mind's ear; had become more blasphemous still, for now he seemed to hear instead: "Don't speak to us of Goddle Mighty! There isn't any, or He wouldn't let us suffer so!" And once he had heard it thus, he was never again able to think 'God Almighty.' He could only think of Goddle Mighty, the addled Goddle who makes a muddle of all matters; a fat clumsy toddler.

Goddle Mighty. He could not help it.

There are crimes that are not sins; there are sins that are not crimes. But blasphemy is both sin and crime. To "asperse, ridicule, vilify, and bring into contempt the Christian religion and the Holy

Scriptures" was to risk not only eternal damnation, but also to invite prosecution; was to risk imprisonment, and heavy fines, and felon's treatment. The Edinburgh booksellers Robinson and Finlay did it quite deliberately, and were imprisoned for it, and served their terms, and were released laughing, and did it again. Well, they sold obscene publications, too—but only by special order; only to the prosecutor's undercover agents who requested them; it was never proved against them that they exposed those for sale. The freethinker Thomas Paterson set up a bookshop in Edinburgh called the Blasphemy Depot and boasted of the handsome profits he made by selling his scurrilous *Oracle* to agents of the law, his best customers. When in 1843 he was sentenced to fifteen months' felon's treatment in Perth Penitentiary, and the Blasphemy Depot shuttered, his assistant Miss Matilda Roalfe carried on—by opening an Atheistical Depot in Nicolson Street. When she, too, was arrested and imprisoned—for selling such publications as *A Home Thrust at the Atrocious Trinity*—her friend William Baker came from London to help keep up the excitement.

Mr Gunn had contemplated ridicule, and the ridiculous; and had arrived at some conclusions. First, a thing which strikes us as utterly ridiculous may nevertheless be perfectly true. Indeed, the more he thought of it, the more apparent it seemed that ridiculousness might rank among the prime principles in all creation: a law of ridiculousness. Consider this, from the author of *Vestiges*: "Who, upon becoming acquainted for the first time with the circumstances attending the production of an individual of our race, would not think them degrading? And be eager to deny them? And exclude them from the admitted truths of nature?"

Nevertheless, we know this fact to be true beyond contradiction: this preposterous, degrading, and ridiculous act—*this* is how babies are made.

And if it hath pleased Goddle Mighty to arrange matters thus—

His wondrous works to perform, by such ridiculous means as these!—have we any choice but to submit? And surely we are permitted to notice that it *is* ridiculous; and we are permitted to ridicule what is ridiculous? To a Goddle Mighty who so clearly cherishes ridiculousness, ridicule must constitute not blasphemy, but worship?

Those are blasphemous thoughts. Put them away from thee.

Presently he fell to thinking about "the circumstances attending the production of an individual of our race." Remembering that. His wife, in those days: succulent, lubricious. The thick plaited rope of her black hair, lying between her white breasts. Or across her strong white back. Their bed; and the acts they had so ardently, so hungrily, performed there. That bed, a good one; contrived so strongly that it did not creak, no matter how they rocked it. That bed, somewhat damp, and smelling of themselves: like crab-meat; like frilled, trembling oysters; like bearded mussels, that tiny meat between hairy black shells opening willingly to heat, not force. Ah, Musselburgh! Its inexhaustible mussel beds! That ardency, that urgency. And then . . . the babies: the naked, wet red-and-blue squalling newborn sons, with their surprisingly enormous—ahems!

He stood up; straightened his back, which ached. Stretched. Those are obscene thoughts. Obscene memories. Obscene acts. Or were they? His wondrous works to perform.

He could not help but often hear the Chambers girls, in their play, or their squabbles:

"Miss Slip-slop! If you were a bird, you'd be a pigeon, and build a slip-slop pigeon nest!" (For in the wild, pigeons and doves build their sketchy nests on rock ledges and cliffs: a few sticks, a few straws; just structure enough to keep the squabs from falling out.)

"No, she'd be a guillemot, and never bother with a nest at all." (For guillemots don't; they, too, lay their eggs on bare rock ledges, not troubling with even so slatternly a nest as a pigeon makes.)

"Then it's very clever of them, you must admit, to lay pointed eggs." (For guillemot eggs are elongated, and pointed. If disturbed, they roll around in a circle, not off the rock ledge.)

"Oh, clever! But it is not cleverness, not in the least. No, they cannot help but lay pointed eggs."

"But what about the hatchlings? Don't they fall off the edge?"

"Not all of them, it would seem."

"Only the bold, rash, imprudent ones."

And, thought Mr Gunn, the unlucky ones.

3

"BUT DADDY: How does a bird know what sort of nest it is meant to build?" asked Tuckie's high piping voice one evening. Constantia, nursing Charlie in her own room, could hear her through the thin partition wall. "How does a wren know it is meant to build a tidy wren's nest—and not a messy slapdash jackdaw nest, in a chimney?" This seemed to Constantia quite a good question, and she regretted that it went unanswered, swamped by Jenny-or-Lizzy's next question: "And Daddy, where do the jackdaws make their nests, if no chimneys are nearby?"

"Or before chimneys were thought of?" added her twin.

"Oh, there have always been chimneys, haven't there, Daddy?"

"Nay, lass," said their father's voice. "Not always, and not everywhere. Even now, the highland crofters have no more than a hole in the thatch, for the smoke to find its own way out."

"But where do highland jackdaws build their nests, then?"

"They find a suitable nook elsewhere," he said.

"Fancy standing upon the edge of the nest," said Tuckie, "just about to leap into the air for the very first time. How do fledglings know how to fly?"

"I know how to fly," said Annie. "If I had wings, I should be able to fly directly, without any lessons."

"As when you leapt from the roof of the garden shed?"

"Nay, that was mere experiment; I found that arms are not suitable; wings are wanted—except in dreams. I do know how to fly, from my dreams."

"Oho!"

"Do you not fly in your dreams? Never? Oh, it is grand! Wearying to the arms and shoulders, but worth the effort—such sights from above, you can't think! And so convenient for escaping the wicked folk, too."

"Cannot the wicked folk fly as well, in your dreams?"

"They cannot. I can aye be away from them, just out of their reach—and they, leaping with rage below."

"Oh, but *why* did God not give people wings? *So* delightful, to have wings," said Lizzy-or-Jenny.

"Silly, what do you take angels for, then?" said her twin.

"But are angels a sort of human, Daddy, with wings stuck on? Or are they some other sort of creature entirely?"

It seemed to Constantia that there was a moment's consideration before their father's voice replied, "*Homo volans*? or *Angelicus sanctus*? I suppose you know that naturalists, when determining the affinities of a creature, closely examine its skeleton; its bones and teeth. But no one, alas, has ever yet had the opportunity to examine the remains of an angel—for never a single specimen has been found. Never so much as a tooth. "

"Oh, but why not, Daddy? That is most curious, isn't it?"

He might, thought Constantia, perhaps have gone on to list the vicissitudes to which skeletal remains were subject; or mentioned the inferred incompleteness of the fossil record—but instead Annie's voice said, "Because angels are immortal! Aren't they, Daddy? How could they leave their remains lying about for examination while they still go about in them, using them?"

"*Are* angels immortal, Daddy?"

"You had better ask your mother," said he.

"Or Lady Janet," suggested Jenny-or-Lizzy.

"But Dad, angels haven't got skeletons," said Mary.

"No skeletons!" said Lizzy-or-Jenny. "How horrid and jiggly they must be, then—like jellyfish!"

"Nay, Lizzy," said her twin. "Never could an angel be like a jellyfish."

Nina's voice now joined this discussion: "I have read that angels are unburdened with actual bodies; neither flesh-and-bone, nor jelly, nor any corporeal existence, at all," she said. "They are celestial spirits, emanations of the Divine Will, and they assume just the semblance of a body only when they require to be seen."

"That seems dreadfully popish," said Mary, "like saints and ghosts. But Lady Janet will know."

"She will certainly know," said their father, in what sounded like agreement.

✻   ✻   ✻

LADY JANET, a nuisance in herself, brought with her an additional nuisance in the form of the cabinet she was japanning. She called it japanning, though her craft had nothing to do with Japan. She was very gradually—with pen, ink, and brush—transforming a plain pale-wood cabinet, about four feet high, into an "ebonized" cabinet decorated with pale-wood flowers and birds and "chinese" figures in "hindoo" landscapes, under "oriental" trees. In minute strokes, she inked in the entire background, leaving these figures as pale silhouettes; then she drew faint lines and hatchwork to delineate the details of the figures. Japanning had been a popular pastime twenty-five years earlier among ladies whose leisure was a burden to them, but it had since fallen out of fashion.

Usually ladies had been satisfied with afflicting some small item—a tea caddy, a workbox, a watch-stand—with this painstaking form of ornament, but a few were inspired to attempt something larger and more permanent. Lady Janet had by now been working on this cabinet for some time, and several large areas of its surface were completely decorated. Alas, her drawing was awkward; her eyes, weak; her taste, indifferent. Consequently, the cabinet was not going to be a great success. As she possessed however the virtue of persever-ance, it travelled with her to the various houses she visited as guest. There, space had to be made for it in the corners of various drawing rooms; and space not only for it, but also for her bottles of ink, and fine brushes, and quill pens, and penknives. All this had to be kept safe from the children of the household. Lady Janet had declared more than once that it was important to set an example of industry, not idleness, to the children.

Who was this Lady Janet, guest ad perpetuam? A rich relation? With a fortune to dispose of? No; only a connection of Mr Cham-bers's brother's wife—which is no relation at all. Nor had she any evident fortune, to live on, or dispose of. She had been staying in Edinburgh with the William Chamberses until they had set off upon an extended Italian tour; then, needing a place to live until their return, she had removed temporarily to the Robert Chambers branch of the family at Spring Gardens. There she had been received out of pure kindness and generous principles, soon regretted. As the Wil-liam Chamberses were due back from Leghorn very soon—within a matter of weeks, now—the family at Spring Gardens stuck to their principles, and did their best with a stubborn virtuous forbearance to tolerate Lady Janet for just a little longer. "Were she rich," Mrs Chambers had said to Mr Chambers, "we might turn her off without compunction; but as she is poor, there is nothing to be done but suffer her company in patience."

* * *

"GOSSIP AND idle tittle-tattle are not at all to my liking," said Mrs MacDonald to Mrs Chambers one afternoon in the garden, "but it were better that you knew something of Mrs MacAdam's personal history, so as to avoid any awkward situations or remarks which might otherwise arise by chance; and so that you can judge what measure of sympathy and kindness are due her—for none of it is her own fault." The two of them settled side by side onto a bench which stood in sunshine at the end of the yew walk. Though the day was not warm, they had come out because they did not wish to be overheard by Lady Janet, who was toiling over her cabinet in the drawing room. "Where shall I begin? She was born Miss Constantia Babcock, in India, just when her father—or so everyone thought him—a lieutenant in the service of the East India Company, had been carried off by one of those tropical fevers. Then she was left entirely an orphan at only nine or ten years of age when her mother died, too. All this was in the deepest jungles, the wilds of Assam or Burma, or some such remote place—where there are scarcely any white people; but she was fortunate enough to be taken under the wing of a black queen there, called the Rani of Nungklow, a friend of her mother's. In any case, when the Rani and her grown-up family came here, via America, some four or five years ago, Miss Babcock sailed with them, in hopes of finding her father's people—or her mother's people—or someone, at least, still belonging to her. It was then that I first became acquainted with them all, though my husband and his sister had known her mother, and the Rani too, many years previously, under very different circumstances. Oh! But there is Lady Janet, coming this way."

"Do not interrupt your agreeable tête-à-tête, pray," called Lady Janet as she approached. "I am in search of nothing but these last warm rays of sunshine."

Taking Mrs MacDonald's arm, Mrs Chambers rose, saying, "Allow me to recommend this excellent seat to your ladyship. No, you do not incommode us in the least; indeed, it is so excessively warm here that Mrs MacDonald and I were just on the point of seeking the shade of the allée." And so the two of them walked off arm in arm to the linden allée, leaving Lady Janet in possession of the sun-warmed seat.

"Where was I?" said Mrs MacDonald, when privacy had been secured once more. "Aye; four years ago. From her mother's papers,

Miss Babcock had learnt that this Lieutenant Babcock hailed from Wivenhoe, in Essex; and there, she and the Rani at length made their way. Their inquiries presently turned up his people; indeed, they found his elder brother, still living in the family house. A farming family, of a middling sort. But she got a dreadfully cold welcome, because . . . just imagine her distress, upon learning—well!—upon learning that this man Babcock had never been legally married to her mother at all! For there, still living at Wivenhoe, was his widow— whom he'd married quite correctly at the parish church, before ever he went out to India! *And* a grown-up daughter!"

"A previous wife, still living!" breathed Mrs Chambers.

"But listen, my dear, there is worse to come: Only then did Miss Babcock learn from the Rani that this bigamous lieutenant was not her father after all; and that her mother was already some months gone with child when he had married her—or rather, when he had *pretended* to marry her—and that her mother had previously been known as Mrs Todd! Indeed, when the Rani—and my husband, too—first knew her, she was a young bride accompanying her husband Mr Todd on their honeymoon voyage out to India."

"No!"

"But this Mr Todd was shot dead in Cape Town, in some sort of affair of honour—"

"Oh, no! *Too* bad! You are making up romances, now!"

"Indeed I am not," protested Mrs MacDonald. "I have not so lurid a fancy. My husband was there at the time, and most dreadful it was, by his account. Oh! Shall we turn this way?" she proposed—for Lady Janet had left her seat and adopted a course which might intersect theirs.

"Quite excessively warm there, just as you observed!" cried out Lady Janet, as she entered the linden allée—just as they turned out of it toward the doocot at the bottom of the garden.

"But you will already have perceived," continued Mrs MacDonald in a lower voice, "that the misconduct of her parents is no fault of Miss Babcock's—Mrs MacAdam's—whatever we are to call her—

who was then only an unborn babe, innocent as a lamb. But she, having once discovered all this, was entirely at a loss, poor child; at a standstill. She was left with no family at all—knowing only her father's surname and her mother's Christian name. She resolved then—this was some three years ago—to go to France, upon the invitation of some American ladies who had befriended her during their voyage here. These ladies had by that time established themselves in Paris, and were pursuing there, I believe, chemical studies of some kind at the museum of natural history. As I say, she accepted their invitation—was helped to some work of her own there, through their connections—and there, soon afterward, quite soon afterward, she met and married her husband—"

"Or so she *claims*," called Lady Janet's voice from behind them.

"But what is the great mystery in connection with him?" said Mrs Chambers quietly, ignoring the interruption. "Why must his name remain a secret?"

"A Frenchman—*if* he exists at all!" interjected Lady Janet, who was gaining rapidly on them.

"No indeed, my lady," said Mrs MacDonald, turning to Lady Janet. "He is a Scot, I am given to understand; no Frenchman. I am not certain whether it may be a matter of—perhaps a debt—or something else . . ."

"You will allow me to observe that something dark and discreditable—if not actually criminal—must lie at the bottom of it," said Lady Janet a little breathlessly, having now caught up to them. "French wickedness, and French dresses; horrid colours! If that is the fashion in Paris, I want none of it."

"But how vastly romantic a situation is hers!" said Mrs Chambers. "She is utterly nameless; her mother's name, her father's name, and her husband's name, all unknown—to us, at least. She is Mrs Anonymous."

"If she has a husband in France, why is she here? Why is she not there, with him?" demanded Lady Janet. "*That* is her proper place."

But Mrs Chambers, resolutely unruffled, said, "She has made it plain that she will stop with us here only until Hogmanay; that I shall have to find another wet nurse before the New Year, when she is pledged to be away, and rejoining her husband."

"Mark my words," said Lady Janet. "When the time comes, she will not go. Husband there is none; nor ever was."

Constantia's dresses, so alarming to Lady Janet, were indeed French; and she had two of them. They were made of fine light roller-printed cottons, ideal for a Parisian summer, but somewhat too thin for a Scottish September. Upon close inspection, the bright busy designs printed on the cloth were astonishing: teeming squiggles, or dizzy speckles, or floating enigmas—rods, blobs, pointed ovals—sprouting spikes or hairs. What were they, these exotic shapes, in strange clashing colours, superimposed upon tangled backgrounds of seaweeds, or corals, or crystalline crenellations? Their appearance was very odd; to Scottish eyes, ugly.

Odd they most certainly were; but in Paris they were new, and wonderful; not ugly in the least. They were all the rage. The French manufacturers called such designs "bizarres," and nothing could have been more of the moment, and more knowing—not only for frocks, but for furnishings, too. These bizarres derived not from the fevered imaginations of artists, but from such unremarkable objects as a droplet of pondwater (rather, the infinitesimal denizens thereof); or a translucent slip of onion skin; or a horse's worn molar—these, as seen through that marvelous device the microscope. Through powerful new lenses, astonishing structures, minuscule flora and fauna, preposterous animalcules—all unsuspected hitherto—were to be seen, and drawn. In France, science was fashionable—and the fashion, just now, was scientific.

Constantia owned a microscope; had earned money by it. She had left it packed away in the Paris attic (sixième arrondissement) where she and her husband had been living before coming to Britain. Through that microscope's eyepiece, she had seen and drawn the very designs she now wore as cloth: the animalcules squiggling in a teeming droplet of water brought in from the gutter outside the front doorstep. She sold her drawings—sheaves of them, each carefully tinted in gouache—to the cloth manufacturer who often bought her designs.

Her forms and compositions were based upon what she saw under the lens of her microscope, but her palette was quite another matter. Recent advances in chemistry had made for new dyes, producing colours never until now fast on cloth: mustard! green! purple! in bold juxtaposition. This was by no means the palette of the old masters; it was new, new, new. Even the famous old Oberkampf toile factory at Jouy, failing to adopt or adapt to this new fashion, had dwindled and, three years since, died.

Constantia had made up her dresses herself, taking the precaution of leaving extra depth in the seams, to be let out for such contingencies as maternity, and nursing.

"Is it true, Mr Chambers," Miss Toulmin asked, one drowsy Sunday afternoon when everyone (except Lady Janet, at kirk again for the afternoon service) had come out for tea on the grass under the beech tree, "that no one has ever found the ancient fossil remains of any human being?" Besides Mr and Mrs Chambers and Miss Toulmin, there were Mrs Crowe, Dr and Mrs Moir, and Constantia, with Livia at her breast. Constantia had just fed Charlie who, in his mother's arms, was attempting to focus upon the enchanting silver spoon which she dandled before him. Nina sat before her easel nearby, engrossed in copying a botanical engraving: a *Musa*.

"Aye, it is quite true," said Mr Chambers. "There have been claims of such finds, from time to time; but all of them have proven baseless. Dr Buckland found a human skeleton some years ago in a cave in Wales, in just the same sediment layer which gave up the bones of a mammoth, but soon concluded that the remains had been buried there much more recently, in Roman times; perhaps by a murderer disposing of his victim. And the famous skeletons found in Guadeloupe, embedded in hard limestone apparently of great age, were eventually pronounced—by no less an authority than Dr Cuvier—to be of recent origin, and the stone only calcareous sand quite recently cemented by natural processes common on tropical beaches. No authentic human fossil has ever been found—not convincingly embedded in rock, you know, not in rock of any antiquity—nor with the remains properly petrified—turned to stone, as is the case in what we generally speak of as fossils; as is true of any ammonite, for example."

"'Fossil' . . ." said Mrs Crowe thoughtfully. "What is the origin, Dr Moir, of the word?"

"From Latin *fossa*: a trench in the ground," replied he, without hesitation. "Originally, 'fossil' referred to any article which has been dug from the earth. But nowadays it is generally taken to mean the petrified remains of a creature which was formerly alive—usually preserved by petrifaction—"

"Rather than lost to putrefaction, the usual fate of most earthly remains," said Mr Chambers.

"But just how does this petrifaction of remains occur?" demanded Mrs Crowe. "If not in consequence of a Gorgon's stony glance?"

"Oh; well; Dr Moir?" said Mr Chambers. But Dr Moir was happy to let Mr Chambers explain, if he could; and he did, saying, "It is a natural chemical process which may sometimes occur in buried remains, if the liquids which bathe the surrounding soils or rock are suffused with particular dissolved minerals, which may, under certain conditions, precipitate and fill the space formerly occupied by the buried remains—indeed, perfectly replacing those remains, as they decay—"

"Rather like cire perdue, then; the lost-wax method, for casting bronze mounts and that sort of thing," suggested Mrs Chambers, who had often seen her father, a clockmaker, use that technique in his work.

"Just so," said her husband. "I have sometimes fancied us—the animated tribes, with our soft mortal bodies, our brief life spans—as mere wax models, if you will; only a preliminary, a preparatory form to be melted away in the casting of those far more durable stone figures, which are the Divine Sculptor's ultimate design for this, His Creation."

"A pretty conceit," said Miss Toulmin, "though not entirely flattering to those qualities we most admire in ourselves."

Mrs Crowe said, "Yet among all His durable stone figures, no ancient humans. Remarkable. What are we to make of that?'

"Now that we are bound, in these enlightened times, to scoff at Bishop Ussher's calculations," said Mrs Moir, "is it permitted to consider whether humankind may be of very recent origin, after all?"

"Perhaps we have not yet searched long enough, or hard enough, or in the right places."

"Either the incompleteness of our researches, then—or, the incompleteness of the record."

"Perhaps both."

"It has been suggested that we are taken bodily into heaven," offered Nina, having set aside her drawing.

"Somehow vacating our earthly graves, well before the Day of Judgment?" said Miss Toulmin. "How might so macabre a notion be investigated? Are we to go in search of some unimaginably ancient necropolis—to be opened, and found empty?"

"It has been proposed," said Mrs Crowe, "that our remains are composed of some lofty material which does not petrify—in which case we ought perhaps to call ourselves *Homo ephemeris*, rather than *Homo sapiens*: the 'wise brotherhood.'"

"I beg your pardon, ma'am; *Homo sapiens* means nothing of the sort!" cried Dr Moir, roused to contradiction. "For *homo*, Mrs Crowe, we must look to the Greek, not the Latin. *Homo* is from humus: dust, earth; so, earthling. *Sapiens* is respectable enough Latin: 'tasting'—from *sapere*, to taste. So: the earthling which tastes. We are the 'tasting earthlings.'"

"'Tasting'! No, no!" declared Mrs Crowe. "Here is some mistake—for was I not taught that *sapiens* meant 'wise'? Though I have often thought, privately, that it smacked of hubris to claim wisdom for our kind in particular."

"Tasters . . . of the fruit . . . of the Tree of Knowledge, I suppose," said Mrs Chambers slowly.

"How Mr Linnaeus rises, in my estimation!" said Miss Toulmin, as appreciation dawned. "I had thought him merely an assiduous naturalist—no mean thing—but he was more than that. He was a poet."

"Knowledge—there is the crux of it," said Dr Moir. "So, the Knowing Ones: the connoisseurs, if you like, of all Creation."

"Let us say, rather, 'savants'!" cried Miss Toulmin. "It is not only the natural philosophers naming specimens in museums who deserve to be called savants; we are, all of us, all humankind, savants—are we not?"

"No; but hold up, for a moment. Say that again," demanded Mrs Crowe. "Might it—mightn't it be the naming itself—the lordly naming of all the creatures—indeed, the very act of distinguishing among kinds—which distinguishes our kind? As, we are told, Adam named them all—and certainly *before* his fateful encounter with that forbidden fruit?"

"As Mr Linnaeus did, too, so very thoroughly," said Dr Moir.

"What would you have named humankind?" said Mr Chambers.

"Oh! Well!"

"No, but this is immensely interesting; not to be taken lightly," said Mr Chambers. "We might devote some serious deliberation—an hour, or even two?—to so momentous a task as this."

"Let us each propose a name after dinner, then—instead of music," said Mrs Chambers. "Tonight you need not sing for your supper—for your tea afterward, I should say—but only propose a suitable name for our kind."

And that was the origin of Adam's Game—as it came to be called in the Chambers household. All of the family's friends and regular guests were soon introduced to it, and any new acquaintances quickly learned that they, too, were expected to propose a name. The name ought to be original, not previously proposed by someone else. And true, in distinguishing humankind from all other kinds. And it ought to be clever.

Lady Janet, when she heard of Adam's Game, would have nothing to do with it. She considered it gross materialism, a grievous error; and said so. Every human being, she told Mrs Chambers, was created in the Divine Image; and was elevated to a rank distinct from and incomparably superior to the beasts by possessing an immortal soul. Mrs Chambers on this occasion courteously refrained from pointing out to Lady Janet that she had just played the game; and made this observation only to her husband, in private.

"Aha! Here you are! I have found you at last, my wife, my Camera Obscura!" cried Mr Chambers. He burst out of the conservatory door onto the broad granite step, where Mrs Chambers had come to sit with Constantia and the two babies in the final two minutes of September afternoon sunshine. "I have been hunting you all over the house, my dear, and not finding you. But you cannot elude me forever; I shall always succeed at last in running you to ground. I am sorry, but it *is* rather urgent, and not a business which any mere husband is qualified to sort out—" And away went Mrs Chambers with him, to attend to some household matter.

Constantia wondered at this. "Camera Obscura"! Did it not mean "dark room"? Was it not also a species of device for making images and portraits: daguerreotypes, calotypes? As a term of endearment from husband to wife, it was certainly unusual; she supposed it must contain some meaning personal to the two of them.

The absent landlord of Spring Gardens owned a fine old library, but evidently he distrusted either his books or his tenants, for the doors fronting his bookcases were fitted with brass mesh, and locked. They were dangerous things, books; best locked safely away in cages, like the fierce beasts in a menagerie. There was nevertheless plenty to read in the library, for the Chamberses took in all the journals and reviews; these covered every table and overflowed onto the chairs and sofas. There was *Blackwood's*; and the *Edinburgh Review*; and most especially there was *Chambers's Edinburgh Journal.* There was an abundance of books, too; and Constantia had been invited by Mrs Chambers to carry off anything she liked; to treat as her own anything that was not locked away.

Beneath the window stood the writing table where, Constantia knew, Mrs Chambers devoted her mornings—and some of her afternoons as well—to a copious correspondence. The table now stood bare except for inkstand, blotter, and a large horn paper knife, for Mrs Chambers always fastidiously cleared away her papers upon completing her day's work. Upon the chimneypiece over the empty fireplace were not the usual porcelain garnitures or bronze figurines, but an assortment of rocks and shells; the window sills, too, were lined with rocks. Under Constantia's examination, these unconventional decorations revealed their remarkable qualities.

"That, Mrs MacAdam, is my husband's dearest possession; his best fossil ammonite," said Mrs Chambers's voice, startling Constantia who, having come in search of the mislaid *Vestiges,* had been distracted instead by the remarkable fossil at the center of the chimneypiece.

"It is very fine," said Constantia, and thought of the little fossil *Potamides* (or was it a *Tympanotonos?*) given her by her husband. It was now—indeed, always—in the bottom of her pocket. "Where did he find it?"

"Oh!—inside a box, truth be told. He did not collect it himself, but bought it, sight unseen, from a dealer in London. He has found several interesting fossils, these last few years, but nothing so fine as that. Here is a Sphenopteris he found near Burdiehouse; and he collected that fragment of ancient fern here in Musselburgh. When other men go out to walk, they stride along with their heads high, their eyes raised to distant horizons, gazing upon the sublime; upon mountains or sea or waterfalls or skies. But my husband's sights are fixed upon the ground beneath his feet; no further. He says he is haunted by the thought that he might, all un-knowing, tread upon something wonderful—might fail to recognise some prize, some treasure, beneath his very boot. Once he told me of a nightmare in which felons, breaking rocks for railway beds, were smashing up the most marvelous fossils: the earthly remains of God's most astonishing creatures."

✧ ✧ ✧

NOTHING HAPPENS; and nothing happens; and still nothing happens. Everything remains the same . . . or so it seems. But the truth is that everything is changing imperceptibly all the time. The pressure of these infinitesimal changes mounts. In the solid edifice, unseen cracks deepen and widen. Eventually, something ruptures—a cog in the cosmic engine slips—and everything crashes at once, into new stasis.

Wait for it.

Some twins are not much alike, but Jenny and Lizzy were all but identical. Constantia could see that one was slightly taller and slimmer than the other, just now. And the shorter one had a little more sunburn across her nose, this week. So they were distinguishable—only just—to a discerning onlooker; but this taller girl, was she Jenny? Or was she Lizzy? Constantia did not feel quite certain which name went with which twin. Within the family they were sometimes addressed as "Twinnies" when together, or "Twinny" if separate. They had not the slightest objection to this. Were they as identical in character as they were in body? It was clear enough that they did not share a mind. Each had to learn her lessons for herself; she did not know what her sister knew. But what was a mind? And what was a character?

Twins! Two, exactly the same! How could this happen? What could it mean? Are we not each a unique creation, then, after all? Had some mistake been made? By whom?

Constantia's twins had been unalike: a son and a daughter. Her daughter was thriving; her son lost beyond all finding. A stranger had slid into the world through her body, but had not paused here; had slipped along again, further, immediately, forever. Gone. Had some mistake been made? By whom?

From her high window Constantia watched the two little boys, Jemmie and Willie, in the garden below, one warm afternoon. As the tight-fitting frocks in which Hopey dressed them each morning buttoned down the back, it was usually possible to keep them clothed. But left unsupervised together for the quarter of an hour, they conspired on this occasion to unbutton each other, and succeeded in promptly shedding their clothes. Even from this distance, Constantia could see that the air and the sunshine on their white skin delighted them; the sensation of freedom delighted them; and the liberation and parading and accessibility of their hairless pink genitals especially delighted them, for these were their favourite parts of themselves. All too soon their sisters found them, and put an end to such pleasures; the boys were required, briskly, to put their clothes on again. Why? To the little boys, it must have seemed unjust. Tuckie's puppy, Bunty, was not required to wear clothes; nor did Bunty seem to notice or care whether the little boys did or didn't.

Jemmie, at four, could very nearly read, but not quite. Mary had undertaken to teach him, and Constantia often overheard their lessons in the day nursery. Jemmie recognised most letters; could sometimes remember their names and, if prompted by pasteboard pictures of animals associated with them, could even repeat the sounds they purported to represent. Constantia still remembered her own difficulties in learning to read, and felt sympathy for Jemmie. "Cuh, for crow" seemed reasonable enough, as one often heard crows say just that: cuh! caw! But dogs certainly did not say "Duh." Tuckie's puppy said many things, such as "Wah! Wah!" and "Ip!" and "Yiyiyi!" and sometimes "Grr," or "Mmm?"—but he never said anything that sounded like "Duh."

The puppy, Bunty, could very nearly understand English, but not quite. There were many utterances he did understand, such as "Walk?" and "Naughty!" and "Cat" and "Dinnertime!" When Mary had begun teaching Jemmie his letters, Tuckie had quietly begun to administer the same lessons to Bunty. Constantia found her at it one day in a corner of the garden.

"But Bunty is as clever as Jemmie," explained Tuckie, "or cleverer; and he is very hardworking—have you seen him dig? He never wants to give it up—so I suppose that he can learn to read."

"Has he learnt any letters yet?" asked Constantia.

"Not *yet*," said Tuckie. "Not *quite*. But I am sure that he will, for he is keen, and I am patient. Learning to read was perplexing when I was little, I remember; but then I found quite suddenly that I *could* read—and now that I can, Mrs MacAdam—oh aye, I have been able to read for years, ever since I was four!—and now, when I see a word, the very sound of it bursts instantly upon my mind, without the slightest effort."

"I know just what you mean," said Constantia. "Once one has got the knack of it, it is impossible *not* to read. I wish you luck with your pupil." She left them at it, but watching from nearby, soon saw girl and dog go to the barred gate which gave upon the street. There Bunty raised his nose into the breeze and growled quietly; the fur along his spine bristled. "What is it, Bunty?" Tuckie said to him; and she, too, lifted her nose and sniffed the air. Constantia herself could smell honeyed linden; wet soil; pigeon dung, the smell of the doocot; coal smoke; rotting seaweed upon the shore not far away; nothing unusual, nothing alarming. Tuckie patted Bunty; and the fur along his spine lay down again. Perhaps, thought Constantia, he revered her for her imperturbable calm, even though awash in terrifying scents of dangers. Perhaps he mistook this calm for courage. Probably it was inconceivable to him that this calm was the result of obliviousness, and ignorance. How could smells *not* be smelled?

The dog apprehended language, Constantia supposed, about as well as the child apprehended smells.

After midnight, while feeding the babies by candlelight, Constantia listened to the silence of the house. It was deeply silent, or so it seemed . . . but how much, she asked herself, do we miss? Do sublime ragas and celestial symphonies constantly play, at pitches we cannot hear? Too high? Too low? Too quiet, or too loud, for humans to hear? Too slow or too fast, for human ears to apprehend? Are there exquisite chords, counterpoints, and harmonies? or is it noise, cacophony, that music of the spheres? Does it roar, that Ocean of Music? Or does it murmur?

Do great volumes—sagas, epics, chronicles—of scent blow across our skin at every moment? Do we breathe them oblivious, illiterate? Is it a stench, or is it a perfume? Are vast libraries swirling around us, breathed in and out by us unsuspected, unapprehended? Do we breathe the eloquent air as a puppy chews a book left on the floor, or out in the rain: only for the irresistible feel of it?

4

THE THICK FOG which had swaddled the entire Northumberland coast for five days and nights melted suddenly away—in less than an hour—to clear sunshine, at mid-morning of the sixth day. The timing could not have been worse. Hugh Stevenson climbed to the rim of the gryke and ventured to raise his head enough to look shoreward. Three-quarters of a mile distant across green sea stood the ruins of Warkworth Castle. Below it, the town of Amble presided over its tidy harbour at the mouth of the River Coquet, in air so clear and cool it seemed nearer. And from the town, he supposed, this wee island—Coquet Isle—must appear equally near and clear.

Mr Stevenson had been relying upon the fog to conceal his fires. The fires, a line of five, were well down inside the gryke, one of two deep, jagged, vertical fissures which snaked inland through the low white limestone cliffs at the north end of the little island. Even with the fog as cover, he had waited until first light to kindle his fires, so that that any glow, as seen from the town, would be swamped and backlit by the usual light of dawn, as well as diffused through fog. Their smoke should have been swallowed by the fog, too.

Now the last wisps of fog had melted to nothing.

The fires were burning well by this time, hot and clean, with little smoke. He had coal enough at hand to last for several more hours.

The underlying stone was not yet heated sufficiently for his purposes. At least two more hours of heating would be required before he could attempt the split; and three hours would offer something like a guarantee of success. This necessity was to be weighed against the risk of discovery.

The wind had come up, and he saw that three boats had already got under sail and out past Amble's harbour jetty. Two lug-rigged cobles were on an easy broad reach to the southeast, heading for the usual fishing grounds. The third, a yawl whose red sails had faded to pink, had turned northward instead, tacking into the freshening wind. As he watched, she came about once more. Headed where?

If he stopped to listen, Mr Stevenson could hear the surf. The sound of this surf was so constant, so unceasing, that after many weeks on this island, he no longer noticed it unless he purposely listened for it. There it was, a dull murmuring and a muttering, rising and falling, like the sound of a great angry crowd at some distance.

He climbed down again. It was warm inside the gryke out of the wind, with the sun beating down from above, and the row of fires heating the line he had scored into the broad ledge of limestone on which he stood. His decision made, he shoveled more coal onto each of his five fires. Very little smoke indeed, he assured himself.

Presently, taking up his two buckets, he made his way along the jagged defile of the gryke toward its mouth. The sound of the sea grew louder, and occasional brisk gusts found their way into the fissure too, until, as he rounded the last winding of the gorge above the open sea, he was suddenly knocked off-balance against the rock wall by the force of an oblique blast. Then he rounded the last bulwark, bracing himself against the eroded limestone wall—and here was the sea, bright lapis-blue now under sunshine, and breaking in white foam over the limestone shelves and shoals which, surrounding and guarding this north end of the island, extended several hundred yards seawards, below the abrupt little cliff of the island's edge. At lowest tides, these shoals would be partially exposed, but now, at high tide, there was little of them to be seen. The wind boxed and buffeted his ears so that he could hear nothing but its roar.

In deep blue water out beyond the shoals, he could see the shining dark heads of two seals. In a moment, two more popped up. They bobbed in the water, watching him as he watched them. Mr Stevenson climbed carefully over slippery rocks down to a pool that was filled with clear sea-water, and filled both his buckets. Then he lugged the heavy sloshing buckets back up again, to the mouth of the gryke; and into it; and along its length some fifty yards or so, back to the site of his fires. There he emptied the buckets into a barrel; shoveled a little more fuel onto his fires; and returned again for more water. He made this journey three times.

At the salt pool for the third time, Mr Stevenson looked up from filling his buckets and was appalled by an unexpected apparition to seaward: bounding into view beyond the vertical rock to one side came the bowsprit—the foresail—and then the bow of the pink-sailed yawl, heeled hard over. She was much nearer than she should have been. Stevenson ducked instantly behind the nearest boulder large enough to conceal him and crouched there, fearing even to look out. He had left his buckets in plain view. He could hear shouting from the yawl, but any words were shredded on the wind. No one would dare to land here, over the rocks—but what brought them here at all? And if their recklessness should bring them to grief onto the rocks, would he not be bound to leave his place of concealment to aid them? This made him angry: by what right did trespassing strangers endanger his enterprise, so long in the making—at this critical moment!—by their unwelcome inquisitiveness and incompetence and recklessness?

He heard no more shouts. After several minutes, he ventured to look out from behind his boulder. The yawl was not to be seen. Presumably she had safely passed beyond the field of view visible to him from this narrow slot in the cliff. Like a blinkered horse, he could see only straight ahead; what lay outside the limestone walls bounding his view to both sides?

He watched for some time. Presently the yawl glided into his field of view again, now on the starboard tack, and much further out. She disappeared once more beyond the left-side cliff. He waited, and eventually saw the pink sails, further out still, cross once more and disappear toward the right. At last he emerged from his hiding place, and retrieving his buckets, turned to check for smoke rising behind him. It was hard to tell from here, upwind, whether his fires were producing plumes of smoke; if there was smoke, it must be blown away from him. He returned along the gryke once more to feed his fires.

After a time, he climbed again to the rim of the gryke. From here, he could see the pink-sailed yawl to the southeast, at a reassuring distance. She had only made a long detour—though much too close—around the north end of Coquet Isle on her way to the fishing grounds. Why? He checked twice more during the following hour, but saw her only recede toward the south. His anger and alarm receded with her.

At noon, Mr Stevenson readied his tools and his mind for the critical operation. Then, taking up a steel rake, he quickly swept the line of burning coals and ash off the limestone ledge, into the damp gorge below—and in the next moment, threw six bucketsful of cold seawater, one after another, all along the underlying slot he had scored in the stone where he desired it should split. Nothing happened. He waited another instant. Still nothing. Seizing his sledge-hammer, he raised it to strike the desired line of fracture—but before he could strike, a dull crack like a bolt of underground thunder was heard, and a split appeared in the stone at his feet. In the time it took to draw his next breath, the split ran, halting but inevitable, the whole length of the ledge, exactly as he had intended. Hugh let out a whoop of triumph. This stone was conquered. What God had joined together, he, Hugh Stevenson, had put asunder.

There remained a great deal of putting asunder to be done; perhaps months' worth. During the long operations which lay ahead—

sawing, hammering, filing, chiseling, drilling, splitting, reducing, and painstakingly teasing apart this vast block he had split off the limestone ledge—there would be plenty of time for worrying, planning, and remembering. It amused Mr Stevenson now to remember his terror when he had first encountered ancient remains, in this very gryke. Then a barefoot stripling of eleven years, he had been stricken with horror at actually stepping upon—too late to stop himself— the unmistakable knuckly ridge of a spine standing proud of the limestone, like a submerged sea creature breaking the surface of the water; breaking into the air. The hairs of his body had stiffened—his appetite for solo exploration and adventure had curdled—and he had bolted from the spot, not daring to mention even to his quarrymaster father what he had seen in this cleft in the earth.

By the time he was fifteen or sixteen, however, and of some real use to his father (and fancying himself already an adept in the stonecutter's art), he had become accustomed to fossils. By then, he knew of the Annings, brother and sister, and of the astonishing— and valuable—monsters they were extricating from the Lias cliffs at Lyme Regis.

To what ancient creature had it belonged, that spine he had stepped on here, all those years ago? No one would ever know. Upon returning to Coquet Isle this summer, he had searched diligently; but no traces of it remained. During the intervening two decades, north wind and North Sea had eradicated it. It had been eroded to gravel and washed to the bottom of the sea.

But then he had found something else; something that even the Annings might have rejoiced to find.

Here, off an English shore, forty miles south of the mouth of the River Tweed, Mr Stevenson thought often of Scotland. As he worked, he sometimes would soothe and delight himself by counting over his native land's long inventory of riches, for even Scotland—so poor in so many of the materials of life—is rich in stone; exceedingly rich in stone. He loved the resonant poetry of the names: travertine, serpentine, celestine. He loved the gems: garnet, malachite, amethyst, jasper, carnelian, cairngorm, chalcedony, agate, druzy crystal, and quartz. He loved the ores: ironstone, galena, talc. He loved the douce sandstones of Craigleith, Binnie, Humbie, and Kingoodie. And he loved and respected the granites of Aberdeen and Kirkudbright, adamantine as Scotsmen themselves; so much of which (and so many of whom) had gone to pave London and Liverpool.

But his favourites above all were the limestones in their marvelous variety and utility: lithographic, bituminous, hydraulic, oolitic, crinoidal; marble in all its extravagant colours, veining, and variegations; alabaster; fluor; arragonite; gypsum, compact or fibrous; asparagus-stone; tremolite; lucullite; stinkstone; domolite; rhomb-spar; brown-spar, foliated or columnar; travertine; tufa; coquina; coral rock; chalk; Lias; clunch. Not to forget stalactite and stalagmite. All these were limestones.

All of it, treasure. Requiring only to be found, then won; wrested from the grip of the earth. Best of all, this treasure was inexhaustible: the whole vast earth beneath his feet was made of stone. A farmer knows his soil is his treasure, but soil—especially Scottish soil—is only a thin deposit atop the underlying stone; only the merest skin, be it ever so comely, over the bony skull. The good honest stone which underlies everything is an infinitely deeper store, of stronger riches.

Strong, but not invincible. A quarryman knows each stone's secret weakness. He knows how to conquer it; how to break it; how to split even granite, basalt, gabbro, porphyry, quartz, gneiss, trap rock.

I am Man; I can break anything. Anything.

Working quite alone, Mr Stevenson was able nonetheless to move immense blocks of stone with ease and precision. His crane, brought from Paris at such cost and inconvenience, was a movable beam type, like that used by the celebrated engineer Robert Stevenson (a kinsman at some remove) when building the Bell Rock lighthouse. There was little space here for manoeuvre; finesse was indispensable.

Mr Stevenson had not much use for books. The earth itself was his book. Who sees the earth as the quarryman does? Who prises apart the very layers of the past—teases apart the uncut pages of the earth's history—as the quarryman does? The very limestone he splits into blocks is the remains of ancient creatures; indeed, some of it is nothing but the remains of ancient creatures. What tremendous creatures have quarrymen down through the centuries not cut into—carved up—and thrown away as useless rubble, rather than the good sound building-stone they seek?

Though he had not much use for books, Mr Stevenson had been reading a borrowed book by brief fits and starts, in the few minutes before sleep overcame him each night. He read meticulously; therefore slowly. *Vestiges of the Natural History of Creation* had been pressed upon him by his friend Mr Darling, the keeper of the lighthouse at the south end of Coquet Isle. Mr Stevenson found the book moderately interesting, though perhaps a trifle belaboured and over-elaborate. Was it not familiar knowledge that various conditions, operating during immense periods of time, upon various materials, had produced the various species of stone?

Was it not self-evident that the same must hold true of creatures? That those same conditions, varying as they did, operating mercilessly during those same immense periods of time, upon various living materials, must have produced the various species of plants and beasts, both surviving and extinct, which inhabit those very situations to which they have (in a phrase he had read somewhere) "superior adaptation and greatest power of occupancy"? There was another phrase that had been haunting him too, these last few weeks: "the weaker, less circumstance-suited, being prematurely destroyed." Where had he read that? It marched, repeatedly, disturbingly, through his mind.

It troubled him that he could not remember, for he had, generally, a capacious and tenacious memory. Indeed, this was one of the reasons he seldom read: He had already a vast store of matters to think of, and little need to pile up more such ore in his mind.

Was it not familiar knowledge that the older the stone, the stranger are the creatures to be found embedded in it, and the less resembling living examples? The stranger the fossil, the older the stone. And the older the stone, the stranger the fossil. Thinking about this while he chiseled a dog-hole in a block of stone, he suspected a logical fallacy—but, fallacy or not, it was true; as true as anything that could be proved.

When daylight failed, he laid down his tools in good order and drew a tarpaulin over them, to keep off the damp. From the rim of the gryke he surveyed the surrounding waters for boats tardily returning to harbour and, seeing none, climbed up and walked the length of the little island in ten minutes, toward the lightkeeper's compound at the southern tip.

As always, he paused at the dovecote to look for any newly-returned pigeon, which would be recognisable by having tied to one leg a ribbon; and to the other a message. He saw no beribboned birds, but only the usual un-ribboned residents chuckling and muttering to themselves as they settled for the night. He was not surprised, for it had been some time since he had received any bird-borne messages. Nor was he disappointed; indeed, he felt a small remission of dread, a brief reprieve—for any message was as likely to bring sorrow as joy. His dear wife!—his poor son! (prematurely destroyed)—his precious daughter! To be a married man and a father was a far weightier business, he now knew, than being a bachelor.

In dusk, Mr Stevenson encountered Mr Darling at the bottom of the lighthouse tower stair. Mr Darling had just descended, having lit the lamps for the night. Together they walked down to the landing-place on the jetty, to unload the coble tied up there after Mr Darling's quick crossing to Amble and back, where he had fetched the letters, and domestic necessities such as flour and milk. As Mr Stevenson shouldered a sack of flour, Mr Darling said, "I was asked in town about the smoke from that north end of the isle."

"And what did you say?" asked Mr Stevenson.

"I said that will be Mrs Darling burning the refuse, a grand heap of it."

5

O N A F I N E C H A I N at her throat, Constantia wore a pearl. It had been her mother's. Livia would reach for this pearl as she nursed, but Charlie took no notice of it. The pearl was no longer round; the back of it, where it lay against Constantia's skin, was wearing flat.

Until now, Constantia had cherished only a few authentic memories of her own mother. She had seldom indulged in bringing them out for contemplation, for fear of wearing them out, wearing them smooth; of rubbing off the sharpness of their features—for she had noticed that they, like the pearl, were becoming flatter over the years.

But now, while she fed the two infants in nearly constant rotation, Constantia was surprised by floods of fresh memories that would whelm up and engulf her. The memories seemed to let down with her milk. Moments, hours, whole days from her past washed over her, as minutely detailed and complete as present moments. Some of the memories were joyous, or lovely; others very sad; some remained as frightening as to the young child she had been.

Her earliest memory was of her own baby-hands and bare knees upon a tiger skin. Of being lifted off it, by her laughing mother. Of longing to touch it again: the dusty fur, the meandering streams of colour, of gold and not-quite-black, and the edges of the stripes where individual hairs of gold overlapped the dark, or dark overlapped the gold. She remembered the rumpled little tags of ears, too, and the long tail—all flattened upon the dark floor planks. Her mother lifting her off it. Her mother laughing, scarcely scolding at all.

She remembered snuggling with her mother under a blanket, while thunder rolled and epic torrents of rain—rain that could drown you, there was so little air to breathe in it, only water, like a waterfall—crashed just beyond the edge of the roof thatch; of feeling safe, sheltered from the monsoon beneath thick muffling thatch, and tucked under her mother's arm.

It was a soft round freckled arm, most beautiful; and the smell of her mother's skin and hair, and of her mother's blanket, was wonderful. Oh, her mother's hair! "Mamma's hair . . ." the very small Constantia had used to murmur to herself, stroking that yellow springy hair when her beautiful mother would lie down beside her, to help her go to sleep; "Mamma's hair . . ."

Later, when little Constantia would awaken in the night, in darkness, she was alone; her beautiful mother—far more beautiful than all the other mothers—was not there. "Mamma's hair," Constantia would murmur to herself in the nighttime, for comfort; and she would stroke her own hair, finer than her mother's; and think of her mother, and think of how glad her mother would be to see her, in the morning, in the daylight, in the sunlight.

Constantia had been astonished when other children, her friends, claimed that their own mothers were the most beautiful. How preposterous! Had they not eyes in their heads? Constantia had pitied the other children not only for the inferior beauty of their mothers, but also for their mistaken judgment.

Constantia sometimes now found herself humming to her own drowsy Livia a song that her mother had used to sing to her. She had not thought of it in years.

* * *

On occasion a pair of squabs was brought upstairs to Constantia on her dinner plate, but no matter how hungry she might be, she could not eat them. It was the ribcages that appalled her; too like that final glimpse of the body of her son: his ribs deflated for the last time, his final agonised breath drained out of him. Stilled.

The two infants, Charlie and Livia, throve, and grew fat cheeks and redundant chins, and creases at their wrists as though tight threads encircled them.

It sometimes happened that both babies fell simultaneously into a frenzy for milk. It was all but impossible to peaceably give suck to one while the other was raging and howling five feet away, apparently in danger of bursting a blood vessel by the violence of its fury and need—but it was equally impossible to pick up the second, if the first was already suckling. On those occasions, Hopey would come in, if she was within earshot. She would pick up the second baby and place it within Constantia's encircling arm, and help her uncover her other breast; help position the nuzzling furious baby at the nipple. Then she'd step back, hands on hips, and say, "Now, there is a pretty sight, Mrs MacAdam! I wish you could see for yourself, the pair of them, the round bald heads of them at you together. I mind very well how it was, when I was nursing my Jenny and Lizzy." Once the babies were positioned, Constantia could hold and satisfy them both. She didn't need more breasts; only more arms, as Hindu goddesses had.

Afterwards, there was the difficulty of disengaging; of shifting one baby safely to a cradle or cushion, or sometimes, to the floor—without dropping or unsettling the other. If they had fallen asleep at the breast, they were sure to startle awake again.

If they had not fallen asleep, it was because they had—or soon would—soiled their clooties, and required therefore to be undressed, cleaned, and reclothed. Again, it often happened that one screamed while she tended the other, gently wiping and cleaning the creases and folds of their surprisingly exaggerated infant sexes: so very male! or so very female! All that pale milk, changed into this: yellow curds. What strange creatures we are; and what a strange and disgusting process was this digestion! Could we not have been formed to live upon air, water, soil and sunlight—as blameless plants did? Humans might be a high caste: Kashitryas, the caste from which spring kings and warriors—but were not plants of the highest caste of all? Doing no harm, were they not the true Brahmins of creation?

What a talkative, playful clan these Chamberses were! Often Constantia could not help but hear them chattering unreservedly beyond the thin partition wall.

"Well, if it isn't Mr Balderstone," she heard Nina say one evening, as her father entered the day-nursery, "come upstairs to sit for a time with his daughters, the clever, good and beautiful Misses Balderstone. Is he come to glean material for his paper? Aye, the usual notebook emerges from the waistcoat pocket—and the usual dull pencil. 'Shall I sharpen that for you?' offers the eldest Miss Balderstone, as is her kindly habit."

"Ah!" sighed Mr Chambers; and Constantia heard his usual chair creak as he settled into it. "What a fortunate man he is, to find the eldest Miss Balderstone, in company with her charming sisters, and all of them prepared no doubt with acute remarks and clever mots—"

"Do not forget her penknife, as keen as her wit—"

"—for him to appropriate, and put into his paper, and pretend they are his own, and all without the slightest trouble to himself," said he.

"And if Miss Balderstone were to reserve her acute remarks and her bons mots to herself?" said Nina. "For her own use?"

Said Mr Chambers, "Mr Balderstone, a man of some native wit and middling-quick understanding, cries, 'Aha! Has Miss Balderstone a novel in progress to tuck them all into?'"

"Well; and if she has?" said Nina.

"She says it is not genteel to use her own name, whatever," said Annie, "so we have been thinking up elegant noms de plume for her. I proposed 'The Dove of Midlothian.'"

"Too lofty and sentimental," said Mary. "'A Caledonian Gentlewoman' is far better, and would look vastly well on a title page."

"But Daddy, why do you never sign your articles in the *Journal*?" asked Annie.

"Sign them! Why should I?" said he.

"Because I wish to know who wrote a thing."

"I should do so, then, merely to satisfy a vulgar curiosity?"

"Oh, Daddy, never vulgar!" cried Mary. "The Misses Balderstone could never be vulgar, for there is no set of sisters so untainted by vulgarity as the Misses Balderstone! But their spirit of serious inquiry is not easily turned aside. Mildly, Miss Mary Balderstone repeats her sister's question, with a most becoming and maidenly modesty: 'Oh, Daddy, sir: Why not sign your own name?'"

"It is a good question—but one that Mr Balderstone cannot answer. Mr Chambers can, however, if you saucy lasses will admit him to your presence."

"We will."

"I do not think I have ever told you," said Mr Chambers, quite seriously now, "that I was present at that memorable public dinner—its purpose to raise funds for some worthy cause or other, though what it was I have forgotten—when Sir Walter Scott was for the first time publicly named and acclaimed as the Author of *Waverley*, and of all those subsequent works of his incomparable genius. It is true that Sir Walter's authorship had been an open secret for some time. Ever since Ballantynes' had failed during the distresses of 'twenty-five, everyone had known, though only in a private and not-to-be-spoken-of sort of way. It was Lord Meadowbank who breached the ban at last—not by any carelessness, or thoughtless slip of the tongue; nay, he was not fuddled by wine; scarcely even warm! Rather, having privately sought and received Sir Walter's consent, Meadowbank got upon his legs after dinner and proposed his toast, somewhat in this vein: 'The clouds are dispelled at last—the darkness cleared away; and the Great Unknown—the minstrel of our native land, the mighty magician who has rolled back the current of time, and conjured up before our living senses the conduct of men and manners of days which have long passed away—sits here among us. Distinguished for his towering talents, he has opened to the world not only the sublime beauties of our country, but also the selfless courage and gallantry of our illustrious ancestors. Before the world he has burnished the reputation of our national character, and bestowed on Scotland an imperishable name, were it only by her having given birth to himself. Gentlemen, I propose to you the health of—Sir Walter Scott!'

"The assembled company climbed upon the tables—of course no ladies were present—and the huzzahs went on and on, fit to deafen us all. Thus taxed, Sir Walter did not deny his authorship, but graciously received the acclaim. But when someone then addressed him as the Great Unknown, he said—and this has stuck with me ever since—'No indeed, sir,' he said. 'Henceforth, I am only The Small Known.'"

"Ah," said Nina.

"Nina understands me," said he, "but Mary looks perplexed. The point is this: So long as the author of those prodigious books had borne no bodily shape in the eyes of his fellow-countrymen, he might indeed have been more than human; a very angel of literature. But once their authorship was known, were not those noble works somewhat diminished by their association with little—old—lame—mortal—flawed—bankrupt—Sir Wat? He thought so, at least: a modest and exceedingly amiable man, who tolerated me kindly, though he must have known that I—then an eager callant of twenty-five—dogged him with the intention of publishing a Life, so soon as he should oblige by dying—which he did, a few years later. That was the first of my books to sell quite well; due entirely to the excellence of its subject, however—and not, regrettably, to its own merits, nor those of its author."

✳ ✳ ✳

ADAM'S GAME penetrated even the nursery. One cold morning when the east wind blew, Jenny said mournfully over breakfast, "I do wish we might have a fire."

"Aye, to toast our bread and cheese, in front of. How vastly agreeable that would be!"

"And I long for a baked apple," said Jenny. "It's many a long day since we had any."

"Do you suppose that when Adam and Eve had their apple," said Lizzy, "they baked it first?"

"And with honey," said Jenny fervently.

"Ah . . ." breathed Nina; and then: "Is it only humans who cook their food? Do none but humankind use fire? I must tell Dad: *Homo prometheum*."

On another occasion, Nina reported to her sisters Mrs Crowe's opinion: "Mrs Crowe says that humans are the sorting creatures, the distinguishing earthlings, *Homo distinguit*; that we divide everything into kinds. We distinguish between This and That. Between Us and Them."

"Do none of the beasts distinguish?" said Mary. "They must distinguish between male and female, at the very least; how continue their kind else?"

"But there are a great many creatures not particularly male or female. Aye, it is so; I read it in a back number of Dad's *Journal*. Not just animalcules, as are seen in their multitudes in a drop of pond water—but also snails and slugs, and earthworms, and some of the fishes."

"No one can distinguish cock pigeons from hen pigeons."

"Nay; only watch them together," said Annie. "The cocks are the ones strutting and puffing—"

"You fancy that you can distinguish, Annie," Mary said, "but it may be that hens puff and strut, too!"

"The pigeons distinguish well enough, if we cannot," said Hopey. "Well enough to fill one nest after another with squabs, all the year round."

"The gardener told me that some very industrious pairs may even fill two nests at once," said Annie.

"How do they manage without help, I wonder?" said Hopey.

"So handsome, still, this shot taffeta stuff!" said Mrs Chambers, holding up an old dress of hers in front of Nina's shoulders in the drawing room one evening. For once, all the family was at home without any guests but Lady Janet at her cabinet in the corner, and Constantia. "These tints better suit your complexion, Nina, than mine; and you are nearly of an age now to wear so elegant a stuff. I could not quite bring myself to part with it—but nor could I wear it, for my waist never was the same again, hinney, after you were born. I daresay that Mrs Brown might be equal to the remaking of it. The bodice must be recut, to be sure; the neckline raised and the waist lowered—"

"But Mamma, those sleeves!" cried Mary. "How mortifying for Nina to go about in such preposterous sleeves!"

"Aye, they are something monstrous," agreed her mother cheerfully. "Yet at the time, you know, we thought them the very summit of elegance. Still, mancherons and perhaps a pair of lace undersleeves would change everything; and there is plenty of stuff in them to be re-cut—"

"I should say so!" said Nina, spreading out the enormous width of the bouffant upper sleeves which had been so killingly fashionable fifteen years before. "Why, there must be three yards to each one."

"I can scarcely believe my ears!" declared Lady Janet from her corner. "I should never have thought to hear such a spoilt and ungrateful reply from any well-brought-up girls, to a mother's offer of a handsome present. It is demeaning to prostrate oneself to the fickle whim of fashion, and I assure you—though you will not believe me—that in fifteen years' time the present fashions will appear equally ridiculous to you. This present mode of arranging the hair is the silliest thing I ever saw; even the queen goes about with her hair contrived in swags and draperies around her ears, for all the world like an upholsterer's display. I am sadly disappointed in her. Worse still are those preposterous ringlets one sees everywhere, all a-dangle at either side of the face, like—like sausages hanging in the butcher's shop!"

This was more than usually tactless of Lady Janet, for all the girls—and their mother, too—arranged their hair each morning very much as the pretty young Queen Victoria did, with smooth glossy wings of hair looped around their ears. It cost them some time and trouble, and gave them great satisfaction, to contrive those very swags and ringlets so derided by Lady Janet.

Lady Janet's scanty white hair was scraped back into an old-fashioned cap; and her ears stood boldly forth ungraced by any swags, drapes, wings, ringlets—or indeed by any feminine softnesses or graces whatever. Although the girls could not admire Lady Janet's toilette (and her whiskery lip and chin horrified them), they supposed that her advanced age put her hors de combat; and their courtesy was so far superior to hers that they could not have dreamed of dropping even a hint that her appearance might be improved in any particular.

It was Constantia who broke the awkward silence which had fallen. "They are quite inexplicable, these revolutions of fashion," she said. "Someone devises a new trimming, or new waist, or new sleeve—and at once the previous style, though it had been until that moment the smartest thing going, is utterly extinguished! As old-fashioned as—as—"

"As a farthingale," supplied Nina.

"As a suit of armour," said Mary.

"As a mammoth," said Annie.

"But how do fashions change?" said Mary. "How can enormous puffed sleeves ever have been smart?"

"One might as well ask why mammoths are extinct," said Annie. "How did mammoths fall out of fashion?"

"Perhaps, having no warm clothes to put on when the east wind blew, they froze to death, each and every one," said Jenny, who had been complaining all day of the cold.

"Oh, silly," said Lizzy.

"Perhaps not so very silly," said Mrs Chambers thoughtfully. "Is it not curious that none of the animal tribes wear clothes? Only humankind does so. Humans are the earthlings who clothe themselves. Do you hear that, my dear?" said she, turning to her husband who, engrossed in his book, had succeeded at hearing none of this frivolous chatter. "It may be our universal appetite for attiring ourselves which distinguishes humankind from the beasts: *Homo vestitum!* What do you think of that?"

"Jemmie and Willie are not human, then," said he, not looking up from the page, "for they are determined to escape their clothes."

"A trifling objection," said Mrs Chambers. "Over time they will develop into humans. It is a matter of development."

"No, it still will not answer," said Mr Chambers, laying aside his book. "I have been reading the account of a voyage recently published by an eminent naturalist—the highly intelligent and observing geologist Mr Darwin—who reports that even the full-grown men and women of Tierra del Fuego often go entirely naked."

"But surely this Fuego must enjoy a tropical climate? Where clothing is only a discomfort and a hindrance?"

"Not at all. Fuego lies in nearly the same relation to the South Pole as our Shetland Islands do to the North, and with a comparable climate. Yet the author reports the sleet falling and thawing upon the naked bosom of the naked mother, while she suckles her equally naked new-born infant."

"They can hardly be human, then."

"They are undoubtedly human."

"How very disagreeable it is to hear such matters spoken of," said Lady Janet from her corner. "In the drawing room, too."

*　*　*

Upon seeing her father wind the hall clock on a Saturday morning, as was his custom, Tuckie—who had only recently learned to interpret its round face, its unequal hands—said, "It is only humans who can tell time. Isn't that so, Daddy?"

"An intriguing notion," said Mr Chambers, stepping down from the ladder. "But how are we to account for the dog who knows when to expect his master's return, and goes to await him in the high road at the end of the day's work? How to account for the birds who know when it is time to fly south?"

"Oh," said Tuckie, crestfallen.

"It is a valuable thought, whatever," said her father. "We are perhaps the only creatures to have devised ways of measuring time—indeed, of measuring anything. We ought perhaps to be called *Homo mensor*—the measuring earthling."

"*Homo mathematicus*," proposed Mary to her father, one evening when he had come upstairs with slippers, notebook, and dull pencil. "None but humans are able to perform mathematical operations." For Mary had been instructed by her mother that very afternoon in the useful Rule of Three.

"Mm," said her father. "But a ewe, having borne twins, is not content if only one of them is by her; she knows that the other is missing, and goes seeking it. And if she has borne triplets, and only two of them are by her, she knows that the third is missing, and goes seeking it."

Said Annie, "If that is true—"

"Mr Hogg, who ought to know, has assured me that it is. A great and amazing fact."

"—then ewes—even silly ewes!—can do maths; can count to three, at least."

"Which is more than Jemmie can do!" crowed Lizzy.

"One, two, three!" retorted Jemmie. "Six, seven, eight!"

"You forgot four and five!"

Mrs MacDonald, who was accustomed to children and quite liked them, would often pay them the compliment of engaging them in conversation, and even in argument, as though they were her equals. One afternoon when she had come down from town, the three older girls were admitted to downstairs tea. In the rambling and wide-ranging course of their table-talk, Annie, somewhat exhilarated by two cups of strong tea, ventured to declare that it was only humans who made use of symbols.

Said Mrs MacDonald, "I beg your pardon, Miss Anne—but consider, pray, that so too do dogs."

"What do you mean?"

"Dogs use their excrement as symbols, to intimidate their rivals. Why else are dogs so determined to leave their droppings in the high road which everyone uses?"

"Is it not to infuriate all those who are sure to step in it?" said Mrs Chambers.

"As I did, on my way here?" said Mrs MacDonald. "No. It is meant as a public notice to other dogs: a warning to would-be interlopers that a well-fed and valiant dog is already here, in this district, and they had best go along, somewhere else."

"Horses make a tremendous monument, too, of their dung, and for the same reason," observed Nina, "though geldings and mares do nothing of the sort."

"This is no fit subject for respectable company," said Lady Janet.

"In Daddy's *Journal*, dung is called 'effete particles,'" reported Annie. "Aye, it is; and some naturalists have made great studies about it, haven't they, Mamma?"

"Quite true," said Mrs Chambers. "Both Dr Buckland and Dr Mantell have established some very interesting and valuable facts deriving from their studies of fossil, ah, 'coprolites.'"

"Oh, 'coprolites,' is it? What a splendid word!" said Mrs MacDonald. "Where is Dr Moir when we need him?"

"Not at all nice," said Lady Janet.

Jenny, playing on the lawn with the puppy Bunty, said to her twin, "Lizzy, if we are the crown of all creation, why cannot we hear and smell as keenly as a dog?"

Lady Janet, passing within earshot on her way into the conservatory, seized upon this opportunity to instruct. "Let it be a lesson to you, miss," she called out. "It is a sign that we are not to be at the mercy of our senses—for we, God's creatures which He has made in His own image, are endowed with something immeasurably higher, and better. You know what that is, I hope?"

"Mm; reason?" hazarded Jenny, without much confidence.

"No, certainly not Reason! Reason may lead us dangerously astray—indeed, Reason is no more reliable a guide than is Sensation. I refer, of course, to our immortal souls. And you ought certainly to know that, at your age. Have you children had no religious training at all? You are as ignorant as infidels." She passed into the house through the conservatory.

Jenny flopped down on her back in the grass, thus inviting delirious Bunty to tumble all over her face and neck, licking her eyes, nose, and ears. She shrieked with laughter until, when the licking and tickling became unbearable, she had to push him away and sit up again. Wiping her sleeve across her face, she said, "Lizzy, do dogs suppose that they are the ones made in God's own image?"

"Aye, they must," said Lizzy. "Just fancy: God with four legs and fur, and a long pink tongue, and a tail to wag when He is glad."

☆ ☆ ☆

ONE DAY, as she was passing by the open nursery door, Constantia was arrested by Annie's voice saying, "Nay, Lizzy, you blockhead.

Mammifers are the creatures which nurse their young. That is why they are called mammifers. That is what 'mammifer' means."

Constantia stopped to listen.

"Oh! Like 'Mamma' then," suggested Lizzy.

"But that cannot be so," objected Tuckie, "because Mamma does not nurse Charlie. She has Mrs MacAdam to do it for her."

"She might, though, if she wished."

"Nay, but she cannot," said Tuckie. "She did try, mind you, after the wicked nurse went away—and she could not, for she had no milk."

"And Daddy, never," said Jenny. "Does that mean that men are not mammifers?"

"No, the males of the mammifer tribes do not themselves nurse their young, but they are mammifers nonetheless . . . because they were nursed by their mammas," insisted Annie.

"But we were not nursed by Mamma," said Jenny. "It was Hopey who nursed us."

"Oh! You are too stupid to talk to! A scanty and defective development of life! Of course you must know what I mean!"

"Mrs MacDonald says it is only humans who laugh; that we are the laughing earthling."

"But Lady Janet never laughs. Have you ever seen her laugh?"

"Nay, nor even smile."

"Miss Toulmin says that we are the only creature that weeps."

"Daddy never weeps—but Tuckie does, nearly every day. A cry-baby."

For nursery meals, the two little boys were belted into high chairs drawn up to the table, but all the girls were tall enough and mannerly enough to sit upon back stools or chairs. Even at nursery meals, where Hopey presided, dining-room manners were to be practised. It was impermissible to leave the table until excused under any circumstance but one: suddenly seized by a musical idea, any of the girls might leap up at once and run to her instrument. It was understood by all that musical ideas were so fragile, so evanescent, and so precious that they were to be snatched from the thin air upon the very moment of their wafting into existence; they might otherwise evaporate as quickly as they had precipitated, never again to be recovered. No chances could be taken with them; it was a duty to bring them into the world. Constantia became accustomed to seeing an inward distracted stillness fall over the face of the girls; any of them might, even in the midst of nursery-supper noise, fall silent for a moment; then spring from her chair, to run to the pianoforte—the harp—the violin.

One night in the dark small hours when Constantia was sitting up with Charlie at her breast, she heard the harp in the drawing room downstairs. Someone picked out a long cascading scale—and then a developing series of melodic phrases, deliberately and meticulously elaborated, elucidated. This nocturne lasted some twenty or thirty minutes.

In the morning, Mrs Chambers apologised for the disturbance, saying that a most exquisite melody had come to her in a dream—a melody so ravishing that it had wakened her from a sound sleep; that she had been compelled to rise and fly to her harp to capture and transcribe it before it went the way of all dreams. "There is no need to apologise," said Constantia. "It was the loveliest thing I ever heard, of a night."

Mrs Chambers cherished a tea-set of Staffordshire manufacture, white with dainty handpainted gold decorations; her own, not the landlord's. One saucer in particular was kept aside for her exclusive use because of its pitch: it chimed a perfect A, whenever a spoon rang against it, or a cup was set down upon it. Each of the saucers had its own pitch, each slightly but discernibly different, and all pleasant to the ear. But only one of them rang a perfect A; and that was the one which Mrs Chambers invariably preferred. Her daughters had once, for fun, replaced it with another saucer, identical in appearance; but their mother, setting down her cup with ink-stained fingers, immediately knew the difference. The cups and cake plates and slop bowl rang too, a little, but the saucers had the purest tone. The girls had, on another occasion, ranged the saucers in order of their pitch, from lowest to highest. All fell within a whole note (they had checked, against the pianoforte)—but each was slightly different from the next. Alone, each note was lovely, and sufficient; Constantia—and indeed all of the girls except Tuckie—could reconcile herself to that tone; that tone could be taken for the tonic, and any scale built from it. But Mrs Chambers and Tuckie each had somewhere within herself some absolute reference pitch, which she could consult with complete confidence; and compare. To them, the saucer which rang A was preferable by far to all others.

One evening, two of the Misses DeQuincey performed a violin duet. Constantia admired the grace of the girls as they plied their bows across the strings, and fingered the fretless necks—though the elder had a distracting way of sniffing, a noisy intake of breath at the end of each bowed phrase; probably she was quite unaware of doing it. Constantia had been told that the DeQuincey girls lived with their grown-up sisters at a place upstream called Lasswade. She imagined a shallow ford, a clear burn where the DeQuincey lasses and their friends, the Chambers girls, might tuck up their skirts on a warm summer's day—the single warm summer's day—and . . . wade. How picturesque.

Constantia could sing in tune, and was a useful participant in a round, able to keep up her own part, in her proper time; but she knew herself to be not finely attuned to music, not as real musicians are. She was hearing just now a pretty melody and its harmony; and, if she concentrated, she was able to compile some sense of direction and of pattern; a sense of where the music was going, where it repeated itself; its passage from one point to another. But as she listened now beside Mrs Chambers, Constantia was distracted by curiosity: What was Mrs Chambers hearing? Her experience of this music must be far richer and more complex than Constantia's own. Where Constantia knew herself to be hearing only melody, harmony and, if she attended closely, progress, was Mrs Chambers hearing intervals, meanings, relationships and ancestries, resemblances and reminders, all plaited together, complex as a tartan?

And to Mrs Chambers's knowing ears, was the experience perhaps less pleasant than to Constantia's unsophisticated ones? Were the instruments ill-tuned? Were the players clumsy? Did Mrs Chambers's finer sensibilities increase her pleasure—or diminish it? Perhaps the defects of the performance (if defects there were) even caused her some discomfort. The players concluded—and Mrs MacAdam thought that as Mrs Chambers clapped her hands in appreciation, she also exhaled a long sigh; it might be of relief.

Then the Twinnies clamoured for a turn, offering to sing—as they often did—"The True Lovers' Farewell." "Very well, my dears," said their mother, "but I want you to attend very closely this time to your enunciation. And let Jenny take the young man's part, for a change, and Lizzy, the lass's."

Their enunciation was exaggerated to the point of brittleness; but for the first time, Constantia found herself attending not only to the pretty melody but also to the ache, the longing and loss in the words of the old song. Jenny sang:

> *Farewell, my love! I must be gone*
> *And leave you for a while.*
> *But wherever I go, I'll come back again,*
> *Though I go ten thousand miles, my dear,*
> *Though I go ten thousand miles.*

(No, thought Constantia, not ten thousand . . . less than a hundred miles, as the pigeon flies.)

Lizzy replied:

> *Ten thousand miles! It is so far*
> *To leave me here alone,*
> *Whilst I may lie, lament and cry,*
> *And you will not hear my moan, my dear,*
> *And you will not hear my moan.*

(What good can come of lamenting and crying? thought Constantia.)
Jenny sang:

> *The crow that is so black, my dear,*
> *Shall change his colour white;*
> *And if ever I prove false to thee,*
> *The day shall turn to night, my dear,*
> *The day shall turn to night.*

And Lizzy replied:

> *O don't you see that milk-white dove*
> *A-perched on yonder tree,*
> *Lamenting for her own true love,*
> *As I lament for thee, my dear,*
> *As I lament for thee.*

(Doves and pigeons pair for life, Constantia knew. But men? And
women?)
Both girls sang the last verse together:

> *The river never will run dry,*
> *Nor the rocks melt with the sun;*
> *And I'll never prove false to the one I love*
> *'Til all these things be done, my dear,*
> *'Til all these things be done.*

(Alas! thought Constantia. How was comfort to be derived from such lover's promises as those? Rivers do run dry! Rocks do crumble, and wash to the sea! All of them do, eventually. She could not help but remember the petty rajahs and chieftains of the hill tribes above Assam, who, as a token of contract and agreement, would present each other with a stone, and these solemn words: "Until that stone crumbles into dust shall our friendship last; and firm as its texture, so firm is our present resolution." Those contracts, agreements, and alliances were sometimes long-lasting; sometimes not. Stones always do crumble, eventually. Do they not? Constantia fingered the flat-backed pearl on its fine chain at her throat.)

"Who has not given us a song?"

"Mrs MacAdam has not!"

"You must give us a song too, Mrs MacAdam! Do, pray!"

"Indeed you must!"

"But I do not know any songs," protested Constantia.

"No songs! Surely you must. Everyone knows songs."

"Sing us something savage—from the jungle—from the Indies!"

Shirking was impossible; sing she must, among this company. Constantia drew a deep shaky breath and, clasping her hands tightly together to conceal her trembling, was astonished to hear her own voice in the room, actually singing. It was a song her mother used to sing to her; the old song that Constantia now sometimes sang under her breath to the babies:

> *A fair maid going by the jail-house door*
> *heard a prisoner bemoan himself there.*
> > *She was the fair flower o' Northumberland.*

(But do not think of her! my mother!)

"Fair maid," said he, "will you pity me?
If ye'll steal the keys and let me gae free,
  I'll make you my lady in fair Scotland."

(nor of that soft freckled arm)

  She's went to her father's stable,
  She's stown a steed baith wight and able,
    To carry them on to fair Scotland.

(nor of her hair)

  They rode till they came to Crawfurd muir,
  He bade her light off; they'd call her a whore
    If she didna return to Northumberland.

(Mama's hair!)

  When she went thro her father's hall,
  She looted her low amongst them all,
    She that was the flower o' Northumberland.

(nor of what happened to her)

  But spake her mother, she spake with a smile,
  "Ye're nae the first that his coat did beguile,
    Ye're welcome again to Northumberland."

Constantia felt herself faltering, but plunged into the last two stanzas nevertheless. Upon the last line of the last stanza, however, she could sing no more. Her throat closed, choking upon a thick sob, and she turned away from them, to hide her tears.

  "But that's all right, Mrs MacAdam," said Mary's voice.

"Hinney, oh hinney, don't cry, then," said Jenny, and Constantia felt herself patted and caressed as the girls closed around her; and one of them said, "Do you know, Tuckie used to cry, sometimes, when she sang, but now she never does. It's ever so much easier when you get used to it, you know."

"And it's a sweet voice you have, Mrs MacAdam," said another.

But Constantia, though she tried to compose herself, could not stem her tears; and after a few moments, unwilling to distress them with her own distress, she withdrew. She got as far as the broad landing of the stair and sat, quite unexpectedly, on the top step, for her legs would carry her no further. She pressed her blazing forehead against the chilly iron baluster and tried to steady her breathing. How mortifying! She had upset Tuckie, too; on her way out of the room she had caught a glimpse of Tuckie's face puckered and red, tears of sympathy glistening in her eyes. When she could, Constantia fled to the privacy of her room, and the comfort of warm heavy babies.

At length there came a tap at her door, and Mrs Chambers entered. Constantia stood with Charlie in her arms and said, "I beg your pardon, Mrs Chambers; I am so sorry to have distressed the children, and spoilt the evening—"

"Oh, never mind that, Mrs MacAdam. They have forgotten all about it already. We erred in pressing you so hard. Or, perhaps, the song itself . . . ?"

"My mother used to sing it to me. My late mother."

"Oh aye," said Mrs Chambers gently. "May I sit down? Northumbrian, was she?"

"From round about Newcastle, she told me."

"It is a fine old ballad, and one of my favourites, that 'Fair Flower of Northumberland'—although it must be conceded that we Scots do not come off to advantage in it. A great many variants there are, too; some of them more to my taste than others. But I don't think I have ever heard any precisely like yours."

"No? My mother always sang it to me thus."

"I have never heard that conclusion. I should be very much obliged if I might hear it again."

"Oh, but I—I don't think I could bring myself . . ." said Constantia, ashamed at feeling tears well up once more.

"The last two verses? Will you say them, perhaps, if you cannot sing them?"

It is a disgraceful old ballad. The loveliest girl in Northumberland, taking pity upon a handsome Scots prisoner, springs him from jail and rides north with him, casting her lot with his, body and soul—until, upon crossing the Tweed, he declares himself already married, and sends her back, ruined, to her old parents. Matters arrange themselves satisfactorily, however, in the concluding verses. Constantia whispered them:

> *A swain once scorn'd she's recall'd the next day,*
> *Now she's yielded, she's let* him *take her away—*
> *Across the border to fair Scotland.*

> *Comes their firstborn child, a gift from heav'n,*
> *No nine-months' baby— nor scarcely seven!—*
> *Now she's the fair flower of Northumberland!*

(Now *she's* the fair flower of Northumberland! her mother would sing to her, and kiss her until she laughed; and little Constantia had known—known!—herself to be her mother's dearest darling, her beloved, her very own fairest flower!)

"Clever!" said Mrs Chambers. "Where did your mother get it, I wonder? I suppose you miss her dreadfully."

"I do, very much indeed," said Constantia, "especially now that I am become a mother myself." And the room swam before her eyes again.

"If there is anything I can do," said Mrs Chambers, and let her hand fall over Constantia's. "I would not press you, not in the slightest—but if there is anything I can do to ease your lot—your husband at a distance, too, during this difficult time!—I beg you will not hesitate . . . I think I can promise discretion, and sympathy. Certainly we owe you a great deal more than that, on Charlie's account."

Eve must have looked just thus, when offering Adam the apple: so kind, so gentle, so generous; fine eyes shining with affection and sympathy for a fellow creature. Constantia was tempted, sorely tempted! to confide her secret. A secret was so hard to bear! So heavy a burden for one alone! For a long moment, she held her breath for fear that she might speak; not daring even to exhale, for fear that some words, a whisper, might escape with her breath.

But no secret was safe, once eased; once the burden of it was shifted, shared with another, it remained secret no longer.

"You are very good to me," said Constantia at last. "You and Mr Chambers do show me every possible kindness." But (she did not add), there are some things which cannot be helped; which must only be endured. She could not even meet Mrs Chambers's frank gaze, in case it might penetrate too far into her thoughts. How dreadful it felt, to repay Mrs Chambers's warmth with such coldness! And no explanation was possible. Mrs Chambers could not be expected to sympathise with the necessity of concealment for a husband's sake.

Presently, Mrs Chambers patted her hand once more, and rose, and went out.

The book *Vestiges* went missing for several days, until Constantia happened to find it behind a sofa cushion in the library. The orange thread she had been using for a bookmark was gone, but someone had left a copy of the newest *Edinburgh Review* tucked into it. She carried it all upstairs to her own room, hoping to find time soon to resume reading.

That night, having fed both babies to bursting once more, Constantia took gratefully to her bed, aching for sleep. With luck she might snatch four or even five hours of sleep before one (and then the other) of the babies awakened again, howling with hunger. But sleep, alas, would not, could not, quite engulf her, for she was startled awake—over and over again—by the bark of Willie's cough from the adjoining nursery, where both he and Jemmie had been put to bed with heavy colds. Constantia could have wept with fatigue and despair; but after a time, harrowed into hopeless wakefulness, she sat up and relit her lamp. As she took up *Vestiges* from the table beside her bed, the *Edinburgh Review* slipped out, onto the floor. She leaned down to retrieve the thick quarterly; she could reach only a corner of it, and it flopped open as she drew it onto her lap.

Someone had written all over its pages.

These pages of the *Review*, she saw from their header, contained that notorious critique of the *Vestiges*; that sarcastic, contemptuous, unsigned review said to be—nay, known to be—from the pen of the eminent Dr Sedgwick. Someone had annotated these pages minutely; had underlined Dr Sedgwick's phrases, lines, even whole paragraphs; had starred and bracketed and commented; and had filled the margins, top and bottom, left and right, with a small dense black handwriting. She turned over the pages. Page after page was annotated thus.

Whose was this handwriting? It was unknown to her. She could not even guess whether this hand—this Annotator—was a man or a woman.

She held the *Review* close under her lamp, riffling through the pages until her eye was arrested by a constellation of asterisks and underlinings. Where Dr Sedgewick's printed text read, "It is true that we see polypiaria, crinodes, articulata, and mollusca; but it is not true that we meet with them in the order stated by our author"— the Annotator had written furiously in the margin, "humiliating to answer an objection so mean as this! no claim made that the animals came in this order! only the words are in this order—in accordance with scientific usage!"

Where Dr Sedgwick had identified "three distinct propositions, and all three are false to nature, and no better than a dream," the handwritten comment in the margin was this: "which party is the falsifier and the dreamer?"

Where Dr Sedgwick had written of "a grand and at the present day an unpardonable blunder," the handwritten comment in the margin was "another dream of S's! & proof of his recklessness in making charges—"

Where Dr Sedgwick had written "But who is the author?" and proceeded to discuss whether the nameless author's style of mind betrayed more of manliness or of womanliness, the Annotator had written, "How could it matter? Why does S suppose it matters?"

Dr Sedgwick had declared, "We have spent years of active life among these ancient strata—looking for (and we might say longing for) some arrangement of the ancient fossils which might fall in with our preconceived notions of a natural ascending scale. But we looked in vain, and we were weak enough to bow to nature." That grand editorial "we" at its most sarcastic and condescending had roused the Annotator to triple underlines which nearly scored the paper through, and the scribbled comment: "Having studied one little patch of the earth, S believes it to be a criterion for all the rest. As though, having met plenty of grown men but never an infant in arms, he were to declare that he bows to nature in pronouncing babes a mere fancy!! Has yet to learn that knowledge is acquired by communication as well as examination."

Where Dr Sedgwick had complained of "difficulties in the way of this theory," the Annotator had written: "What difficulties, sir? Why do you not state their nature? so that the argument may be reframed so as to satisfy you?—risky and arrogant too, so dogmatic a tone in a field still so uncharted—"

Dr Sedgwick had gone on to declare that "species were found, in living nature, to be permanent. To this law not one exception has been found." Opposite this the Annotator had written, "bald falsehood."

Dr Sedgwick referred to "a personal and superintending God,

concentrating his will on every atom of the universe." He wrote of "a personal and superintending God, who careth for his creatures." And all the contrivances of nature, he asserted, "are wise and good." In the margin beside each of these statements, the Annotator had written, "Evidence to support—ex scripture??"

Constantia's lamp flickered; the wick needed trimming. The house was still; no one even coughed.

Many people do annotate their books and papers. It is a practise of attentive, thoughtful readers. Anyone—any intelligent, keen, well-informed reader—might have written these comments into this copy of the *Edinburgh Review*. There was no way of knowing whose comments they were; and Constantia did not want to know. They were private. They were something she ought not to have seen, just as she ought not to hear Mr and Mrs Chambers in their bedroom below. Rising, she donned her dressing gown and carried the *Vestiges* and the *Edinburgh Review* downstairs. Moonlight flooded the staircase. At this hour there was no one on the stairs; no one in the passage; no one in the library. She returned the borrowed texts to the place where she had found them, behind the sofa cushion.

One or two mornings after this, when Constantia was in her room nursing Livia, Hopey appeared in the doorway and said, "The gardener asked me just now to bring up your book. He said he picked it up in the garden, some days ago, and meant to bring it up to the house directly—but found it just now lying forgotten among his hurdles, and begs your pardon." She set the book on the table under the window. It was the *Vestiges*—with the orange thread that served as a bookmark, just as Constantia had lost it, marking the chapter about the Origin of the Animated Tribes.

6

─────────

"MR MACAULAY! *His* facts beyond dispute!" burst out Constantia, provoked at last to rude contradiction. "There can scarcely exist, Lady Janet, another man whose utter disregard—nay, whose contempt!—for facts equals Mr Macaulay's!"

"Indeed," said Lady Janet, offended.

When Mrs Chambers had been called out of the room by some catastrophe in the kitchen, Lady Janet profited by her position of temporary authority to read extracts aloud to the girls from a recent speech given by Mr Macaulay at Westminster. Nina, at her easel, and the other girls, cutting out silhouettes in red paper, were paying scant attention; and Constantia managed to keep silence until Lady Janet, in conclusion, had commended "the excellence of our Member, whose factual arguments are always beyond dispute."

"I have known of Mr Macaulay's imaginary 'facts' ever since his unfortunate posting to Calcutta," said Constantia, "when he wrote that infamous Minute on Education. Oh yes, my lady; though I was only a girl at the time, I remember very well the disgust—yes, disgust!—excited by Mr Macaulay's ignorance and arrogance, among the people with whom I then lived, in India. Six months after Mr Macaulay's arrival in India—still the rawest of griffins—he felt himself qualified to declare that in all of Sanskrit literature, there was nothing worth reading! And that the language was not fit for conducting the education of Indians. And how had he reached this conclusion? Had he learned the language, so that he could study its literature, and arrive at a proper and informed estimate of its value? No, my lady, he had not. No! He admits in the Minute itself, quite coolly, that he had not bothered actually to learn any Sanskrit—"

"Well, of course he had not; I daresay it is a very strange and difficult language," said Lady Janet.

"I beg your pardon, my lady, it is not; certainly not as compared to Greek or Latin," said Constantia. "It is rich in nuance; it is subtle; it is vigorous; it is expressive—but it is also refreshingly simple and logical in its grammar, and even its vocabulary has a surprisingly familiar feel to speakers of English. Yet Mr Macaulay—who fancies himself quite the linguist—oh yes, ma'am! has he not boasted of beguiling his leisure re-reading the Greeks: Euripides and Aeschylus, Hesiod and Pindar? and of learning German, on the voyage home? Has he not declared that he could learn any language in a matter of four months, if only he set his mind to it? But he did not set his mind to learning Sanskrit; he could not be troubled."

"Jenny, dear," said Lady Janet (to Lizzy), "you are spoiling your tucker."

"Can you read Sanskrit, Mrs MacAdam?" asked Nina.

"Yes, well enough," said Constantia. "And write it, too. But if Mr Macaulay would not learn Sanskrit," she continued, "did he make any attempt to read the classical works of Indian literature—in translation? Did he make himself acquainted, even in translation, with the Vedas? The Upanishads? Or, if those were too laborious, perhaps he read *Mahabharata*? *Ramayana*?—for these, you know, ma'am, are the great epics of India, her *Iliad* and her *Odyssey*. Did he read the *Charyapada*, or the works of Kalidasa, or any of the Sutras? Well, it may be as he claimed, that he glanced over a page or two, here and there, when he was not too much engrossed by Homer and Horace and Herodotus. But it is clear from his comments that he cannot have done so with any energy or attention. No, my lady; he only inquired of his sister's fiancé—a man who had arrived in India some months before himself, and whom he took therefore for an expert—a man who was full of schemes for baptising all the Hindus and Moham-medans of India—whether any of it was worth reading; and upon being assured, by this pious and bigoted future brother-in-law, that it was not—that it was all a pack of unscientific lies and blasphemous superstitions—he concluded that he need not trouble to acquaint himself with any of it."

Mrs Chambers returned, in time to hear Mrs MacAdam's indig-nation in full spate: "I daresay that the only natives he ever spoke to," she was saying hotly, "were his servants! his khansaman, his syce, his bearers and sweepers. The only natives he encountered were those to whom he gave commands. Perhaps he never met a cultivated Hindu—but if he did, I daresay he had not sense enough to know it. Quite possibly he ordered a learned scholar and poet to—to prepare his hookah! to fetch his slippers!"

"I doubt that Mr Macaulay ever degraded himself so far as to have anything to do with a hookah," said Lady Janet. "I have met him in company on more than one occasion, and he is a thorough gentleman. Furthermore, I will venture to remind you that a decent respect is due the office, even from those who may presume to disapprove the man. He is, after all, our Member."

"Whose Member is he, ma'am? Who elected him?"

"Why, the electors of Edinburgh, of course!"

"And who are these electors? Who are these elect and justified few, anointed to elect the fewer still? The fewer still who, once set above us, then presume to make laws, meant to be binding upon us all—all!—under penalty of fine or punishment?"

"Why, you sound nearly as bad as those Chartists!" said Lady Janet.

"I hope so, ma'am," said Constantia. "I am proud to declare myself a Chartist."

"I cannot believe it of you. I suppose you mean to provoke me."

"Not at all. I became a Chartist long before I ever had the honour of meeting your ladyship; and without the slightest intention of pro-voking you."

"Ah! And I had made such efforts to think charitably of you! But no reasonable person can possibly wish that traitors and criminals shall have the direction of our civic affairs! Are we to sink into anar-chy, as in France? What can ensue but bloodshed and brutality, riots and strikes?"

"Chartists are neither traitors nor criminals," said Constantia. "As for the strikes, it must be clear to everyone that they worked quite against the operative classes. The stoppages instead favoured the mill owners, who rejoiced in the excuse to halt operations—to idle their mills while there was no market for their produce—and then, upon resuming, to reduce pay yet again—"

"That is a perfect example, then," interrupted Lady Janet. "Are ignorant labourers, unable to discern even that their actions are not in their own interests—are these people fit to fashion the laws of the land?"

"You quite mistake my point, my lady; do you not see that the strikes—and the riots too—were instigated by spies and infiltrators, in the hire of the mill owners for their own pecuniary interests; or else of the government, to bring disgrace upon the movement?"

"Spies! What nonsense! Name me one."

"I shall name you six: Hartley. Harrison. Goulding. Frowen. Grif-fin. Cartledge. That is only six among untold scores; only six whose infamous names happen to lie at the tip of my tongue."

"Stuff!" scoffed Lady Janet.

"And the mails opened—" said Constantia.

"Stuff!" said Lady Janet again.

"Indeed they are! It is a fact that Patterson and Cooke were con-victed at Manchester upon the evidence of intercepted letters—and letters not from them, but to them."

"Blether, I say! Our mails are inviolate, and the best in the world."

Here Mrs Chambers entered the fray, saying, "I fear there is very good reason to suspect, Lady Janet, that the mails are watched, and sometimes intercepted."

"Anyone who is no criminal has nothing to hide," said Lady Janet.

"I am no criminal," said Mrs Chambers, "but I may nevertheless have secrets which I had rather not share with—everyone. With the world at large."

"Mamma, may we be excused, please, all of us?" put in Mary hastily; and permission granted, she and her sisters and dog all escaped to the garden.

More calmly, Constantia said, "Even the operative classes are required to pay taxes. Even the operative classes are required to turn out for militia duty. Why, then, may they have no voice in shaping the laws of the land? Why, then, are their opinions branded as 'sedition'—and their persons liable to arrest, imprisonment, and transportation—merely for voicing those opinions?"

"Well; there was a Chartist candidate, as I recall, who made a great noise and a fuss, about standing against Mr Macaulay in the last election," said Lady Janet. "A stone-mason, or a miner, I believe; some such fellow—"

"I suppose you mean Mr Stevenson. A quarrymaster," said Constantia.

"Quite possibly that was the man's name," said Lady Janet. "But if memory serves, he failed even to make an appearance at the hustings. No doubt he was too frightened to ascend the platform, when the time came."

"Not at all, my lady. The truth is that he was prevented from going to the hustings because a false writ for debt had been sworn out against him—"

"Oh, a debtor! A bankrupt! I might have known. Well, if the Chartists can do no better than that—"

"A false writ, I said; a perjured writ, sworn out expressly to prevent his appearance at the hustings! A low, cunning stratagem, a conspiracy among the supporters of Mr Macaulay—for they were fearful of the humiliation that should have attached to their candidate, when it became clear in the show of hands there, that he was by no means the choice of the majority!"

"We cannot be ruled by mobs, Mrs MacAdam; nor by bullying majorities. I do think it is a pity that we in Scotland have no property qualification for Members, as they have in England. We would be spared these agitations, these undignified displays—these circuses; and crowds of mountebanks and vagrants at the hustings. There is a great deal too much lawlessness, upon these unfortunate occasions—"

"Ah; there is a point on which your ladyship and I can agree. If poverty is deemed a crime, there is a great deal too much of that crime about!"

"Of course that is not at all what I mean. And you ought to know that these people are not nearly so poor as they pretend to be, or they would not be so very ready to down tools and go out, upon any pretext, or none at all. It is only an excuse to become drunk and riotous. Or how do they afford such quantities of intoxicating liquors, do you suppose?"

"I assure you, ma'am, they are desperately poor—and so ill-paid for their labour that, whether in work or out of it, they face starvation just the same. It is desperation that drives men to desperate measures."

"Desperately ignorant, to be sure. Surely you cannot deny that the gross ignorance of the entire class disqualifies them to function as electors!"

"I do deny it, though, my lady. But even if it were so—which I deny—why then does the present government strive so mightily to keep the laboring classes in deepest ignorance?"

"How absurd. There is not a shred of truth in so ridiculous an assertion."

"I beg your pardon; it is quite true. Or why is it that only poor men's newspapers are taxed? Only those newspapers costing less than sixpence are subject to the Stamp Act, you know—while rich men's newspapers are exempt! Do you know that it is illegal to lend a newspaper? And as it is illegal for the workers to combine, how, then, can the Corn Laws—which protect the combined interests of the great landowners, at the expense of everyone else who must subsist upon a mouthful of bread—how can the Corn Laws have become the law of the land? And how can there be justice in a Master and Servant Act which provides that a worker's transgression makes him subject to criminal arrest—while employers, under the same Act, are liable only for civil penalties?"

"Why, what in the world is the use of lodging a civil action against a labourer—who hasn't got a shilling to pay the fine with?"

"Precisely, Lady Janet, just so! And having robbed their workers, penny by penny, of every shilling due them in justice for their labour, the masters now resolve to rob them of the sole possession still remaining to them: their very bodily liberty! Having deprived them already of their ancient right—their right, ma'am!—to participate in electing the lawmakers whose laws will be binding upon us all—having subverted and degraded that lawmaking body to its present shameless condition, where it legislates solely in its own class interest, and against all others—"

"This is a very dangerous style of talking, Mrs MacAdam, and I advise you, for your own good—"

"Excuse me, Mrs Chambers, and my lady," interrupted Hopey, poking her head in, "but you are wanted in the nursery, Mrs Mac-Adam, hinney. Most urgently wanted, I am afraid! Quite in a swither! Upstairs, I mean. As for bread and corn, who can say?—but milk is the thing for bairns, now; milk—"

"—of human kindness," said Mrs Chambers, quietly, as Constantia went out.

Then, another point occurring to Lady Janet, she went out after her, and called up the stairs: "We are obliged, each and all of us, to submit to laws not of our own making, Mrs MacAdam; and those are the laws of nature: God's laws!"

When Lady Janet returned to the drawing room, she found Mrs Chambers sitting quietly, apparently absorbed in her book of household accounts. Lady Janet took a few turns up and down the room; and presently, having composed herself and marshalled her resolve, she said, "Dear Mrs Chambers, nothing but a deep sense of obligation and friendship toward you and Mr Chambers could induce me— nay, compel me!—to presume to say something, on a subject which is properly no concern of mine; but I cannot feel easy that the sweet children should be exposed—should live on so intimate a footing with such a person as this sly 'Mrs MacAdam' reveals herself to be. Her views are dangerously republican, and she seems a great deal too familiar with the doings of those Chartists."

"I do agree, Lady Janet, that the Chartists have been most unlucky in their leaders," said Mrs Chambers, setting aside her household book. "Certain of them do their cause more harm than good. Nor can I approve their more extreme tactics and rhetoric. But I think it is a pity they have not found better men to lead them, for—as regards their principles, at least—I am a bit of a Chartist myself, you know! Aye, but I am, my lady; for the Charter itself is only plain justice and good sense. I am quite in earnest, I assure you. Those Six Points of theirs must become the law of the land, sooner or later; and Britain will be all the better for it, whenever it shall come to pass."

"How can you . . . ? Every man, to have a vote? Every pauper, every vagrant? Every drunken brute? Every atheist? What will become of us all?"

"Not just every man, Lady Janet; but every woman, too."

"Oh! And every dog, and cart-horse, I suppose!"

"I should like to cast a vote. And if I am to cast a vote, Lady Janet, I daresay that you should like to have a vote as well—with which to nullify mine, if nothing else. And if we are to eliminate the property test for voters, it must also be eliminated for Members—not only in Scotland, but throughout the kingdom. And Members ought to be paid a moderate salary for their work, so that any worthy men—even those not born to independent fortunes—may take their seats in Parliament without dooming their families to starvation; any Member who feels himself demeaned by his salary may turn it back to the Exchequer, if he likes. And as I ought not to be subjected to intimidation or retaliation from others for casting my vote according to my own conscience, the ballot ought to be secret. There is no shame in that; it ought to be as private as the post, at least—not that our mails are so very private, I fear. Of course the constituencies ought to be as nearly as possible of equal size—in numbers of electors, I mean, so that every vote carries approximately equal weight. And Parliament must know that its deeds and acts are under the close superintendence of the electors, who may promptly recall them if they are displeased; hence Parliaments ought to be brief—perhaps not so brief as one year, as some argue—but certainly no longer than three years. There! Those are the Six Points, Lady Janet; and I do subscribe to them, shocking though it may seem."

Upstairs, Constantia sat by her open window nursing both babies at once, and a grudge against Lady Janet; but eventually she fell into contemplation.

Who has made the laws which govern men and women? Who must obey those laws? Is this state of affairs just?

Who has made the laws which govern the universe? Who must obey those laws? Is this state of affairs just?

Why would anyone suppose that justice has anything at all to do with anything? Justice!

The human faculties lead unavoidably to occasional error.

Soon after this, Constantia contradicted Lady Janet again, quite inadvertently. "How I wish I could fly!" Tuckie had said, to her sisters.

Lady Janet, from her seat at her penwork cabinet across the drawing room, lifted up her voice to admonish her, saying, "If God in his infinite wisdom and goodness had meant us, his creatures, to fly, he would have endowed us with wings."

"But we can fly," Constantia declared impulsively. "By our ingenuity, we do fly, despite our sad lack of wings—such an unaccountable oversight, that! Oh yes, but we do, Lady Janet, using hot air balloons. I saw such an ascent myself, when I was a child, in India."

(For suddenly—this instant—she had remembered herself, a little girl on a palace terrace, in dazzling early morning sunshine; and remembered the little wicker boat suspended under an immense balloon sweeping upward, plummeting upward! falling upward! The handsome Englishman in it—such a splendid moustache—had bowed in passing to Constantia's supremely beautiful mother, whose hand Constantia gripped.)

"That is not flying," said Lady Janet. "Flying is what birds do, upon their own God-given wings."

"And angels," said Jenny.

"Bats, too," added Lizzy, "though they are so prodigious ugly. It does not seem right, does it, that they can fly?"

"But if you had to choose between having wings, and having arms with hands at the ends, which would you choose?" said Mary.

"Oh! Wings instead of arms! Nay, I could not possibly manage without arms, and hands."

"You would have to peck at your food with your face, like a bird."

"Willie does. Look at him, with grease on his nose: 'A scanty and most defective development of life.'"

"Jenny, that is very rude," said Lady Janet.

"But Mamma says it; I have heard her."

"She does not say it of her children."

"I should like to have wings and arms."

"And legs, too?"

"Certainly legs!"

"You would have six limbs, then; you would be an insect!"

"No; but plenty of insects have six legs—and a pair of wings."

"Angels have arms and wings. And legs. Haven't they, Lady Janet?"

Lady Janet took this opportunity to declare that there was no scriptural warrant for attributing wings to angels. The children, unlike Mrs MacAdam, were polite enough not to contradict Lady Janet to her face, but later, when she had gone out, they agreed that she was quite mistaken. It is familiar knowledge that angels have wings.

That night, in quiet darkness with Livia at her breast, Constantia examined this newly-emerged memory. As though with sable brushes and burin and sandpaper, as though freeing a new-found fossil from its stony matrix, she brought it forth.

Dil Kusha—Heart's Desire.

"You are my Dil Kusha," Constantia's mother had whispered to her, on the verandah of the Dil Kusha palace in Lucknow, amidst a great crush of people, both Indians and Englishmen. "My fair flower! my Dil Kusha."

And the handsome English balloonist coolly doffed his hat to Constantia's mother and bowed, as he was borne swiftly upward. Her mother released Constantia's hand for a moment; then sought it again and squeezed—as man, boat, and enormous sausage-shaped balloon were borne aloft. Up, up they swept, past the Nawab and his nobles and notables, all assembled upon the big verandah of the Dil Kusha palace. How strange, how like a vision in a dream, to see the little wooden boat sailing—in midair! The enormously swollen balloon from which it was suspended seemed its big-bellied sail. For a moment Constantia felt herself underwater, looking upward at the keeled boat sailing through the brilliant blue above. The marvelous machine shrank rapidly, diminishing each minute against the blazing March sky until it appeared no larger than a water-jug; then a lofty air current seized it, and bore it off to eastward. A regiment of horse galloped out of the Dil Kusha park, to follow it. Constantia was six and a half years old.

The Nawab's more important guests presently retired to a breakfast laid out for them in an inner room; and the less important guests, such as Constantia's mother, regaled themselves upon a lesser—but still sumptuous—repast in a larger outer room. Constantia shared the food from her mother's silvery platter, beautifully arranged around the edge like the numbers on a clock face. There was a sweet made of honeyed carrots: delicious. Afterwards, Constantia's mother convinced a khansaman to show her and her companions the other rooms of the handsome mansion, and of course Constantia went, too. Constantia did not like to lose sight of her beautiful mother, especially in such a crowd as this. The khansaman who led their little party from one room to the next spoke very good clear English. Dil Kusha, he explained, meant Heart's Desire. The palace had been built for the Nawab by an Englishman some forty years earlier, to a plan identical to that of a famous English palace.

What palace was that? demanded someone.

Alas, admitted the khansaman, at this particular moment his memory failed him; at this particular moment he could not quite recall its name. But after a moment's thought, he ventured to assert that it had been a work of a famous English architect whose name was Sahib Fonnabrew.

This too met with uncomprehending silence, until someone cried, "Ah! Vanbrugh, you mean; Sir John Vanbrugh."

Blenheim, suggested someone, doubtfully.

Surely not, said another. This house is not at all like Blenheim.

Grimsthorpe Castle, proposed someone else.

No, said the khansaman unhappily, he did not think that was it. He had been told that the palace whose name just now unfortunately eluded him had burnt down some time since . . .

"Oh! Seaton Delaval!" declared Constantia's mother, and the khansaman was delighted, for this was certainly the precise and correct name which he had momentarily forgotten. Constantia felt very proud of her mother, who was as clever as she was beautiful.

Seaton Delaval! Seaton Delaval! How lovely it felt in the mouth, and how musical to the ear, this beautiful name! So beautiful a name must belong to a beautiful place. "But I knew Seaton Delaval very well," explained Constantia's mother to the Rani Anibaddh, who walked with her, on her right side—for Constantia, as always, kept hold of her mother's left hand. "When I was a girl . . . I am from Northumberland, you know. And I remember very well the night when—when it burned. But I had the strangest presentiment of familiarity, upon coming into *this* palace! I could not say just what it was that seemed familiar. Yet now I do recognise . . . And the river, there! Just as Seaton Delaval overlooks the sea, the shore of the North Sea—so this palace overlooks the river. What is this river called? The Goomtee? What an amusing name!" she exclaimed, and laughed. Constantia knew from the laugh that her mother was excited; and she tugged her mother's hand just a little, to remind her that she, Constantia, the Fair Flower, was there.

"Fireplaces, even here?" said Constantia's mother. "I wonder at that, in this climate."

Constantia's mother was distrustful of fire. She never would bank a cooking fire and leave it, not even when she would have to make one all over again an hour hence. Before going to bed at night, she always made sure that every flame had been extinguished. Constantia was not allowed to bring a lamp into their bedroom. "Nay, hinney, you don't want it," her mother would say gaily. "Close your eyes a moment; then, when you open them, you'll see in the dark, as a tiger does." Or, if Constantia, complaining of cold, wanted the comfort of a fire, her mother would say, "Cold? Not this. A January in Northumberland, now: *that* is cold. Here, snug this about yourself," she would say, and wrap Constantia in one of the striped silk shawls she had woven herself. The shawls were not very expertly woven, nor very warm; but after she had tucked the tickly fringe under Constantia's chin, she would pat and rub her thin shoulders in a most kind and comforting way.

Another palace, in Lucknow: Moti Mahal—Pearl Palace.

Servants had raised umbrellas and canopies over the portico, and all during the hot afternoon, the Nawab's guests were treated to the spectacle of animal combats staged upon the the banks of the Goomtee: a tamasha. The Nawab's pleasure barge sailed back and forth upon the river, upstream and down, bearing the band of royal musicians, who pounded upon gigantic kettle drums and blew nine-foot-long trumpets. The barge was shaped like a fish; it had golden scales, and was bedecked with brilliant pennants and canopies. Constantia had never dreamed of anything so sumptuous, of such crowds of people, of such sunlight and dust and noise. The Khasiya hills were nothing like this.

But tigers, elephants, buffaloes, and rhinoceros were all well-known to her, for they roamed all over those hills. Within a large enclosed court built against a wall of the Pearl Palace, half a dozen well-grown young buffaloes milled about. At the drop of a banner, a hatch in the wall opened, and a pair of heavy tigers was turned loose among the buffaloes. "Oh! It will be a slaughter!" cried Constantia's mother and, gripping Constantia's hand, she craned forward over the parapet, the better to see. Constantia was only just tall enough see if she stood on tiptoes; but the tigers did not leap instantly upon the buffaloes as she had expected. Instead, they slunk around and around the walls seeking any gap by which they might escape, their long heavy tails carried low. Eventually the tigers lay down, not far from one another, panting through open mouths. Constantia studied them. She had never seen a tiger like this: lying down; lying still; vulnerable to examination, suffering the gaze of all. Constantia felt sorry for them, and sorrier still when the buffaloes formed ranks against them. Three or four buffaloes lined up, massy armoured heads low and, shoulder to shoulder, advanced slowly across the enclosure upon the unoffending tigers, pausing to snort and stamp their heavy hooves from time to time. Still, the tigers would not be provoked, and remained lying down. They would not look at the buffaloes, and only the tips of their long tails snapping up and down in the dust betrayed their agitation. Constantia marveled at their self-command. But when at last a phalanx of stamping buffaloes approached within a few feet of the smaller of the tigers, the alarmed tiger lifted a paw—and was promptly tossed into the air upon the horns of the largest buffalo, landing painfully upon the horns of another—was tossed again—gored—impaled— then dropped, to writhe bleeding in the dust for just a moment until the buffaloes closed upon it, and trampled it to tatters—to stillness. Within ten minutes, the other tiger had met a similar fate.

Oh! the poor creatures! Constantia had never felt sorry for a tiger, and had never expected to. In the Khasiya Hills, tigers were an ever-present threat; to venture out after dark was to invite a tiger to dine. Nor were the daylight hours entirely safe, not even in the villages, for tigers sometimes snatched up children playing on their own doorsteps in the sunshine, and carried them off. Constantia was never allowed to run about alone after dark, and prudent adults avoided it too, unless for irresistible, inexplicable, but excellent reasons of their own, such as her mother had.

Yet even tigers, Constantia now saw, were not invincible.

Other combats followed, in the enclosure below the palace: bears against bears (comical); rams against rams (the shock of impact when they crashed head to head was like an earthquake); hyenas against a remarkably vicious horse (which trampled three hyenas and retired victorious); and a python (which pursued, crushed, and swallowed a goat).

But these matches, it turned out, were only preludes to the main event of the day: the elephant fights. These were to take place on the far bank of the Goomtee, a flat dusty plain, and safely removed from the important guests crowding the Pearl Palace's rooftops, but just too distant, alas, to be seen quite clearly. Multitudes of the common people had gathered on the far bank, too, at what was supposed to be a safe remove (unless it might prove to be within harm's way) to see what they could: occasional tumults, through clouds of dust.

Presently two immense bull elephants were brought out, to a great fanfare of trumpets and drums. The elephants appeared so well-matched in every respect that they might have been brothers; and perhaps they were, for they showed no inclination to fight, despite the urgings and goadings of their mahouts. Indeed, why should they? They were then made to swallow balls of human earwax—a stimulant which, as is well-known, enrages even the most pacific and sweetest-tempered of elephants. But when this, too, failed, their mahouts retired them to opposite ends of the pitch, while a beautiful female elephant was brought to the central ground between them. Then the bull elephants were turned round once more and, perceiving now in one another not a brother but a rival, battle was joined at last.

It was at first merely a shoving match, but as they grew angrier, their tusks and trunks came wickedly into play. With their thick trunks entwined, they grappled, squeezed, wrestled and twisted at one another, as determined and deadly as pythons. It went on for some time, and it was very exciting to see; and riveting—except to Constantia. To her, the thick groping intertwined trunks were horrible and disturbing. She relinquished her mother's hand and went to sit down upon a ledge nearby in the hot shade; closed her eyes to shut out the glare, and thought of home: cool high green wet hills; rushing streams; butterflies. When a cry went up from the spectators around her, a collective gasp, she opened her eyes. What had happened? Something shocking, something terrible; what was it? She peered over the parapet, at distant veils of dust. There were several brilliant flashes, followed by a sound of explosions; rockets and fireworks were thrown at the battling elephants, to separate them, and one of the elephants was with difficulty turned by his mahout and ridden down to the edge of the water. The other elephant pursued, still furious—but where was his mahout? There was no little figure clinging to his back. A knot of people had gathered on the trampled ground where the elephants had been, clustering around something dark on the yellow sand.

"It was certainly deliberate," said an English voice, above her head. "I saw it perfectly. It stepped to one side, and set its foot upon the fellow quite *deliberately*."

And that put an end to the tamasha that day.

Later, everyone had returned to yet another palace nearby, called La Constantia, where the Nawab's European guests lodged. Muslims never slept there, because the embalmed corpse of the Christian general who had built the palace still lay in a mausoleum vault beneath it, a permanent desecration. Constantia did not much like the idea herself of sleeping above his moldering corpse. The general's personal motto was carved in stone above the magnificent doorway: LABORE ET CONSTANTIA. Constantia was glad that the palace was not called Labore instead; glad that she herself was not called Labore.

The handsome English balloonist had somehow returned, sunburnt and celebrated. Everyone sought an opportunity to address a few words to him: questions; congratulations; invitations to repeat the feat at other venues nearby; or to tell him of other balloon ascents they had seen. If they could not speak with the young man himself, they addressed his uncle instead, who traveled with him as an assistant. Constantia was of course holding her mother's hand when he was introduced, when he made his bow to her mother, for the second time that day. Constantia was afraid that he might ask her name too, for gentlemen sometimes did, when they met her mother. But he didn't notice Constantia at all. He was smiling at Constantia's mother and she was smiling, too; and even when other people, with the press of their introductions and remarks, separated him from them, Constantia could see that he was still looking about, from time to time, for her mother. Of course he did! She was the most beautiful woman in the room. Always; in any room.

* * *

Livia, at Constantia's breast, had fallen asleep, and a line of thin blue milk dribbled from the corner of her mouth, fallen open now against Constantia's freckled breast.

Why did nursing make Constantia think of her mother? Was it the constant company of her own breasts? Her memories of her mother always included the pillowy freckled plumpness of her mother's bodice, just at Constantia's (then) eye-level. Very low-cut bodices had been the fashion in those days; remarkably low; but the fashion had changed since then, and no one went about décolletée nowadays, except to a ball. Until now, Constantia's own figure had never had the plumpness of her mother's. But now for the first time in her life her milk-swollen breasts did resemble her mother's. Perhaps that was why nursing these babies made Constantia remember her mother.

But it was not only her mother. It was everything. Every thing.

In the guest quarters at La Constantia that night, Constantia had sat up abruptly, suddenly awake; what sound had roused her? It seemed to echo still in her mind's ear: the quiet click of the door latch. There was only a rumpled shawl on her mother's side of the bed. Constantia slid from the bed, crossed the room, and opened the door just enough to see down the long corridor. There were shaded lamps and, at intervals, servants sleeping on mats. She opened the door further and stuck her head out to see in the other direction—and there she caught the briefest glimpse of her mother's back, just as she whisked around the corner, and was gone. Constantia nearly cried out, terrified of being abandoned, left alone here by her beautiful mother, but knew that her mother would be angry, and bit back her distress. Instead, she ran after her, on silent bare feet. She might have lost her in the next reception room, quite dark; but then a rectangle of light had suddenly gaped in the far wall, and her mother's form was silhouetted in it for a moment as she had slipped through a far doorway into a better-lit place beyond. The rectangle of light was extinguished, but Constantia had taken her bearings; she crossed the large empty hall and found the far door almost immediately. Silently she then followed her mother across a moonlit verandah; down another long corridor; up a stair. There she crouched in her nightdress upon the shadowed landing at the top, for this stair led only to a rooftop pavilion, open all around to the night air. Moonlight spilled between the slender pillars which held up the curvy roof shaped like a parasol, and laid dark moonshadow arabesques across the pale marble flagstones.

Constantia's heart battered against her ribs, and thrummed in her ears, so that she could hardly catch the sound of her mother's voice, her excited laugh. Another shadow disengaged from one of the pillars, and came forward, and caught at her mother. A man. A man was there.

Constantia listened with all her ears, but they weren't speaking. They had melded into a single figure. For a moment the single figure divided into two; then again became one. In the bright moonlight, Constantia could see their arms: entwined; grappling. Like pythons, crushing; like the trunks of embattled elephants. Terror rose in Constantia; terror for her mother, terror for herself, if her mother should be crushed and destroyed by this man with whom she was locked in mortal combat. Constantia couldn't help it; a whimper escaped her. Instantly the two figures broke apart, and her mother was at her side. Quite unhurt. "You followed me!" whispered her mother.

"I was afraid," Constantia had sobbed, humiliated.

The man turned aside, harmless. As the moonlight fell across his face, Constantia recognised the handsome English balloonist.

Even now, remembering, with Livia asleep at her breast, Constantia felt a tide of heat rise in her. It was a return of the humiliation she had felt then; but it also had other feelings in it. She assayed them: Shame, at her then-ignorance. Embarrassment, to match her mother's. A married woman's understanding, now . . . no, more than that; a sharing, now—of the amorous urgency which had moved her mother, then. Which had moved her mother, always! And last, late, but increasingly, there was a deep sorrowful compassion for the frightened, perplexed, powerless child she herself had been. Childhood for some, it seemed, was happy and carefree; but not for Constantia. These Chambers children, for instance, seemed quite happy—except for Tuckie, who thought too much. Constantia studied Livia's still-formless pudding-face, asleep, slack. Pink curved wet lips; the dimple in her chin. And wanting for nothing, at this moment. For nothing at all.

7

A narrow snip of blue silk grosgrain ribbon.

A square of vermilion velvet, frayed.

A scrap of plain grey linsey-woolsey.

Four inches of grubby apron-string.

A swatch of moth-eaten tartan in green and blue.

A tatter of red worsted.

A splinter of wood.

A patch of worn leather.

WERE THESE THE identifying tokens left pinned to the blanket of a baby relinquished on the kirk steps—in case its mother might someday find herself in a position to return and reclaim it?

Not at all; they were authentic relics of Bonnie Prince Charlie himself, preserved upon the end boards of "The Lyon in Mourning," the eight-volume manuscript collection of journals, narratives, and memoranda relating to every circumstance of the Forty-five Rising, compiled by Bishop Forbes—and now the cherished property of Mr Chambers.

"Supposed to have been snipped from his Garter ribbon," said Mr Chambers to his daughters, as he smoothed the blue silk ribbon. He was arranging these eight volumes, open, upon the library table, so as best to display these precious relics attached to their end-boards. "And the velvet is from the hilt of his sword. What do you deduce from that, Lizzy?"

"I don't know," said Lizzy.

"Jenny?"

"Don't know," said Jenny.

"Twinnies do not know, and do not wish to know," said their father. "Polly, did you ever hear of a sword with velvet to its hilt?"

"Oh, Dad! You know very well to call me Mary. 'Polly' is a nickname fit only for babies."

"I beg your pardon, my dear Mary. It was only the force of ancient habit. But what do you make of a velvet-hilted sword?"

"Might it have been a French sword?" she proposed. "Brought with him from France?"

"I daresay it might well have been, and no Highland claymore. Now, this plain grey stuff is supposed to have been from the dress he wore when disguised as 'Betty Burke,' and the string is from the apron worn over it. The tartan and the red worsted are from the suit of clothes given him when he left off being 'Betty Burke' and became a man again. The splinter of oak is a memento of the boat that carried him over the sea from Borodale, after the catastrophe at Culloden. And the leather is from his shoe, or so Bishop Forbes assures us. Authentic Vestiges—of the Natural History of Prince Charles Edward Stuart. Nina, did you get all that?"

Nina, whose handwriting was deemed the most elegant, was writing little pasteboard cards to explain these relics laid out upon the library table among various other books and curiosities, for the entertainment of the guests expected today, the Prestonpans Gala Day; or—as the family had taken to calling it—Our Day o'Treason. "To spare us the necessity of explaining, all day long," said Mr Chambers. "How tedious it is to furnish endless explanations!"

*   *   *

Of course no one was a Jacobite in any serious way, these days; but anyone less earnest than Lady Janet (who had absented herself from the occasion) was glad to come and pretend; glad of an afternoon's sentiment and excitement. A pleasant jaunt down from town; an easy stroll to the old battlefield; plaids and blue bonnets to be worn; pipe music (in merciful moderation); a banquet at long tables under the trees, with toasts to be drunk; perhaps some breathless reels to be danced by the young people; all to be concluded by a bonfire after dark, and fireworks. Some seventy or eighty friends were expected.

At the ordained time they began arriving, in their droves.

The conservatory door leading out to the garden was braced open, and tides of guests drifted happily inward and outward, back and forth, all afternoon. Two floors above this doorway was Constantia's little room, and from her chair at her open window she could hear perfectly the lively chat and laughter which gusted upward. From behind the scrim of the voile undercurtain, she could see, too, without being seen.

When the time had come to progress to the historic Prestonpans battlefield—a mile to eastward—quite a number of guests declined to accompany Mrs Chambers, preferring instead to loaf about the ground-floor reception rooms and the gardens with Mr Chambers, eating bowlsful of strawberries and drinking punch. It was by greatest good luck a fine warm day, and just now there was a party gamboling up the walk from the doocot at the bottom of the garden. Constantia could hear men's voices; women's voices; children's high voices; laughter; railliery. The pigeons, disturbed by the unaccustomed commotion, had taken to the air, and were wheeling about. Livia, at her breast, was nearly asleep. Charlie, already sated, slept in his cradle across the room.

There floated up to her a man's voice, declaiming: "Certain things have actually happened. These events are facts. Other things have not happened. They might have happened; for there is nothing in natural law to have prevented their happening. However, they did not happen. The things that actually happened, in their actual sequence, are History. That is what History is made of: a series, a mere series of occurrences; of events. 'W-A-H,' I call it: What Actually Happened. Much of History is deeply obscure; it is no easy task to ascertain What Actually Happened—and what did not. And in what sequence. The difficulty, however, of ascertaining What Actually Happened is no excuse for pretending that it does not matter; or that we cannot know; or that our guesses are as good as knowledge. It is no excuse for failing to distinguish between what, in fact, did and did not happen. For failing to make the attempt, at least." His loud braying voice—who was he?—became inaudible as he passed into the house. It was very annoying, that voice; and therefore annoying that his words should nonetheless strike Constantia as important.

"This actually happened." In her memory she could hear Hugh's voice saying those words. At Neuilly on a gusty autumn day, at a wide bend of the glistening river. Halfway down the river bank was a limestone outcropping, a ledge. Hugh, his coat thrown aside, was kneeling over his task, bent and intent. Deftly he applied an engraver's tool, a burin; then a small dry brush; then he bent closer still, to blow away the dust he had made; spending his breath upon the object he was uncovering, discovering, freeing from the matrix of limestone in which it had been encased for so long, unimaginably long. His shirt-sleeves were rolled up, so that the play of sinew and muscle showed in his forearms, where the hairs sprang lively, ardently, from his golden dust-covered skin; but what a clean floury dust it made, this pale limestone! How miraculous, the wrists! Look, how they rotated! She had had to look away from the length of his back, from the long ridge of muscle to each side of the spine under his linen shirt. How well made he was: neck, arms, shoulders, and chest, muscled by years of working stone; years of lifting, splitting, drilling, channeling, mauling, bullying, coaxing stone, ever since he was grown big enough to swing a sledgehammer. Just then it was grains of dust that he dislodged, not blocks of stone. "Ah! Come up, now; come up, hinney!" he murmured; and it came free: a Potamides (or perhaps it was a Tympanotonos?) once alive, now turned to stone. He had rubbed it against his shirt. Spat on it, and rubbed it again; held it up to blue sky. Taking her hand, he had turned it over; placed the shell on the center of her palm, saying, "This actually happened. It lived; it died; a hundred millions of years before us. Here is the proof. And look, it is still here."

At that moment Constantia had fallen in love with Hugh. That is a fact; it actually happened.

She now reached into the pocket she wore beneath her skirt to feel the elongated prickly shell of the little fossil snail. It was still here. Where else would it be? She did not need to bring it out, or see it; the mere feel of its familiar ridges was enough.

But she had nothing at all of her unchristened son. No lock of his hair—he'd had no hair. What could she have kept? She wished she had thought to take a paring from his fingernail, a transparent little crescent of himself. What remained of him? His lifeless small body had been wrapped in linen; placed in a small casket; committed to the churchyard, while her childhood friend Jeebon Sing—Dr John Sing—who was a piper, had played a lament for him. Her nameless son was still there, in the churchyard; where else would he be? But he had been here. Had lived; had died. He was a fact.

But why have certain things happened? And other—equally possible—things not happened?

There came a tap at her door. "May we come in, Mrs MacAdam? It's Mrs MacDonald," said the familiar voice of her friend, at the door. "And I've brought you a very special visitor, a dear old friend of yours; you'll never guess who is come to see you!"

How she had aged, this visitor, this dear but least-expected of old friends! "Why, it's Mrs Fleming!" said Constantia. "How astonished I am! How glad to see you! And here, of all places!" The hair, formerly flame-red, was now nearly white—but the bright eyes still smiled from the same face; the affectionate smile was the same; the slim grace of her as she bent to kiss Constantia was the same.

"By merest good fortune," said Mrs Fleming, "I accompanied my husband on his jaunt from Antwerp, knowing full well that I should find Jeebon here in Edinburgh—but I did not dream that I should have the pleasure of meeting with you, my dear! You were only a girl when I saw you last—in Calcutta, wasn't it? How the years do pass! Now I see you wife and mother."

Saying that she was wanted downstairs to help Mrs Chambers set aright the place-cards which someone had shuffled about, Mrs MacDonald excused herself and left the two of them alone together.

"Dear girl, darling Constantia," said Mrs Fleming gently. "How well you are looking. And is this your own babe—or Mrs Chambers's?"

Constantia drew back her shawl to show her sleeping daughter, a milky bubble at her lips. "Mine," she said. "My own Livia."

"She is perfectly beautiful, the prettiest baby I ever saw. Just your very dimple to her chin, too! But how sad it is that her brother has been taken from us. Twins . . . Mary told me."

"Yes . . . they came rather early, too—"

"Twins often do, I believe."

"Yes . . . and I was a seven months baby, myself," said Constantia.

"Were you? I remember very well the first time I saw you, a nursling in your mother's arms—just as I see you now, with yours."

"Won't you sit with me a while, Mrs Fleming, and talk to me about my mother? Do, pray! I find myself thinking of her a great deal, these days. Tell me: was she not the most beautiful of all the mothers? So she always seemed to me."

"Indeed she was; very lovely," said Mrs Fleming, settling herself comfortably. "You are rather like her, you know. Aye, you are—as to appearance, I mean; though quite different in temper. She was always so gay that some folk thought her a little frivolous, I daresay; and she had never had any advantages of education, which she was always first to admit. But under that giddy manner, she had remark-

able pluck. Aye; and courage, and resolve, and self-command, though
one might not know it just at once, for none of it was showy or obvious. She had a generous compassionate heart, too. I remember once,
when you were very small, we all had gone for a picnic—with the
Rani and her children, too—at a garden pavilion near Dacca. And
your mother, reaching under a stand for a water pitcher, suddenly
drew her hand back, quite sharply. I asked what was the matter, for
she looked quite frightened for a moment; but she laughed and said
it was nothing; and made us all go and play on the swing, swinging
all you children higher and higher, to thrill you. It was only later that
evening that I found her tending to—what do you think?—a little
wound on the back of her hand! She had been bitten that afternoon
by a wee snake, coiled in the shadow under the water jars—but, seeing that the snake was not of the venomous kind, she had pretended
that nothing was amiss. Because, she told me, she had not wanted to
frighten the children."

"Ah!" said Constantia, gratified by this proof: courage, self-
command, compassion. Presently she said, "I seem to remember that
you, in those days, were always stitching, stitching at a vast piece of
canvaswork . . ."

"Oh, that! I came to the end of it at last," said Mrs Fleming. "It
was meant originally to cover a sofa, but by the time I had com-
pleted it, the sofa for which it was intended was nowhere to be found.
Instead, I had it mounted into the headboard of our bed, after Mr
Fleming and I had returned to Antwerp—and I have never taken
up a piece of canvaswork since. That was more than enough for this
lifetime."

"You knew my father, Mrs Fleming, did you not? I mean, not
Lieutenant Babcock, but my father, Mr Todd?"

"I did, briefly; during some two months, I suppose, aboard ship."

"Yes, before the fatal incident at Cape Town; the Rani told me of
that. What sort of man was he?"

"But I know almost nothing. Let me try to remember. It was so
very long ago, wasn't it—twenty-two or twenty-three years ago?—

before you were born." Mrs Fleming considered for some moments; and presently she said, "He was English, you know, not Scottish. He had an open and manly countenance. He was well-made, of medium height and complexion, with a lively manner, when in a good humour. He enjoyed the society and conversation of others. Of rather uncertain temper, however; and, though he loved a prank, I fear it was sometimes . . . at the expense of others."

"Do you know his Christian name? Or where he came from? His people?"

"I do not think I ever knew his Christian name, nor where he was from—but the names Todd and Dodd are frequently heard in Northumberland. And your mother was certainly Northumbrian, for she once happened to mention that she had lived near Newcastle all her life . . . until she had, ah, eloped, with Mr Todd."

"I don't suppose you know what my mother's name had been before she married?"

"Her Christian name was Maria, I remember—for I once had a letter from her, signed thus—but if ever she told me what her family name had been, I am sorry to say that I do not recall it."

"I do wish," said Constantia, "that the Rani had seen fit to tell me, much sooner than she did, that the bigamous Babcock was not in fact my father. I do not blame her—but matters would have gone far easier for me, if she had. So much time wasted, all on the wrong track! If I had known, I should never have squandered my efforts in looking up his people; I should have gone straightaway to look for my Todd relations instead. Indeed, I mean to do so yet, whenever I shall find the necessary time and resources at my command."

"I daresay the Rani meant well, however," said Mrs Fleming.

"I am sure she did. She said that as my mother had not seen fit to tell me, it was not her place to do so; and of course she'd had not the slightest grounds for suspecting that my mother's marriage to him was a sham. No, I cannot blame her. Yet it is painful to belong to no lineage at all; to descend from nowhere, and from no one. Indeed, Mrs Fleming, I sometimes feel myself scarcely human. It may seem odd—I can hardly explain why it seems a matter of such importance and even urgency to me, to find out my ancestors—but so it is, and especially now that I am a mother myself. I cannot tell when any opportunity may offer—probably not soon!—but I do still cherish a hope of finding someday the record of my parents' marriage in the parish registers at Gretna Green, or in that vicinity."

"Oh; indeed?" said Mrs Fleming.

"If, however," Constantia continued thoughtfully, "my parents eloped to Scotland from Newcastle or thereabouts, as you suggest, I ought perhaps to direct my researches first toward Berwick and the other border towns in that eastern part of the country."

"Mm," said Mrs Fleming.

"I have often wondered why she named me 'Constantia.'"

"That I can tell you with certainty," said Mrs Fleming, "for she told me herself. You were named for the celebrated sweet wine of Cape Town, which was a great favourite of hers."

Meanwhile, downstairs, the energetic contingent which had trudged with Mrs Chambers to the former field of glory at Prestonpans returned hot, thirsty, and conscious of superior virtue. The punch bowls were soon drained; and presently the doors to the dining room, where the buffet was laid out, were thrown open. Ceremony was not to be stood upon; everyone helped themselves and their neighbors to all the good things within reach; and then guests streamed out of the house again, on the garden side, carrying well-laden plates down to their appointed places at the long banquet tables set out in rows on the grass under the trees.

Hopey came upstairs, bearing a plate for Constantia. "Not a one of those jellied quenelles remained by the time I reached the buffet," she said, "but I did snatch for you a slice of the galantine of venison." The plate was heaped high with ham, the aforesaid galantine, beetroot salad, prawn paste, buttery rowies, marmalade, and a honey cake.

Mrs Fleming kissed Constantia and left her, saying she must go and find her husband and Jeebon.

Constantia dined in the privacy of her room, looking down over the wagging heads lining the long tables. Such chatter, and clatter, and laughter, and talk! From this lordly height, she could pick out the heads of Mrs Fleming and Mr Fleming and Jeebon at the far end of one of the tables and, nearly across from them, Mary and Annie with the DeQuincey girls. Mrs Fleming, happening to look up, saw Constantia at her window; she spoke to the others, and they all turned to wave: Come down! Join us! But Constantia with a smile shook her head no, and gestured behind her, into the room, toward the babies. This noisy gala was more agreeable from here.

Before long, the orations and toasts and songs began. From these, Constantia gradually pieced together the reason behind the day's revelries—for, until now, the historic events commemorated on this day had been embarrassingly sketchy in her mind, she not having been born to them, as everyone else had been.

This was the gist of it: One hundred years ago, on this date, on this ground, an "army" of some 2,500 Highlanders under the command of Prince Charles Edward Stuart—scion of the exiled Stuart dynasty—had, in the course of twenty minutes just at daybreak, surprised and routed an "army" of 2,300 Lowlanders and raw English recruits under the command of General Sir John Cope, loyal to the reigning Hanoverian dynasty. A century ago, just here, the Redcoats had broken and run away—and here, therefore, a century later, the Blue Bonnets still gathered to exult.

That had not, of course, been the end of the business. Queen Victoria, now in the ninth year of her reign, was the great-great-granddaughter of that Hanoverian king whose "army" had so disgraced itself on that occasion—whereas the Stuart dynasty had dwindled meanwhile to nothing, to extinction; had dwindled to the Sobieski princes, who—handsome, lazy as lions, with legs that looked remarkably well in hose, and wearing their tartan with an air—were really, as everyone secretly knew, only the Allen brothers from Wales. No one could seriously wish them ascendant.

But the fatal reverses suffered by the Stuart cause since that glorious battle at Prestonpans made it all the more poignant to gather on this anniversary; to salute that auspicious event, when—briefly—Scotland's future had seemed so bright.

The toasts were well under way, and someone was on his legs, declaiming: " . . . though we observe the occasion a day early—"

"You are mistaken, sir!" interrupted a loud braying voice. "We are twelve days early! Aye; because the twenty-first of September 1745 was an Old Style, Julian calendar date—occurring before the switch to the New Style in '52. To be quite correct, we ought to celebrate this anniversary on . . . just a moment, I am counting . . . nine, ten, eleven . . . on the second of October!"

This was too bewildering even to contemplate.

Other voices rose, to muddy matters further: "Not only are we hard-pressed to determine exactly what happened—but also to state precisely when it happened. But something certainly did happen; and it was approximately a victory, approximately hereabouts, approximately one hundred years ago."

"Surely we may be quite certain as to where it happened!"

"Approximately so; probably very near the place we laid our wreaths today."

"Do you claim, sir, that all facts are only approximate?"

"No sir; some are exact, and precise. The men who died at Prestonpans did not merely approximately die; they completely—entirely—exactly—and precisely died, each one of them."

Constantia heard Mrs Chambers's voice, happy and excited, passing into the house by the doorway below her window. "Oh," she was declaring to someone, "I cannot say what a good Jacobite may do—

but as for myself, I shall gladly drink any number of toasts, today at least, to any number of rebel princes!"

At dusk, Jeebon struck up his bagpipes at the bottom of the lawn. Constantia had just succeeded in getting both babies to sleep, and she promptly shut the window, for fear that the magnificent howl of the pipes would awaken them again. For a few minutes she watched over them, but they seemed only to withdraw into a deeper sleep; and presently she went downstairs, to listen from the open doorway of the library.

"It is Dr Sing," she overheard a man on the lowest step in front of her say, to the lady standing beside him. "The *Piper nigrum!*" He sounded like the same overbearing man who had been laying down the law—setting everyone straight, on all counts—throughout the afternoon. Perhaps he was slightly deaf? Though Constantia could see not much more than the shape of his head in the deepening dusk, she thought she recognised Mr Anstruther, of the prodigious side-whiskers, who had once sat across from her at dinner. "*Piper nigrum,*" he repeated to his companion. "That is the Linnaean name for pepper, you see; black pepper; ha! This particular piper—well, take a good look at him. I warrant you that even Black Donald of the Isles was never so black as this fellow! His mother was a black African slave, from America, and his father a Chinaman. Well, not a Chinaman, precisely; no, a Burmese prince, or rajah, or some such thing, as I understand it. But he is a doctor nevertheless, our *Piper nigrum*—fresh from the university at Glasgow."

Constantia knew the piper very well. Jeebon had been her friend and playmate since childhood; Jeebon had played the lament at the burial of her nameless baby boy. For some years Constantia's mother had served as companion and court attendant to his mother, the Rani Anibaddh Lyngdoh, queen of a very small principality in the Khasiya hills between Assam and Burma. After Constantia's mother died, it was the Rani (born an American black slave, true—but how did Mr

Anstruther know that?) who took in Constantia and brought her up with her own children.

Here in Scotland, where Jeebon had come to study medicine, he had adopted the name John, which saved a great deal of explanation. His brother Bajubon (now known as Benjamin, for the same reason) had been studying law in London—for, alas, that very small principality in the Khasiya hills had unfortunately fallen under the control of the East India Company; and Bajubon was now preparing a lawsuit by which to wrest it back.

"Quite a pretty piper, too," Mr Anstruther was saying. "He has been well taught. And I have heard Angus MacKay—the younger, of Raasay, of course; I am not old enough to have heard the first one, whatever you may think, madam! I have heard John Bain MacKenzie, too, in my day—and they are the cream of the family Piperaceae—ha! The typical; the best-developed of their circle, exhibiting the highest degree of perfection—as the author of *Vestiges* would have it! Have you read it? Indeed! Your husband permits it? I would not permit any wife of mine to read that book."

"If you had a wife, sir, you would never make so absurd a declaration," said the lady who, by her speech, was English, not Scottish; and not so young as to feel intimidated by any Scotsman, be he ever so loud, assured, and bewhiskered. "Now let us hush, for he has begun."

"No, he is only tuning, still," said Mr Anstruther. "Turned aside from us, as you see, and pretending that we are not here; while we, for our part, are politely pretending that he is not there; that we cannot hear him. They are the devil to tune, are bagpipes. Pipers spend thirty per centum of their time tuning, it is said . . . and the other seventy per centum—out of tune! Ha! Well, that's as close as we are to come, I daresay. He has got a serious commencing look about him now, and turns his face to us at last. Well, doctor: what is it to be?"

He stopped talking long enough to hear the first phrase of the tune—and then whispered loudly, " 'Rout of the Lowland Captain'— of course! The rout of Johnny Cope himself! A very suitable tune, for this day. Now, madam, let us listen very well to this urlar. That is the ground—the ground floor of the building, the foundation upon which all is built. Piobaireachd, you see, is a theme-and-variations business. Not that the underlying theme itself is ever actually played—never so bald, so naked as that. No, even the urlar, the ground, is decently clothed; well-wrapped in its plaid. But it is slow, as you hear; stately, and entirely free from the indignity of conforming to any particular beat or meter. Not a march; never a dance tune! No, quite free from any particular rhythm. Unconstrained by time; we have all the time in the world, for something so important as this. Ah! did you hear that? That phrase, that little question mark, that inversion? I call that the hinge; it is the place where we turn around and look back at the statements, the assertions we have heard thus far. We turn; look back; and from this side, with the light shining through, we can see where the thin places are: translucencies. Then we roll it up again, from this end, so to speak. Here we come, down to the finish, a sense of completion, even of reconciliation—but without any hint of grandness or pedantry. Ah! Ah! Well done, piper! Go it, doctor!

"Now we shall take this musical idea, to which we have been so patiently, so thoughtfully introduced—and we shall elaborate upon it, in a series of set variations. We shall now construct the upper storeys of our building, so to speak." For some moments during the first variation and its doubling, he fell silent, but was unable to suppress for long his helpful commentary. "Ah! the taorluath variation," he whispered loudly. "What a difference a change in the rhythm of the ornaments makes! But still one hears the underlying theme; still those notes shine through the carven-stone screen of the taorluaths . . . oh! Exquisite, the doubling, now!

"Are you ready, madam? You are; and here it is: the crunluath, the crown of ornament upon it all, the most extended and drawn-out of the quick rhythms, the lift of the music now elongated—extended—and sustained—almost beyond—bearing; beyond what anyone would have thought possible! Ah! The hinge; the reconciliation! The shuddering panting, melting, slowing . . . finish! Ah! Silence, now, for the doubling . . . Oh! Oh!

"And will our good piper give us a crunluath a mach? Oh, good doctor! He does! We are airborne; flying; freed from everything which had weighed upon us . . .

"Then soberly, at last, we return to the urlar—the ground. It is always necessary to return to ground, sooner or later, is it not? No matter how lofty the flights we may have achieved, we always are compelled at last to return to ground. A relief, too. How different this urlar feels to us, now! What once was strange is now familiar. What once seemed arbitrary, made-up on the spot, random, improvised— is now revealed as utterly necessary, a fixed reference point. Now we know what it means."

The piper reached the end; and stopped.

No flourishes; no crashing chords or crescendos or arpeggios of conclusion. Just stopped. Thick silence struck, sudden as a thunderclap.

There are no rests, no breaks, no drawing of breath in pipe music. The music is a single long breath, an unbroken exhalation, a sustained sigh. To exhale forever is immortality; is divine.

After a stunned moment, there was applause, and cheering; and someone shouted a request: Can you play "Johnny Cope"?

Mr Anstruther was summing up for the English lady: "Beginning with our solid rusticated ground," he was saying, "we constructed our sober and dignified Doric; topped that with our interesting and intricate Ionic—and then we attained at last to the exquisitely elaborated Corinthian capital, the baroque crown atop our architectural orders!"

She asked him some question, which Constantia could not quite hear.

"Improvised!" cried he. "Oh no, indeed, none of it is improvised; not a single note, not a single ornament of it! What in the world gave you such an idea? No, madam, I assure you: every piece of the great music, the ceol mhor, is a fixed and time-honored composition, handed down to us from the great pipers of old. To change a single note of it—a single phrase or spring of it—would be nothing but error. Indeed, the thought is horrible; only decay, destruction, the overthrow of civilisation. The piper does not read it, no—because he has perfectly memorised it. Perfectly."

Constantia withdrew through the library. The thought of improvisation was not horrible to her, whose ears from earliest infancy had received the classical music of India: raga, an exquisite music (structured strikingly like the ceol mhor)—but always to some degree improvised. Some of the greatest musicians of Hindustan had achieved in her hearing undreamt-of, unplanned, uncomposed flights of beauty, never to be exactly duplicated. Never. Was that fact unbearable? Or was it exquisite?

Was music not meant to be played? Surely that was the proper use of music, to be played—not performed; studied; memorised. Music is play, surely?

Played. Plaid. Plaited. Pleated. Woven, twisted, knotted. Patterned, yes; not a lawless tangle; but how not? Planned, designed? Or produced by its own operation? Her eye fell across a miscellaneous assortment of curiosities—various grimy scraps of cloth displayed with pasteboard labels, amid a wealth of books on the library table. The largest and most impressive of the books thus laid out was *Vestiarium Scoticum,* a handsomely-bound and lavishly-illustrated volume of authoritative heft, purporting to be the ancient text by which certain tartans were, from time immemorial, associated with particular clans; setting forth the ancient, true, and authentic model for each tartan. It lay open to show, for the benefit of guests, a flattering inscription on the title page from its "editors" to Mr Chambers. Alas, this extremely dubious book, of spurious antiquity, "discovered" and "edited" by those Sobieski Stuarts, was known to be as fraudulent as themselves; her old friends Jeebon and Bajubon were far better princes. *Vestiarium Scoticum* was no more authentic than the *Ossian*— "discovered" and "edited" by the nobody James MacPherson, a generation ago—which had played upon the same vanities, with the same near-success. Played; plaid; plaited; pleated. They were pretenders twice over, those Sobieski Stuarts. To pretend that one's own book was the work of someone else was very different from presenting a book—*Vestiges,* for example—unsigned, unattributed. There was nothing dishonest, at least, in publishing a book without its author's name. An author might be entitled to conceal; but not to deceive. Not to deposit her egg in the nest of another. Constantia made her way upstairs again.

When the fiddlers launched into an irresistible reel, the chairs emptied; who can sit out a reel? From her window Constantia, with Charlie in her arms once more, overlooked the pairs, foursomes, and eightsomes forming and reforming their patterns on the grass below. Even these patterns seemed to pose again that all-important question: Is this universe, and all that is in it, a fixed composition, the work of a Composer, a Designer, an Author—a Creator? Or is it an improvisation which spins itself into existence in accordance with certain parameters of the possible (aye, they are certain, these parameters, despite the difficulty of discerning them; let us remain within this scale, this mode); an improvisation which might, at any juncture, at any of an unimaginably vast number of points, have played out differently? And may do so yet?

The fiddlers played at a spanking tempo, and the dancers, though not quite up to the pace, were undoubtedly exhilarated by the effort. There are rich pleasures to be gleaned from the familiar, from recognising a known tune; discerning pattern; feeling rhythm. There is delight and even comfort in ease of recognition; in expectations precisely met; in certitude satisfied. In the unchanging; the reliable; the same, in each and every iteration; where like begets like; what always was, and always will be. All is fixed, world without end, forever and ever, amen.

Still, the familiar is not devoid of tedium. There is ennui, boredom, doomedness, sameness; the fore-ordained failure of everything, in precisely the same fore-ordained, forseen, and unforestalled manner. There is no hope.

Meanwhile, delights beckon from around the bend of the unfamiliar: the charm of surprise! of novelty! of a joke! Here resides the wondrous notion of Infinity; of infinitely rich possibility. The joy of change; of promise; of advent. The chance, even, of improvement; minute, perhaps, and only incremental; seldom vast or astonishing. Still, where change is possible, progress is possible. Matters might play out differently—and better—this time.

But the horrors of the unfamiliar surpass all for dread and revulsion. Matters might play out far worse. Deformities and monstrosities might engulf us all. And then, eradication of everything we knew and loved; even—especially—our selves, and our descendants, and everyone resembling us. Extinction. All might come to an end.

Even the dancing, as night fell.

At the bottom of the garden, a pillar of fire flared upward, and someone detonated a squib. The night breeze wafted the bonfire's column of smoke away from the house, toward the fisherfolk's huts at the shore.

The bonfire had posed a difficulty: What was to fuel it? The gardener had protested that his garden was so well in trim that nothing—no boughs, no prunings—could be spared for immolation. But upon consideration, it was thought that boughs and prunings might be obtained from the adjacent estate belonging to long-absent Dalrymples, whose shrubberies and woodlands had been growing wild for years. It was not quite clear to Constantia whether permission had been sought, or given—but here, somehow, was a fine bonfire illuminating the ruddy faces of over-excited children and adults alike. A good fire was a thrilling thing, a little frightening and deeply fascinating; who could forbear to gaze into it? Who was immune to its bewitchment?

Abruptly the fireworks commenced: a grand barrage of serpents, wheels, sky-rockets, Roman candles, Chinese fires, and tourbillons; each one dazzling, and strangely rousing; each detonation delivering a thump to be felt in the chest, like artillery fire. These were met with cries and shouts, and finally, when it was over, cheers. Someone started singing "Awa' Whigs Awa'," and all joined in, at uncertain tempo and pitch, but very loudly. And when that was concluded (to more cheers), it was time to go home. The tide of guests began its rapid ebb.

Sunday passed in merciful quiet at Spring Gardens. There was left-over food to eat. No one came, or went; and not even Mrs Chambers went to kirk.

Overnight, the weather changed, and Lady Janet returned on Monday morning through a drenching rain. The Monday morning post also brought a letter for Constantia, the first she had received at Spring Gardens. She did not know the handwriting and, what was more curious still, the letter was very closely sealed, three times over. She lifted the seals and, unfolding it, looked first for a signature. It was from her mother's old friend Mrs Fleming.

> Edinburgh
> 22nd Septr.

Dearest Constantia,

> What matchless delight I had, from the sight of you and your darling baby, on Saturday! What pleasure, from talking over the old days with you!—and from remembering your dear mother, of whom you remind me so much, and of whom, alas, we know only too little.
>
> Yet there is one fact more I know of her, and of your father

Mr Todd. I did not speak of it on Saturday, for I was not then
certain whether it is a matter which ought to be spoken of.
I rise this morning convinced—or nearly so—that I must
tell what I can, before I re-embark today with Mr Fleming;
nearly convinced that Truth, be it ever so disagreeable, must
be preferred over error and ignorance, by persons of sound
principles and mature judgment, as I believe you to be.

It is this, dear Constantia: Upon that dreadful occasion
in Cape Town, under the most distressing circumstances
imaginable—under the first shock and agony occasioned by
Mr Todd's death—your mother (then pregnant with you)
told me that she and he—though he called her his wife,
and she was known as Mrs Todd—had never in fact been
married at all.

I could not then be quite certain that she knew what
she was saying, for she had been given a strong draught of
laudanum and several glasses of fortified wine, for the sake
of their sedative effect; and it was certainly the case that after
this harrowing event, she again habitually referred to Mr
Todd as her late "husband."

But on one subsequent occasion, when she and I were
alone together once more, she again referred to the irregularity
of her connexion with him. This was soon after your birth,
when I met her by most surprising chance up at Goalpara in
Assam. By then, poor Lt Babcock had already succumbed
to fever—and you were a babe in her arms, not much older
than your two nurslings are now. But on that occasion she just
mentioned to me—almost in passing, it seemed—that she
was, this time, in truth a widow. "A pukka widow this time"
were her very words. They shewed, as I supposed then, that
she remembered telling me that she and your father had never
been properly married. Indeed, I do not know, even now, what
else she could have meant by it. I never asked her anything
about it, and she never again referred to the matter.

I hope I am right, dear Constantia, to tell you this. What your mother—or your father—might have thought right for you to know, if they had been spared to us, we cannot guess; nor shall we ever know why they did not chuse to enter into matrimony.

You remarked on Saturday that the Rani might have spared you a great deal of distress and disappointment if only she had earlier confided in you the truth that Lt Babcock was not your father. Further, you spoke of your determination to find out the record of the marriage between your mother and your father, whether at Gretna Green, or elsewhere. It is with the wish, then, of sparing you another fruitless search that I now write—for it is plain that no diligence can turn up any record of a marriage which never took place.

What some people call the stain of illegitimate birth is, to my way of thinking, merely imaginary; but (as my India-born nieces and nephews know only too well) the world at large takes quite another view. I have never said anything of this matter to anyone but yourself, nor do I suppose that I ever shall.

I remain, dear Constantia, your devoted friend,

Catherine Fleming

8

_____

SUCH A LETTER as that merited a treble seal.

Lady Janet's voice was ringing through the partition wall, her tone more didactic than usual. Mrs Chambers had gone up to town for the day to settle some matters relating to the furbishment of the Edinburgh house, leaving her children at Spring Gardens undefended; vulnerable to improvement. "'Yet since I became a pilgrim, they have disowned me,'" declaimed Lady Janet's reading voice, "'as I also have rejected them; and therefore they were to me now no more than if they had never been of my lineage'"

Constantia pressed her hands against her ears. Until the age of nineteen, she had been Miss Constantia Babcock; had supposed herself the posthumous daughter of Lieutenant Babcock, an Englishman and a surveyor in the service of the East India Company—her mother's "dear, dear Babcock," dead of fever some weeks before Constantia's birth. Had her mother intended to tell her, sometime, that dear, dear Babcock was not her real father; was merely her stepfather? Constantia had been ten years old when her mother died. When might her mother have intended to tell her? At twelve? At fourteen? Never?

The Rani Anibaddh could have told her much sooner than she did. Why hadn't she? "Why should I tell, if your mother never did?"

she had said upon that dismal evening at the damp inn at Wivenhoe, when the tawdry truth had finally come to light. "Who ever suspected that Babcock was a cheat? He was kindness itself to your mother, you know—and I was in a good position to judge, because I was still your mother's servant then, when the fever took him, not long after he'd married her—I mean, pretended to marry her. No, he made fools of us, me and your mother both. Who'd have guessed he had a wife living? But now—now that he's proven a knave, a scoundrel!—I think you should know the truth: you are no bastard of his. No; your real father was your mother's first husband, Mr Todd. Oh, yes; Babcock knew all about it. Your mother was well along with you when she married him, and she was no deceiver, whatever he may have been. How furious I am, to think that Babcock deceived us! Not the generous step-father willing to receive an unborn step-child; no! But a bigamous scoundrel, a liar, a cheater of women! Not only your poor mother, who thought she was truly married to him—oh yes, before witnesses, by the chaplain of his regiment; I was there myself!—but his real wife too, that dried-up old widow who spat at us today; and her dried-up spinster of a daughter. I'd spit in his face, if I could!"

Constantia had begged the Rani to tell her everything, anything that could be remembered about this new father—this Mr Todd! What sort of man was he? Were they very happy together, this young couple who had sailed for India from Edinburgh, all those years ago? And how had he died so tragically, so soon?

"Very much in the first transports of the, ah, joys of the married state, they seemed," the Rani had said. She described Mr Todd as convivial, sociable, very fond of company and fun. Gently, she had told of the fatal incident in South Africa, during the voyage to Calcutta; he was buried at Cape Town, in the English cemetary.

By telling her of Mr Todd, that evening three years ago, the Rani had redeemed Constantia from sudden illegitimacy.

Now Mrs Fleming's astonishing letter plunged Constantia once more into a new, second illegitimacy.

Illegitimacy! What a word; what an idea! Fatherless. Nameless. Anonymous, in the most literal meaning of the word: unnamed, unclaimed, unowned. Ignominious.

But after all, why did it matter? The misconduct of her parents had taken place long in the past, before she was born. This disgraceful fact had always been fact, even though she had not known of it. Here, now, unchanged by new knowledge of this old fact, was herself; equally unchanged was her daughter. Nothing was changed, nothing.

"'Yes, I met with Shame,'" rang Lady Janet's voice through the partition, "'but of all the men that I met with in my pilgrimage, he, I think, bears the wrong name. The others would take No for an answer, at least after some words of denial; but this bold-faced Shame would never have done.'"

Still it rained. Though both babies were, for the moment, perfectly content in the night nursery with Hopey and the little boys, it was too wet for Constantia to escape to the garden. In hopes of muffling her disagreeable reflections—and the disagreeable voice from the next room—she took up the book which lay at hand: *Vestiges of the Natural History of Creation*. Red cloth cover; no author's name on the title page; anonymous. Look, here is the book itself. Judge that; do not trouble yourself over the question of who made it. That is no proper concern of yours.

She tried to read. "Were we acquainted for the first time with the circumstances attending the production of an individual of our race,"—(oh! the tangling of limbs, in darkness! the panting! wetness! the force of it, the urgency!)—"we might equally think them degrading, and be eager to deny them, and exclude them from the admitted truths of nature."

What sort of a woman, then, can my mother have been? The most beautiful woman in any company, yes; tender and generous indeed— but was it only to Mr Todd and Lieutenant Babcock? What sort of man, then, was my father? And why, why had they not married?

Of course my mother was not eager to explain to me that I was no child of Lieutenant Babcock's.

"She was very lovely, your mother," Mrs Fleming had agreed.

But why did it seem to matter?

Constantia tried again to read, starting over at the top of the paragraph. "Is not this degrading? Degrading is a term expressive of a notion of the human mind, and the human mind is liable to prejudices which prevent its notions from being invariably correct."

Was she incorrect, then, in feeling degraded by the circumstances attending the production of herself?

She turned back a page: Are we to draw back, asked the author of *Vestiges*, from our investigation of God's works, "lest the knowledge of them should make us undervalue his greatness and forget his paternal character?"

His paternal character!

Her disagreeable thoughts only aggravated, she set the book firmly aside.

By this time Lady Janet had finally gone downstairs, and now it was Nina's voice that could be heard, continuously, through the partition. What was Constantia to do with this damning letter? If there had been a fire in her grate, she would have fed it to the fire—but the only fire in the house was in the kitchen. Instead, she tucked the letter safely alongside the Potamides in the pocket she wore under her skirt, and went to the doorway of the day nursery.

Nina was reading aloud to her sisters while they worked. Each of the girls was silently hemming a handkerchief—cut out by Lady Janet from threadbare old sheets. ("I, for one, am perfectly content to wipe my nose on an unhemmed square of linen," Jenny had told Lady Janet. "It is not for you, miss," Lady Janet had replied tartly. "It is for the deserving poor. You might think of someone other than yourself. Do you ever see me sitting idle? No; there is always useful work to be done. But I shall leave *The Pilgrim's Progress* here with you, and Miss Nina is to go on with reading it aloud to you girls as you work. You have had nothing but pleasure for many days now; it will do you no harm to devote a morning to the good of others." And at last she had gone downstairs to her cabinet, satisfied that the girls were now well provided with useful work to do, and an improving book to do it by.)

Nina read aloud, " 'The misfortune of your birth ought to make you particularly careful as to your associates. There can be no doubt of your being a gentleman's daughter, and you must support your claim to that station by every thing within your own power, or there will be plenty of people who would take pleasure in degrading you.' "

This was decidedly not *The Pilgrim's Progress*—which lay discarded on the table beside Nina, handy to be snatched up quickly in case of Lady Janet's coming upstairs again. Instead, for the improvement of her sisters' minds, Nina had substituted *Emma*, and was reading from the first volume of that novel. Its other two volumes lay upon the low bookshelf beside the doorway. As Nina continued reading aloud, Constantia picked up the concluding volume. It fell open near the end, where her eye fell upon this: "The stain of illegitimacy, unbleached by nobility or wealth, would have been a stain indeed." She turned back to the title page. *Emma* was, of course, "By the author of *Pride and Prejudice*"—for here was an author, yet another, who chose to withhold her name, though it was no secret; who would not own the offspring of her own pen.

Plenty of people would take pleasure in degrading you. A stain indeed.

Constantia fetched her mantle (Parisian, prettily embroidered, and with two rows of deep fringing; but not quite as warm as one might wish when in Scotland, in late September) and plunged downstairs, across the glistening granite doorstep outside the library. She needed to be outdoors, despite the drizzle which still fell into the little walled paradise of Spring Gardens. She needed to be in the open air; to pace up and down the dripping-wet garden walks; to walk herself, if possible, into composure before the babies should require her again.

✳   ✳   ✳

THE CHAMBERS FAMILY had taken the house and grounds at Spring Gardens for the summer months, while their Edinburgh house at 1 Doune Terrace in the New Town underwent improvements and repairs. Unfortunately the Edinburgh builder had fallen behind (through no fault of his own, he stoutly asserted; he blamed the building-stone supplier and the treachery of the slaters) so that at Michaelmas, the 29th of September, the house in Edinburgh still was not habitable. It was agreed therefore between landlord and tenant to extend the family's tenancy of Spring Gardens until the Scottish term day: Martinmas, on the 11th of November.

There was only one difficulty: fires. Fires were not permitted by the terms of the Spring Gardens lease, as the chimneys had not been swept since no one knew when.

In September, afternoon sunshine had still streamed warm and golden across the grass, though the nights grew very chilly; but early in October there came a day when white frost remained all day long in the blue shadows to the north of the house, and on the roof. Everyone complained and shivered in their summer clothes, and the children congregated in the warm kitchen, which annoyed the cook. "Mr Balderstone," Mrs Chambers had declared to her husband early the next morning, "we must have fires. We cannot do without fires in the library and the day nursery, at least."

Mr Gunn in his bothy at the bottom of the garden had just downed his breakfast dram when there came a tap at the door. He folded away his newspaper and opened to the tenant who, with lidded hamper over his arm, was trailed by three of his lasses, each shivering with excitement, worry, and cold. "Good morning to you, Mr Gunn," said Mr Chambers. "We have come to gather a few pigeons for a day's outing. Not for the table, no; but for the carrying of a message. The birds are quite accustomed to you, I suppose? Aye; perhaps you will come out and advise us which ones to take, and help us to catch them."

"But how will they find their way, Daddy?" piped one of the lasses. "Will they not be lost?"

"No, they will not be lost."

"And so a great distance, from Edinburgh to here!" cried another. "Can they fly so far as that?"

"A mere matter of eight miles? That is nothing to pigeons, nothing at all," their father assured them.

At the door of the doocot, Mr Gunn had to knock loose its frosted bolt. Then, ducking under its low lintel, he led the others inside.

"They can do far greater distances than that," their father was saying. "Hundreds of miles; over mountains, across the sea. And cover the distance more rapidly than the swiftest horse, too. How else do you suppose, my lassies, that those Rothschilds on the London 'Change have managed to gather up such a fortune, these last ten years? By getting their intelligence first, you see—even before the express couriers could arrive from the Continent. Aye, they set up a pigeon express of their own across the Channel; and it answered very well indeed, until the general brokers banded together and refused to do any business until the papers—the second editions—should have come to hand, bringing the same news to all; and thus was pared away the advantage that the pigeon-men had held for a short time."

The stone-built walls of the round doocot tower rose some fifteen feet high, to open eaves where the pigeons passed in and out as they pleased, just beneath a slate roof. It was surprisingly warm inside, out of the sea breeze; and smelled of feathers, dung, and grain, rather ripe. There were shelves, perches, rails; but most of all, there were nest boxes lining the walls, all the way up and all the way around; dozens of pigeon-holes, like the inside of the post office. Scores of birds fixed their round bright eyes on the intruders; perhaps fifty or sixty birds, in every shade of iridescent blue, grey-blue, dove-grey, creamy-grey, all mottled and striped like mica or slate, and pure white, too. On some nests dwelt a patient complacent parent; its mate might be nearby, or out feeding itself. On ledges inside the open eaves were birds strutting, birds preening, ruffling, flapping, gossiping, courting, purling, chuckling, and flirting softly with one another. Some nests stood empty; some held pretty eggs by the pair; some held a pair of gawky half-fledged squabs.

"Now, Mr Gunn," said Mr Chambers, folding back the lid of his basket, "shed me a few braw birds, if you will be so good. Two or three sturdy cocks would do best, I suppose."

"Nay, but the sexes cannot be distinguished, one from the other," said Gunn. "Not to look at. Sir."

"Those must be hens, though, sitting on their eggs," said Mr Chambers.

"Nay, they are quite unlike barnyard fowl," said Mr Gunn. "Among pigeons, you know, the cocks and the hens sit alike, turn and turn about."

"Do they? Well, there is a doughty well-grown pair, quite equal to a day's work, I should think," proposed Mr Chambers, pointing to a nest rather overwhelmed by a plump complacent-looking couple of dull grey birds.

"Those will never do," said Mr Gunn. "Sir. For they were eggs not three weeks since. Though quite of a size now to have their necks wrung, and make their appearance on a dish at dinner. Aye, bigger, and heavier too, than full-fledged birds—for they do nothing but sit, all the long day, and devour the food proffered them by their hard-pressed parents. But they have never yet stirred from that nest, and cannot fly at all; not so far as the garden wall."

"What do you say, then, to that likely-looking bird? Already caught for us," suggested Mr Chambers, of the lone pigeon confined to its separate pen in a small annex off the doocot.

"Nor that," said Mr Gunn. "That bird belongs to—to the wet nurse; 'tis not Spring Gardens–born, and would never return here; indeed, if it got the chance it would fly away instantly, to wherever it came from. That one is not to be let out on any account, poor creature."

"Well, Mr Gunn. Well. Perhaps you will be so good, then, as to select two or three eligible birds for us. Are there no idlers here with nothing better to do than lounge about and eat up the grain that should go by rights to honest birds bringing up families?"

Quickly, Mr Gunn caught two sturdy birds for them: a stout dark one; and another, pale, with a frill to its hose. The birds scarcely struggled when Mr Gunn wrapped his quiet hands around their bodies, holding their wings. When he turned each bird over, so that one of the lasses could tie a short red ribbon around one of its legs, the birds lay quite still, only craning their necks around to keep their world upright. Once captured and flagged, they were popped into Mr Chambers's hamper.

"One more, for luck," said the tenant; and Mr Gunn caught them a third, a slim purply-blue bird with iridescent black bands to its tail.

"Now, Tuckie, my lass," said Mr Chambers, "you and your sisters are to watch for the return of these messengers—each bearing its red pennant, to mark it out from all the others. I shall be sending a message for your mother later this morning."

"But the wives, or husbands, of these birds in your hamper— won't they be wretched?" asked one of the lasses.

"Not knowing what has become of their dear ones?" added another.

"Ask Mr Gunn," said their father.

"Won't they, Mr Gunn?"

"Nay, lass," replied Mr Gunn, "never fear. Your birds will be home again before their mates notice they are away. Pigeons are like the ewes at lambing, or the salmon at spawning. Or like your own dad. Pigeons always do find their way home, swifter and more faithful than Her Majesty's penny post. And free besides."

"If the cost of their feeding is not reckoned into account," said Mr Chambers. "Thank you, Mr Gunn."

Mr Gunn watched Mr Chambers, limping, lead his lasses back up the garden walk to the house. Mr Rhubarb with his lasses, thought Mr Gunn . . . for rhubarb was Rheum. It was familiar knowledge (throughout the Lothians, and beyond) that this Mr Chambers and his brother—now the respectable publishers of the extremely popular *Chambers's Edinburgh Journal*—had raised themselves by their own fortitude, frugal self-denial, and honest industry from an early poverty full of hardship and humiliation to their present state of prosperity; of affluence and influence. Hadn't this very Mr Robert Chambers formerly been—some twenty-five or thirty years ago—that thin, lame boy, Bob Chambers, living at nearby Joppa Pans? Thin, lame Bob Chambers, who walked every day (for there had been no tram, in those days) from here to Edinburgh, and back? In every weather, and limping all the way?

Of course Mr Gunn said nothing of his recollection—one does not say, I remember noticing you, years ago, when you were wretched!—but he was quite sure that this was the same Robert Chambers. The profile was distinctive, and so was the limp.

In those days, Mr Gunn had been in his own strapping prime, just past thirty; lusty and strong; with a hale happy wife and three young sons, all thriving. And suppose I too had chosen, Mr Gunn thought, to make of myself a writer, a scribbler, a publisher—and not a gardener? I might have done so, for I, too, am a reader, a thinker; I, too, started with nothing and have made my way by honest industry. But this garden would have been much the poorer without me; who would have fostered the linden walk; the clipped yews; the orchard; the rose beds? True, all were blasted now by frost (except the yews, which never changed), but all would revive next spring. My own labour produced this. My own life has not been wasted.

All three of the Spring Gardens pigeons returned, together, before noon. Mr Gunn caught the birds and helped the girls detach the messages they carried: three tiny notes, each rolled into a cylinder and tied to the leg of a bird. The girls carried these little quills, numbered 1, 2, and 3, to their mother, who smoothed them flat and read her husband's message in three parts:

1. Landlord declines expense of chimney sweep for comfort of mere Balderstones.
2. Landlord insists No Fires—until chimneys are swept.
3. Mr B begs Mrs B engage sweep earliest, at Mr B's expense.

"Very shabby, I call it," said Mrs Chambers, of the landlord's conduct, to Lady Janet. "How he can call himself a gentleman, I do not understand, be his name ever so ancient." She sent immediately for the chimney-sweep who, with his assistant, arrived within the hour.

The rest of the day was required to clear the chimney in the library; and all the next morning to clear the day-nursery's chimney. From above and from below, the sweep and his assistant knocked down and hauled out bushels—amounting to a cartload—of sticks, litter, straw, bird droppings, soot, mud, feathers, dust, old eggshells—and the desiccated carcass of a half-fledged jackdaw. The children were fascinated, and loath to leave their observation post, not even for meals. All their talk and all their study was of the marvelous jackdaws—clever, ingenious, industrous jackdaws!—which had dropped all this filth, litter, tinder, and kindling down the chimneys, to make nests for their hatchlings "Cawdaws," the sweep called them; and declared that they mated for life, more faithful than men—or women.

"Ha! 'The swans will sing when the jackdaws fall silent,'" Hopey had retorted, as if to herself.

When the sweep had finished his work and gone, the Twinnies together dragged upstairs a scuttle filled with sea-coal; and Hopey lit the day-nursery's first fire since no one knew when—just as a sleety rain commenced to stream down the window panes. The children drew the thick curtains and lay, elbows on the hearthrug, chins on palms, admiring the flames through the tall nursery fender, praising the luxurious warmth; and so fulsomely did they petition ("Oh! Dear, good, kind Hopey! Sweet Hopey! Beautiful Hopey! Do say yes!") to have their tea there, on the rug, that fond Hopey agreed.

There Constantia found them, their flushed faces lit up by fitful flames, while they turned buttered stale bread over the fire on toasting forks. How beautiful, those glowing young faces! Then her eye was arrested by the thing which stood upon the mantle, leaning against the chimney breast. Shaken, she went closer, the better to see it.

"Isn't it grand?" cried Annie. "Mary made it!"

"Very clever indeed," said Constantia. Of course it was not a fossil; it was only the bird skeleton which had been recovered from the chimney, salvaged by Mary from the sweep's cart, and now, transformed. Mary had dissected it, bone from hollow bone, and then glued these bones onto a piece of pasteboard in a lifelike—though flattened—airborne pose. She had written beside each bone its name in ink: upper and lower mandibles; furcula; coracoid; sternum. Both wings were fully extended for flight, complete out to the dainty phalanges.

The children were still full of the wondrous ingenuity of jackdaws, especially of their being so thoroughly jackdawish without, presumably, the benefit of lessons: "But how do jackdaws know what sort of nests it is proper for them to build?" asked Tuckie. "How do they know they ought to look for chimneys, to drop sticks down?"

"It is instinct," declared Annie, very positively. "They know by instinct."

"Extinct?" asked Jenny.

"No, silly; instinct. Quite different."

"Jemmie stinked!"

"Did not!" cried Jemmie hotly.

"Did so!"

"Ha! Dropped it! Jemmie dropped his bread in the fire!"

"But 'instinct' only means 'inborn,'" said Nina. "It is only a word, only the name of the phenomenon; and merely pronouncing the name of the phenomenon is no explanation. The question is, how can it be inborn?"

"It's the quills I wonder at," said Annie. "Do the bird's own quills, embedded in its skin, poke it unbearably? A feather mattress or a pillow is bad enough—but imagine a whole skinful of quills, poking without mercy!"

"Perhaps that is why birds are so very restless; so flighty," said Mary. "Never so easy nor comfortable as cats, napping in their fur."

Constantia watched for her opportunity, and a day or two later, upon finding the day nursery briefly deserted while its fire still flickered in the grate, she burned the letter from Mrs Fleming, poking it to a crumble of grey ash.

One Sunday evening when the parental Chamberses had gone across the river to Musselburgh to dine with Dr and Mrs Moir, Lady Janet came upstairs to conduct the weekly catechism of the children. This was a duty properly their father's, though by him sadly neglected. She appeared so suddenly and unexpectedly that Constantia, who had been helping Tuckie sort her collection of feathers, had no time to retreat to her own room. "A coal fire!—in the day-nursery!—and before Martinmas!" exclaimed Lady Janet from the doorway. "How excessively luxurious! My father never dreamed of such a thing. You are most fortunate little children. I hope that you have been studying your questions? No? I am very sorry indeed for it. I daresay that you, Mrs MacAdam, might hear the children in their questions, when you find yourself at leisure of a Sunday evening. Ah, leisure! how pleasant that must be! Now, what is this little book? The infamous *Vestiges*! Still! In the day-nursery—and on a Sunday!" She opened the little red-bound volume at random, and for a moment her eye roamed the page. "Miserable twaddle," she said. "Listen: 'That enjoyment is the proper attendant of animal existence is pressed upon us by all that we see and all we experience.'"

The children exchanged surreptitious glances with one another, but no one ventured to speak, until Constantia said, "But what objection can your ladyship have to that?"

"My objection? Only that it is heresy. What is the first question, Miss Mary?"

Mary looked perplexed, and Lady Janet said sternly, "In the Catechism, of course."

"Oh, the Catechism," said Mary, stalling for a moment; but then she had it: 'What is the chief end of man?'"

"And Miss Anne, I hope, can oblige us with the answer."

Annie could, and grudgingly did: "'Man's chief end is to glorify God, and to enjoy Him forever.'"

"There, you see," said Lady Janet.

"But I do not see at all," said Constantia. "Even the Catechism concedes that we are made for enjoyment." Then, finding herself perilously near to engaging in yet another argument with Lady Janet in front of the children, she excused herself and retired to her own room. There she was at liberty to indulge in vehement imaginary arguments with Lady Janet, such as this, on the controversial subject of coal:

LADY JANET'S (IMAGINED) DECLARATION: "Here is yet
another instance, only one of the Almighty Creator's
many contrivances both wise and good, only one proof
of His personal and superintending will wrought upon
every atom of His universe—and that is the existence
of coal! Coal, we are told by the naturalists, is the fossil
remains of the primeval forest which covered much
of the earth in former ages, untold eons before God
created Adam. Rich and inexhaustible are those deposits
which He hath caused to be laid down! Coal—which
fires our furnaces, our mills, our steam engines—and
cheers our hearths as well, from the grandest castle to
the most humble cot! Coal, which fuels all that is best
and most advanced in human endeavor and progress!
Now, Mrs MacAdam, what reasonable person can doubt
that this gigantic forest was called into existence by the
personal and superintending will of an Almighty God

who careth for His creatures; proof of His goodness—
His foresight—His great plan—His generosity? For no
other purpose than to provide for the future needs of the
human race, His beloved children, whom He even then
intended to call into being, in His own image, in the
fullness of His own good time? Is not Coal an irrefutable
proof of God's goodness; of His might; of the vastness—
and also of the minuteness—of His great plan?"

CONSTANTIA IMAGINED FOR HERSELF VARIOUS REPLIES, SUCH
AS THIS: "No, although it would be pleasant indeed to
think so. No doubt it was pleasant to suppose, in former
days, that our Earth must lie at the center of the Universe,
a yolk cradled in the center of its egg. Alas, that it does
not! Alas, that it spins instead, we know now, at the
edge of an unremarkable galaxy, among countless other
galaxies! But let us now consider bed-bugs, Lady Janet.
Or, if you prefer, lice; or mosquitoes. By your logic, you
are obliged to conclude that the Author of us all created
humankind not out of any great or particular love for
us, not because we are the apple of His eye, but only by
way of provision for those insects, apparently so beloved
by Him, which thrive upon our bodies. Did the Creator
provide humankind as their playground, their Eden,
wherein they might thrive? Are we   our very bodies—
provided only to succour them? Are they the crown of
His creation; is it they who are created in His own image?
And is not humankind, then, demoted to a role very like
that of those prehistoric forests, now coal? What then of
your personal, superintending, wise and good God?"

OR THIS: "No. Coal is proof only that primeval forests
existed, during former ages of immense duration.
And humankind's enthusiastic use of those fossil

remains, in this present age, demonstrates that thus
far, the ingenuity and luck of our kind has been
sufficient to obtain our survival; sufficient, thus far, to
permit of our perpetuating our own kind, drawing
upon only those materials which do exist, though
they are far from ideal—for there is nothing else;
quite literally, and by definition, nothing else!"

OR THIS: "No. Coal is, as you say, important to our continued
existence, our advance in the courses of civilization.
But the infinite trouble, danger, and great expense of
painstakingly and laboriously extracting that coal—
of delving it from the depths of the earth—would
tend to prove instead that the deity to whom you refer
cannot possibly be paying attention. It will occur to
everyone that a great many far superior arrangements
might have been devised, by any truly superintending
Creator—who careth for his creatures—Almighty and
all-wise! Might, and ought, to have been devised! Does
this look like the careful husbandry of a loving Father?
(Aye, like that of Abraham, filicidal Patriarch!)"

LADY JANET'S (IMAGINED) RETORT (FOR SHE WAS DETERMINED,
EVEN IN THESE IMAGINARY ARGUMENTS, TO HAVE
THE LAST WORD): "Well! Sea-coal is to be had, easily
enough! Free for the picking-up, off the sands!"

* * *

TUCKIE, the youngest of the girls, was of a serious disposition. She
could not always bear the noisy society of the day-nursery, and sometimes asked to come into Constantia's little room. One evening, while
quietly studying an atlas on the rug at Constantia's feet, she looked up

from a map of the Antipodes and gravely said, "But Mrs MacAdam, what are people for?"

Constantia took an instant's consideration before she replied, "A very good question—and many clever and good people have devoted their lives to studying just that. Some people believe that they know the answer. But as for myself, I do not know; and I am not convinced that anyone truly knows."

Tuckie nodded, and turned to the next page in the atlas: Japan.

But later, Constantia thought, what are people for? What is the chief end of man? Such good questions.

✳   ✳   ✳

ON THE 22ND OF AUGUST IN 1833, when Constantia was ten years old, she had been jolted awake in the middle of the night, not by her mother's careful return to their bed, but by an earthquake. The beams overhead creaked, complained; and litter rained down from the thatch upon her head in the darkness; still the jolting went on; and there was a deep rumbling which she first took for heavy iron-bound carriage wheels on a wooden bridge; and then for thunder. It was neither wheels nor thunder, but the groaning of the earth.

Sleepily, she had turned over and, finding herself alone in the bed, had instantly sat up, fully awake.

A tall cabinet toppled, crashed. Voices cried out, nearby, within the house and the outbuildings; and further away, in the town below: male and female voices, oaths and prayers. There was another crash in the next room, and a cry. The end of a beam smashed down upon the loom which stood in the corner, crushing its web, destroying the length of striped silk which her mother had been weaving. Constantia rolled off her mattress and crouched on the floor with her blanket over her head, too frightened to squeak, her fragile spine awaiting the smashing blow whenever the heavy beams overhead should come crashing down.

On; and on; and on, the jolting continued. When would it stop? Why didn't it stop? It could not go on, and on! could it?

Would it stop? Would it get worse? Would it continue like this, henceforth?

Constantia had felt plenty of earthquakes in her ten years, where she and her mother lived in the Khasiya highlands between Assam and Burma. A jolt, a shaking, a rumble, a rattling. Earthquakes were common enough, though not nearly so frequent as the torrential rains which fell so heavily here, so steadily, that for months at a time it was like living under a waterfall—and earthquakes were therefore less quotidian, more remarkable, more fun. "Ah! Did you feel that?" her mother would say, amused, when the writing-case rattled on the shelf, when the stew pot hanging over the fire swayed on its chain, when ripples suddenly chased each other back and forth across the surface of the water in the basin. "Just a little one. Didn't you feel it?" If you were outdoors—playing, climbing, wading, running, always moving—you might not even notice an earthquake; they were more noticeable when you were inside a house, where you had to be still. A jolt, or two, or three; then it was over and you laughed; how exciting, that the earth, too, could move! Even the earth.

Constantia almost always fell asleep beside her mother, in the bed they shared, in the quarters they had to themselves, in the Rani's mansion. Her mother would lightly rub her back, and Constantia would stroke her mother's hair as they fell asleep together. Lately, though, Constantia had sometimes awakened in the night to find herself alone in the bed. When that happened, she would lie awake, rigid with dreadful imaginings, until her mother came back. Sometimes it was nearly daylight before her mother came back. She would creep silently into their bed smelling of . . . what? Not herself. Constantia always pretended to be asleep, but she was not asleep.

When day dawned hours later, revealing the appalling wreckage wrought by the immense earthquake, Constantia's mother hadn't yet come back. At noon, she still hadn't come back; and after that, she continued not coming back. Went on and on that way, not returning.

That is when Constantia had been brought by the Rani Ani-baddh to live with her own children, and study under their demanding tutors.

✼　✼　✼

WHEN CONSTANTIA had parted from her husband, she had brought away with her four sturdy pigeons for carrying messages back to him, at that place where he was to remain. It was true (as Mr Gunn had observed) that she knew little about pigeons; and that little, picked up during her India childhood, was quite foreign to any Scottish pigeon-keeper's ways. In India, breeders would distinctively perfume the bath-water of their various flocks, so that birds indistinguishable to the human eye could be sorted by scent. The birds of this line, this loft, might smell of sandalwood; those, of vetiver; while still others, when they flapped their wings, filled the air with jasmine—attar of roses—holy basil—or cinnamon. While a clean well-tended doocot in Scotland might smell of ripe (or overripe) grain and guano, a pigeon-loft—a kabootarkhana—in Lucknow or Patna smelled like heaven.

Or, perhaps, more like the zenana, the women's quarters in an Indian palace.

To Constantia, the pigeons she had brought with her smelled of their place of origin: of salt grass, and lamp oil, and the wind off the leaden sea . . . not so very distant from here.

She had by this time flown three of her pigeons back to her husband, carrying three messages. First, on the 24th of July: "Twins, boy and girl, 21st July."

Then, on 28th August: "Our girl christened, Livia; but our poor boy lived only 34 days."

And, on September 1st: "Going to Mrs Robt Chambers, Musselburgh."

She had sent no messages since then, though she sometimes tried composing them in her mind. They had to be so very brief! They had to be so very important! But nothing worth the sending was to be told in ten or a dozen words; and her one remaining pigeon might be required for carrying some future message of great importance.

☆   ☆   ☆

EARLY IN NOVEMBER, Lady Janet gathered up her goods and chattels—her cabinet, pens, pen-knives, inkbottles and brushes—and quit the Robert Chambers family at Spring Gardens. It was time for her to return at last to the house of Mr and Mrs William Chambers, who had come belatedly home from their extended Italian tour. Upon her departure she offended the Spring Gardens servants by tipping them stingily—and mortally insulted Mrs MacAdam by tipping her, too, and presenting her with a little book of sermons.

"Of course four months is nothing, in geological time," said Mrs Chambers to her husband that evening in their bedroom, as he undressed, "but in Spring Gardens time—in Balderstone time— well! I had begun to suppose that she might never go! I had begun to fear that she might indeed remain here with us upon a geological time scale: for an epoch—an age—an era! Bullying the children all the while! She advised Nina, by way of farewell, that by drawing anatomical subjects she was blighting not only her own marriage prospects, but those of her sisters also; and counseled her to stick to flowers—or butterflies, if she must."

"My brother tells me that at his house, lacking children to scold," said Mr Chambers, climbing into bed beside his wife, "she endeavors instead to improve the morals of his servants. Well, there was not much of pleasure to be had from her visit—and it must have been far more disagreeable for you, my dear, than for me—bearing her company as you did, day after day."

"I had to bite my tongue nearly to bleeding, on several occasions; but I can declare in good conscience that I never quite said anything altogether rude to her, despite severe provocation. Though I did run dangerously near it, once or twice, in defense of Mrs MacAdam."

"Paragon! Virtue beyond compare!" said he, teasingly.

"Nay, it was only because I had resolved never to owe her any apology; so it was pride, you see, which regulated my speech; not virtue at all."

"Well, as your conduct has been blameless, we need not inquire too closely into the purity of your motives. You have earned garlands of laurels, and wreaths of olive branches. But I should like to point out that Lady Janet—vastly trying though she was—has demonstrated during her residence with us an important principle of great interest to geologists."

"Has she? What do you mean?"

"We have had demonstrated in our own house, under our very noses," said he, "the immense cumulative result which can be effected by even a puny and minuscule cause—such as erosion, or sedimentation, or a lady with a pen—when in operation over a sufficiently vast span of time. I believe that she quite nearly finished blackening one entire side of that cabinet, one slight penstroke at a time; and in so doing, she has—unwittingly—furnished evidence in support of a theory which she would probably disapprove on doctrinal grounds. She has proven the Adequacy of Actual Causes."

"Oh! Aye, she would disapprove that principle, to be sure, if ever she heard of it," said Mrs Chambers. "As for my part, I am only relieved that her pens, her brushes, her terrifying bottles of ink, are well away at last, out of the reach of Jemmie and Willie. During all these long months, I have been dreading a catastrophe to the landlord's carpet; it might have happened at any moment."

"Oh, aye, might have happened," he agreed easily. "But—like so many of the innumerable catastrophes which might engulf us all at any moment—it did not. Come, Mrs Balderstone, give me a kiss; and tomorrow I shall bring you laurel and olive, if any are to be had."

Of course neither laurel wreaths nor olive branches were to be had in Edinburgh, but he brought an armful of pungent flame-coloured chrysanthemums instead.

9

LATE IN NOVEMBER, the Chambers family moved at last into their Edinburgh house at 1 Doune Terrace. Under Mrs Chambers's generalship, this arduous manoeuvre—this Great Flitting—was executed almost as swiftly and silently as the Jacobite army's flanking night march at Prestonpans. So it seemed to the children, at least; and to Mr Chambers who—having slept at Spring Gardens and gone up to Edinburgh by tram as usual to work all day at his premises in Roxburgh's Close—upon emerging at dusk turned northward; crossed the Mound; and, walking up Castle Street and Gloucester Lane, arrived in twenty minutes' time at his new house, where his over-excited children and a quantity of tables, chairs, japanned trays, beds, lamps, and carpets all awaited him. Dinner, too.

The new house was tall, north-facing, many-chimneyed. On the street front, the windows were large and regular, but in back, levels did not line up; inside, odd brief flights of steps, three or four at a time, married the front storeys of the house to the back. There was no garden to speak of; only a small walled enclosure lay behind the house, but across the street was unbuilt ground sloping down to the Water of Leith, where the children were allowed to play when weather and waning daylight permitted.

Constantia was allotted a room at the back of the house beside the night nursery, on the second (or was it the third?) storey in the south-west corner, where afternoon sunshine sometimes played briefly, even in late November. She missed the spaciousness of Spring Gardens, but Doune Terrace was far better built; here, stout walls of timber, plaster, and stone—not plank partitions—contained the family chatter and clatter within rooms.

There was no doocot. Constantia's last remaining pigeon had to be billeted where it and its fellows had been housed before the jaunt to Musselburgh: in the chicken-coop behind Mr and Mrs MacDonald's house at nearby Deanhaugh, just across the Water of Leith.

✻ ✻ ✻

IT WAS HIGH TIME that Jemmie, nearly five years old, should be breeched: taken out of frocks and put into trousers. Mrs Chambers issued a few select invitations to this important occasion marking her son's development from child to boy; and one Saturday afternoon, a small company of relations and tolerant, kindly friends gathered, to fill every chair ranged around the new-furnished drawing room. Jemmie and his father were not to be seen. To ease the expectant waiting, Mrs Chambers and her daughters passed trays of cold refreshments: scotch eggs; prawn paste on crisp toasts; caraway shortbread. Presently—at last!—the door opened, and Jemmie appeared in breeches and jacket for the first time in his life. Mortified, reluctant, and very near tears, he was drawn into the the room by his father.

"O the darling mannie!" and "Our braw wee chiel!" exclaimed the ladies fondly.

"It's bonny callants they fancy themselves, every one," said Lady Janet.

Sweets from the ladies soon quelled his bashfulness. Better still, the gentlemen offered him pennies, to be put into his new pockets. Before long, sucking upon a butter toffee, he was confident enough to show his Uncle William (a portly man, all round belly, seated upon a stout settee) the buttons of his new garment. "Very handsome buttons, to be sure; and such a great many of them!" said Uncle William.

Jemmie—gaining rapidly in the urbanity and assurance conferred by wearing trousers—asked, "And have you buttons to your breeches, Uncle William?"

"Indeed I have, young chiel!" replied Uncle William briskly, "very nearly as neat as your own!" and stood up to prove it, by showing them—to gales of laughter from all present.

✧   ✧   ✧

"ARE YOU still quite fixed in your determination, my dear, to be away at Hogmanay—at the New Year?" Mrs Chambers asked Constantia, soon after this. "Cannot we induce you to remain yet a while?"

"It is not in my power to remain any longer," said Constantia, "although I shall be very sorry to leave you and Mr Chambers; and my darling Charlie, and every one of the children, too, for you have all become so very dear to me, and been so very kind to me; but I am sure you will understand that I am exceedingly eager to rejoin my husband, after so long a separation, and am pledged to do so at the New Year."

"I shan't try to dissuade you, then; and had better lose no time in finding another wet nurse to take your place. And as for that other matter . . . of—of Charlie's operation, to have off his extra fingers and toes: I had hoped to delay it for a little longer—but it is best, I suppose, to have it over and done while you are still with us—oh, aye, yourself, Mrs MacAdam; so calm, so steady! Dr Moir says the operation is next to nothing, now; but it will be a far more serious matter if we wait until he is older. It is true that they heal quickly at this tender age, and practically without scars. All the same, it is dreadful to a mother's feelings. I remember only too well when it was done to my poor little Jemmie. He was just the same age; four months. But in

Jemmie's case, it was only one supernumerary finger, on his left hand. He did heal very quickly—and remembers nothing of it. All four at once is best, Dr Moir assures me; both hands and both feet, all at once. They scarcely feel it, he says, although . . . oh, Mrs MacAdam! I am sure he is wrong about that! But my husband, too, tells me that it must be done, and the sooner, the better. He knows whereof he speaks, for he himself was five years old when his superfluous ones were taken off. Aye, from both hands, and both feet, like Charlie's. His feet have never been quite right since, and he has often said it had been better done sooner. His brother had them too, you know; aye, Mr William Chambers had them. It does run in families, and most often in the male line."

"But why must it be done at all?" said Constantia. "May not Charlie go through life quite well just as he is? What a harpist he would make, with that extra finger!"

"Ah! No," said Mrs Chambers sadly. "Indeed, we harpists do not even use all the fingers we have. The smallest finger is never used, of either hand. I do not know why; it simply is not done, c'est tout."

The surgery was performed by Dr Moir one morning in the nursery, with an assistant from the medical school in attendance, while Mr Chambers was at Roxburgh's Close, and Mrs Chambers stayed downstairs in her room. Even in this well-built house, Constantia could not help but hear it. It was not over quickly; it was four times performed.

By the time Charlie was brought to her afterward, he had fallen quite silent and still: stunned by shock. His hands and feet looked like clubs wrapped in their layers of gauze dressings; like the tree branches one sometimes sees along Paris avenues: pollarded. She put him to suck, but he nursed only briefly, feebly; and slept within moments. Constantia, though warned (and, as she supposed, braced), felt horror; she could not look away from this gauze-swaddled paw, like a kitten's, resting upon the swell of her breast. Laid gently in his cradle, Charlie slept for twelve hours, and when he woke, he did not cry or squirm or kick off his bedclothes as usual; he only lay still and looked, blinking, again and again, as though he could not believe what he saw.

What did he see there, in the air above his cradle?

On the third day following the amputation of Charlie's surplus fingers and toes, a putrid inflammation set in. The virulence began in his left hand. Dr Moir, after an overnight vigil, conducted a cleansing operation, excruciating to all concerned. It did no good, however, and two days later, the baby's left hand, now gangrenous, had to be amputated just above the wrist. By the following morning, his right hand was seen to be affected as well. "Morgadha," whispered Hopey, reverting in her distress to Gaelic: "mortification." Everyone in the house spoke in whispers, even little Willie, who didn't know why. Our darling, our darling! The inflammation and fever acted with all deliberate speed; within ten days of the initial operation, Charles Edward Chambers was dead, having lived nearly twenty-one weeks in this world.

Hopey sought solace in a tune. She sighed it to herself—in and out, upon each breath—whenever she was not asleep: "Tha Loingeas fo breide"—A Nurse's Lamentation for the Loss of Her Foster Child.

Once more, Constantia's breasts were painfully hard and heavy; engorged with far too much milk, just as in the days after Livia's twin had died. Now, as Livia suckled at one breast, the other breast leaked, dripped, sprayed. O the sad waste of it! Constantia's clothing was wet, no matter how often she changed her linen. She was drenched not only with milk, but with tears. Tears ran down her face as she suckled Livia; tears for Charlie and for her own dead nameless son; and for waste, loss, terror, pain, grief. For all the horrors; for all the unbearable pain that must only be borne.

* * *

Mr and Mrs Chambers had lost two children before this one. Veterans in affliction, they understood that letters containing sentiments such as these, from Lady Janet, were intended to console:

> Our Almighty God hath entrusted unto you the dear babe, to be brought up for Him; knowing, as He knoweth all things, that no one, could fulfill His purpose so well. Now your task, Mrs Chambers, has been done; aye, well and faithfully done; know that the sweet dear babe, all garbed in white, walks now with Him; walks now in joy with his, and our, Heavenly Father.

10

G o. Now.
Constantia had expected to remain in Edinburgh with the Chambers family for some weeks longer, until the turn of the year; but one morning soon after Charlie's burial she awakened to an impulse both imperative and urgent: It is time to be away. Now. Her milk was no longer necessary to anyone but Livia. Before breakfast she found Mrs Chambers at the writing table in the library, and declared her resolution of taking a place on the next morning's southbound mail coach.

Drawing a sheet of foolscap over her writing paper (black-edged, for mourning), Mrs Chambers set down her pen. "I knew this day must come," she said, "but I did not expect it quite so soon. How are we to part with you, Mrs MacAdam? I trust that fortune will contrive to bring us together again, in this life. And you must promise, my dear, to send word from time to time, wherever you go, to let us know that you are well; and darling Livia, too. Oh! But wait; I have something for you. Aye, we did know that this day must come, sooner or later; and while we have all admired your pretty fringed mantle during the warmth of summer—well! I have been annoying the mantua-maker for weeks to finish something warmer for you—and here it is, my parting gift to you," she said, bringing out a large paper-wrapped parcel from a cupboard. "Something to remind you of us, and of Scotland."

Opening the parcel, Constantia unfolded a new long cloak in a tartan of pink, green and brown wool, with a capelet over the shoulders, crimson gimp trim, a green quilted satin lining, and an ample hood. It was achingly fashionable, the most clever and knowing thing going in Edinburgh just now, and Constantia (though suspecting that it might appear very curious indeed on the boulevards of Paris; even astonishing) was much moved. The gratitude she expressed was sincere: So beautiful! So ample, the cut! Such softness and warmth! What charming colours! So generous of Mrs Chambers to think her worthy of so handsome a garment! She would do her best to live up to its elegance, and would cherish it always as a memorial of the warmth and kindness she had enjoyed enfolded here in the bosom of the Chambers family.

"Oh, the bosom! But that is yourself!" exclaimed Mrs Chambers.

At breakfast the girls tried to dissuade Constantia from leaving so soon; and Tuckie wept. "Nor will you get to meet Mam'selle, which is a great pity," said Mary mournfully—for the returning governess was now expected any day.

But after breakfast the girls all came to her room to assist, discuss, advise—and to amuse Livia while Constantia put her belongings in order. Livia could now sit up with some help, and she was always enchanted by the girls, who would tirelessly play peckaboo with her. Constantia had no trunk, only a carpet-bag; and made presents to the girls of inessentials that would not fit into it: a light summer bonnet in need of refurbishing; a parasol, still useful though not quite pretty; and that small volume of sermons bestowed by Lady Janet.

"But I daresay that Mamma might gladly spare you a trunk, Mrs MacAdam," said Nina. "The box-room is crammed with them."

"No, thank you, my dear; no trunks for me. I have resolved to take no more than I can carry myself, as porters and footmen are scarce, where I am going."

"I do wish you would say where," said Annie plaintively. "We are quite wretched, not knowing. I do think you might tell us."

"It is dreadfully heavy," said Mary, testing the carpet-bag's weight.

"How are you to carry Livie and your gear too, if there are no porters?" asked Jenny.

"And your pigeon, in its creel?" said Lizzy.

Bags, parcels, cases, trunks, and creels were rightfully the business of porters and footmen, not of their owners. Even babies of the more comfortable classes were not always carried by their own mothers, but were likely to be entrusted instead to the arms of nursemaids who followed close behind. Such babies were generally dressed in very long embroidered and laced gowns, which cascaded decoratively halfway to the ground. Livia's gowns, while long enough to satisfy convention, were rather plain. Constantia's carpet-bag was stuffed with additional baby-gowns, caps, and waistcoats, equally plain; an abundance of well-washed clooties, woven of diapered flax; and a sheepskin pilch to spare, oiled for waterproofing. How were people to know that Mrs MacAdam was respectable, if she carried her bag and her plainly-dressed baby herself?

"I shall carry Livie like this," said Constantia, knotting her long paisley shawl over one shoulder to make a sling across her chest. She tucked Livia snugly inside, as poor women do the world over. Still, it was not easy to arrange Livia securely and comfortably inside this sling, and Livia protested at having her face pressed against her mother's bodice; she squirmed, and slid downward, precariously. But when Constantia turned her around, to face outward, the shawl did not support Livia's head properly—unless it covered her face, which, to judge by her protests, was intolerable.

"You look like a fisherwife, up from Newhaven," said Annie.

"In paisley, not stripes, whatever," said Mary.

How did those Newhaven fisherwives manage to carry their babies thus? How did those barefoot young mothers in India manage? Hopey might have known how the knotted shawl ought to be contrived, but Hopey was out, having been sent to fetch a parcel from the apothecary. "I suppose it may be a matter of becoming accustomed," said Constantia, dubiously. "But perhaps I had better make a trial of this arrangement—just as far as Mrs MacDonald's house. I must go make my farewells, and fetch that poor lonely pigeon, too."

Do let us come with you! clamoured the girls, but as Signor Ricci the dancing master could already be heard moving the chairs against the wall in the drawing room, they were obliged to go down to their lesson instead; even in mourning, these essential lessons continued. Constantia, with Livia tied snugly against her, descended the steps to the street unaccompanied.

How cutting, this wind! How glum, this sky! Constantia almost turned back for the new cloak, but instead pulled the shawl well up to Livia's cap and went briskly onward. The knotted shawl was not entirely satisfactory, for she was obliged after all to support Livia within one arm—but only one. It was not far, however, down the hill and across Leith Water to Deanhaugh.

But the MacDonalds were not at home. The maid who opened the door welcomed Mrs MacAdam kindly; drew her into the hall out of the wind; admired Livia, who (with her twin) had been born upstairs in this very house; but could not say when her mistress might return. She ushered Constantia, however, into the drawing-room, and left her there at a writing table furnished with paper, pen, and ink. Constantia would have liked to dwell upon her letter of thanks and farewell; would have liked to sit quietly and think, and feel, and remember, and put all her grateful heart into it, but Livia, no longer a compliant new-born, prevented anything of the sort. She reached for the pen, the inkwell, and the sand-bottle; and drooled upon the blotter. She was markedly heavier these days; far more alert and attentive; and seldom inclined to daytime naps of any convenient duration. Constantia could only quickly scratch a few affectionate and grateful lines. She folded the notepaper and left it on the writing table.

The MacDonald henhouse—not a proper doocot at all—was at the bottom of the garden. There Constantia's last pigeon languished, disconsolate in the company of hens. The pigeon-creel of woven wicker was there too, dirty but still serviceable. Livia had to be set down in the grass, which she began to pluck and taste; Constantia hoped that a little of this was harmless. "Come, my fine fellow," she said to the pigeon, a sturdy blue one. Its pen was small, and she had no trouble catching it. Constantia stuffed it unprotesting into the creel, and fastened down the lid. Then she noticed something remaining in the corner of the pen: a pretty little egg. "A fine fellow, did I call you? I beg your pardon, madam!" she apologised to the pigeon.

This was not an egg that might hatch, as the pigeon had been in a state of involuntary celibacy for months. The egg might be eaten, or left to rot. The pigeon would not know or care. Constantia felt that it ought not go to waste; but how was she to carry it? It would be crushed in her pocket. It could not be carried inside her bodice, not with Livia pressed against her. She loosened the ties of her bonnet, and tucked the egg up into the nest of her coiled hair on the back of of her head; then retied the bonnet snugly over it again. She could scarcely feel the egg. Do not forget, she told herself, when you get home and take off your bonnet.

Then she set out for Doune Terrace once more, Livia on her left arm, and the handle of the big wicker pigeon-creel over her right. What a long climb, back up from the bridge which crossed Leith Water! At length Livia fell asleep against Constantia's pounding heart, despite the wind and the joggling; or perhaps because of them. How ridiculously large, how excessively heavy, this hamper! How disagreeably it bumped against Constantia's legs! If the Chambers girls had accompanied her, as they had wished to do, they could have helped, thought Constantia; and she conceived, as she trudged up the slope, an unreasonable grudge against Signor Ricci the dancing master.

She was much warmed however by the exertion, despite the scouring wind that blustered in from the North Sea. She had been unaware of any weather at all during the past days and weeks of catastrophe and sorrow; such trivialities as season and weather had ceased to matter during the crisis of Charlie. Now it was forcefully borne in upon her that wintry December was well under way; had arrived despite her inattention.

By the time she gained the top of the slope, she had formed a new resolution. Although it had been her intention to bring this pigeon for future use, she was obliged to conclude that it was too much to carry; she had much better fly this bird now, with a last message.

She attained Doune Terrace at last, and there, having stowed the pigeon in its creel beside the kitchen stair out of the wind, went upstairs. When she came down again (without Livia, for Hopey had by now returned), she had ready—written, folded, and rolled—a message, in minuscule letters upon a slip of paper as thin as the skin of an onion. She reached into the hamper, and with a red satin ribbon (impossible to go unnoticed when the pigeon should arrive at its destination) she tied the message to the pigeon's leg.

The bird, once turned onto its back with wings held lightly, did not struggle, but only stared from a round bright uncomprehending eye. Behind that eye lay neither feeling nor intelligence; but how bright, nevertheless! It would know its way home from anywhere, even from this distant place where it had never been before. Mountains, seas, snowfields, were no obstacles to it. Imagine being blindfolded, thought Constantia; and led—for months, or years—through a labyrinth whose existence you cannot even suspect. Suddenly the blindfold is removed; your captor vanishes; and you are left to find your way home. From here, it might be anywhere.

Constantia carried the bird to the open ground across the street, and there threw it into the gusty sky. The pigeon circled twice, ascending, wings beating strongly; falling upward like that hot-air balloon in Lucknow, so long ago. Was it strong enough still, this bird which had been confined and unable to fly, for so long; for months? The pigeon circled once more, very high and small now against the clouds; nearly the same colour as the clouds; and finally headed fast and straight toward the southeast, across the wind. The correct heading. Shivering, Constantia watched the speck disappear beyond Edinburgh's slatey roofs and granite chimneys. Good luck, good luck. Go faithfully home. The message carried by this pigeon was this: "Leaving Edinbr mail-coach Tues 11th; expect us Wed."

Later, when Constantia took off her bonnet, the egg she had forgotten fell and smashed on the floor. Small golden yolk, slick clear fluid-of-life, shattered calcium shell: O the pity of it! the sad waste of it!

During the night, the wind ceased. Then, in silence, snow began to fall.

By morning, snow lay six inches deep upon the pavements of the city, creaking-dry with cold. Constantia kissed all the Chamberses, dismissing their urgings to remain until the weather should improve. Mr Chambers, who had never before gone to Roxburgh's Close by cab, found he must have one on such a morning as this—and how very convenient, he said, that their destinations lay so near each other! Though she knew perfectly well that the cab was entirely for her sake, Constantia pretended to believe in this kind fiction, and was grateful for it. Carrying well-wrapped Livia within one arm, her carpetbag upon the other, and wrapped in the remarkable tartan cloak, she mounted Mr Chambers's cab, and was in due course put down at the coaching-inn on the Calton Road (which was not near Roxburgh's Close); there to wait with other passengers in the smoky parlour.

But as the day wore tediously on, the mail-coaches did not arrive; neither the one from the west, nor the one from the north. The one from the south straggled in six hours late, at three-o'clock dusk, having twice run off the indiscernible road into snowy ditches; and twice been dragged out again. Not until tomorrow then, said the coach-agents to the exasperated passengers who had waited all day. Nothing is going south tonight.

Carrying Livia and the carpet-bag, Constantia set out on foot across the city toward Doune Terrace, to sleep there once more. It was already quite dark and, though still, very cold; the footing was treacherous. To fall, carrying Livia, would be terrible. Constantia's progress was dreadfully slow, and she was glad, by the time she arrived at St Andrew Square, to hire a cab to carry her the rest of the way. How would she ever have managed with two babies?

The Chamberses welcomed her delightedly, tucked her into the best easy chair nearest the drawing-room fire, commiserated with her, gave her the usual hearty supper, and finally sent her upstairs to her bed—which, Constantia discovered, had been stripped already of its sheets. This punctuality, she told herself, was only the sign of a well-run household; it was not to be construed as any gladness about her departure.

But snow fell again that night—another ten inches or more. When red-nosed Constantia, Livia, and carpet-bag returned next morning to the coaching-inn (in another cab ordered by Mr Chambers, just as before), the agents declined even to predict when any coach might be able to get along the coast road to the south. Her fellow passengers—all familiar by now in feature, voice, and character, after the previous full day's acquaintance under vexing circumstances—were conferring with one another. "The steam packets are sure to be going," said one, a stout widow in a redoubtable black beaver bonnet, who knitted as fluently as she talked, without looking at her hands. "Steam never minds the cold, and saltwater never cares for snow."

"There's no wind. If only we can get down to Leith, I daresay we can be off by the next ebb-tide," said a travelling commission agent who traded in worsteds.

"What is the state of the tide?"

No one knew, though someone ventured an opinion that the ebb must have begun by now.

And so someone arranged for a wagon drawn by two sturdy horses, the expense to be split among those going down to the harbour at Leith on the Firth of Forth, just down the long slope north of the city. "But where is the lady with the cloak—and the babby?" cried the industrious knitting widow in the flurry of departure. "Come, hinney, aren't you going with us? Where is it you're bound? Where? Amble? Amble! You want the express packet to Newcastle, then, with me. I'm bound to Newcastle myself; and from there you can get yourself back up along the coast to Amble, easily enough. Come along, then! Pray, move over, Mr Elliot; make room for this lady. Up you come! And you, Dickie, put up her bag; what are you waiting for? Come now, no more time to be lost! Time we were off!"

The big carthorses went mincingly on the icy pavements, and steam issued from their nostrils as though they were dragons, or steam locomotives; but presently the wagon brought its passengers and their baggage safely down the long road to the Leith waterfront. The still-knitting widow knew just where to apply for times and tickets, and by purest good fortune, found the express packet to Newcastle due to get under way within the half-hour. "Not knowing if you wanted first cabin or second, I've got you a place in the second by me," said she, upon returning to Constantia where she waited in the lobby. "This way, now; and that gangplank, there, is where we go aboard. Oh aye, many times before; I know all about it. Now down this passage; and take care, hinney, to duck your head." Almost before she had time to consider, Constantia was settling herself and Livia into a place in the second cabin of the Leith and Newcastle Steam Packet Company's iron steam-ship *Britannia*.

"There's some as must have the first cabin, or a private state-room, even, but the second cabin suits me very well," said the widow, as the little iron vessel throbbed, strained, and then drew away from the dock; the ribbon of iron-grey water widening, widening behind as it vibrated and throbbed and whiffed its way out onto the deep channel.

"I like to walk about, and talk with comfortable folk," she added, her needles clicking steadily, "and eat my own homely provisions—and it's scarce ten hours to Newcastle. I hope I am not yet so feeble that I cannot sit up among other pleasant folk for ten hours. Look, we'll be coming alongside of the Bell Rock lighthouse—I do always like to go up and see the waves breaking on it. Oh; not quite well? I'm a seasoned old sailor myself, but if you're liable to the sea-sickness, hinney, you'd better come up on deck with me. Always better in the open air, sure. Come along and I'll show you a snug place out of the wind near the boilers, where you and the babby can be just as warm as ever you like. The first cabin is no better—you'd be quite as sick in there, and cost you three shillings more. Fresh air is the thing, plenty of fresh air. That's a fine thick cloak you've got, prodigious handsome, and babby quite snug, too. There now! Better? Aye. You had better stay up here. Look, 'tis clearing; I see blue sky on its way, though none the warmer for it. That snow will lie aground for a good while at this rate, and it will be days, I'll warrant you, before the mail-coaches can win through. Pretty, though, aren't they, those snowy hills, from here? Well enough, from this comfortable distance; but not to be struggling along the roads of them, and the drifts five feet high against the stone walls. We are getting along past them smart enough!"

In the lee of the smokestack, grateful for the remarkable cloak, and warmed by the coal-fired boilers below, Constantia soon felt better. She was not the only one to prefer the deck's open air and long views; others came and went too, and shreds of their talk were carried to her, on eddying gusts of wind.

"That is Siccar Point," she heard one top-hatted first-cabin gentleman tell another, much younger; "where Mr Hutton found his celebrated and most excellent illustration of the junction between the ancient greywacke, all tortured, folded, and tilted—and the much newer Old Red sandstone laid down atop it, eighty millions of years later. 'A beautiful picture of this junction washed bare by the sea' were his very words—of this very place. And so it is, although from here it appears quite unparticular; only resembling all the rest of the rocky cliffs and coasts hereabouts. But if we were to go in close— much closer than is safe—we might peer, as he did, into the deep recesses of the past, down the long echoing hallways of time. We might read here—indeed, anywhere along these cliffs—the very pages of the book of the earth's history; might riffle the edges of the volume wherein are written its long periods of peace, its paxes— and its revolutions, its upheavals and convulsions. Not Infinity, no; there is a beginning, and an end. Unimaginably long; but finite." They walked off, making the circuit of the deck, perhaps for exercise; or, evidently, several circuits—for they passed in front of Constantia three or four times.

Some time later, on one of these circuits, they paused once again nearby, and she heard the same poetical gentleman say, to the much younger companion, "See, here, the muddiness of the water; that is solid land washing down into the sea, grain by grain—for here is the outfall of the River Tweed. There, northward, lies fair Scotland. Here, southward, lies merry England. We have crossed. Here, two breeds, two tribes of mankind, rub up against each other; wearing away at each other, like land and sea, water and stone, warily."

Pray, do stay here and let me hear you talk! thought Constantia; for this is talk worth hearing! Occasionally, at least; perhaps not continually. The younger gentleman spoke not at all; was he weary of this incessant instruction? Were they tutor and student; bear-leader and bear? It is wearying to be constantly the object of improvement. But they did not stay; and presently she saw them enter the first-class cabin together.

The kind widow, her needles clicking busily, appeared from time to time to make sure that Constantia and the babby were not cold; to share the provisions she had brought aboard (pork pies, cheese, bread); to hold and play with Livia for a while. Livia was at first a little frightened by the formidable black bonnet, but soon overcame her shyness and let the widow stand her on the deck to bounce and sway upon her own feet, held up by the hands. "She'll be in leading-strings before you know it!" predicted the widow. Constantia was glad of this opportunity to ease the ache of her back—until Livia tired of this play and had to come back into her arms again.

"What islands are these?" Constantia heard a lady with a French accent inquire, some time later, of the stout Englishman whose arm steadied her, at the rail. "Is it the Holy Isle?"

"Oh no, the Holy Isle is well behind us; these are the Fernes," said the Englishman. "A dangerous bit of shore, too. There, you see—that black pile atop that head—that's old Bamburgh Castle. And the lighthouse on that island is the very one where Grace Darling lived. Well, Grace Darling, of immortal fame! Can you really not have heard of Grace Darling? The lighthouse-keeper's daughter? The heroine of the age?"

At the mention of this name, Constantia listened harder, for she had a particular interest in Grace Darling.

"Is it possible," said the French lady, "that the fame of your English heroines may not have penetrated quite *every* corner of the world? But," she added, coquettishly, "you may tell me of her, if you like."

"So I shall," said he, evidently enchanted. "It must have been five or six years ago; the *Forfarshire*—a new steam packet, very like this one, in fact—was making the run between Dundee and Hull, and carrying on that occasion some forty passengers, along with another score or so of crew; about sixty souls, altogether—when, just as a storm blew up, her boiler sprang a leak; and then her pumps failed. They went adrift, with the northeast wind blowing; and though they set the sails to try to keep her off the rocks, it was too late, and she went onto the rocks, just about there, at three o'clock in the morning—"

"Brrr!" said the lady.

"—and broke in half almost immediately. Some six or eight got into one of the lifeboats, but the other boat was carried off by a wave, in the confusion. The alarm guns had gone off at the Castle, but it was far too rough for the lifeboats from the Castle to get out to them—though to see it today, it is hard to imagine. But the desperate cries of the survivors attracted the notice of Grace Darling, who was the twenty-two-year-old daughter of the keeper of the Outer Ferne lighthouse; yes, that one. And just at daybreak, having spied living beings still clinging to the wreck, she and her father determined to attempt a rescue, despite the raging of the storm, and the mortal peril to themselves. By greatest courage, determination, and skill, the young heroine and her father rescued nine survivors from the rock, and carried them to the safety of the lighthouse—where the refugees had to remain for three days more, so fiercely did the storm rage on, before they could be brought ashore. Hers was a heart of oak!"

"'Was'? Does she not live still?"

"Alas, no; she went to her heavenly reward within this year, or the last, at the age of twenty-six. A consumption, the papers said."

"Left she any children?" asked the lady.

"No, she died a maid," said the Englishman.

"La pauvre!" said the lady, and the two of them sauntered off arm in arm, leaving Constantia to reflect. Died a maid! Now, what was the good of that? A matchless courage, a dauntless generosity—a prodigious individual, snuffed out, without issue in the world! Cut off. The pity of it, the sad waste of it! Here is a prodigious seed—fallen upon barren rock. Never mind; some day, some age, there may be another equally prodigious seed . . . which may, or may not, meet with better luck. What is the hurry? Why does it seem to matter? The natural economy—the divine economy—is a profligate one. Efficiency and thrift, those human virtues, are strikingly absent from its workings; from its slow, inefficient, uninformed, careless, and accidental workings.

Constantia contemplated the lighthouse: Pharos. Draped across glistening rocks at the base of the squat tower she could make out a congregation of fat grey-brown slugs: slumbering seals. The name

Pharos brought another: Proteus. In such a place as this the changeable god Proteus might haul himself out from time to time, to sleep among his seals. And here, at the juncture of land, sea, and sky, he might be apprehended, and made to tell the truth about past, present, and future—if mortals could succeed in seizing him, and in holding fast to him through all his terrifying changes, his exuberant mutability, his disposition to sport. *His* principle was quite opposite to her own: Constantia. Constancy; unchanging, always the same. Mrs Fleming had said she'd been named for the celebrated sweet wine of the Cape, but Constantia doubted this, guessing that the name signified instead her mother's longing for that quality which had ever eluded her: constancy—fidelity—in her lovers, and perhaps, in herself. In constancy, like produces like, up from the past and down into the unlit future, forever and ever! World without end, Amen! But Proteus embodied the opposing principle: Change. Changing, changing, always changing. Never the same. Not just caterpillar becomes chrysalis becomes imago—but stranger than that. The impossible is commonplace. Everything changes: caterpillar becomes bird becomes tree. Everything disperses, shatters. Everything, even hardest rock, wears down to dust, washes into the bottom of the sea.

Where new rock forms, under the influence of heat. And pressure. And *time*.

Might we breed a winged horse? How beautiful!

Might we breed a human with six arms? How divine!

We have succeeded in breeding a human endowed with a thumb and five fingers on each hand. Not just four, but five. How monstrous! Let us cut it off.

O the pity of it. The sad waste of it.

The steam packet made some five or six knots; enough to produce a moderate bow wave, two curls of ocean peeling away on either side of the bow which cleaved its ruffled surface, carved away like a pair of endless ringlets of wood whittled from a stick; like heavy soil turning, falling black and wet off the moldboard of the plow. Upon this bow wave rode dolphins, at least four of them; perhaps more. It was hard to count, as they kept disappearing and reappearing; and then, while dolphins might distinguish easily between individuals of their own kind, it was not so easy for Constantia. Still, she counted four visible at once; and it seemed to her that their dolphin-faces (if dolphins could be said to have faces) wore grins (unless that was only the habitual set of their features). They had good reason to grin; why accompany the packet if not for sheer enjoyment? "A disposition to sport"—the phrase sprang again into her mind, though it was not at all what the gardener Mr Gunn had meant, when he was telling her of the pigeons he had been breeding. Then it came washing over her again: her astonishment and alarm at the mutability of things; of this fabric of nature. The *Edinburgh Review*'s reviewer—the contemptuous and contemptible Dr Sedgwick—had declared that "Species were found, in living nature, to be permanent. To this law not one exception has been found." O, permanence! How reassuring to believe that something, anything, should be permanent!

Was this "disposition to sport" carelessness? Or was it playfulness?

Was it error? Or was it joyous and exuberant improvisation?

If the musician introduces a note outside of her scale . . . what happens then? How far outside? How wrong? Sharp. Flat. Out of tune? Or a change of key?

Did none of the self-evident truths stand up to a minute and painstaking examination?

Water is level. But this water, at this moment, was far from level; the steely surface was ruffled in every direction, and the deck of the steam-packet lurched and heaved. There were swells, quite abrupt ones, at irregular intervals, and moving in various directions. The wind blew the tops off the thinnest of these. Against the distant shore, waves rose up (inspired by what force?) and crashed against the rocks; and fell back again, to be succeeded by others without end. Then there were the tides, water rising, and falling, immense masses of it, in rhythm with the moon. Streams ran downhill; joined, became rivers, always running down to the sea—except when they ran up! overwhelmed in their beds by the force of the tides. Indeed, if the savants could be believed, the oceans themselves—"sea level"—had not always lapped against the margins of the land at the same height as they now did. And on a minute scale, even a still glass of water was not truly level—for a thin film of it rose up against the inside wall of the glass—quite visible, if only you looked.

So: Water is not level. It is only approximately levelish.

Here is another self-evident truth: Like produces like. A mare always produces a foal, never a tiger cub—nor even a lamb. But a mare might produce a mule. A brown mare might produce a black foal. A four-legged mare might produce a five-legged foal; a monster. Like produces similar. Usually.

Here is my Livia. Like me. And like her father.

Ah, her father! . . . "O my dove, let me see thy countenance, let me hear thy voice; for sweet is thy voice, and thy countenance is comely." Was Solomon indeed the author of that lovers' song of longing? Solomon, it was said—with an enviable degree of certainty—was himself the son of David and Bathsheba. Lucky child, of such certainty! (But why did it seem to matter? Why did anyone want to know?)

That Song of Solomon, that ghazal, was quite unlike any other book of the Bible. Christian missionary preachers gave the Song of Solomon a wide berth, even in India—whose own stories and songs it markedly resembled. In India the divine relationship—the relation between divinity and humanity—was that of lovers: amorous, rapturous, reciprocal. In Christendom however, the relationship was paternal, not (shamefully!) amorous. Divinity was father, and humanity, child; their proper relation was infinitely unequal, stern, authoritarian—except for the Song of Solomon, a cuckoo's egg laid somehow in the Christian nest.

* * *

She could smell the man (second cabin, to be sure) who paused just now, to windward. It was not the smell of gin, as was so often the case here in Britain; nor of garlic, as in France; nor of cumin, as in India. It was just the scent of a man who has not washed his skin and hair, nor changed his shirt in some time. It was the characteristic scent of a human being. Dogs smelled of Dog, cats of Cat, horses of Horse—and men of Man. We are the earthlings who emit that particular smell.

Presently, as daylight failed, Constantia recognised flat white Coquet Isle, though the packet passed it at a considerable distance to seaward. She recognised the squat lighthouse near its southern tip. Beyond it she could just make out the fishing town of Amble on the low shore of the mainland; and on the hill above that, the ruin of Warkworth Castle. Scarcely any snow was to be seen here. If only they could be put off here, Livia and herself, on that wee isle! But even if it could be done—which was out of the question—it would raise suspicion; and suspicion must on no account be raised. Still, it was heart-rending to come so near, and be obliged nevertheless to pass on. Birds—pigeons and gulls—wheeled in the sky, scribing curves.

If only she had saved that last pigeon for now—for here—so near its home! It would cross this water in a scant minute; would land there, on that white rock; it could not help but go there. Indeed, it undoubtedly had gone there. Constantia had flown the pigeon from Edinburgh on Monday, around midday; it should have arrived at Coquet Isle within two hours, perhaps three. Constantia had sent word that she would arrive Wednesday (for who, on Monday, had forseen snow?) Now that it was Wednesday night, was Hugh agitated by her failure to arrive? She feared that he might go ashore—into the town, or beyond—in search of her. My darling, she thought, do not on any account go ashore. Stay safely where you are. Stay there, on Coquet Isle; wait for me there. Wait for us there.

How homesick she felt! Despite having no home, and despite the heavy homely warmth of Livia against her, she ached for home: a safe, familiar, private place. For being surrounded by people well known, not strangers. For knowing how things work; for not being wrong, as strangers find themselves in the wrong, not knowing how to behave: "I know not how to goe out or come in." She longed for water that tasted like the first water she'd ever swallowed, the way water ought to taste. She longed for an always-known landscape; for seeing just far enough, not too far; shadows falling where they ought; known grasses, trees, flowers, vines; knowing which berries to eat, and which to shun; the easy stirring of soft hazy air; the delicious fall of the land; familiar scents and stenches; familar barkings and birdsong; and all of it ending in an intimately known horizon: that bump; that slope; that peak where the light lingers last at sunset. Oh, home! Home is meeting the eyes of one's husband, after a separation. Darshan: seeing, and being seen. Drinking up the sight of him. Being drunk up by him. Go out; come in; it does not matter how. Any way one likes.

Then, as she watched, the lantern atop the lighthouse suddenly came alight: a hot spark in the purple dusk. Never fear. All will be well.

As night fell, the steam-packet entered the channel of the Tyne just behind the last of the fishing boats. Livia nuzzled, suckled, and slept again. The cordial widow reappeared, this time to insist on sharing the last of her porkpies with Constantia. The Tyne's channel was deeply cut, its banks high and steep; the black city seemed to lean scowling over its black river, ill-lit, unfamiliar, and unwelcoming, during the long passage upriver.

"There's plenty of lodging houses up around the Black Gate, for second-cabin travelers such as us," said the widow, drawing her cloak closer about her as the packet sidled alongside Newcastle's torch-lit steam wharf, to tie up at last. "The one I always go to is just past the Castle keep, not too far. The landlady keeps a good fire and a hearty supper—but her charges are moderate for all that. What's more, I've never been bitten by bugs in her beds, unlike some other houses I might name. Come with me, if you like. She'll have a bed for any friend of mine." They disembarked and Constantia, knowing of no other place to go, was glad to follow a guide. "The entire district is likely to be cleared, before long," called the widow over her shoulder as she led the way up the steep muddy street—still knitting, by feel, in the darkness. "There's talk of building a railway viaduct through here. Where's all of us second-cabin folk to lodge then, I ask you?"

The lodging house was better than Constantia had feared, and the landlady greeted them like old friends, saying, "So here you are after all, Mrs Todd! I was just saying to my girl, 'How sorry Mrs Todd will be at missing that funeral!'—with the roads all stopped by snow, and no mail-coaches getting through from the north. But you've won through somehow, for here you are, and brought your young friend, too."

"Quite right," replied the widow. "Just off the steam-packet from Edinburgh. I never would miss that funeral, not if I could help it. As for my friend, here, and her little babby—well, I never did ask your name, did I?" she added, turning to Constantia.

"I am Mrs MacAdam," said Constantia. "And did I hear aright? Are you indeed called Mrs Todd?"

"I was born a Carter, and married first a Barnes and then a Norris. But my third husband, may the good lord have mercy upon his soul, was Samuel Todd, of South Shields."

"My father was a Todd," said Constantia.

"Was he, now? From hereabouts?" said Mrs Todd.

"What was his Christian name?" said the landlady.

"Indeed, I do not know," admitted Constantia. "He died before I was born, and my mother remarried soon afterward. But he and my mother both hailed from Northumberland, and I should be very glad to find their people—if only I knew where or how to look for them."

"Well, as it happens, Mrs MacAdam," said the widowed Mrs Todd, "I expect to see the entire tribe of them tomorrow; of Todds, that is—all my late husband's people—at the funeral. Oh no, a very old woman, quite her time. Won't be a sad occasion. If your business permits, you might like to come with me and make your inquiries. There'll be a crush of talkative old folk—older and more talkative than myself, just fancy!—who can tell you all about every Todd—and Dodd—that ever was. Can and will. There's no need to go to the graveside; I'm not going myself. No, I'll be far too busy helping to lay out the breakfast that's after, at her daughter's house. It's just out the West Gate road. You can walk there with me—and help with the breakfast, too, if you like."

"How kind!—if only my time were my own!" said Constantia. "Unfortunately I am obliged—most urgently obliged—to post back up the coast to Amble at the first opportunity—by tomorrow morning's earliest coach."

"Not in the morning you won't," said the landlady. "The steamer bringing the London mails don't come in until half-past three o'clock in the afternoon, at the soonest; and then the northbound bag gets loaded onto the coach that'll be waiting at the Tower Arms. The coach don't leave for the north until four o'clock, or quarter-past, sometimes, if the steamer's late—then to drive on all the night through."

"So, you see, hinney, there's all the morning—if you like to come along with me to that funeral breakfast," said Mrs Todd.

Matters might have turned out very differently, Constantia knew. Chance! What is that? Is there such a thing? It is an event not intended, and not accounted for; it is neither divine design, nor fitness to circumstance. It is not God. It is not Nature. Both of these imply direction, and efficacy. Both imply implacable cause; and inevitable effect: that is to say, Law! which, whether divine or natural, is not to be trifled with. But chance is quite another thing. It is, for example, the precise location of the hidden mole hole in the pasture—stepping in which, the galloping colt snaps his foreleg. Or, missing which, he does not. It is the gust of wind which causes the plummeting hawk to miss its quarry; to wearily proceed, therefore, to another attempt, in which this pigeon is knocked out of the sky instead of that one. It is the depth and width of the plowshare which—by a hair's breadth—snags and brings up a gold torque, betraying the hoard below. Or—by the same hair's breadth—misses it.

Our words for this phenomenon are unsatisfactory: Happenstance. Circumstance. Luck. Accident. Some matters, some eventualities, it seems, do lie within the jurisdiction of certain forces which may be law, either divine or natural. But other matters—even those of immense eventual significance, of colossal consequence—fall prey instead to lightest, most capricious chance. At any of a great many points, things might have turned out quite differently than they did. It is very hard to think about this, for nothing seems so inevitable as History, the sequence of things which did happen (not least because history has quite obviously conspired to produce the very flower of the universe: one's own magnificent self).

But suppose the tiger had hunted eastward that night, instead of westward? Or suppose the hornets had, the previous day, abandoned that nest for another, somewhere else; and did not rise to sting, when stepped upon? Suppose no one had been passing below, when the teak tree dropped its massiest branch? Suppose the creature whose remains formed an exquisite fossil embedded in the limestone of Coquet Isle had been devoured instead by a passing monster; had been digested, transformed into lowliest excrement, ephemeral dirt; into nothing?

In natural law, Constantia knew, there is no justice.

Suffering does not matter at all.

Waste does not matter at all.

Time does not matter at all.

But what an unbearable thought! Despicable!

We have a better idea than that; for we are the human beings: *Homo sapiens*, the tasting earthlings. Rasikas, tasters, connoisseurs, savants, persons of goût, of discernment! of judgment, of justice! of ingenuity! We have a better idea than that despicable one. We can imagine something far better. We have imagined it; do imagine it;

and we call it God. This idea, of our very own creation, inevitably has our fingerprints all over it. We make our idea Just, Loving, Attentive, Wise, Thrifty, and All-Powerful.

To humankind, Wisdom is justice; Solomon was called wise because he was just.

The Redress is in reserve.

Is it?

11

"JOSEPH DODD, did you hear that?"

"What's that?"

"They eloped, she says. No, *eloped*; that means they run off together in secret, just the two of them, to Scotland, where anybody can be married just as hasty as they like, without banns or decent waiting."

"There was Simon Todd's son, who ran off with that hussy—that sempstress from Yorkshire."

"Oh, aye; but those two settled down in Jarrow at last, steady as deacons, though no one expected it. And that wasn't but ten or twelve years ago, so it can't be them. When did you say all this—this, business was, then, Mrs, ah . . ."

"Mrs MacAdam," supplied someone.

"It must have been 1822," said Constantia, "as I was born in 1823." All the elderly Todds and Dodds, seated on chairs ranged around the walls of the steamy farm kitchen, were inspecting her and Livia with frank curiosity.

"Oh, that was a good while ago. Joseph Dodd, did you hear that?"

"What's that?"

"It was back in 'twenty-two. Now, that was the year the King came north, wasn't it? Sailed right past us—never stopped in to have his hand kissed, even. Didn't we all practice our curtseys, though, just in case! Do you mind that, Miss Mary? Just about the time your sister's boy went to Canada."

Miss Mary, a very elderly wrinkled person in a starched though yellowed cap, was puffing juicily upon a tobacco-pipe. Abruptly she pulled the pipe from her lips to say, "Poor old Robert Todd at Tynemouth had a boy who sailed to the Indies."

"Nay, will it not be to China that poor old Robert Todd's boy sailed?"

"It was to China that he sailed at first. But not caring for the work when he got there, he quarreled with his master, and threw up the place his father had bought for him—cost him a pretty sum, too!—and came sailing *back* again, to all kinds of trouble, until he went off once more to the Indies, that second time."

"Oh, *that* boy . . . whatever became of him?"

"Is that where he went? A rascal; a scoundrel. A trial and a sorrow to his poor old father unto his dying day."

"He never came back again, did he?"

"Plenty of folks go *out*, but not so many come back," declared Miss Mary. "Sailing here, and sailing there. Best to stay at home, where the Almighty has seen fit to put you."

"Joseph Dodd, don't you remember him: poor old Robert Todd's boy? What was his name?"

"What's that?"

"What was his *name*? Upon my soul, I can't recall it. It'll come to me."

"Ask Mr Cotton. He'll know," said Miss Mary. "He was Mr Turner's man of business in those days."

"Oh, Mr Cotton; spare us a moment, pray. Now think back, sir; do you remember poor old Robert Todd's boy? The one that got a place in the Indies, or the Chineese, back in the year 'twenty or 'twenty-two?"

"Nay, I can't say that I do."

"Oh, but if you'll just put your mind to it, Mr Cotton. We know yours for the most wonderful memory."

"Miles," said Miss Mary, suddenly removing her pipe. "Poor old Robert's boy was called Miles. Young Miles Todd."

"Oh, that one!" said Mr Cotton.

"And wasn't there some bad business about a girl, about the time he went away, for the second time?"

"More than one, I'll be bound," said Mr Cotton.

"Aye, there was, now that you remind me. There was a girl up at Seaton Delaval. The gardener's daughter—gamekeeper's daughter—"

"Housekeeper's daughter. The housekeeper who was sound asleep when the fire started—all of itself, she swore it! Now, what was *her* name?"

No one knew.

"Well, well; Miles Todd," said someone at last, comfortably. "I'd forgotten all about him."

"What's that?" said Joseph Dodd.

"*Miles Todd.*"

"Good riddance," said Joseph Dodd.

"Her father, she said?"

They looked at Constantia and Livia with increased interest.

"She doesn't *look* much like a Todd, but she's pretty enough all the same," said Miss Mary from her wreath of smoke. "Favours her mother, I expect."

As easy as that? As common, as squalid as that? Constantia asked herself as she walked with Livia on her hip back to Newcastle's center. The sun now shone so that the town, though grimy, wore a less forbidding aspect than it had the night before.

Miles Todd, then? Perhaps.

Now, for a father, she had (perhaps) Miles Todd, wastrel son of poor old Robert Todd, of Tynemouth.

Why had she wanted to know this? Why go any distance at all out of her way to find out so discouraging a fact (perhaps) as this?

Why had it seemed to matter?

Once she had deposited her heavy carpetbag at the coaching inn, Constantia felt less burdened. Two hours of agreeable and unaccustomed leisure lay before her until the northbound mails would arrive and then leave again. With Livia warm in her arms, Constantia sauntered in sunshine along the pavement that curved around the garth under a massive square medieval keep, a vestige of the eight-hundred-year-old "new castle" from which the town took its name. Presently she found herself strolling along a busy street lined by the shops of grocers, saddlers, wine merchants, mercers, hatters, drapers, newsagents, and booksellers, their goods framed behind large clean windows. If these were not the marchands-merciers of Paris's rue St-Honoré, neither were they the fishmongers of Musselburgh, by any means.

In a bookseller's window, her eye was caught by a book with a familiar red cloth binding and embossed gold lettering. She meant to pass on—almost succeeded in doing so—but was compelled instead to go into the shop, and inquire.

"Only just published, ma'am," said the bookseller, handing her the book. "By the author of *Vestiges of the Natural History of Creation*. Have you read *Vestiges*? You have? This, you see, is the author's sequel; a reply—no, a retort!—to the critics of that book."

So it was. It was the same size and binding as *Vestiges*, though slighter; and from the same London publisher; the spine carried the same gold lettering. She opened to the title page.

EXPLANATIONS:
A Sequel to
"Vestiges of the Natural History of Creation."
BY THE AUTHOR OF THAT WORK.

"If this stirs up as great a sensation as the *Vestiges*, my five copies will all be sold by this time tomorrow," said the bookseller. "At only five shillings."

Constantia opened the book; riffled through its heart. Her eye alighted upon a phrase: "The dew-drop is, in physics, the picture of a world."

Livia, drooling, reached wet fingers toward the book. She was growing restless and plaintive; and Constantia, reminded of her maternal duties and responsibilities, could not bring herself to part with 5 shillings; not even though she longed to possess this book; longed to plunge into such a world—this world, our world!—constituted of a physics manifest in dew-drops. Reluctantly she relinquished the little red volume to the bookseller, and went out.

Down the street and around the corner, she came upon a fine view of the deep river gorge, and of the bridge springing from here to the south bank. Livia cried and squirmed, hungry again, and Constantia found a seat in a quiet corner against a stone wall, in sunshine. The sun-warmed stones against her back were pleasant; even the lowering sun in her eyes was pleasant. Unfastening her bodice, she placed Livia comfortably to the breast. No one took any notice of so ordinary a sight.

No one, that is, but a well-dressed elderly lady on the far pavement, who stopped and watched for a moment. Then, dodging traffic, the lady crossed the street and startled the drowsing Contantia awake, saying, "What a pretty picture you make, you and your bonny baby! You make me think of my own dear babes—now bearded men, all three of them, and living so far away in South America! Now, do not be affronted, hinney; but only take this as a present—because one fine day, when I was a young mother nursing my eldest in the market square, just as you are doing, an old lady, a stranger, stopped and presented me with just such a token. Here," said the well-dressed lady—tears suddenly, alarmingly, brimming in her eyes—and she pressed a large heavy coin into Constantia's hand. "You must take this, and buy something for yourself—for yourself, mind, not for baby!" Then, not waiting to be thanked, the lady briskly turned and crossed the street again, and was gone, out of sight around the corner, before Constantia could think what to say, or whether to accept, or to consider herself insulted.

It was a silver crown. Not all English coins were familiar to Constantia, but this, she knew, was worth 5 shillings. She studied the obverse: the young queen in profile (just a few years older than herself, but already a mother four times over); her hair dressed à la grecque, and the inscription VICTORIA DEI GRATIA—Victoria by the Grace of God. On the reverse, the crowned shield of the royal coat of arms within a laurel wreath, and the inscription BRITANNIARUM REGINA FID: DEF—Ruler of Britain, Defender of the Faith.

A pound would have been too valuable to spend. A farthing would have been beggar's alms. But a crown; 5 shillings: at this moment, how significant; even providential! As soon as Livia was sated, Constantia returned to the bookseller's, and bought the book *Explanations* after all. The man took his time wrapping the little red volume in brown paper, and tying it with string. As she waited, she heard a bell strike the time—half-past three—and was suddenly filled with a sense of urgency. At last, the transaction concluded, she hurried back to the Tower Arms. The London mail had come in, and hostlers were backing fresh horses into position to be hitched to the Royal Mail coach.

The inside seats were taken already, and no one offered to give up their place to a young mother with a baby. Constantia saw her carpet-bag loaded with the other baggage and then, with Livia, mounted to an outside seat on top. It would be cold. Blessing the remarkable tartan cloak again, she wrapped it well about herself and Livia.

What is your name? Where did you come from? Where are you going?

In India, everyone expected to be asked these questions by strangers, fellow travellers; and everyone asked these questions, too, in turn.

Indeed, it would be impolite not to ask; not to manifest this degree of respect for and interest in others, not to acknowledge their human dignity by courteously inquiring as to name, origin, destination.

Here in Britain, manners were very different. Here, Constantia had found, polite strangers thrown together by circumstance seldom unbent enough even to murmur, How d'ye do? Which meant nothing at all; no candid reply was expected, or welcome. As hours and days passed, one might eventually—as yesterday, with Mrs Todd—learn by chance a fellow traveller's name. But not before the hours and days had duly passed.

Outside passengers, however, were generally not so genteel as inside ones; and the three other passengers atop the coach this evening—a woman and two men—were, it seemed, one another's old acquaintances. By the time the coach gathered speed upon the high road in the gathering dusk, they were already gossiping and laughing loudly together, ignoring Constantia.

Constantia was revolted by their vulgarity; their loudness, coarseness, and ignorance; and glad to be ignored.

Then she felt annoyance toward herself, for her instinctive revulsion. Was it necessary to be so exceedingly nice? Was she lacking in some element of simple humanity?

And was her revulsion apparent?

Perhaps it was, to the old woman. Or perhaps it was some generous impulse to include a stranger in their warm little social circle which moved her presently to lean across and say to Constantia, "And where are you and the baby bound this cold night, hinney?"

"Oh! North," said Constantia, "to rejoin my husband."

"Well, you're on the right coach then, if you're bound north! We're all bound north, aren't we, Tam? Did you hear her, Bob? I asked her where she's bound, and she said she's bound *north*!"

The two men laughed, as though this were a very good joke indeed.

"To join her *husband*!" the woman added gleefully, at which they laughed again. "Well, where north, hinney? It's a big place, north," said the old woman, turning back to Constantia once more. "Where's this husband, that you're going to join? What's his name?"

Now Constantia saw that she had been right to be disgusted; and, unwilling to be the butt of any further jokes, she drew herself up and said, "Why do you ask?"

"Only out of curiosity, I suppose," said the woman, suddenly mild and confidential. "Though mother always told me, curiosity killed the cat."

"Ah," said Constantia, and attended to wrapping her cloak more closely around Livia.

The old woman waited some moments, still expecting to have her curiosity gratified; then, having waited in vain, she turned to her companions and said, "Well! What monstrous luck for us, Tam: just fancy, we've got the Quality up here with us, on the outside seats! Us common folk mustn't make a nuisance of ourselves though, by expecting polite conversation, or hoping for a civil reply to a civil question. But I already know where she's going, for I axed the coachman, and he told me she is going to Amble. Unless she decides to get down sooner, to get away from *me*. She doesn't like me. I can see that much. Her Ladyship doesn't like me at all."

"Sure she does. She likes you fine," said one of the men.

"Nay, she does not."

Constantia thought, I was willing to like you, well enough; but now I find that I do *not* like you. I do not like your inquisitive bullying. I do not like your vulgar and impertinent curiosity. Have you given me any cause to like you? Why will you not leave me in peace?

What is your name? Where have you come from? Where are you going?

Why does everyone want to know?

The moon rose nearly full, washing the fells at either hand in silver: the heights in repoussé; the shadowed coombs, chased. A bold young hare darted out upon the road and, beholding the approaching coach, promptly lost all presence of mind. There it squatted until the coach was nearly upon it. At the last possible moment it broke and ran across the verge to safety; then abruptly it doubled back into the roadway again and darted madly under the right rear wheel. The long arc of the ironshod rim rolled over the lower part of the hare's long back, shattering the long hollow chain of vertebrae; bursting the spleen and liver, crushing stomach, intestines. From her high perch atop the coach, Constantia heard the hare's cry, a breathy high wail; she had never heard a hare's voice and did not know they had any. She could not help looking back, and in the moonlight saw it writhing against the rutted roadbed, thrashing, the short front legs running futilely in weakening spasms. For some moments longer, its strong heart, lungs, and nerves continued to work at their utmost pitch. It was still twitching in death spasms when it was lost to view as the coach rounded the next turn.

Her milk let down. It was the hare's cry that did it; the hare's paroxysms. She felt the surge, the flush in her breasts; then the wetness spreading into her bodice. She drew her cloak closer about herself and her sleeping daughter.

It is not so much the dying, thought Constantia, as the suffering. Why should that be necessary? Why permitted? Are we to emulate our Deity in this respect? Are we, like Him, to cultivate a lofty disregard for the sufferings of creatures less exalted than ourselves?

No, we are better than that. We are the compassionate earthlings. *Homo misericors.*

Some of us. Sometimes.

The night was still, and coal-smoke lay heavy in the low places. At each small town, the guard threw down a mailbag to a waiting postmaster or postmistress and took up another; the coach scarcely paused, for the steaming horses must not get cold. Constantia did not know where she was, for all the towns, and the houses in them, looked very much alike in the gloom; all their chimneys smoked very much alike. Drawing the hood of her cloak up over her quilted bonnet, Constantia burrowed deeper into the rug furnished by the Royal Mail for the use of outside passengers, and succeeded in dozing a little from time to time despite the cold; her arms holding Livia were cramped to stiffness, like wood petrified.

An abrupt voice awakened her: "See that dome, Bob," the rude old woman was saying, "just nosing up above the treetops? That's the moslem of the Delavals."

Hearing this, Constantia could not help but peer out of her rug. A Mughal dome? Here, so far from India? So far even from the Royal Pavilion at Brighton?

"That's the moslem that Lord Delaval built for his only son, the last of that line. Aye, and the place passed to the Astleys afterward, by the female line—as they were called before they became Lords Hastingses. But never a dead body has been inside of the moslem, because Lord Delaval couldn't agree with the Bishop of Durham over his fee to consecrate it."

The old woman meant "mausoleum." Only the lead dome itself was visible, rising above the overgrown thicket of leafless trees. It was not at all like a mughal dome, for it was perfectly classical, and in the streaming moonlight Constantia could just make out the Doric capitals which supported it.

"The Bishop it was, that made the difficulties," said the man called Tam, "not approving of the Delavals. The heir wasn't twenty when he died, but already a Delaval through and through—none of 'em ever died in their beds!"

"Not in their own beds!" said the woman.

"Not alone in their beds!" said Tam.

"They say it was a kick from a laundry maid in defense of her honour that killed him," said the woman.

"A mighty kick then it must have been," said Tam.

"And well-aimed," added the man called Bob.

"Caught him in a—ha!—a particularly tender spot, they say!"

"While he had his—ahem!—his 'guard' down!" crowed the old woman. "Oh, guard—did you hear that? His 'guard' was down!"

"Down, do you say—or was it up? Eh? Ha-ha!" laughed Bob.

The guard seated behind the coachman pretended not to hear them.

"It's haunted, or so they say," said Tam.

"What, the moslem?"

"And Seaton Delaval Hall."

"There is no ghost at the Hall."

"But there is. She is sometimes still seen in the window of the tower."

"The housekeeper dusting the blinds, I fancy."

"Impossible, for there remains no floor below those windows that any mortal woman could stand upon—it was burnt away in the fire."

"Besides, Mrs Turnbull is the frowdiest housekeeper in the world, and never thought of dusting a blind in her life. Why the family keeps her on I do not know."

The guard behind the coachman now spoke for the first time, to say gravely, "The Almighty God hath served the unrighteous with the fruits of their wickedness; His justice hath been meted out at last: the family extinct and their palace burnt to ashes."

But Tam said, "Nay, they weren't so bad as all that. Lively and clever, and very free with their money! Nothing mean or miserly about the Delavals! Plenty of folks hereabouts still talk of those good old times when, rent-day coming round, they used to go up to the Hall—not to pay money—but to receive it! To be paid, for all the good things they'd furnished to the family: beeves and hogs, mutton and chickens, butter and eggs, ale and beer and bread. Wasn't there a lot of it, in those days!"

"And the laundry at that house!" said the old woman. "None of this mean every-week business, nay; why, there was a good three months of linens and bedclothes belonged to that family, I tell you;

and the laundry, when it was time—not but quarterly, mind you—kept half a dozen laundresses at work for a full week! The coppers! The fires! The stirrings and tramplings! The boilings, the bleachings! Why, a factory at Birmingham is what it was like."

"Nothing like these mean threadbare times. The family was clever, and high-spirited too, every one of them, men and women alike—and devilish handsome, forby."

"Oh, aye, devilish! We can agree there," said the guard. "The family that has it now is far from saints, either."

"Who has it now?" asked Constantia, after waiting a moment for someone else to ask; but no one did.

"Why, Lord Hastings, to be sure," said the guard.

"What!" said Constantia, "The very Lord Hastings who was Governor-General of India, back in the 'twenties? Or perhaps his son may be the present Lord Hastings?"

"Nay, nay," said the guard, having now abandoned all his virtuous reserve. "Out in India it was the Marquess of Hastings—a different family altogether. But our Lord Hastings is Baron Hastings, who was just Sir Jacob Astley, until Parliament raised him up three or four years ago."

"They wanted him out of the way, and kicked him upstairs to the Lords," said Tam.

"One good kick deserves another!" declared the old woman gleefully.

"Nay; to make it up to him that he could not have his divorce when he wanted it," said the guard.

"Why could he not?" asked Constantia.

"Where have you been, not to know?" said the guard. "When Sir Jacob's wife Lady Astley ran off with that scoundrel Thomas Garth—"

"And that's another scandal, in the very—highest—circles of all!" breathed the old woman with relish. "Eh? Garth? Oh aye; the royal bastard! But you're too young to remember any of that. The Princess Royal! With her father's equerry!—"

"Nay, it was worse than that—the equerry just a tale, to cover up the sordid truth—"

"Hsst!" said Tam.

"—leaving her two little boys behind," said the guard, as though he had not been interrupted, "Sir Jacob lodged a suit for divorce and twelve thousand pounds in damages."

"Did he not succeed?" asked Constantia.

"Garth's solicitors brought evidence that Sir Jacob had—habitually . . . ah, had been a frequenter of prostitutes—of, well, the very lowest kind—so that Sir Jacob was awarded—what do you think? not twelve thousand pounds, nay!—but one shilling! One single shilling! And the divorce denied! Unable to remarry, all those years."

Now the coach was rolling past the ruined mansion itself—Seaton Delaval Hall—its massy silhouette still superb at the top of its drive; its flanking wings and broad court still magnificent; sequestered behind high iron gates. After a moment Constantia asked, "Do the family come here still?"

"Never; London suits them—"

"And they, London."

"From here, at night, with the moonlight on those towers, you wouldn't know it for burnt and roofless," said the guard. "It makes a splendid ruin."

"It made a splendid fire, too," said Tam. "I saw it burn. Aye, I was a labourer at the bottleworks by the sluice, back in 'twenty-two. The coldest January in living memory; the old folks had been freezing to death in their beds, that winter—and the ground so hard they could not be buried; the corpses were stacking up like cordwood at the sacristan's, awaiting a thaw. I remember waking to the bell—we all ran to help—dragged the fire engines into position—but not a drop of water could we pump, for all was ice, frozen solid! Loads of the valuables, pictures and statues, was carried out onto the grass—until the leads of the roof began to melt; aye, the very leads melting and running down like rain! No one dared risk passing beneath such a shower as that. Well, it made a magnificent bonfire—and the heat of it something wonderful, in the midst the winter. My hair and eyelashes were scorched, though I stood well back. Oh aye—you might not think it, but in those days I had hair aplenty!"

"It was the kitchen fire that started it, I suppose?" suggested Constantia.

"Nay, it started in the east wing that was, then—in a corridor of upstairs bedchambers, where jackdaws had stuffed a chimney with their nest."

"Ah!—so the family was home at the time?" Constantia asked.

"Sure they were *not*—and had not been for many months."

"How came there to be a fire, then, in that part of the house?"

"Well might you wonder!"

"The ghost," said the old woman.

"Ghosts don't start fires."

"Who can say what a vengeful ghost might not do?"

"What, the doughty laundry maid?"

"Nay, nay, quite a different ghost," said the guard. "A different maid; and a different Astley; a—a younger relation, not the heir. Matters got sadly crossed up somehow, by a generation or so; the amorous scion of the 1750s met with an unwilling laundry maid, and died of it; and an amorous housemaid of the 1820s met with the faithless scion who sailed for India after the fire, leaving her to perish in bringing their bastard into the world; her ghost haunts the place still."

"That's all flum," said Tam. "It's true enough that the man who sailed for India after the fire went by the name of Astley, but he had no right to it, coming as he did from the wrong side of the blanket. He was here, the night of the fire. I remember often seeing him here that winter, idling about, waiting for his commission to come through—and trifling with the housekeeper's very pretty daughter. Nay, it was the previous housekeeper who was here in 'twenty-two, at the time of the fire—not the present Mrs Turnbull, though she knows all about it, and will be glad to tell anyone who is curious enough to ask her. And that girl never made a ghost, for she ran off shortly after her lover sailed—and in blooming health, to put it politer than she deserved. I remember her very well, a fine fresh girl called Polly, far too pretty to be good; and she certainly did not die in her guilty childbed, but ran off to Scotland in good time—with a rascal from Newcastle who deserved the horns he got. What was his name, now? Fox? No, but something foxey . . . Todd, or Dodd."

"Dafty! Didn't he know?" said Bob.

"Who can say what she chose to tell him?"

"There's husbands as will believe there's such prodigies as seven-month babies," said the old woman. "Or six. Even five, sometimes."

Still the coach rolled onward; the topless towers of Seaton Delaval Hall were receding into the night. Abruptly Constantia called out, "Coachman, stop! Pray, stop at once! I should like to get down—here."

"What, here! Nowhere! At this hour!" said the coachman. But she insisted, and he wrested the horses to a standstill on the frozen mud of the road.

"What possesses the woman? Is she mad?" said the old woman. "And her with a bairn at the breast."

"It's yourself who's to blame, you old carlin," said Tam. "Who can fault her, if she won't bear to hear such loose, vile, scandalous talk? Why don't you curb your tongue like a decent woman?"

"I told you Her Ladyship does not like me."

"And the carriage money she has paid, to be lost!" said Bob.

"Thank you," said Constantia to the coachman, and climbed down with Livia, against the advice of her fellow travellers and of the guard who handed down her carpet-bag.

The noise of the coach receded—wheels, hooves; fainter, then gone—and the winter night's stillness expanded around her, clear to the stars. There was a steady whispering, a murmuring, from the east: the sound of waves assaulting the shore.

12

CONSTANTIA WALKED BACK along the road for a hundred
yards, to a place where she could see the form of Seaton Delaval Hall straight on, high and black against the starry sky.
Though unroofed, it stood tall and stately upon its plinth; though
ravaged by fire, it retained its distinctive towers advancing at each
corner of the main central block. Its broad high flights of steps were
like the ascent to a temple. It was magnificent still, this ruined moon-
washed masterpiece of the celebrated architect Sir John Vanbrugh;
this original of the Nawab's Dil Kusha palace at Lucknow.

The sight transported Constantia, so that for a moment she
ceased to shiver, as she remembered sun-dazzled Dil Kusha—Heart's
Desire. She remembered just how its rooms intersected, how they fit
together, inside; knew their clever interlocking volumes. Knew how
the stairwells served them. Knew its balconies and galleries, its land-
ings and passages.

But the bitter cold of the Northumbrian night soon recalled her
to the present moment, and her present difficulties. Just what was
she to do now? Now that she had—suddenly, impulsively—broken
her journey northward? A single light showed from a small low window in the flanking west wing of the mansion; all else was dark.
There was a pair of carriage gates in the iron railing at the broad

drive which entered the grounds, but these were chained shut. A little further along she came to a man-gate, but it too was locked. In her dismay, she rattled it hard and long. The clatter—cold iron on cold iron—rose into the black sky, futile.

Livia now awakened with a start, and began to cry. Constantia, as she considered what to do and where to go at this hour of the night, kissed her, rocked her; but Livia would not be comforted. Was she hungry? Must she be fed? Again? Livia howled louder, and there was nothing Constantia could do but set down the carpetbag and tender her breast there and then, in the high road at midnight. Just as she had got Livia quiet, she heard a man's rough voice, a shout—and saw through the iron railing a moving light: a bobbing hand-lantern approaching from inside the grounds of Seaton Delaval.

The watchman was apprehensive until he saw what he had to deal with: only a vagrant slattern feeding her bastard. "Be off then! off with you!" he said roughly. "You can't stop here."

But when she rose, and spoke, he was not so sure. Was she not rather too neat, modest and clean for a whore? It was hard to be certain, by lantern-light. Well-spoken too, like a gentlewoman—though a stranger, undoubtedly. "I have come to speak with Mrs Turnbull," she said again.

At this hour of the night?

"I am called Mrs MacAdam; I am an old connection of the family," she said.

Not that he had ever heard of; and old connections of the family did not generally arrive unannounced outside the gates at midnight. But doubt was sown; and after a moment, he unlocked the gate to admit her. There was no knowing who might not come to speak with Mrs Turnbull the housekeeper, with whom he was not on good terms—but whose window was, unusually, still lit. If he admitted this visitor, would Mrs Turnbull be annoyed? If he denied this visitor, would she be more annoyed? While opportunities to goad Mrs Turn-

bull were welcome, she had proven capable of revenge. In any case,
this stranger was unlikely to steal the burnt building stones which
still remained in the high grass where the ruined east wing had once
stood; so as these, his main concern, seemed safe, he decided to open
the gate. "My bag," she said. He carried it up the broad expanse of the
entrance court for her, lighting the way toward that single illuminated
window in the west wing.

Mrs Turnbull's lamp burned so late only because she had failed to
extinguish it and go to bed; had instead fallen asleep in her chair,
slumped forward upon the deal table before the dying fire, her gin
bottle empty. A clatter at the door and the voice of the despised
watchman roused her; angrily she heaved herself up and flung open
the door, her cheek embossed in red where it had been pressed against
the pine board.

The watchman, a teetotaller, did not miss the bottle on the table
or the smell of gin. He heard the stranger introduce herself, apolo-
gising for the lateness of the hour, but he did not believe that she—
this Mrs MacAdam—was an old connection of the Astley family.
He himself had no right to receive and entertain friends of his own
upon the Astley premises, and he doubted that Mrs Turnbull had any
such right either. In short, he thought he smelled not only gin, but an
opportunity to stir up trouble; perhaps even blackmail. "Night callers,
is it now, Mrs Turnbull?" he said, a leer in his tone.

Mrs Turnbull, who waged an unflagging campaign against presumptuous and encroaching inferiors such as the watchman, retorted,
"I do not see what concern it can be of *yours* if I receive respectable
callers, in my own rooms."

"At midnight," he said, insinuating something.

"At any hour I please. Pray, won't you step in, ma'am," said Mrs
Turnbull genteelly to the visitor, enunciating with extreme care. "Do
come and warm yourself and the baby at my fire." The watchman

was not permitted to have a fire in his guardhouse unless it was actually snowing.

"We'll see about that," said the watchman.

Mrs Turnbull shut the door in his face and turned to this unknown visitor. The proffered fire, unfortunately reduced to embers, emitted only a faint warmth, but the stranger was warming her hands and her baby before it. It was a handsome cloak she wore, and her bonnet was more than respectable. What had she said her name was? What had she said her business was? Mrs Turnbull felt herself a little unsteady; perhaps not quite up to entertaining a visitor, after all. She got herself safely into her chair, however, and heard the visitor say, " . . . I beg your pardon . . . so very late an hour . . . better perhaps in the morning instead, if you can give me a bed for the night? For what remains of it, at least?"

And so it was that a miserable sleepy ten-year-old maid of all work, roused from her bed by Mrs Turnbull's bell, was ordered to conduct the visitor by candlelight to a spare bedchamber behind the kitchen. The candle showed a small low room with a large patch of damp beneath the window, an old bedstead, and a strong smell of mildew. "Nor can I leave you the candle, ma'am, as it's strictly against orders, for the family is exceeding wary as to fire, even now; but there's a moon to see by. And water . . . aye, there's some," observed the girl— a thin pale child— tipping the jug on the table. "Just enough . . . no, there'll be none hot at this hour, only the cold." And then the little maid withdrew, leaving the visitor and her baby in full enjoyment of that dismal chamber of near-perfect discomfort.

By moonlight Constantia drew back the coverlet and, feeling the damp chill of the wretched old featherbed's ticking, resolved not to undress; she only wrapped herself and Livia in her cloak, and lay down. It was a vile bed, damp and musty, an envelope of mildew and deep cold which relentlessly drew the warmth from her, and did not return it. Livia slept; Constantia did not—or so she thought. But when she opened her eyes again, it was to moonlight in her face; some time had passed and the moon was descending to the west. Constantia lay and considered the strangeness of being here; of sleeping in this house. This house, of all the houses in Britain! Presently, in the same way as memories would sometimes let down with her milk when she nursed the babies—as underground springs rise, whelming upward between rocks to the air—as faint musical phrases sometimes wafted unbidden into the minds of the Chambers girls—a memory now welled up her. Most wonderfully, this memory of her mother was a fresh one, never remembered until now. It had a raw bright distinct quality, not yet worn down by examination and handling. A pearl still round, not yet rubbed flat in back; not yet dissolved by repeated handling—but round, fresh and full, entire, new:

Her beautiful mother, licking her own fingers to smooth Constantia's hair away from her face; and then smoothing her own hair too, and smoothing the cloth of her gown over her belly; and adjusting the bodice of her dress, and her bosom within the bodice. Waiting, so tiresome. Dusk. Hot. Waiting with her mother in a small octagonal room windowed all round, overlooking the Nawab's dusty garden; in the distance lay the sluggish grey-green river. This was Dil Kusha, she knew; a room atop one of the corner towers. Presently an English officer came in, a tall man with yellow hair brushed back, wearing military dress and polished boots. He spoke, quietly, to Constantia's beautiful mother, who replied in a voice Constantia had never heard before. What did they say? Constantia could not remember. They were not speaking to her. But her mother made Constantia curtsey to the officer. He dropped to one knee to look in her face, while holding her two hands. She did not like this. It had greatly embarrassed her to be looked at so intently; she had scowled at the floor, twisting away instead of looking at him. Still, an impression remained with her: His dark wiry moustache. His gold-green eyes; his straight brows. A dimple to his chin, like her own.

That was all. This fresh new memory was constituted almost entirely of boredom and embarrassment—but these remembered sensations were so pure and so strong as to convince Constantia that this memory must be a true one; a real artefact, of real experience.

Hadn't her mother been very gay, afterward? Laughing a great deal at supper? Very lively and high-spirited at the nautch that followed? And wasn't the English officer there too, among the guest-spectators, beside a Hindu woman who was his wife; a beautiful woman who reclined upon a litter, and did not walk, but was carried by bearers? After that, Constantia did not remember ever seeing him again.

Was it later that same night that Constantia had followed her mother? Had surprised her in the embrace of the handsome balloonist?

That was all. How odd that she never had thought of this before.

How odd that she remembered it now.

Despite the moonlight in her face, Livia slept, her tiny lips slack. Veins showed blue through the transparent skin at her temple, which fluttered to the pulse of her baby heart.

At dawn, Constantia—stunned by broken sleep and cold— found angry red raised welts on Livia's neck and wrists. There was no looking-glass in the room, but Constantia felt suspicious itching raised places on herself, too; and did her scalp crawl only with doubt? Or with something worse?

"I hope you were comfortable, ma'am," said Mrs Turnbull civilly, over breakfast. She had resolved to conceal that she could not remember this visitor's name or her claim to be here—if indeed these had been told, last night. Most of the people who came wanted to see the ruined house, and Mrs Turnbull confidently anticipated a gratuity; perhaps a handsome one, to judge by the quality of this visitor's tartan cloak.

"Oh—well enough!"

"The bed not damp?"

"Well—perhaps—rather damp," admitted the visitor.

"I feared as much. Those featherbeds are dreadful to keep dry. And we're not allowed to put them to the fire for airing—not after what happened. I mean our fire, of course—all those years ago."

"Oh! But what have featherbeds to do with that? Was not the fire caused by a jackdaw's nest in a chimney?"

"Nonsense. Oh, a jackdaw's nest had something to do with it, sure enough—but the housekeeper's daughter was to blame for that fire. A previous housekeeper: Mrs Wilson was her name. Well, not apurpose—I would never say that—nay, the girl's wickedness was of another kind altogether, if you understand what I mean. Will you take coffee? Ma'am? And there is some butter if you want it for your bread. Does the baby take a rusk yet? There's crasters, too. Her mother was to blame; *she* should have kept a stricter watch over such a girl as that. A pretty face is not always a girl's fortune; it may very likely prove her downfall, instead. But there, I mustn't clack on about all that old scandal—of no interest to anyone, after so long a time."

"On the contrary, Mrs Turnbull, there is nothing I should like better than to hear about that long-ago fire. I beg you will tell me *all* about Mrs Wilson—and her daughter—and the fire—and featherbeds, and jackdaw nests."

"Ah? Well; if it is of any interest to you . . ." Mrs Turnbull paused to gather her thoughts, and to re-estimate the tip that might be had by gratifying this nameless visitor's unexpected taste for stale gossip. "Aye . . . well, Sir Jacob—as he was then, you know—always would write a week or two in advance, to advise that he would arrive on such a day, and would bring so many gentlemen with him; and to desire that Mrs Wilson should light fires in the necessary bedchambers for at least three days and nights—oh, the chill in those rooms, in winter! three days and nights of fires round the clock, just to get them passable warm! And she was to put the featherbeds before the fires, of course, to air and dry them—for this is not a *dry* house, and never was, not on *this* shore—not even in those days, when there was a roof over it. And the beds and their sheets all to be slept in for three nights at least before their arrival—"

"Slept in! Why?"

"So him and his friends wouldn't be bit to pieces, of course, by hungry bugs! Mrs Wilson and her three daughters would all have to go upstairs each night to lie in all those grand beds—aye, in the new east wing that was, in those days, along the upstairs corridor. I'll show you after breakfast, if you like, where it was. They must have come down each morning chewed to bits. Oh, there's no getting rid of bed-bugs; they creep through the walls, and hide in the cracks, and behind the tapestries and the pictures; and even if you chase them from one room, it's only as far as the next—and then they'll creep right back again, the nasty bloodsucking creatures. A body can't help but won-der what the Creator thought He was up to, when He created them. But once they've fed they'll leave a body alone, for a few nights. And so Sir Jacob always wanted the beds well slept in—the bugs well-fed, you see!—before he'd come here, him and his friends. Another craster? Well, if you like to come along then, I'll show you the house. Now, Jeannie," she interrupted herself, turning to address the pitiable little maid, "I want you to sift the meal while I conduct, ah, this lady over the house. Oh, aye, ma'am, teeming with weevils, this latest sack of meal; dreadful stuff! We'll go up this way; mind the steps. Often? Oh nay; even then Sir Jacob came here only seldom—and Lady Geor-giana never, for her second baby was just new-born—and they were living together, mostly, at Melton Constable, and in London. But he'd bring a party of gentlemen, from time to time. 'Gentlemen'! I suppose they must have been, though you might not have thought so, from their antics. Fancy dress; and theatricals; and tableaux wearing noth-ing but Roman togas—*if* so much as that. London must be a very odd place. Or sometimes Sir Jacob would come for a fortnight or so, with just his valet. What bad luck he had with valets! There seemed to be a new one every time he came. I was just a girl at the time, an under house-maid in my first place, up the coast—but everyone knew, and the matter was much talked of, though I did not understand it then. Now, you are about to see our celebrated, our magnificent hall," said Mrs Turnbull, unlocking the door and standing politely to one side.

Entering, Constantia was startled by an explosion—but it was only the beating wings of a score of pigeons taking flight, climbing up into the open grey sky that was the immense hall's only roof. For a moment Constantia fancied the house's ghosts—the Grey Lady, the White Lady—embodied now in these pigeons; and wasn't there still a faint whiff of smoke, a ghost of calcined stone and burnt timber? "Forty-four feet long, and forty-four feet high," Mrs Turnbull was saying, in a loud practised manner. The floor, a broad chequerboard of black and cream marble squares, was filthy, littered with leaves, twigs, bird-droppings. "There's talk, now and again, of re-roofing it, but nothing ever comes of it. You wouldn't think it could happen so fast, but see how the very marble of the floors is weathering, under twenty winters of snow; twenty summers of rain—"

"Twenty-three, is it not?" said Constantia.

"Let me see . . . the fire was the night of the third of January, in the year 'twenty-two," said the housekeeper, "so that will make it . . . aye, twenty four years, on the third of January next; so it will. How the years do fly by."

The water-stained walls rose three storeys. Let into them were tiers of Roman niches, each still occupied by its life-sized classical figure. Crammed against the plinths at the feet of each figure were pigeon-nests, on which a great many birds remained, peering warily down. "The statues large as life," the housekeeper was declaiming, "executed by the best Italian artists, and each one holding her own symbols and 'tributes representing the fine arts such as, Music, Painting, Geography . . ."

Constantia could feel the mist falling wetter on her upturned face, and pulled Livia's cap well down over her ears. The statues were horrible, leprous; and Constantia saw that they were—had always been—frauds; not carved from stone at all by those best Italian artists, but only hollow skins of plaster over armatures of wire, their burnt heads now dangling on their breasts from shreds of wire and plaster; like incomplete suttees, widow-immolations; like half-cremated corpses on the banks of the Ganges. " . . . Architecture, Sculpture, and . . . Stronomy," trailed off the housekeeper, sounding increasingly doubtful.

The marble fireplace was undamaged; caryatids supported it still, headachy but uncomplaining. The masonry of the walls was exquisitely worked, and the stone a luscious russety-pink hue as though bathed in the glow of a permanent sunset. "What is this beautiful stone?" asked Constantia. "Such an unusual colour."

"Well, it is our limestone, from the estate quarry. It *was* creamy, near white, but the fire burnt it pink," said the housekeeper.

The housekeeper now led the way to the splendid saloon. This, she asserted, measured seventy-five feet long and thirty feet wide, and its ceiling, "when it had one, before the fire, was painted by Signor Vercelli, an Italian, of goddesses and nymphs without any clothes on." They proceeded then through various lofty apartments—dining-rooms, drawing-rooms, sitting-rooms, business-rooms, libraries—and arrived eventually at one of the grand spiral stone staircases, "a full *seventeen* feet in diameter. And up there, you see, at that landing, was the doorway that led formerly to the new wing built by the last Lord Delaval—where the fire started." Constantia could see a wide doorway which opened into thin air, grey sky. What remained of the iron stair baluster writhed over empty space where a few of the steps had fallen away. The stone was burnt a darker pink here; this stairwell filled with fire, thought Constantia, must have been like the chimney of a furnace.

"Now we'll pass outside again by way of our magnificent portico—of the Ironic order, and each column *three* feet in diameter—to the south front, formerly the pleasure grounds; and from here you can see where Lord Delaval's handsome new wing had been." With a wave of her arm, the housekeeper sketched the vanished wing in the air: "Two storeys, four*teen* rooms: bedchambers, dressing-rooms, sitting-rooms—each with its own fireplace."

The mist was turning to drizzle and Constantia drew her cloak around Livia; how heavy she was becoming! Here, Constantia could see once more (from outside now) the high doorway which opened upon air. A few stone supports and corbels still jutted from the wall of the house, but in the rank grass below lay only a few—surprisingly few—large blocks of building-stone, burnt pink; not enough ever to have constituted so large a wing. "What has become of all the stone?" asked Constantia.

"Stolen," said the housekeeper. "So much easier, and cheaper, to steal, than to pay good money for new-cut stone from the quarry! The folk hereabouts have been helping themselves for years—until the new iron fence was put up. You need only stroll about the district with your eyes open to see where it has gone: there's garden walls, and byres, and entire cottages all in the telltale pink of *our* stone. Now we've a watchman at night, but he's worse than none; I'll warrant you he's been selling off what little remains."

"Do the family not come here?"

"Not them. Why should they? Why leave the warmth and ease of Melton Constable? And London?"

Constantia studied the building again, so strangely familiar. Just there, upon that balustraded terrace above the magnificent portico, she had held her mother's hand, and watched the handsome balloon-ist sail his boat upward into the blazing Lucknow sky.

Just there, in the hot airless room atop that corner tower, she and her mother had waited, and waited; waiting for the yellow-haired English officer who, when he came at last, held her hands and her gaze as though he would swallow her.

"How did it start, though—the fire?" asked Constantia.

"Aye, I was coming to that . . . where was I? "

"Bed-bugs," said Constantia.

"Oh, aye. Come along out of the rain . . . this way, now, to the stable wing. Its chief apartment measuring no less than sixty-two feet long, and forty-one feet wide, and twenty-one feet and *four* inches high—and each stall and hay-manger built of dressed stone."

"All untouched by fire, I see," said Constantia. "You were just about to tell me how it started."

"So I was. Well, as I've said, Sir Jacob had wrote to Mrs Wilson desiring her to ready the house for a party of gentlemen to arrive soon after the new year, so there was fires in all of those upstairs bedchambers in the new wing, and Mrs Wilson and her girls setting the featherbeds over the fenders in front of the fires each morning, and then putting them back onto the beds to lie in them each night. Only, that night—the third of January—one of the girls, the middle one, Polly, the pretty one—well, *was* she in her bed and sound asleep, where she ought to have been?" She turned to Constantia for a reply.

"Was she?" said Constantia obligingly.

"Nay, ma'am," said the housekeeper. "I tell you she was *not*. And that featherbed she ought to have been sound asleep *on*—where was it?"

"Where indeed?" said Constantia.

"I will tell you: it was left draped over the fender, in front of the bedchamber fire. Just so near that when an old jackdaw nest came atumbling down the chimney, alight—well! Ticking and old dry feathers; imagine! They'd go up like tinder, you can be sure; and the stench of it! But was anyone there to see it, or smell it, or throw the water-jug onto it, or raise the alarm?"

"Was no one there?"

"Nay, ma'am; no one, I tell you. And where was the girl, then, if not sound asleep where she ought to have been?"

"Where was she?"

But the housekeeper only pursed her mouth and shook her head, saying nothing. She led the way now through a door which led into the vaulted basement beneath the main block of the house: chamber after chamber of dismal damp offices, passages, and store-rooms, with low dressed-stone arches between. Presently she stopped at a heavy timber door, and fumbling through her ring of keys, unlocked and opened it. Constantia followed her into the dim room lit by a single glazed window set high, and as her eyes adjusted to the darkness, she saw that it was stacked to the vaults with upturned chairs, and filthy tables, and chests, and crates, baskets, trunks, wardrobes. "This store contains everything that was saved from the fire," said the housekeeper. "Only this." She drew back a tarpaulin to uncover a stack of old framed pictures leaning against a wardrobe. Tipping three of them forward to reveal a fourth, she wiped it tenderly with the hem of her apron; then waved Constantia near, to see a three-quarter-length portrait of a man in uniform.

Young; only recently entered upon the virile beauty of his full manhood; frank and level of gaze, his moustache darker than his yellow hair. His brows were straight and flat, and his eyes an unusual greeny-gold, rather feline; a deep dimple in his chin.

"Who is that?" asked Constantia. She leaned closer, to see the engraved plate affixed to the frame. "'John Fenwick Astley,'" she read aloud.

"Jack. With him, that's where," said the housekeeper. "She was in Jack Astley's room."

"Sir Jacob's room, do you mean?"

"Nay, not at all! I mean this cousin, Jack Astley; that is, Mr John Astley—not a legitimate cousin, mind you, but only a natural one, from the London branch of the family—nay, he was waiting for his commission that his guardians were trying to get for him in the service of the East India Company, for him to go out there and make his fortune, if he could—but there was some delay . . . and so, having no place to wait but here—well, here he waited: smoking in Sir Jacob's library, and shooting at Sir Jacob's game, and drinking Sir Jacob's wine, and making himself agreeable—rather more than agreeable—to the daughters of Sir Jacob's housekeeper. Ah! But he had a way with him, hadn't he? And handsome! the picture doesn't do him justice. The result was just what any reasonable person might foresee and expect. And prevent! But who's to say that was not just what Mrs Wilson was hoping for, all along? A young man bearing that name, and with such prospects, even though illegitimate, would have been a fine match for any of *her* girls, and I'll warrant you she'd have been relieved, not to say triumphant, to have had one of them taken off her hands by young Jack Astley, and away with him to the Indies. And that's where that girl Polly was, that night, when she ought to have been sound asleep on a featherbed in the new bedroom wing. She was in Jack Astley's room instead, off the upstairs gallery in the old central block." The housekeeper jerked her thumb upward.

"Oh! It was not Mr Todd, then? Not Miles Todd, from Newcastle?"

"Him!" scoffed the housekeeper. "A day late, and a pound short, that one. Only just in time to get a pair of horns fastened to his forehead! I'll say that for Mrs Wilson: she rarely missed a chance. There's not many as could have been her equal, in her day, for turning any situation to advantage. I daresay there's a great deal more to it, that she might have told *if* she pleased—but too late now. We'll never know."

"That is a pity—for I should very much like to have met her. When was it she died?"

"Died! Where did you get that idea? Nay, she is quite alive, though childish and unable to speak, nor stir from her chair, these ten years now. Aye, she is looked after by her eldest daughter, Mrs Russell, who does for old Miss Huthwaite of Seaton Lodge. Oh aye; they live in the cottage hard by—with the younger daughter too, the evangelical one. Far? From here? Not at all! It's just down the road by the Sluice, across from the bottle works."

Mrs Turnbull's anonymous visitor, with her baby and her carpet-bag, took leave suddenly, even hastily; but the tip pressed into Mrs Turnbull's outstretched hand exceeded even that greedy woman's utmost expectation.

The watchman who let her out the gate watched her walk away along the muddy road toward the town, beneath a thickening drizzle now turning to frank rain. To his surprise, she had tipped him too.

13

THE WALK to Seaton Sluice, in a light gusting rain, took ten minutes. Within the shelter of Constantia's cloak, heavy-lidded Livia nodded, drooling. A single line from the song her mother used to sing sounded over and over again in Constantia's head as she walked; she could not banish it:

> No nine-months' child, but only seven . . .
> No nine-months' child, but only seven . . .
> No nine-months' child, nor scarcely seven . . .

Each of the six conical chimneys of the bottle works streamed its stinking black plume of smoke toward her, for the breeze blew fitfully off the sea. At the bridge across Seaton Burn, she paused. A bottle sloop tied up at the quay on the opposite shore was being loaded; from one of a pair of black gaping holes opening into the bank itself there issued clanking railcars laden with crates—from tunnels leading underground to the bottle works. What a thriving, bustling, dirty, stinking, noisy place! The shores of the Burn were bare mud, without grass or any growing thing. The opaque brown water of the Burn seemed scarcely to flow at all. She heard shouts of men, and groans and shrieks of machinery; but no birdsong, no plashing of water. A short distance upstream she could see another, smaller bridge thrown across the Burn; a footbridge, which led from the brick-built ranges of the bottle works on the far side to a large but plain thatched house on the near side: Seaton Lodge. Tucked in beyond the Lodge she could see the servants' cottage; and from its chimney, there rose a meagre thread of smoke.

Constantia went first to the cottage and knocked at its door, but no one came. After a moment she turned to follow a much-trodden flagstone path to what she supposed must be the Lodge's kitchen. And so it proved. Here, the stout door was opened to her knock by a lean woman with floury hands, who stood halfway behind the door, with a question in her face: Who dares bother me now? Behind her a vast black range squatted in the fireplace; a work table stood at the center of the flagged floor. Steam and the smell of warm tallow wafted out.

"Mrs Russell?" said Constantia.

"Aye," said Mrs Russell; and waited, not with any air of patience.

But Constantia hardly knew what she wanted. (Why do we want to know? Why does it matter? Why does it seem to matter?) She was aware that her mouth was open; that no words came from it; that she must present a picture of imbecility.

But once again the caped tartan cloak did its office, and Mrs Russell took pity on her. "It's a wet day for standing on doorsteps then, hinney, with the door open wide, and my coffer paste cooling in the draft," she said. "Come you in from the rain, and warm the baby beside my hot range."

"I went first to the cottage, seeing smoke from that chimney; but no one came to the door," blurted Constantia at last, coming in.

"No, only my old mother is there, but she cannot stir from her chair, nor speak a word to you if she did. I am obliged to keep a fire in each kitchen, running back and forth between the two; it seems a sad waste of coal—but we've plenty of that. Miss Huthwaite never grudges us the coal, though she's particular enough about the tea; and the sugar."

"Ah! Your mother . . . Mrs Wilson?"

"Aye," said Mrs Russell, and resumed briskly kneading her hot-water-crust pastry.

"And yourself a Miss Wilson, then, formerly?"

"Of course I was, a long time since; before I was Mrs Forster, and then Mrs Russell. And who might you be?"

"And hadn't you a sister?" said Constantia, trembling. "A very pretty sister, called Polly Wilson?"

Mrs Russell had been standing over her dough, roughly pummeling it with her knuckles, but she now sat down suddenly. "Polly! Why do you talk to me of Polly? Who are you, to talk to me of Polly?"

"I am . . . I am her daughter. And if she was your sister, then you are my aunt. And your mother, down at the cottage, would be my grandmother."

"Polly's girl! Polly! Can it be? It's many a long day! Let me look at you."

Like the man who had looked in her face, at Dil Kusha, all those years ago—as though he might swallow her—so Mrs Russell looked at her. But this time, Constantia gazed back, seeking her mother's likeness in this woman; and finding it.

"My sister's girl!" said Mrs Russell. "My Polly's girl! Preserve us! A tonic for the shock; just a drop. Aye, you must let me pour one for you, too; you with a baby to feed. Well, here's to Polly, then. Polly! And you Polly's girl! . . . How old are you?"

"Twenty-two."

"Born in . . . ?"

"Eighteen twenty-three."

Her glass drained, Mrs Russell gathered up her coffer paste into a rough ball. She divided off a quarter of it and set it aside; the larger portion she then patted flat on her floured table.

"In the Indies."

"Oh aye, we'd thought as much. She will have gone out to the Indies, we said. With him."

"With . . . ?"

"Him." Mrs Russell was now leaning well onto her rolling pin, rolling out the pastry. When it was broad enough and thin enough, she lifted one edge and turned it back over her rolling pin; then, lifting gingerly, she deftly slid the heavy roundel across the top of her wide, deep pie dish.

"My father?"

Mrs Russell patted her coffer paste down into the corners of her dish, and did not reply. She took up a bowl filled with parsleyed potatoes and small gutted, plucked, beheaded, footless birds—squabs— and emptied it, bones and all, into the pastry crust; then she topped it with a generous sprinkling of big sticky flakes of salt from the saltbox beside the range. Turning out the remaining paste onto the floured table, she patted it flat, and began rolling out a lid. "Is she there still?" she asked presently. "In the Indies?"

"My mother died in 1833," said Constantia.

"Oh! We never knew." Mrs Russell downed her rolling pin once more and splashed another dram into her glass. Constantia's nearly-full glass got none.

"No. I am sorry," said Constantia. "I was only ten years old, and none of us—no one knew—to whom to write . . ."

"I cannot say I am surprised. Still, we'd continued to hope, all these years . . . But I think Todd might have let us have a word, a word about it. He need not have grudged us that."

"Miles Todd, was that?"

"Who else?"

"Is that who she went away with?"

Mrs Russell drained her glass instead of replying.

"But he was not my father, was he?" said Constantia.

"Will that be what she told you?"

"She told me nothing. I was only ten years old when she died."

"Poor Polly! What will it be, then, that carried her off?"

(That "carried her off"! Constantia was assaulted by a far-too-vivid image, of her mother being "carried off," by—!) She could not speak.

"One of those fevers, I suppose," said Mrs Russell, easing the edge of her pastry lid backwards over the rolling pin; then she lifted and draped it over her pie.

"I slept last night at Seaton Delaval Hall; the surviving wing," said Constantia.

"Mrs Turnbull . . . ?"

"Treated me kindly."

"Hm! Very fond of gossip, not to say slander. Don't you want your dram?"

"It burns my throat."

"Waste not, want not," said Mrs Russell. "You might have said so. If you're not droothy, I'll drink it for you."

"Do, pray," said Constantia, but she held on to the glass, saying, "I should like very much to know about . . . my mother . . . and my father."

Mrs Russell trimmed the lid with a knife, and crimped its edges neatly to the lower crust. With the round handle of her spoon, she poked a hole in the center; then, from the pile of feathers and potato parings in a basin under the table, she selected a pretty pink curled pigeon's foot, and inserted it in the hole, toes upward.

"About my mother. And . . . my father, Mr Astley," said Constantia.

"What would I know?"

"A sister may know a great deal. A sister may even be trusted with secrets."

"A sister may know how to keep them, too."

"My mother is beyond all harm, now, from their being made known." Constantia slid her glass across the table toward Mrs Russell. "May not the sister's daughter be trusted, as well as the sister herself? A grown daughter, after all these years; myself a mother? Have I not some right to know?"

Mrs Russell swallowed Constantia's dram. "Happen you might," she conceded, reluctantly. Then she opened the hot oven and carefully set the pigeon pie inside. "I've to go down by, and look in on Mother," she said. "Come you with me."

* * *

"Mother, here's one come to call," shouted Constantia's aunt at a crumple of linsey-woolsey slumped in the chair in front of the cottage hearth; and she threw several lumps of coal onto the dull fire.

The old woman stirred in her chair. Constantia saw pale blue eyes, blinking; a skin thin, ashy, deeply wrinkled. No lips showed at the crease of the mouth; they were drawn inward over toothless gums. This crone is my beautiful mother's mother: my grandmother.

"And where will Susan have gone to? She was to have fetched water." Mrs Russell tipped the jug at the back of the stove and, finding it empty, turned her attention back to her mother. "Mother, this is Polly's girl!" she shouted. "Polly's girl, just fancy! And the bairn is your great-grandbairn!" Then, more quietly, to Constantia: "Her eldest? Her only? Aye. Born when, exactly?"

"In the spring of 1823, in Assam," said Constantia. "April first, I've always been given to understand, though there exist no parish registers or anything of that sort to be consulted."

"Aye, that'll be right," said Mrs Russell, counting on nine fingers. "By the end of that July—in 'twenty-two—Polly knew she was in for it. Well, it's not bad blood, the Astleys, no matter which side of the blanket. What are you called?"

"Constantia . . . MacAdam. She christened me Constantia."

"Of all things! She longed for just the thing she could not have, then. Nor to be, poor Polly!"

"But I do not quite understand the timing of all this," said Constantia. "Did my mother and Mr Astley carry on, ah, their courtship, even after the fire?"

"Aye, didn't they. He went away for a few weeks, but returned before the turtle doves in the spring. At the Red House he had to lodge, then—complaining of it, too, as beneath the standard of comfort he had enjoyed at the Hall. But he wasn't often in his lodgings, was he? Him and Polly spent every minute of every day together—and rather too much of those short summer nights, too—as it turned out."

There was a tumult at the door, and then a red-nosed woman let herself in, staggering under a yoke with a sloshing pail of water at each end. "I had to go right up to the well at the church," she explained breathlessly, "because Taylors' cows had got out and fouled the spring again. And then I thought I might just stop at Mrs Reid's for a moment; and as Mr Harvey was there, we got to discussing a point of scripture—Rebecca at the well, in fact!—but here I am at last."

" 'Discussing'! Aye, you mean an hour on your knees, I suppose—and our mother left here alone, with the fire burnt down to nothing."

"Nay, Rose; I built it fairly up before I went out, and I was nowt like an hour."

Mrs Russell turned her back on her sister and, without any effort to introduce or explain, spoke only to Constantia, saying, "Mr Astley had promised to take Polly with him—or so she said. But when it came to it—when his commission came through at last—he sailed away without her. Polly thought she'd die of him leaving, just die of being left. And that's when Miles Todd became convenient again. She'd sent him about his business pretty sharp, the year before . . . but now, now she let him come round again. And didn't he come right along, the gowk! Our mother did her best, too; contriving to leave them alone together—"

"I tried to warn her, didn't I, that Miles Todd was up to no good with Polly," said the red-nosed Miss Wilson.

"Aye, and nearly spoilt all our plans! There you were, keeking and sneaking—in stairwells, behind curtains, spying and darking, carrying tales and tattling! Interfering, and trying to put a stop to—the best thing that could happen!"

"Miles Todd, the best thing? Miles Todd, good enough for our Polly? A fearful come-down he was, after Mr Astley! And so soon!"

"Not a moment too soon, hinney. We were lucky to get her off when we did."

"What can you mean?"

"Just that there was not a day to be lost—for Jack Astley had left her a wee token—a little remembrance of himself—which wouldn't stay hidden under her heart for long . . ."

"Nay, Rose!"

"Oh, aye. And here she is, before you: our niece, Constantia MacAdam—Polly's girl!"

"Nay! But you never told me!"

"Of course I did not; you, a child of eight years. You'd never have held your tongue."

"I have not remained a child of eight years. You might have told me any time since."

"Still cannot hold your tongue."

Livia was fretting and drooling again, and Constantia put her to nurse once more; then said, "My mother sometimes hinted, though, that I was a seven-month baby—in which case I was not conceived until the first of September, or so—"

"Nay," said Mrs Russell, "I daresay she might pretend to Miles Todd that it was a seven-month baby, and he might have believed such a thing. But I remember it all very well. She knew she was in for it by the end of July. It was just after Jack Astley's trustees had finally got him his commission—away he sailed! —and still early in August when she ran off to Scotland with Miles Todd, and the neighbors none the wiser yet. Smart work, even for so pretty a girl as our Polly was then."

"And Mr Astley? What became of him—in India, and after?"

"Oh, he did very well, we heard—he was in Sindh and the Punjab even before the fighting broke out, first as an aide-de-camp, and then had a command of his own. But when his leg was broken—well, no; his pony fell with him, at polo—he never got right again afterwards, and was buried at last at—at—where was it, Susan?"

"At Peshawar," said Miss Wilson promptly. "In the Christian cemetery; you may take some comfort from that."

Whatever troubled Livia, it was not hunger, for she suckled only a minute or two before wailing, arching backward. She did not feel hot, nor cold; she was not wet, nor soiled. At a loss, Constantia offered her breast once more—and then cried out in pain.

"Bit you?" said Mrs Russell. "So did mine—just the once! Teething, is it?"

"At five months?" said Constantia, but she rubbed her fingertip across Livia's lower gum. "Oh! But see these two hard little ridges! Nothing of the kind, three days since!" How precocious she was, this darling daughter! Constantia rubbed Livia's sore red gum, and wiped her chin again.

"It's a coral the bairn will be wanting," said Miss Wilson.

The crumpled old woman blinked; stirred; sat up, just a little, in her chair before the fire.

"A thick trough-shell is just the thing; that's what I gave to mine," said Mrs Russell. "How he cherished it! Carried it about until he was nigh five years old, though the big boys mocked him for it. Aye, those surf clams—so stout, and the shells so ridgy. As many as you want down on the sands after any storm."

The old woman shuddered; and slowly raised a tremulous arm, a palsied claw; her shawl fell from her shoulder.

"Why, Mother! What's the trouble, then?"

The old woman opened her withered mouth, and gave voice: a croak, a bleat. "What's got into her? What is it then, Mother? Whatever does she want? Up there, on the shelf? What, the tea-caddy? No? The Staffordshire jug? Oh, Polly's jug! Lustreware, and far too good to use . . ." Mrs Russell reached it down from the high shelf above the fire, and blew a coating of dust off it. Something rattled inside and she looked into its dark interior. "Bless my soul! Fancy her minding, all these years! I'd forgotten all about it—but here it is still, after all this time: the coral that Jack Astley sent, for Polly's baby. Poor Polly never knew, for it didn't come until too late—long after she'd gone off with Miles Todd."

"For Polly's baby . . ." said Miss Wilson. "But that's yourself, isn't it, ma'am?" she said, turning to Constantia. "Go on; take it. 'Twas meant for you; sent for you. To think that you've turned up, after all! His mysterious ways! Here, take it; do."

Unlike the corals one sometimes saw, bedizened with tiny jingling bells and rattles and whistles, this one was unadorned: slim, straight, plain; quite old-fashioned. The pink coral end was slightly curved, the size, shape and colour of Constantia's smallest finger, but hard and rough as—coral; as pumice stone. The other end was a smooth loop of black metal. She rubbed this and saw the tarnish lift, for it was silver. The tender pink hue of the coral was still pristine, still pink as a maidenly nipple, pale beside the blackened silver; for no baby had ever yet gummed it, chewed it, sucked it, drooled on it, doted upon it. A folded sheet of notepaper was rolled around it, tied with a narrow yellow silk ribbon, very dusty. Constantia untied the ribbon, slid the paper off, unfolded it, and smoothed it flat.

There was a faded handwriting inside the curl of paper. It was a man's handwriting: Astley's handwriting. Her own father's handwriting, handsome, plain and old-fashioned, like the coral. He had written:

A SOLDIER'S WELCOME TO HIS FIRST-BORN,
NEVER SEEN

> *You're welcome, bairn, on Earth's sweet soil,*
> *you pledge and proof of amorous toil!*
> *Brought forth by woman's travail and moil*
> *—Eve's daughters must—*
> *Let new-made fathers then be loyal,*
> *worthy of trust.*
>
> *You're welcome, bairn! Who'd still deplore*
> *such fash and clash as came before?*
> *Though now embarked to distant shore*
> *—life's e'er in doubt—*
> *yet if I'm spared to home once more,*
> *I'll seek you out.*

'Tis pride and joy to claim, as father,
my love-begotten son—or daughter!
Though idle tongues make scornful clatter,
*   citing shame or name,*
I know—none better—'tis no matter
*   how nor when you came.*

God grant that you may full inherit
your mother's looks, her grace and merit!
And your father's heart and spirit,
*   without his faults.*
Our good name, Astley! Blithely bear it
*   e'er in your thoughts.*

—J.A. GRAND CANARY. SEPTR 1822.—

"But where is the letter?" Miss Wilson was saying to her sister.

"A letter there never was," said Mrs Russell repressively.

"Aye, but there was, Rose; a letter came with it, and banknotes, too," insisted Miss Wilson.

"Hush, Susan, you talk too much, and know nothing."

Livia was drooling around her fingers jammed in her mouth. When Constantia placed the tarnished loop of silver into Livia's other hand, Livia grasped it eagerly and brought the coral tip to her sore gums.

Miss Wilson said, "Now then, that's better, isn't it? Heaven be praised! Our Almighty, All-Merciful Father leads our every step! Forsees and prepares! Provides! Smooths our path before us! If only we will submit our will to His! Wonderful are His ways! Wonderful His wisdom and goodness! His mercy! And to think that our mother remembered about that coral, all these years! I do recall my puzzlement when it came; Mr Astley fancied Polly still here with us, no doubt, not married and away—but why a present for a bairn? ... now, I understand. I do think I might have been told sooner. And to think that you, ma'am, should have been led unto us, here, now—and your bairn wanting a coral!"

"Well, and what led you here, to us?" asked Mrs Russell. "After all these years?"

"Chance only," said Constantia, "for I am on my way northward to rejoin my husband; and it was upon the merest impulse, the whim of a moment, that I interrupted my journey here."

"Chance! Whim! Never indeed! Not at all!" cried Miss Wilson. "It is the Divine Will! His design! His Almighty hand directs us all, in every step along our path, in this, our pilgrim's progress, our earthly journey."

"Yet this journey of mine, so happily interrupted here," said Constantia, "must certainly be resumed as soon as possible—by the next mail coach, if I can get a place—for my husband will have been anxiously expecting my arrival these past two days."

"Oh, you can get a place on tonight's coach, I have no doubt," said Mrs Russell warmly. Constantia read relief written plainly upon her face; relief, perhaps, that a husband existed; relief that she and her baby, near kin though they were, did not hope to stay. Probably Mrs Russell was loathe to share what little they had, that little being only just sufficient for the three of them and no more.

Miss Wilson was saying, "I never thought to hear word of our Polly again. Poor Polly! Will it be one of those tropical fevers that's carried her off?"

"No," said Constantia; and then—because they were glad she would not stay, and had not the courtesy to pretend otherwise—she heard herself speaking the excruciating truth: "No; it was a tiger. A tiger carried her off." Her voice sounded remarkably steady. She felt for the gold chain at her neck; felt for the flat-backed pearl suspended from it. By this, her mother's remains had been identified when at last they were found, more than a year after her disappearance during the night of the tremendous earthquake.

(Her mother often went out at night, but she always came back before daybreak—and then slept until a late hour in the morning. People had things to say about that.

Everyone knew it was dangerous to roam abroad at night, when tigers hunted; and only the most daring, or the most desperate, or the most amorous, did so.

Constantia's mother had been more daring than most; and sometimes desperate; but above all, she was amorous. She was made that way. God had seen fit to make her that way. It was her nature.)

"A tiger! A tiger! Oh! May the good Lord have mercy! poor Polly! Did you hear that, Mother? It was a tiger that ate poor Polly, out in India! I never dreamed . . . oh, Polly! May the Lord have mercy upon her soul, poor weak sinner as she was!"

(Eventually, when the immediate emergency of the earthquake had abated, inquiries were made as to the minor mystery of Mrs Babcock's disappearance. The soldier from a nearby garrison town who had been her lover at the time fell under suspicion, naturally enough; but he claimed that she had not come to him that night; had failed to arrive at their usual trysting place, a hut above a waterfall. Supposing that something or someone had delayed her, he had waited for some time, dozing, until, shaken suddenly awake by the prodigious earthquake, he had run back to his barracks, a league off. Not everyone believed him, but nothing could be proven. And in the aftermath of that stupendous earthquake, there were a great many more pressing problems than the disappearance of Constantia's mother.

Could she have been trapped in a fallen building? This seemed possible, at first. One by one, collapsed houses were dismantled, avalanches of bricks cleared, shattered roof beams dragged free; grateful survivors and unlucky corpses were pulled from the wreckage. This went on for weeks. But Constantia's mother was not found in any of these buildings.

Could she have lost her way? This seemed all but impossible. And even if she had, she should have found it again by now.

Constantia had been horror-struck, and terror-struck, and filled with shame at having been so unlovable as to drive her mother away; as to make her mother stay away, all this time. And no one had much time for Constantia just then—except for the Rani Anibaddh, who had brought her to live and study with her own children.

A boy out hunting had finally found her, a year later. A glimmer of scarlet and gold under a tangle of brush had caught his eye; he had investigated; had found what remained of her. The scarlet and gold was the trim of her shawl. She was identified by the shawl, a gift from Anibaddh; and by the gold chain with its pendant pearl, still oddly intact around the crushed vertebrae of her neck. Here the tiger had dragged its kill, and roughly covered it, in case it chose to return later; but it never had. The tiger had eaten only a little of the meat of her haunch; nor had the vultures been at her.

At the base of her skull, amid strands of still-golden hair, were large triangular punctures, where the tiger had seized the back of her neck in its jaws, and crushed her spine. Those punctures to the skull and the crushed spine were conclusive: a tiger did this. Not a leopard; not a sloth-bear. Not a man. The soldier from the nearby garrison was cleared of all suspicion.

How did Constantia know this? No one had been indiscreet enough to tell a child of ten years so much as this. But she did know. She had pieced this much together, from overheard remarks, and other tales of tiger-kills and tiger-hunts, and comments between adults who imagined that so young a child could not understand their cryptic remarks. She was always—always!—listening for anything she could learn; and she understood a great deal more than the adults talking over her head supposed. She pretended not to hear; not to understand; not to be paying attention—for they talked more freely in her presence if they thought her oblivious. She pretended she was playing; she pretended to hum little tunes to herself. But all the time she was listening; and when she lay alone at night—alone! alone! and stroking her own hair, pretending it was her mother's—she fitted together her gleanings: the things she had learned by listening, thinking, and remembering.

That's how she knew so much.

Later, when she was older, she also knew what had driven her mother to go out, those nights. And why she smelled of notherself when she came back; why she slept so late in the mornings. The most beautiful of all the mothers.)

"She's paid dearly for her sins; dearly," said Miss Wilson. "Our pretty Polly, poor dear."

"Nay, my pie!" cried Mrs Russell. "It'll be burnt to cinders—" and out she dashed.

It was near midnight when the mail coach came. Constantia was waiting at the postmaster's fireside, sleepy Livia on her lap, and was very glad this time to get a seat inside the coach. Inside, no one spoke. Through the rest of the night, she dozed with Livia in her arms; and was jostled cruelly awake again and again—again—again! alas!—by the lurching of the coach.

The silver-mounted coral was now tied to Livia's wrist by the yellow ribbon which had come with it. If the coral was a comfort to Livia, the note that had been tied around it was of far greater solace to Constantia. As Livia wrought her sore gums upon the coral, so Constantia considered, again and again, those verses penned by her father. They changed everything. Each time she was awakened, she fell to wondering, marveling, remembering, supposing:

No doubt my mother and my father made me by accident, without any thought of me. Indeed, the thought of me, when the thought—

nay, the fact—of me did eventually dawn upon them, must have appalled them both. I meant ruin; I meant disaster; I meant shame, distress, and dismay. They made me only because they could not help it. They could not help it.

Nevertheless, the man who was my father had (by the time I was born) welcomed me (or, at least, the idea of me) tenderly, affectionately, open-heartedly. The man who was my father: Jack Astley. John Fenwick Astley.

And though Constantia had no proof at all—not a shred of evidence— still she felt certain, entirely certain that the officer who had, in Lucknow, when she was six and a half years old, once held her two hands in his, and gazed into her face as though he would like to drink her up—he had been her father. Father. She felt this to be true. She was certain it was true.

(And this, she knew, was just how the devout believed in their God—in their Heavenly Father. With as scant proof; and with as certain conviction.)

I have met my maker.

An hour later she awakened to the verses her mother used to sing to her:

> *A swain once scorned she's recall'd the next day,*
> *Now she's yielded, she's let* him *take her away*—
> *Across the border to fair Scotland.*
>
> *Comes their firstborn child, a gift from heav'n,*
> *No nine-months' baby—nor scarcely seven!*—
> *Now* she's *the fair flower of Northumberland!*

My mother did tell me, whenever she sang me that song.

At a later waking, she considered this: By chance the snow came early, blocking the roads from Edinburgh, so I came by the Newcastle steam packet instead. By chance, I could not get a seat inside the northbound coach from Newcastle, and had to sit outside. By chance, a scurrilous old woman and a garrulous old man sat up there too. By chance, the road passes near Seaton Delaval, and by chance, these chance fellow-passengers were moved to speak of the ghosts of the Delavals. And because of what I heard, I decided, upon a moment's unpremeditated impulse, to get down there, of all places. I had not intended to do so. It was all chance; all luck. Not design.

Chance! Never, indeed! God's Will! God's design, Miss Wilson had declared, with utter certainty. Her certainty was like Lady Janet's. Constantia here fell into one of her imaginary arguments with Lady Janet:

C, PASSIONATELY CONTRADICTING: Your ladyship may claim
  it is design, if you please; but I see no evidence of it. A
  person who will believe that will believe anything.

LADY J: Surely you do not imagine that mere chance could
  ever have produced such a result! A person who will
  believe that might manage to believe in God; need
  not boggle at God! To swallow so enormous a chain
  of coincidence as that—but strain at a gnat?

C: But chance could indeed produce this result, I say; and here
  is my proof: it did so. Quod erat demonstrandum.

LADY J: Having the last word does not prove you right, not
  even in Latin.

C: I agree; the last word proves nothing. Go on, then; have it
  for yourself.

LADY J: I shall pray for you.

C: I shall make no attempt to stop you.

LADY J: You've still had the last word for yourself, though,
  haven't you!

C, TO PROVE HER WRONG, HOLDS HER IMAGINARY RETORT.

Later still: Never mind who made it. Here is the Thing Itself; study it. The thing itself is worth apprehending. Then, if still we must know who made it—(But why must we? To judge its worthiness? To determine whether it ought to command our reverence? Or our scorn?)—then know this: Within the Thing Itself (be it poem—painting—concerto—or all Creation—All This, this fabric of Nature) lies the answer we seek; the knowledge we crave. Within the Thing Itself lie the clues which tell Who made it. How. Why. The Author always signs his work. The Author cannot help but impress the shape of his hands upon his handiwork—the mold of his mind upon his casting—his signature upon his design. The sprues of the Made all point toward the Maker, the origin. The Made is the Maker, manifest. Seldom obvious; often obscure; but always manifest. We may learn to read the swirl of those cosmic fingerprints; to read the cipher of mountain, valley, river, dust, air, ocean. Exercise patience; exercise it over fleeting centuries—over brief millennia—over epochs and ages. We must release all our preconceived notions about Time; about how long things ought to require; about the interval of time that has already passed, and the interval that remains yet to pass. Time is immeasurably more immense than we have any hope of imagining, even if we were to spend every instant of our whole brief lives doubling and redoubling our conception of it. Which, of course, we won't.

Later again: Why did I long to know? Why had it seemed to matter so?

But all this does matter a great deal. I cannot explain why, but it does. Where have we come from—all of us earthlings? Where are we going, all of us? And why? What is our proper name, the name of our kind?

What are people for? What is the chief end of man?

Even if it were true that every species, in its pride, considers itself the crowning glory of all creation—may not one of them truly be so?

*   *   *

Yet another grievous awakening: The coach rumbled over cobble-stones, to a halt. The new-risen sun blazed mercilessly into Constantia's eyes from across the water.

Amble, at last.

14

THE TOWN OF AMBLE, at the mouth of the River Coquet, looks out to a low white island three-quarters of a mile off-shore: Coquet Isle. Constantia could make out the squat square tower of its lighthouse. So near! But offshore is offshore; a boat must be had. A quantity of suitable small boats bumped and bobbed against their mooring lines in the little harbour. At this hour, their owners were doubtless inside the several nearby public houses taking nourishment—solid and liquid—to encourage and sustain them against the day's rigours. Constantia, however, skirted all these establishments and, with Livia on one arm and the carpetbag on the other, made her way instead up the broad street which led out of the town, up toward the ruins of Warkworth Castle, which presided above the lowest and last bend of the river, before it widened and became harbour—and then, sea.

Some distance below the castle ruin there stood within private walled grounds a substantial farmhouse of moderate size. The gables of the house were pocked with pigeonholes, each underlined by a guano-frosted stone perch; the perches were frequented by grey, white, and blue pigeons, coming and going upon their early-morning pigeon-business. The sign at the open gate read COBB.

It was not, however, old Mrs Cobb who opened the door to Constantia's knock, but a broad-shouldered, sun-burnt, wind-burnt man in his late thirties. "Oh! Mr Darling—" cried Constantia.

"Why, Mrs Stevenson!" he exclaimed, at the same moment.

"The very person—above all others—whom I wished to see!"

"Not the very person above all others," he said. "I might name another whom you will be a great deal happier to see. And as pleased as I am to see you, his happiness is sure to outrun mine by far!"

"I intended to beg a pigeon of Mrs Cobb to fly to you, asking that you would be so good as to come ashore to fetch me off. But here you are, as though summoned by my mere wish. I hope you have not been awaiting me here since Wednesday?"

"No, indeed! Why should I? We had no idea of your returning so soon—not until the New Year, wasn't it?"

"Did not my pigeon arrive, then? I flew my last bird on Monday, to say that I should arrive Wednesday—but once having done so, I was then sorely delayed—detained by one hindrance after another— and have only just descended from this morning's northbound mail coach. Today is . . . ?"

"Saturday; but we have had no bird from you. Well, it is rather fortunate than otherwise; how distraught a certain person would have been, these three days, at your failing to turn up! Can you bear to wait yet another hour? And take some breakfast with Mrs Cobb and me, to beguile the time? By then, the tide will have fairly turned, and I shall undertake to ferry you out to our rock just as smartly as may be. Come in, do; and show Mrs Cobb your pretty bairn!"

Mr William Darling, keeper of the Coquet Isle light, was of the renowned lightkeeping dynasty. He was a brother of the late lamented heroine of the age, Grace Darling; son of the elder William Darling, renowned keeper of the Longstone light; and brother also of (confusingly named) William Brooks Darling, assistant keeper of the Longstone light. All his other brothers and sisters were settled along this Northumberland coast, too, none of them further than a half-mile from the sea. His wife was Ann Cobb Darling, whose mother lived in this farmhouse.

Mr Darling was furthermore staunchly Chartist in his principles; and a brave, loyal, and discreet friend to Constantia's Chartist husband, for whose detention a warrant on charges of sedition, conspiracy, and treason was still, after four years, in effect.

Within the hour, Mrs Stevenson, Livia in her arms, was seated in the stern of Mr Darling's coble, and Mr Darling was rowing briskly out of the harbour. To row three-quarters of a mile over open sea was nothing to a Darling—though on his own account he might, but for Mrs Stevenson's eagerness, have awaited a sailing breeze. The coble was laden with coals, nails, bacon, turpentine, yeast, tallow, a sheet of glass, and a carefully crated and tarpaulined object: Mrs Darling's Christmas present. Half a mile out, they came to ruffled water and a lively breeze; and here Mr Darling, having boated his oars, hoisted a sail and took sheet and tiller in hand for the remainder of the crossing.

At the Coquet Isle landing-place, the breeze was a wind which tore at Constantia's bonnet. As soon as Mr Darling had tied off the coble to a cleat, he handed Constantia ashore. "Now, ma'am, you must run right up," he said, "don't you wait for me. Run up and get a cloak at the house—and then off you go! You know where he'll be." Then she was in the lee of the wall (white and fine-grained as bread, this Coquet Isle limestone)—and the stout timber door of the house was opened to her knock—by Mrs Darling, surprised (for visitors were so rare as to be all but unknown)—yet astonished, delighted! and unembarrassed even at being caught with her eider-downs ranged across chairs in front of the fire—because Mrs Stevenson, having lived here for some time during the summer, knew very well that Mrs Darling always aired her eider-downs thus every morning. Mrs Stevenson and her darling baby!

"Shall I take you there?" offered Mrs Darling, after their first greeting. "Of course not; you know the way as well as I. But bide a moment, hinney, for an over-cloak, and cover your bonnet. And the bairn? No, take her to him, to be sure!"

Constantia set off northward up the spine of the island, with the wind buffeting her back, and the canvas over-cloak billowing like a spinnaker. The rabbits on the close-cropped green machair scattered at her approach, and the birds rose up before her, taking to this air— this steady wind—without laborious graceless flapping or beating or hopping, but effortlessly, merely by opening their wings to the wind; by embracing it. Gulls, terns, ducks, pigeons, guillemots, eiders—all rose from the earth before her in swarms, in clouds, in their heavenly hosts, mewing and crying. The low green grass and the rocks were all spattered white and grey; the reason for the over-cloak. Birds hung motionless in the sky, facing the wind, balancing there. At a mere hitch of their feather-mail shoulders, they slewed down sideways and crossways; at a shrug they rose, they descended. At will, they dove, they plummeted; from time to time they beat laboriously upwind or crabbed up crosswise, like sailboats beating up into the wind. They cast themselves upon the air in perfect faith, certain of being borne up by it as a skiff is borne up by water; they lay upon the wind as easily as they sat upon their nests—in their thousands on this small rock alone.

It was not far to the north end of little Coquet Isle, to the place where two clefts in the rock run inland: a pair of deep narrow gorges; grykes. His derrick marked the spot: sturdy poles, tackle, and a winch, set up inside one of the grykes, for heavy lifting.

He was here, down in the cleft of the rock below her, out of the wind. She saw his shining head, his brown hair tied at the nape of his neck, uncut since she had last cut it for him, six months since. Hugh's back was to her; he did not see her approach, nor could he hear her footfalls for the wind rushing above his head; nor did her shadow fall across him. Sunshine lay across his rolled-up shirtsleeves; illuminated the pale hairs springing from his forearms. He was murmuring to himself as he toiled there in that moist cleft of the earth—wielding hammer, file, chisel, brush. A few words came to her on the air: very private words, as from love-damp sheets: "Come on, come on up my darling . . ." How rare, how precious, to see him all alone (or so he thought) all unconscious of another; he was only himself, at his most engrossed. Constantia stood mute and still, watching him for some moments. She could not say how long. How could he not feel her here? But he did not; and did not; and still did not.

Until a rock gave way—a bird shrieked—a pebble rolled—suddenly he awakened from his working dream, his lover's dream and, looking up, saw her. Saw them both.

> *O my dove, that art in the clefts of the rock,*
> *in the secret places of the stairs,*
> *let me see thy countenance, let me hear thy voice;*
> *for sweet is thy voice, and thy countenance is comely.*

> *O my dove.*

The square stone tower from which the Coquet Isle light shone out over the sea was medieval, a vestige of the monastery which had stood here since before the time of the Danish hermit Saint Henry; but the light itself was quite new, fitted out only four years before by the Trinity House engineers. In the lantern atop the newly whitewashed tower was a set of stationary argand lamps fitted with large reflectors. These lamps burned expensive sperm oil—gallons and gallons of it—which arrived in barrels on Trinity House barges according to schedule, to be stored in a vaulted chamber beneath the stone tower. It was the duty of the keeper—Mr Darling—to light the lamps each evening at sunset, and to ensure that they continued to burn all night, and every night. The sperm oil was not always perfectly pure; the wicks did not always draw evenly; and even these excellent new argand lamps had their quirks, and required some nocturnal vigilance. Immediately after sunrise he was to extinguish them, trim their wicks, polish the greasy smut from their chimneys and reflectors, and leave all in spotless readiness for the next lighting. He was to repair the damage when flying birds crashed through the glass of the lantern. When passing vessels got into trouble, he was if possible to aid them; to rescue men, rigging, cargoes. And he was required to submit frequent reports to his masters at Trinity House as to the rate at which official supplies were consumed; this was a matter of constant interest to them. The keeper was allowed discretion to light the lamps before sunset or leave them burning after sunrise if a storm made the day very dark, but this was not to happen often, and the masters kept a close watch on expenses. Trinity House provided a dwelling for the keeper and his family; their painters painted it; their slaters kept a roof on it. Trinity House paid his salary of 40 pounds annually, and furnished an allowance of coal for his household; drinking water if the rains failed or if high ocean waves washed into the holding tanks; and a new suit of clothes for himself (though not for the members of his family) each January.

The essence of his duty was to make sure that his light shone without fail during the hours of darkness. To mariners, an intermittent or unreliable light was worse than no light at all. Upon pain of dismissal, he was not to leave the island unless some competent deputy remained to tend the light. In practice, he often did leave the island for several consecutive days and nights, relying always upon his exceedingly competent wife.

The island was—had long been—the property of the Dukes of Northumberland, who generally let out the right to quarry its stone and minerals. Coquet Isle limestone was prized because it was strong, sound, and nearly white; easy to work when first quarried, but becoming both whiter and harder after exposure to weather. The battlements of Syon House outside of London are built of Coquet Isle stone. In 1820, the then-duke had granted a thirty-year lease to a Mr George Stevenson, master mason, quarrymaster, stone-broker. Upon Stevenson's death in 1840, his son in the same trade had inherited the lease's remaining term, along with other valuable quarry properties from Edinburgh to Newcastle. This son—Hugh Stevenson by name—had taken up the Chartist cause; had been so bold as to stand for the Edinburgh seat against Mr Macaulay in the 1841 election; but had fallen afoul of the law—and had in 1842 disappeared. It was supposed that he, like so many other Chartists, had fled to France.

And so he had, for several years.

But by midsummer in 1845, he had quietly returned to Coquet Isle with his new bride. This was a deep secret, as the warrant for Mr Stevenson's arrest was still in effect. Only the lightkeeper and his family knew; and made room for them (unbeknownst to the masters of Trinity House) in the lodging newly built for some hypothetical assistant lightkeeper, not yet appointed.

Briefly, very briefly, was Livia bashful with this new stranger, her father. Quickly she became enamoured of him, even coquettish; quite as enamoured as he was, of her. Encouraged by him, she would babble: Da da da da da da da! She kindled when she saw him; craned to watch him as he moved about the room; and it was while bounced upon his knee that she first laughed, a merry chuckle. When she laughed, the most beguiling dimples appeared in her plump cheeks, to match the one in her chin. Dimples in her cheeks! Constantia marveled that she had not known this about her daughter until now.

As Hugh and Constantia had been unable to communicate during their long separation, except by the four pigeons Constantia had taken with her, they had a great deal to tell each other. All day they talked as they worked side by side, and in bed at night, they still talked. Oh, that bed! The plain bedstead was of stout oak; the featherbeds piled upon it were lofty. The sheets were linen. The pillows and the coverlet were filled with eider-down. There was a north-facing window, and from the bed, stars could be seen wheeling about their hub in the northern sky. This lodging (new-built for some future assistant lightkeeper, in the ruins of the fifteenth-century chapel, and at some distance from the Darlings' house) had thick stone walls; the Stevensons knew they could not be overheard.

"It may yet be nothing," murmured Hugh one night in the darkness of their little bedroom. Rain rattled against the windowpanes; Livia, asleep in an open trunk at the foot of their bed, stirred, sighed, and slept on. "It may prove to be devoid of any interest or importance to anyone; only a fool's errand, a child's delusion, a great waste of my time and, what's worse, of yours."

"On the other hand," said Constantia, "it may prove of immense value and significance! Matchless, peerless, incomparable! Unimagined, and unimaginable, until now!"

"It had better be—as it kept me from your side at a time when I ought not to have been separated from you."

"What choice had we? We were compelled to separate."

"All you suffered, and alone . . ."

"I was not alone; I was surrounded by friends, the kindest friends anyone ever had."

"If I had known!"

"I am glad you did not. It would have changed nothing. Nothing. You could not have saved our son. Very often, I was glad that you were spared—"

"That I was spared what you had to bear. But if it should turn out that while you have been off producing this Incomparable Treasure— our Livia—and I, meanwhile, have only been trespassing upon the Darlings' hospitality these long months, and neglecting my duty to you, so as to devote myself to extracting what may prove to be nothing more than a vast quantity of—of useless rubble!"

"Well—and if so?"

On another night (this one still and cold, under the last full moon of the year), Hugh, awakened by the dazzle of moonlight splashed across his face, turned over and found Constantia awake too, silent tears glistening on her cheeks. He sought her hand curled against her chest in the warm envelope of their bed, and drew it to his lips. "Was he christened?" he whispered, presently.

"No. No, he never was."

"What name had you given him, though, in your mind?"

She shook her head, and smiled sadly. "I have never yet brought myself to say his name," she said. "Even now, when he is beyond all harm. Absurd of me . . ." And so it was. But it was very strong, this instinct to protect the helpless newborn. A baby's name must never be spoken aloud until it has been taken to church and placed under divine protection by christening. "A friend—a piper—played a traditional lament for him when he was buried," she said. "A lament composed for the infant son of some highland chief, I was told."

"'Maol Donn.' Was it 'Maol Donn'? Like this?" Quietly, Hugh voiced the long plaintive first phrase of that old lament.

"It might have been that—but those bagpipe tunes all sound very much alike to me," confessed Constantia.

"'Maol Donn' means 'God's monk, the tonsured one—the bald one.' That's how superstitious old wives refer to an unchristened baby boy, so as to confound the malevolent spirits who would steal him away if they could: 'the bald little monk.'"

After some time, she whispered, "David Alan Stevenson."

"Davey," breathed Hugh. "Our bald wee monk."

"Yes, he was quite bald," said Constantia.

The Darlings and the Cobbs all kept pigeons, not only for eggs and meat, but because pigeons—unlike hens—could be trusted to carry messages. (How comical, the idea of hens—bustling, silly, maternal, foolish, waddling stout hens—carrying messages! Hens, flying! Hens, finding their way, anywhere!) The old monastery dovecot housed Mrs Darling's flock; these pigeons were at liberty to come and go as they pleased; to rustle in and out the little doors in its cupola; to take to the open sky in any weather, of their own free will. They always came in to roost each night just about the time the lamps were lit. Here they chose their mates, built their nests, and raised their squabs. They fed upon grain and washed in water which providentially appeared (provided by Mrs Darling). They built their sketchy nests from straw and twigs they found (set out here and there by Mrs Darling). Sometimes their eggs or their squabs vanished into thin air (taken by Mrs Darling, for reasons inscrutable to pigeons).

But in other, smaller pens were confined other pigeons, pigeons denied the liberty of the sky, because they had been hatched not here, but in the dovecots of other Darlings and Cobbs elsewhere. Those birds longed to return to their native places; if let loose, they could not help but make the attempt. Consequently they could be relied upon to deliver messages promptly to, from, and between those offshore islands rarely served by Her Majesty's mails. When paying visits to one another, the Cobbs and the Darlings generally ferried along a crate of fresh birds to be left, thus replenishing each other's stock for the carrying of future messages. The canny Rothschilds could not have been better organised. The pigeons that Constantia had taken to Edinburgh were of course Coquet Isle–born birds; Mrs Darling's birds.

This homing impulse of pigeons was, like many other truths, only generally true; only somewhat true. It could not be strictly true— or how could pigeons have spread over the whole world? If it were strictly true, they should all, all be in their ancestral place still, the place of their original progenitors.

It had been suggested to the doctor at Amble (a man unfortunately hostile to Chartism, and Chartists) that he distribute pigeons of his own raising to his patients in the district, so that he might be sent for quickly and easily when needed. Somehow this excellent idea had not caught on.

Columba livia is the Linnaean name of these birds, these blue rock pigeons. *Livia* means "blue."

* * *

What is so delightful as to come in from wind and rain? To latch a stout door, two planks thick, against the gale and draw the quilted portiere across it; to doff cloak and bonnet; to enter a warm parlour where a coal fire glows? The wind may whistle and moan atop the chimney, but here the stone walls are three feet thick, and a woven grass mat covers the flagged floor where the children play—without shrieks or tears, at this moment. Their industrious thrifty mother sits under the window, recessed in its deep embrasure of stone, to stitch a ticking. The gale may howl under the eaves; rain and sleet may pelt the window panes; but within, all is warmth and homely comfort. The industrious thrifty mother (not elegant, but resourceful, patient and good) pauses in her work to fill a cup for her guest, who is very glad to get it—and the last potato bap, still warm in its serviette.

"Three times today have I smashed my poor thumb with a hammer," declared Constantia, exhibiting the thumb wrapped in a strip of linen—"thank you, Mrs Darling, so good of you to have saved a bap for me—and I cried tears the third time. I could not help it, for the pain and vexation. Now I am excused from further mayhem, until tomorrow." She opened her bodice and put Livia to nurse. Livia still liked to touch the pearl pendant while she nursed, although she now wore a neat little necklace of her own, of St Cuthbert's beads—fossil crinoids—that her father had gathered and strung for her. "But we have very nearly finished crating up my husband's treasures," said Constantia. "I cannot express, Mrs Darling, how sorry I shall be to leave your snug island again so soon."

"Poor Mrs Stevenson!" said Mrs Darling. "Only just fled from dull Edinburgh—and bound next to dreary Paris! I suspect you, hinney, of trying to make me content with my lot. I assure you it is quite unnecessary, for, strange though it may seem, I am content already."

"And why not? Edinburgh and Paris have their charms, of a kind," said Constantia, "but for perfect homely comfort and the most complete seclusion, I should always choose just such a cosy lightkeeper's cottage as this, on just such an island—and with just such good and kind companions, too."

"Aye, an island is a pleasant private place—until the doctor is wanted. Then, it's hoist the signal and hope for fair seas. How very sorry I was—very unhospitable indeed!—to send you off as we did. But I should have felt myself quite unfit to attend alone at the birth of twins, in case something went wrong."

"I am convinced that I should never have been safely delivered without a doctor's attendance. And my old friend Mrs MacDonald was very good to me."

"And so, too, were you, to her friend, to whom you went in her time of need." Setting aside needle and thread, Mrs Darling took up a plump paper packet and carefully cut a slit in it with her scissors; then she patted its contents into the ticking she had made. Inevitably, some airy tufts of eider-down escaped, and danced erratically about the parlour, rising or falling upon the air currents. Laughing, her children chased these elusive faeries.

"It looks rather small," said Constantia of the ticking, which Mrs Darling now held up.

"Just the size for a bairn," said Mrs Darling. She crimped together its open edges, and commenced to sew it shut. "A bairn called Livia Stevenson." All the Darlings slept under coverlets filled with eider-down, for, after the fledging season, industrious Mrs Darling would gather the down left in the nests of the Coquet Isle eider ducks; wash and dry it; and sell on any excess not required in her own household.

Eider ducks line their nests with down plucked from their own breasts. What are their sensations upon performing this painful rite? What inner compulsion moves them? Why do other sea birds along this cold wet coast not do the same?

The littlest girl, knocked down in the rough play, toddled crying to her mother, who set aside her work and lifted her onto her lap. "Hush, Gracie, hush, lassie," she said. This littlest Darling was the namesake of her intrepid aunt, the one who had died (a maid) three years before. "Oh dear; sopping wet again, already. Are those clooties dry yet, Mrs Stevenson? Can you reach them?"

"Nearly dry," said Constantia, feeling the small-clothes drying on the rack close to the fire beside her. The laundry was a constant chore with babies in the house, and while the washing was arduous enough, the drying was more difficult still, during these stormy winter months.

"Off my lap now, Gracie; here, you may play with this bobbin. Well, Mrs Stevenson, my husband and I have been talking about your husband's limestones, and we hope they will enjoy the greatest possible success among those savants in Paris."

"Yes, so do we; and though limestones to Paris might seem as coals to Newcastle, we cherish hopes for un succès éclatant, for these particular specimens."

"They are no ordinary rocks, he tells me."

"No, quite extraordinary indeed, these particular rocks. Hugh says that when, as a boy, he first discovered fossil deposits in these grykes, he was frightened by them—by the monstrosity of them— and, putting them out of his mind as soon as he could manage it, quite succeeded in forgetting all about them. It was not until he encountered the fossil collections at the Muséum in Paris, two or three years ago, that he thought of them again; not until then did he wonder whether the curious vestiges he had seen here on Coquet Isle—though useless as building stone—might prove precious indeed, to the savants. And so, Mrs Darling, your brave and generous hospitality has been rewarded by our trespassing upon it for longer, rather longer than any of us had anticipated."

"Not at all; nothing; a pleasure," demurred Mrs Darling, embarrassed.

"No, you never can bear to be thanked. But these petrified remains of a vanished creature from the deepest past which he has so laboriously retrieved might be . . . it is possible—more than possible, Mrs Darling—that they will prove to be of very great significance. And perhaps quite valuable too. Or so we dearly hope."

On another of those long winter nights abed, Constantia told Hugh the facts that had so fortuitously come to light regarding her parentage. "Not to mince words," she concluded, "I am, almost certainly, the bastard of a bastard. There, I have bravely confessed; can you cherish me still?"

"Of course," he said. "How could any of that make any difference at all?"

"Does it not matter? I wonder. It did seem exceedingly important to learn who made me."

"Oh, that is important, undoubtedly. Facts do matter. Ascertaining facts—what actually happened—is important, and valuable. I mean only that this question of legitimacy, or of illegitimacy, matters not at all. Not to me."

"To our children?"

"Nor to our children."

They lay in silence for a time. Presently, Hugh said, "But as for that foolish housekeeper's tale about a chimney fire started by a jackdaw's nest . . . it strikes me as most unlikely, my dear. It is far more probable that the builders were to blame. In many of those large old houses built in the last century, such as Seaton Delaval Hall, the flues ran more nearly horizontal than is nowadays deemed prudent. It is difficult to line such flat flues properly, and the masons may well have failed to fully sequester the structural timbers from the heat of the fires. Over a period of years those dry timbers are roasted, little by little, into charcoal—until, some cold windy night, with a good fire roaring, the timber finally ignites, thoroughly and irrevocably. There is no hope of extinguishing any such fire as that; the house burns down—and jackdaws bear the blame. As no one was present when the fire started, its origin cannot be known with certainty. But even if your mother had been in the room, nothing that she or anyone else could have done would stop such a fire. Your mother and your father may have been guilty of certain small and very common failings, but I doubt that they were to blame for burning down Seaton Delaval Hall. And as to their sin in making you . . . for that, my dear, I am more inclined to gratitude than to reproach."

Constantia kissed the palm of his hand. It was rough, yellow-calloused.

Presently he added, "But the most fascinating aspect of all this, I think, is the unlikeliness of your discoveries. I mean the scantness of the chance, the faintness of the whisper of happenstance by which all this obscure history has been opened to you."

"Uncanny, isn't it."

"It is that."

"It is nearly enough to make one wonder . . ." she said.

"Very nearly."

One day soon after this she showed him the verses "A Soldier's Welcome to his First-Born, Never Seen" in her father's handwriting. He was moved; but some time later, he said, "Yet it is striking, too, to note the resemblance which those verses bear to the well-known verses composed by Mr Robert Burns when—well, upon a similar occasion."

"Do they? Well-known, you say? Not to me."

"There is a strong resemblance to Burns's verses, if my memory serves me—and yet, they are quite distinct. I suppose that your father must have known of Burns's effort, and taken them as his model when he composed these—his own—for you."

Constantia told Hugh about Adam's Game, and the various names for humankind that she had heard proposed by the Chambers family and their friends. "What name did you propose?" Hugh asked her.

"None, at the time," said she. "But I have been pondering the matter ever since, and refining my ideas, and have arrived at last, I think, at a proposition which may have some merit. Shall I tell you? I should propose to call our kind *Homo contumax*; that is, the earthling which seeks to overthrow natural law; to overthrow the processes of all creation, of all the universe; to fight its forces; to thwart nature, to master it; and thus, to change and improve upon it."

"Mm . . . There is a bold claim to make for our kind. But let us argue a little, to test the fitness of this idea. It seems to me that other species have changed this earth, and the conditions upon it, far more profoundly than humankind has ever yet done—and that without any design to do so; quite without intent. Consider, pray, all those earliest organic forms—the corals, crinoids, conchs, crustaceans—which first drew the dissolved calcium from the primordial waters, and concentrated it to form their own bodies; those bodies, those carapaces and shells in their countless multitudes, over countless millennia, have drawn calcium from the waters—thus changing the very chemistry of the oceans—and have compiled it, gathered it, collected it, as a solid instead. The remains of these calcareous-bodied creatures drifted down, down, layer upon layer—upon countless layers—to be compacted, during countless ages, to form stone: limestone—chalk, clunch, ordinary limestone of every kind, and marble—now so common upon and within the crust of our earth . . . Or, if you prefer, let us consider the colossal vegetal exuberance—gigantic ferns, immense palms, and other forms of which we have no memorial—which evidently once covered all the lands, wet and dry, torrid at every latitude from pole to pole; a vegetation which drew into itself during long ages vast quantities of carbonic acid gases from the atmosphere—as the atmosphere was then composed—and which, during millennia of decay and compression, have since been transmuted to coal beds—so that by now, still sequestering in their fossil remains those enormous quantities of carbonic acid gases, they have rendered the earth's atmosphere—the air that we now breathe—fit to breathe. No, my dear, it will not be easy to convince me that humankind has, or will ever have, sufficient power to wreak any changes upon the natural world on a scale comparable to those previously wrought, entirely without purpose or intent, by shellfish—and by plants! By the lordly ranks of shellfish and plants!"

"Well," said Constantia, when at last she had an opening, "I see that you, sir, are what Lady Janet would call a Rank Materialist. You are immune to my poesy; deaf to my lyrics; determined to examine ponderous facts, and not to be borne airily aloft by any buoyant theories. Of course you are quite right. And yet! And yet! We are the ones, you must admit, who would reverse the spinning of the galaxies. We would bring it all to a shuddering stand-still . . . and then, slowly, slowly, reverse it in its courses. We would change nature; would remould the universe and everything in it according to our own ideas of how it ought to be. We would recreate it as Just. We—our kind, *Homo displiceo*, the dissatisfied earthling—would create a universe in which individuals are important; where each one actually matters."

"Oh! Yet among pigeonkind, as well as humankind, you know, individuals do matter. Even pigeons choose a particular, an individual mate, and remain more or less faithful, as long as they both do live."

"You are exceedingly squashing," said Constantia. Still, privately, she continued to ponder and cherish her idea, for she could not think of a better.

Some days later, while he was splitting a plank into battens for his packing cases, Hugh suddenly looked up and said, "*Homo ruptor.* We break things."

"But that is the same thing," said Constantia, "as what I said. It is reversing the courses of nature, don't you see? Undoing what has been done. Unwinding what has been wound. Putting asunder what has been joined together. *Homo domitor.*"

What of the pigeon that did not arrive at Coquet Isle, the last pigeon Constantia had flown from Edinburgh? Was it killed by a goshawk? What of the fragile slip of paper tied to the pigeon's leg? Was it torn, bloodied, and discarded by the hawk? Was it dropped unregarded to the ground; rain-wetted, ink-run; salvaged by a mouse for its nest; shredded; eaten; and—as mouse-dung—disintegrated to dirt?

Or was the pigeon perhaps daunted instead by the wind, and the expanse of the sea? Did it abandon its journey and form an attachment to an unmated male dwelling in a chalky cliff near Siccar Point? Did the new-mated pair build their nest and successfully raise offspring? Was the message tied around its leg soon lost in the wind? Did the ribbon which tied it eventually rot and fall away?

This is not known. No record has been found. No fossil has been found. Many facts are lost beyond finding—but they remain facts nonetheless; facts known to no one.

Oh, that stout oak bed! The nights now, at midwinter, were long, very long, and, while Livia slept, this bed was Hugh and Constantia's haven, their paradise, their refuge; the private theatre of their ardent joy.

To her own surprise, Constantia savored—far more now than when she had first been married—an increasing carnal appetite. The long nights were not long enough; and sometimes, as she worked at Hugh's side during the day, a sudden flush of desire for him would be sparked by the sight, perhaps, of the play of muscle in his forearms below his rolled-up shirtsleeves. And this imperative appetite, Constantia now knew, was just what had always—always!—moved her mother, that beautiful amorous mother (who, unlike Constantia and Hugh, had never been properly married at all, though she hadn't known it). Indeed, it was just this abandon which had finally proven fatal to her mother. Now that Constantia herself enjoyed the same peremptory hunger, she knew she would eventually have to forgive her mother everything; forgive even her dying, that final abandonment.

Who claws at the earth as the quarryman does? Defaces and mauls its pages as the quarryman does? What tremendous fossils have quarrymen not cut to pieces—smashed to shards—used as ballast or roadbed—or thrown away as useless rubble, all these centuries? As the puppy chews the book?

What is revealed? What remains concealed? What is destroyed, irrevocably? All depends upon how the matrix is sliced; how it is teased apart.

Constantia helped to crate up the stones—the Useless Rubble—that Hugh had so painstakingly extracted from the gryke at the north end of the island. Embedded still in its ancient limestone matrix, broken but complete, was a petrified creature some five or six feet across. In the belly of this beast were the most astonishing things of all.

On a moonless night just after the New Year, 1846, a French lugger drew in by prearranged signal to the Coquet Isle landing, where Hugh's derrick and crated cargo waited, ready. It took all night to load and secure this heavy cargo. The lugger—with three Stevensons aboard—did not get under sail again until shortly before daybreak. For some time Hugh and Constantia, looking aft, could make out Mr and Mrs Darling still waving their last farewells, smaller and smaller upon their diminishing white isle astern. Then, just as a brilliant scarlet crust of sun pushed upward, emerging from the pewter sea ahead, Constantia looked back in time to see the Coquet light extinguished. Extinct.

The heavily-laden lugger sailed rather deep and sluggish, a cause of some consternation to her captain, a M. St Clair of Le Havre, particularly as the barometer was falling rapidly. Across a fresh northeast wind they sailed southward, into a cliff of dark cloud.

15

R AIN SOON ENVELOPED the French lugger, and for four days
and three nights she beat doggedly into it. On the evening of
the fourth day, by providential design, or good luck, or superior seamanship—or all three—her captain got her into Le Havre
on the last possible moment of slack tide before the ebb. By that time,
Constantia's fingertips were wrinkled with the constant wet; and so,
she saw, were Livia's. And still the rain lashed down, so that Constantia was immensely grateful when Hugh proposed an overnight halt
at Havre. Captain St Clair readily agreed, for his house and family
were here, and he invited the Stevensons—mère, père, et enfant—to
come eat, sleep, and dry themselves at his house. But when Constantia learned that his wife had been unwell for some while, she insisted
upon going instead to the principal inn of the port.

They arrived just too late for the table d'hôte dinner, but in good
time for the ceremonial cutting of the galette des rois, for the date was
the 6th of January: La Fête des Rois, the feast of the three kings. Constantia nibbled dutifully at her slice of galette until another guest—a
pretty young bride—let out a whoop of triumph, having bitten down
upon the fève, and was duly crowned queen. Thus relieved of obligation, Constantia relished the remainder of the almond cake; then,
leaving Hugh to disparage the disgusting weather with the other

men, she carried Livia upstairs. Their bedchamber at the back of the inn overlooked only a small yard, and was quiet. A fire burned in the grate, and a basin and jug of fresh water stood on a washstand. She undressed Livia and sponged away the salt of the past three days; then rinsed her own hair, too. Then, dragging the washstand near the fire, she draped all their clothing over it. Steam rose; and she and Livia fell asleep to the homely smell of drying wool; and to the rattle of rain still pelting the window panes. Hugh slid into bed beside her sometime during the night.

Rain was still falling steadily next morning when they re-embarked for Rouen, just behind the rising tide. The mascaret between Havre and Rouen, like the tidal bore at Calcutta, was not to be trifled with. It could and often did capsize small craft, and tore larger ones from their moorings; and in ascending the river, its effects were more pronounced—as the channel became narrower and shallower—all the way up to Rouen. Captain St Clair timed their departure so as to ride along just behind this rising tide, borne easily upstream upon its surge. At first the river resembled a broad estuary, its banks some three miles apart—until suddenly at Quillebeuf it narrowed to less than a mile.

As the morning wore on, the rain became intermittent, sometimes relenting for entire quarters of an hour at a time. When visible, the river banks here were delightfully picturesque. But alas, the castles, hills, trees, villages, and miles of chalk cliffs under which they passed had mostly to be taken upon faith, for they were so heavily shrouded in clouds, rain, fogs, and mists that Constantia felt herself transported back to the Meghalaya of her childhood: the Abode of Clouds and Mists.

Was there ever so leisurely and meandering a river as the lower Seine? On a bulkhead in the cabin was tacked a chart showing its course—which resembled nothing so much as cranial sutures, the seams where the plates of a skull knit themselves together. Dozing the afternoon away, Livia at her breast, Constantia relinquished first her sense of direction, losing track of the points of the compass—for on so winding a river, the sun and the wind might come from any direction, at any time; only the current held steady; and not so very steady at that. Then she relinquished her convulsive grip on place, and time. What river do we ascend? Is this the Hooghly? Brahmaputra? Ganges? Perhaps this is the Goomtee, at Lucknow?

She awakened unmoored, adrift—but Livia slept within the parenthesis of her arm. A porthole opposite her berth showed sky, clear and blue; showed white cliffs and the hanging woods of the river banks, fresh-washed. Is this still Tuesday? or perhaps it may be Wednesday? Is it early morning, or late afternoon?

Hugh appeared suddenly, filling the hatchway, eager, red-nosed. It was still the afternoon of the 7th of January; and the place was Duclair, a village of no importance a few miles below Rouen. "Have I awakened you?" he said. "I am sorry. I have just been ashore to make some inquiries, and I have a proposal to lay before you. My dear, I should not like you to feel deserted in the least, and you've only to say a word and I shall gladly relinquish my plan. But if you are willing to dispense with me for a few hours—well, perhaps even overnight—I should like very much to make a quick jaunt up to Barentin to see the works going forward there. Barentin? Just five or six miles up the Austreberthe, the stream which empties itself here into the Seine, you see. And then I shall rejoin you at Rouen, if not tonight, then before breakfast tomorrow morning, at latest. The road is not too bad, and I've arranged for a post-chaise."

"A post-chaise . . . Has it a hood? We could go with you then, Livia and I," said Constantia—though, as she spoke, she feared to see his face fall at her proposal.

Instead, he brightened, saying, "I should like it above anything!— unless it may be too cold for our wee lass?"

"This, cold? No, my dear; I assure you this is quite nearly warm, compared to our journey to join you on Coquet Isle. Look, even the rain has stopped—for now." So they all three set off by post-chaise,

Hugh having arranged with Captain St Clair to rejoin the vessel and its cargo up at Rouen.

"Here, as anyone may see, is the turning to the quarry—my quarry," said Hugh, where the road—pretty fair thus far despite the wet weather—suddenly became a morass of muddy ruts and mire. "And still in heavy use, it would seem. Do you mind, my dear, if we turn in here for just a few moments? It is not far to the work-face."

Constantia had no objection; indeed, she was interested in seeing this quarry where Hugh had formerly been the master—until that hot disagreement with Mackenzie, his one-time employer.

As the chaise drew to a halt in the wide turning yard—plenty of room for turning teams and wagons—Constantia could hear drills and hammers. The neatly stepped cliff-face, rain-soaked, rose streaky grey to the grey sky: a gigantic staircase which dwarfed the tiny men who were blasting, shaving, chipping, and drilling shards off it. "I daresay he'll stand," said Hugh, handing her the reins as he got down. Indeed, the meager hired horse seemed only too glad to stop. Across the wide yard stood a laden wagon; a team of heavy horses was being backed into position before it by a couple of teamsters, probably Irish to judge by the oaths they swore at the horses. Another wagon, its wheels well-chocked, was positioned under a loading dock, and was being loaded by men who cautiously manoeuvred a large block of stone on stout timber rollers. The rattle of another vehicle driving in at an urgent pace made Hugh look about smartly—but it was only a wagon returning empty.

Someone recognised Hugh—hailed him—and fetched the foreman, a Frenchman who came forward to shake hands. They exchanged some quiet words, nearly out of earshot, and Constantia could hear little of what they said—but it struck her that there was no laughing or joking; they were quite serious. Hugh's back was to her and she could not hear him, but she could make out this much, from the foreman: "Non, he is not about the line at all, these four or five days—non, tormenting his brother down on the Bordeaux line, on dit—unless it may be that he is having another tooth pulled from his head. Bien entendu, he may turn up at any moment, just when one supposes him at some safe distance."

Between the two of them there was considerable gesturing and pointing—toward the rock face, toward the wagons, toward various distant places or persons unseen. They planted their feet wide apart, taking up a doughty stance, heads sagely nodding, then shaking, then nodding again. They crossed their brawny arms (it is familiar knowledge that quarrymen have brawny arms) across their chests. Then they ascended the steps beside the loading dock to inspect the stone blocks being loaded onto the wagon. Frowns; then the quick flash of a grin. Eventually there was a shaking of hands again in parting, and Hugh returned to Constantia and the chaise. Taking the reins from her, he started the horse once more, but said nothing until they had regained the main road and turned up to continue toward Barentin. "We've only to follow the ruts in the road," he said then. "Warm enough, you and the wee lass?"

"Quite."

"That'll be our stone," he said presently, as they drove past a small farmhouse and its outbuildings, all surrounded by a low wall, all in white stone. "From our quarry."

"Is it? It looks ever so stout and reliable—to me, at least."

"Aye, it's handsome enough," agreed Hugh. "And for this—mere field walls and the like—it will do very well. But some folks think they know better than others, merely because they have had the luck to grow very rich; and will not hear anything they don't like. They esteem their own expertise much higher than is warranted. Consider themselves qualified to judge a stone, only because they have seen a stone before this. Now, what do you call that pretty white stone, my dear? Is it a good sound limestone, do you think? Will it harden properly, exposed to the atmosphere? Will it weather well? Can it bear a load? How great a load? Or do you count only how little it costs; and how quickly and easily it may be extracted? Do you let your judgment be corrupted by how conveniently near it lies to your works? Well; what do you say?"

"I? I say it is a white pretty stone; but dare not pronounce any more than that."

"You show better judgment, then, than some highly-placed persons, who imagine themselves experts. It is white; and it is calcareous. But it is not truly limestone at all, not in the true sense—not in the stone-mason's sense of the word. It is only chalk, indurated chalk: mere clunch. Somewhat hardened; harder than alabaster; it does not fracture or crumble instantly. It is suitable for, oh, decorative features, low farm walls, the facings of embankments, and the like. It is easily cut and carved; and it will harden, somewhat, eventually. Not nearly as soon as some people would like to suppose. Stone will not be hurried. Stone has all the time in the world. But indurated chalk is no more fit for piers—which must bear unimaginably heavy loads—no more fit for the piers, the footings of a railway viaduct—than—than is cheese! or blanc-mange! or hard-boiled eggs! And so I told Mackenzie."

Presently they rounded a turn, and Constantia's breath caught at the sight which now opened out before her. "Oh! Is this it? Is this Barentin?"

"It is," said Hugh, and stopped the horse. The new viaduct was beautiful: twenty-seven very tall arches carried a long curved sweep of brick—an aerial wall of brick—across the entire wide valley. The stream of the Austreberthe, though rain-swollen, appeared now quite inconsiderable passing under it: dwarfed. The top of the viaduct was perfectly level, but the arches which supported it were of differing heights, depending on the uneven sloping river bank below—as though they were suspended from the level brick railbed, as though they reached down to the uneven river bank rather than upward from it. "A hundred feet high in the center," Hugh said, unasked, like the housekeeper at Seaton Delaval. "And six hundred yards long."

Abruptly he fell silent at the approach of a fashionable carriage. Constantia saw him scowling under the brim of his hat—until the calèche had rolled past without slowing, and its occupant was seen to be only an elderly French widow.

The massive footings beneath these high brick arches were built of large blocks of handsome white stone.

Atop the new-built viaduct, out near the middle of the span, men and machines could be seen at work on the railbed. "They're laying ballast already," said Hugh. "Laying an even bed of coarse rock, you see. Broken and angular, not rounded—so it cannot roll away, not even when the cars go pounding over it. That is the ballast. Atop that, they'll lay the sleepers: big oak timbers laid crosswise. Then the iron rails go down atop the sleepers, held in place by spikes. Oh, terrible loads, terrible to think of! And yet, if properly constructed—of good sound stone—it does very well. They have come on rapidly, though; very rapidly indeed. In filthy weather too. I should very much like to get a closer look—just one of these piers, on this side, perhaps. One or two of them, at least. This track, I think, must lead down the bank. Certainly. Look, the tannery remains, in the very shadow of it! But the little farms and market gardens had all to be moved—"

Constantia felt uneasy at the height of the towers looming above her. So very high! And so very slim, in proportion to their height; as spare as a dragonfly.

From the doorway of the tannery a boy eyed their chaise; then he disappeared inside. As Hugh stepped down, the tanner himself came out, brandishing a measuring stick. "Voyons, I do not raise the false alarm, not I!" he declared vigorously to Hugh, in French. "As for myself, no doubt remains, for I have taken measurement! It widens, that first crack; and now others, several others show themselves also. It is vastly unfortunate that monsieur is so much behind his time, for it grows dark already, and it will be necessary to go quickly if monsieur is to view well these alarming developments."

Perhaps he mistook Hugh for some official connected with the railway contractor or the government. Hugh did not correct him, but only replied mildly, also in French, "Cracks; this interests me; and I beg you will show them to me. Tell your boy to come and hold my horse." As he followed the tanner down the bank to the nearest pier, Hugh threw Constantia a look over his shoulder which she took to mean, remain where you are. This she did, watching them from inside the chaise while Livia squirmed in her arms.

From the first pier she saw them proceed to a second, a third, and a fourth, well down the river bank. At each, the tanner gestured, and pointed, and waved his arms, and applied his measuring stick; and Hugh looked: up, down, all around the massy pale stone blocks of the piers. He picked up something from the ground, and examined it; and put it in his pocket.

Presently they returned, and Constantia could hear Hugh's parting words to the tanner: "I fear, monsieur, that you have mistaken me for another," he said in French. "But I assure you, I am not from the Ministère de Ponts et Chaussées. Nor have I any connection with the English contractor. No, indeed, monsieur, none at all! I have no official powers, alas; and I never said that I had; only that I should be glad to see the cracks which you freely offered to show me. If you assumed that I was an official personage, the error is yours only, for I have said nothing to mislead you, nor to misrepresent myself. I am a mason, however—je suis maçon—I have worked stone all my life— and as a mason, I tell you, gratis, that this viaduct is unsound, and unsafe; and in your place—well! in your place, monsieur, I should betake me to any other place! Any place but this! If I were you, I should no more lay me down to sleep under this viaduct than I would sleep across the iron rails of the railway line. It will come tumbling down; it is only a matter of time. If not tonight, then perhaps tomorrow; if not tomorrow, then perhaps by Easter; if not this Easter, perhaps by next Easter, or Easter three years hence. I urge you to remove yourself and your household and your goods immediately. I would not sleep here for a single night. I would permit neither my wife nor my child to set foot under its shadow." At this, he drew back the side curtain of the chaise—and the tanner, seeing actual wife and actual child, was convinced at last that this was no official visit, and Hugh no official personage; and reluctantly permitted them to drive off.

* * *

"Not only is the stone unfit—every bit as bad as I told Mackenzie—but the mortar is infamous. Infamous! I mean the mortar of the brickwork, the brick arches springing from atop the piers. Look: I picked up some mortar that was dropped, spilt, during the construction of the arch, two months since. Two full months, mind you. It is not much better than wet sand; and is not fully set even now, after two months! I daresay they have used local common lime mortar, not hydraulic. They ought certainly to have used hydraulic; there can be no excuse for doing otherwise, particularly in so wet a season as this has been. And onto this—this incompetent structure they even now are loading ballast!"

From Barentin to Rouen the old road ran near the new railway line, and Hugh brooded all during the twelve-mile drive. In the dusk Constantia could see from time to time the signs in his face of remembered or imaginary rows and arguments, revisited, rehearsed, revised: the lowering brow, the flash of the eye, the twitch of the lips, the tightening of the jaw. He inspected other approaching carriages with suspicion; and, when another carriage halted near where they had stopped by the opening of the Pissy-Pôville tunnel, he drove on quickly. It was full dark when they came to Malaunay, but he stopped once more, long enough to walk down the embankment to examine in darkness the piers of the new-built viaduct there.

What is limestone? It is the skeletal remains of dead creatures; of corals and shelled creatures. It is their armatures of calcium, the vestiges of their carapaces, ground to sand, to dust, to powder; washed down and down, bedded at last in the deeps under the sea; there pressed so heavy, so hot, so hard, so long, that these crumbled skeletons form—stone. Young and lightly-pressed, it is mere chalk, crumbling. Pressed hard, long, and hot enough, it is transformed into obdurate marble. Just right, it is limestone, a most beautiful and useful stone, in shades of white and ivory, cream and gold. It is sweet and easy to cut, when first brought to light, first exposed to air; sweet to work, yielding to drill, submissive to chisel. It does not harden until it has been exposed to air and sunlight, above-ground; then it becomes durable. That is limestone.

What is limestone when it has been burnt, then ground? It becomes lime: thirsty. Then, slaked, it may become mortar, grout, stucco; or Roman cement, British cement, Portland cement. Constituted and reconstituted. The same material—the earth itself—is used again and again. Ground to dust, washed down into the bottom of the sea, there to be pressed, over long eons, into new stone; eons later, raised up once more, as fresh-made mountains, up and up; once again to be ground to dust, and washed down. Over and over. There is nothing else but what is here, and has ever been here. Ashes to ashes. Dust to dust. Raised up briefly—a flash of magnificence, of glorious temporary animation, an instant of life—then extinguished again, for long ages and epochs. Extinct. But still *here*. Where else would it be?

The lighted streets of Rouen, at last.

Captain St Clair's lugger had already arrived. Hugh recognised it tied up at one of the old stone quays below the new bridge. As soon as Constantia and Livia were installed at the Hôtel D'Angleterre, Hugh went out again to meet him and commence arrangements for transferring his crates from the lugger onto a péniche, one of the cargo barges which plied the river up to Paris. It was late when he returned—to urge that Constantia and Livia should travel up to Paris without him on the new Paris-Rouen railway, by the next morning's eight o'clock train: "You will arrive by noon! Ease and comfort all the way! Do, my dear; the cost is not much; and I may be delayed here for some time, arranging for the transfer and the carriage of my Useless Rubble. Then, you know, the accommodations aboard a péniche are scarcely better than you might find on a tinker's caravan. And I'm told that the upriver passage has been prodigious slow—two days, or even more, due to flooding and backed-up traffic."

But Constantia refused. She could not bring herself, after so long a separation, and so joyous a reunion, to leave her husband again so soon, not even for the sake of a quick and comfortable journey up to Paris.

Her decision seemed ratified, all the next day, by the easy success which they enjoyed at every turn. Hugh's inquiries led him straightaway to the captain of a good steam tug towing a six-barge train, nearly ready for departure. By some stroke of fortune, there remained on the last péniche of this train not only sufficient deck space to accommodate Hugh's precious crates of Useless Rubble—but also a vacant cabin for the comfort of his wife and child. By one o'clock, all these had been brought aboard without the slightest mishap, and their passage up the Seine's locks and weirs began that same afternoon: January 8th.

Constantia thought, upon surveying the péniche's tiny cabin, that if tinkers lived so comfortably as this, they were to be envied. There was a little coal-stove for warmth; and plenty of coal. There was a kettle and a packet of tea. There was a snug double berth, and one chair, and a lamp on a gimbal mount. From a beam hung a cage containing a pair of finches, which sang. "They belonged to my sister," said the bargeman who owned this péniche, as well as the two others which preceded it in the train. "Belgian buffs. Cover the cage if you want silence. My wife can't bear them." He and his wife and their old fat dog had accommodations on the preceding péniche.

The unremitting rains of the preceding days and weeks had swollen the Seine so remarkably that in some places the river was too high for taller watercraft to pass under the arches of its bridges. Barges, low and flat, could pass downriver on the rapid current, but some of the taller steam tugs that towed them upriver again could not, and anything with masts had to laboriously ship them at every bridge, and then raise them again. All in all, river traffic was a mess.

Ma foi! cried the bargeman to his wife, whenever there was a delay. Or was it mon foie? wondered Constantia. Was it his faith by which he swore, or his liver? Faith, ah; that is a matter for debate . . . but the liver, now, ça, c'est serieux! How odd the French are, thought Constantia. How unaccountable! It is a profound seriousness that they lavish upon frivolities and trifles.

Or perhaps not. Everyone must eat. The bargeman sent back a jar of wine and a cabbage; and lent Hugh a line with hooks, whereby he caught supper: a couple of bream.

For some hours during the night the train of barges lay stalled in the darkness—something to do with a queue ahead where a too-high steam tug had earlier jammed itself under the too-low arch of a bridge—but Constantia and Hugh and Livia dozed, slept, and dozed again, not much worse than usual.

Constantia awakened to daylight and a stench. Leaving Livia and Hugh still asleep in the narrow berth, she emerged onto the cargo deck as the sun rose above the mist. The stink was more vile still. No somnolent fishermen, no red-armed washerwomen were evident along these banks, where the river was so foul. She knew the reason, and could not help waiting to see the horror itself as they finally came abreast of it, and passed it: the sewer outfall at Asnières. A black torrent, a ceaseless vomit, a Styx, a Roman cloaca, the anus of all Paris. Whose fault was this? Whose fault, that all living creatures must piss, must shit? To fail in this is to die.

Above Asnières, the Seine was a river once more, the water smelling as it ought. Fishermen and washerwomen reappeared along the banks. When Constantia went below again, Hugh and Livia were awake. Constantia changed Livia's clooties—and then rinsed the soiled ones over the side, in the green water of the river.

There was a great deal to see along the embankment. It was like viewing a wintry panorama contrived by monsieur Daguerre; like a pretty scenic wallpaper installed by some expensive marchand-mercier. Here were the charming villas, gardens, and promenades of Neuilly, populated by elegant loiterers well wrapped in furs against the chill, and quaint peasants, and bucolic cows. Presently the Bois de Boulogne passed slowly on their left; and then St Cloud to the right, with its pretty church. Later, at Sèvres, the top of the palace which housed the celebrated porcelain works, under the direction of Monsieur Brongniart, could be seen; nothing at all like the muddy potteries of the English Midlands. Slowly they left behind the Île Seguin, slowly rounded the last long curve to the left—and finally, as the winter sun set, too early, behind them again, approached Paris itself: handsome bridges; well-built stone quais. To their left drifted the Tuileries, and then the Louvre; presently the towers of Notre-Dame loomed up in the dusk; and finally, just at full dark, they tied up at the quai of the Halles aux Vins, just below the Pont d'Austerlitz; just below the Muséum and the Jardin des Plantes.

Home.

The evening of January 9th.

16

A T 4:32 ON the morning of January 10th, the Barentin viaduct
was standing.

Then, at 4:33, it fell down.

Who saw it fall? No one; it was still dark. No human person saw
it. A pair of dairy maids, sisters, who ought to have been on their way
to the cows, had both overslept. A baker, who had been up since 3:00
and was thoroughly awake, happened to have his head inside his oven
at that moment. A flock of ducks saw it fall but, being ducks, did not
know what they saw.

The southern end, over the tannery, failed first; there, the weak
chalk stone of the piers cracked, bulged, sagged—and, finally,
exploded under the pressure of miscalculated tonnage bearing downward and outward. The stones themselves burst. The brick arches
above shattered instantly, and the entire viaduct came crashing down
like a file of gigantic dominoes. It collapsed entirely, from the southern end to the northern. The ground shook, and the noise was like
the end of the world. It was the most complete and spectacular failure
anyone could remember or imagine.

* * *

"Have you heard?"

"Tumbled right down!"

"Have you heard? Not one brick remaining upon another!"

"I myself should not care at all for passing over any of their shoddy bridges!"

"Nor under them!"

"Well, and the tunnels; what of those?"

"Just imagine, if a train had been passing over it!"

"Those English contractors, so greedy! so hasty and careless! So vainglorious!"

"The job should have been given to good honest French builders, didn't I say so?" Thus excited and indignant French voices resounded in the street, floating all the way up to the fifth-storey windows just under the eaves, where Hugh and Constantia, warm in a real bed for the first time in days, and still craving sleep, were awakened far too early.

The sensational news came up to Paris by the early train from Rouen, with the milk and the fish. Most incredible of all, it was reported that (by God's good grace) no one had been hurt.

"Were you not engaged formerly, monsieur, upon that very railway?" said the landlady, Mme Mouchy, to Monsieur Stevenson across the boarding-house breakfast table, a little later. "Before you came up to Paris, I believe?"

Indeed he had been, conceded Hugh, in '43 and '44.

"What is the name of the contractors, pray? The English contractors? Brasseur et Méchant? Brassière et Macaroni? Something like that?"

"They are Brassey & Mackenzie," said Hugh.

The newspapers feasted for some time upon the collapse of the Barentin viaduct. The tanner whose tannery had been crushed gave several interviews. By the grace of God, he said, he had moved his family out from under the viaduct only the very day before the collapse. Because an angel had come to warn him. Oui, an angel. He refused at first to describe the angel, but when pressed, let it slip that the angel had been about the size and shape of a typical human being, and apparently wingless.

More than a few sermons were preached, the following Sunday, on the subject of the angel who had appeared to Joseph in Bethlehem, advising him to flee with his wife and her newborn son to the safety of Egypt, just in time to escape King Herod's slaughter of the innocents.

For a few days, Constantia took to addressing Hugh as "your angelship" when they were in private.

But no one had been hurt. No human persons, that is; though within a week there were reports of a tremendous dying-off of the fish in the downstream trickle of the Austreberthe, an unexpected consequence of the immense quantity of lime—both mortar and stone—which now all but dammed its flow, and poisoned the trickle that got through.

The English contracting concern of Brassey & Mackenzie stepped forward instantly to pound its own corporate breast in manly mea culpa, promising to rebuild the viaduct to a far stouter specification, at its own expense, and within the time limit required by its contract. Privately, Mr Brassey blamed the engineer whose design had proven faulty, and the suppliers of the common lime mortar which had not set, and the weather which had prevented its setting. Privately, Mr Mackenzie ordered a supply of expensive but exceedingly reliable stone from a distant quarry of high repute for the rebuilding of the piers at Barentin.

But no one had suffered even a scratch. It might have been much worse; might have been horrific.

The contractors, in consultation with the engineers, also announced that all the other viaducts, bridges, and tunnels along the new line would undergo the most stringent reviews, in cooperation with the Ministère de Ponts et Chaussées; and that certain load-bearing elements of those structures would be reinforced—not out of any particular necessity—for they had complete confidence in them—but to reassure the public; to allay any and all anxiety on the part of the public, no matter how unwarranted.

A series of sensational knife attacks in the Marais some weeks later eclipsed the Barentin viaduct story at last, and drew off the attention of the newspaper-reading public. Mr Brassey and Mr Mackenzie heaved sighs of relief, and got on with their work.

Mme Mouchy, to whose boarding-house the Stevensons had returned, did not hold out for any increase in the rent she charged them for their top-floor rooms. She did, however, exact an additional sum for use of the garden-shed, which they now required as workshop and housing for the crates of Useless Rubble. She had kept their rooms empty for them all this time, she assured them, out of generosity. The real reason, the Stevensons knew very well, was that her rents were so high, and her table so undistinguished, that everyone except les Anglais shunned her establishment.

It stood at the eastern edge of Paris proper, near the Jardin des Plantes, the Muséum d'Histoire Naturelle, and the Halles aux Vins; not far from the Gobelins factory, and the dirty trickle that was the Bièvre River, a sad and bullied and exploited little river, a poxy little street whore of a stream. This was by no means a fashionable quarter; quite the opposite. The only eminent people who slept here were those who could not help it, because they were dead: the worthies (Voltaire and Jean-Jacques Rousseau among them) entombed within the honorable and glorious Panthéon—the quondam Church of St Geneviève—on its hill nearby. But the neighborhood was inexpensive, and convenient, and surprisingly safe, compared to certain other quarters of the city. Workers and students lived here, amid carpet-weavers, dyers, and tanners.

Their top-floor rooms filled with dismal old-fashioned furniture remained exactly as Constantia and Hugh had left them, only dustier. Mme Mouchy was too fat to ascend so far, and her servants too lazy. There was no cradle in the room; Livia slept in the pulled-out bottom drawer of the chest of drawers. Familiar rustlings were still to be heard from the attic overhead. These were not rats. Constantia climbed the ladder on the landing and, raising the overhead hatchway into the attic, opened to a flutter, a bustle: pigeons. Their round unblinking eyes stared at her, unafraid. Did they recognise her? Remember her? Their numbers were undiminished; perhaps even increased, despite having had to fend for themselves for the past half-year. Not even the most knowing Parisian street urchin is better able to scrape, beg, and steal a living than a pigeon.

Among the residents of the house was an American, Miss Julia Grant, who, with her intimate friend Miss Harriet Buckley, an English-woman, occupied the first-floor appartement of two rooms: a little sitting-room in front; a bedchamber behind. Miss Grant and Miss Buckley were overjoyed at the return of their friends the Stevensons, and could not contain their delight over the two new prizes carried home by them: Livia, and the Useless Rubble.

Miss Grant and Miss Buckley doted upon Livia. When they were at home, their laps were ever at her service. They praised the intellect and the character which they claimed already to discern in her features, her changing expressions, her winning way of flinging her coral to the floor for retrieval, and especially in the smiles and even laughter which they frequently succeeded in wringing from her. Livia, for her part, was particularly enchanted by the tinted spectacles that Miss Grant wore.

"Well, yes; we, too, have had some successes during your long absence . . ." said Miss Grant one day in their little sitting room, where she and Constantia sat mending stockings, while Miss Buckley attempted to induce Livia to taste a dish of sops in bouillon.

"Insignificant, of course, in comparison to a baby! nothing so impressive as a baby!" said Miss Buckley.

" . . . but minor successes all the same, in our own way," continued Miss Grant. She and Miss Buckley also shared a well-lit corner workroom in the Muséum d'Histoire Naturelle, where they had long been engaged in a quest to develop a practical technique for what they called "daguerrean lithography." As the precious fossil remnants in the Muséum's collections cannot propagate themselves—cannot disseminate themselves throughout the world—it is the duty of humankind to replicate them; to publish descriptions, minutely detailed, with exact measurements. And with illustrations too, prepared by adepts in the arts of etching and engraving on copper or steel; in mezzotint and aquatint; and in lithography. These illustrated descriptions, correct and complete as print facsimiles upon a page may be, are rendered for study by savants everywhere.

"I do not mean to disparage your particular skill, Mrs Stevenson," said Miss Grant. "You know we are great admirers of your designs. And of course the Muséum's artists and engravers are superbly accomplished—"

"I am glad to hear you acknowledge it, Julia," said Miss Buckley. "It is so tiresome always to have to insist upon it myself. We artists and engravers do hold ourselves and our productions in the highest esteem. Engravers especially."

"But you understand, Mrs Stevenson, that it is precisely the eye and the hand of the human artist which we are determined to eliminate," said Miss Grant; "the artist who, being human, cannot help but exercise human judgment—"

"Whether it is to simplify, or to elaborate; to amplify, or to suppress, unadorned nature; unimproved nature," interrupted Miss Buckley smoothly. "Nature, with its ample scope for improvement. No, we are determined to induce the light reflecting off the relic, through the agency of the camera's lens, to imprint its own image upon the printing plate—"

"Or the printing stone, as the case may be—"

"—by irresistible and infallible chemical means—without the intervention of any human eye or hand, of any human perception or judgment, of any human 'improvements.' As an image inscribes itself upon the silvered plate of the daguerreotype."

"As an image from a calotype negative writes itself upon the salted paper."

"I remember," said Constantia, when she could, "that you were striving, before I went away, to make the daguerrean process bite deeper into the plate, deep enough indeed to engrave it—to make a plate fit for printing by the intaglio process—"

"Alas, we accomplished nothing; we succeeded only in burning holes in our clothing with Julia's vile acids, most vexing!—Oh, come, Livia, we mustn't spit—"

"—but during your absence we shifted our efforts instead to lithographic limestones—"

"We are deeply indebted to Mr Stevenson for his hint, aren't we, Julia?"

"—and have been trying them with a variety of preparations deriving from Mr Fox-Talbot's discoveries; and it seems—it does seem—that we shall perhaps succeed—have indeed actually succeeded—"

"To a very small degree, thus far—"

"—to a small but encouraging degree, in making an image of our model—"

"An elk; we are using the skull of an ancient Irish elk for our patient, long-suffering, perfectly motionless model—"

"—inscribe itself in a hydrophobic material upon the lithographic surface, of its own accord."

"It cannot help it."

"It cannot help it any more than *Homo sapiens* can help but reproduce itself."

"As regards *Homo sapiens*, I believe I have just made an important new discovery," said Miss Buckley. "Which is, that Livia, the present specimen, does not care in the least for sops in bouillon. Who can blame her? Nasty soggy stuff. But such a lovely tooth she's got! Neither the Cylindricodon nor the Cubicodon—no, not even the remarkable Labyrinthodon!—has got so charming a tooth as our Livia's! Don't fuss; where's the darling girl's coral? There, wipe it off; good as new."

"Just a moment, Harriet; I'd like to see that coral; thanks. Ah! A rather good example of *Corallium rubrum*, isn't it."

"No, Julia, it is not."

"Indeed it is, Harriet. I am certain of it."

"But you are quite wrong nevertheless. It is a *Corallium cuvier*. Do I not always freely yield to your superior knowledge in the realm of chemistry? I do; but when it comes to invertebrate identifications, my dear Julia, I wonder that you should think of contradicting me."

"Hm!" said Miss Grant, and then, to Constantia, abruptly changed the subject: "Will there never come a time when it will be safe for you and Mr Stevenson to return openly to Britain?"

"I'm sure I read somewhere that Mr Pickering returned, a year or two ago," said Miss Buckley.

"Yes, Pickering did return," said Constantia, "and, oddly enough, goes about to this day quite unmolested by the Crown's officers, just as though there never had been a price upon his Chartist head. But, by a strange and suggestive coincidence, Mr Cooper and Mr Newton were taken soon after; and tried; and convicted, upon evidence that only Pickering could have produced. Mr Cooper was transported, and Mr Newton was put to two years of hard labour. He broke down after eight months of stone-breaking, and died in his prison cell. I daresay we too might openly return—if my husband liked to betray his old associates."

"Oh! I see. That is disgusting to think of."

"How dreadful it must have been, to feel yourselves in danger at every moment."

"So it was. Hugh loathed skulking about—and putting his kind friends at risk, by our presence. But the warrant for his arrest is still in effect. His face is well known; and of the many bitter out-of-work men roaming the Northumberland coast, one or another among them, upon recognizing him, might well be desperate enough to betray him for the sake of the reward proffered by the Crown. Even before the election, he had a very wide circle of acquaintance, and not only among Chartists. Any stone-carver or mason or builder in southern Scotland or northern England might have recognised him, so he did not dare to stir off—well . . . the secluded place where we cloistered ourselves. And then, when we had to separate after all—when it became apparent that twins were to be expected, or, at least suspected—matters became a great deal more difficult still. For one thing, once apart, we could not communicate freely."

"Not letters?"

"They are opened, you know. Oh yes, Miss Grant, of course they are, by the orders of the Home Office. Opened, copied—then resealed and belatedly delivered. The very postmasters are under the rule of the spies of the Crown. Our friends had evidence that their own mails were under surveillance. Oh yes! I assure you: unaccountable delays; letters clumsily re-sealed and sent along—so we could not feel confident that letters for Hugh under cover to them were safe. Nor was it possible for Hugh to send letters to me, not even by my pseudonym, not even if carried by, ah, our friends to be posted from elsewhere; from some distant town. No, any such doings would have aroused a towering curiosity in any postmaster or postmistress. Instead, I contrived to send only a few essential messages, very brief ones—by pigeon! And though my Scottish friends—the Edinburgh friends who received me for my lying-in—were kindness itself, still, no kindness could compensate for being separated from my husband at such a time."

"Childbirth: bad enough!" said Miss Buckley. "One quails at the thought. But twins!"

"How is one to respect the designer of such a system?" said Miss Grant. "Surely there must be a better solution to this problem of reproduction—of replication. You and I, Harriet—old maids though we are—must redouble our efforts." Seeing Constantia's perplexity, Miss Grant added, "I mean, of course, at daguerrean lithography."

"And your Edinburgh friends—were they in on your secret?" asked Miss Buckley.

"No; they received me for the sake of old acquaintance, having known me formerly when I was Miss Babcock. I abhorred the necessity of dissembling—of concealing so much; even a matter so essential as my name," said Constantia. "Indeed, I could not do it very thoroughly. I made no secret of 'MacAdam' being only a convenient pseudonym, assumed for reasons which, though secret, were not dishonourable. But secrecy has of itself a tint of dishonour; we do place a very great value upon candour. The best I could do was to declare, frankly and openly, that I had a secret, and was determined to keep it."

"As we have got onto the subject of secrets, Mrs Stevenson . . . when are we to be allowed a glimpse of your prodigious fossil?"

"We long to lay eyes upon it."

"We ache to lay eyes upon it."

"You shall be the very first, I assure you," said Constantia, "as soon it is ready to be seen; quite soon now, I hope. We are preparing the specimen for presentation to Professor de Blainville—"

"But first, to us; your promise!"

"—quite soon; certainly before the great conference in April."

"How fortunate that Mr Stevenson's wonderful fossil was still there, in that remote—nameless—place, after all these years."

"And just as he remembered it."

"Oh, but it was not!" said Constantia. "Or we should have harvested our prize much sooner. You will imagine our bitter disappointment upon discovering that twenty years of storms and waves had carried away the relics he remembered from boyhood. But then came the discovery that those same storms and waves had uncovered something . . . even more intriguing. More telling, more valuable, we hope and trust; but also far more difficult and time-consuming to extricate than we ever had anticipated."

"Vertebrate or invertebrate?" asked Miss Buckley.

"Oh, vertebrate, decidedly vertebrate—but I will not be lured into a game of Twenty Questions!"

"No? But you will surely answer me this: Is our understanding of our world to be blown up entirely by what he—and you—have risked your all, to bring before us?"

"That remains to be seen. It is too soon to say."

"Oh, isn't she cruel, though, Julia? Cruel, to taunt us so!"

Whenever Livia would nap or amuse herself for a time, Constantia donned an artisan's smock and set to work. Sometimes she worked in the garden-shed behind the boarding-house, picking at the Useless Rubble. For tools, she had a little chisel-edged hammer weighing two ounces; two emery-stone files, one flat, the other round; a stout embroidery needle; and a badger-bristle brush. At the Muséum she had formerly done this work for months on end. Stone yields to the gentlest of the strong forces: water, and women. Minute, meticulous care and inexhaustible patience were required; in that, too, it was women's work, mothers' work especially. Bent over a worktable, by the daylight falling through the open doorway, Constantia tapped, chipped, blew, brushed, smoothed, removing a few grains of grit at a time; uncovering fossils in their stony matrix. They were to be uncovered, yes; but not freed entirely, for the matrix in which these vestiges were embedded—evidence and proof of their relationship to one another—was of essential importance. Gradually their forms emerged, in high relief. Was she carving these forms, or was she releasing them? She was only releasing them. She gave up will, intent, design; she was the midwife, not the creator. She was helping them to emerge, not making them. She was cleaning them; and cleaning, always and everywhere, is women's work.

A film of white dust overlay everything in the shed: tables, chairs, cloches, watering-cans, and canvas-draped forms. What emerged from the rubble? Marvelous things; surprising things. But it was too soon, still, to say. Do not speak of it yet; do not let the malicious fairies know. Not until it has received the protection of its name.

To be fair, it must be said that Hugh, too, did a share of this work, whenever he was at home. But he was frequently away during February, negotiating the sale of his two-fifths share in a gravel quarry near Tours to his three partners. He had already, through intermediaries, sold the leases of all his quarry properties in England and Scotland—except for the Coquet Isle lease which, with less than four years remaining to run, was of small worth. The Stevensons were just now converting into cash all the assets they could lay their hands on, with a view to buying a Very Good Thing—though it was still too soon to be spoken of. Between themselves they referred to it as Our Castle in the Air—or, sometimes, Our Hole in the Ground.

At other times, Constantia would bring out paper and gouaches, uncover her microscope, and set to work painting designs to be sold to a cloth manufacturer. Others might draw pretty mignonettes and bonherbes if they liked, but Constantia specialised in bizarres: those very dress-prints that had so alarmed Lady Janet. She was paid in francs and—as dessinatrice, the designer—she was also entitled to a dozen ells, a dress-length, of any cloth eventually printed from her designs. Some of these lengths she had made up into dresses, but her need for dresses was finite, and she generally sold the surplus lengths for good money.

Constantia was at work upon a design based upon the elegant architectures of crinoid fossils—that is, of the St Cuthbert's beads which Hugh had strung into a little necklace for Livia. The technically demanding aspect of composition—accurate placement of the repeats, both vertical and horizontal, so that the design could be roller-printed—was finished. She could now attend to her favourite parts: the drawing, and the colours. In her design, these beads (now in shades of mustard and purple) drifted in schools before a background of vivid pink coral arranged in loose zigzags, all upon a seaweed-green ground. It was an arresting composition which had never existed in life; in unimproved nature.

* * *

Whenever Livia was awake and requiring to be amused, Constantia would set down her files or her brushes, stretch to straighten her back, and pick up her baby. If the weather permitted, she would carry Livia to one of the parks nearby, where entry was open to all, and free of charge. Sometimes she went to the Luxembourg Gardens, to see respectably-dressed people strolling about and feeding the swans; at other times, she went to the Jardin des Plantes. The remarkable tartan cloak, wherever she wore it, excited wonderment and stares from the Parisians—though not, Constantia suspected, any great envy.

The Jardin des Plantes adjoined the Muséum, where Miss Grant and Miss Buckley were at work. Constantia sometimes stopped by their workroom on the ground floor, to deliver letters or meals, or to admire their progress in their attempts at daguerrean lithography, or to condole upon their disappointments.

The Jardin housed not only the nation's botanical collection, but its menagerie as well: caged bears, antelopes, sloths, monkeys, and more. Most of these animals huddled miserably from the March winds. There was a rhinoceros, an African one, rather different from the ones Constantia knew from her early years in Assam. There were two elephants, weary, wise, and patient, just like the ones she knew from Assam; probably their second cousins. In the House for Fierce Animals were tigers, which Constantia avoided. Even at this season the menagerie was often crowded with visitors, and usually Constantia preferred the less-frequented regions of the garden: parterres, copses, and groves, avenues of trees pleached or pollarded, all dotted by charming little follies, towers, hermitages; or else the glasshouses, especially pleasant on cold windy days. Another of her favourite places was the Labyrinthe of yew which spiraled up a mount overlooking the gardens, topped by a fanciful iron gazebo. This was the place where, two years ago, she had first understood that Mr Stevenson was essential to all her future happiness.

* * *

Hugh was having disturbing dreams—of Mackenzie, he admitted to Constantia: the railway contractor William Mackenzie who, while in the pincers of one of those ferocious tooth-aches to which he was a martyr, had flown into a towering rage when Hugh (then master of that quarry near Barentin) had challenged him as to the adequacy of its stone. It did no good for Constantia to list the unforseen benefits that had ensued: "His injustice has proven the greatest of boons," she declared. "If you had continued delving away there, all content, you might never have made your way to Paris—to the Muséum—might never have made the acquaintance of Professor de Blainville— might never have set out in search of lithographic-quality stone. You might never have dipped into the Muséum's fossil collections. And without having seen those, you might not have given another thought to the remains you had found on Coquet Isle as a boy, all those years ago. Indeed, if you had not come to Paris, and to the Muséum— to me—then where—when—how—might you and I have met? And if not, how was our Livia to have been born?" Hugh admitted the merit of all her arguments, but his disturbing dreams did not abate.

One stormy March afternoon   too cold for working in the garden shed and too windy for strolling in the public gardens—Constantia, in her lodging at the top of the house, was in search of some cloth which might be made up as new frocks for Livia, who was fast out-growing her first tiny clothes. Constantia's trunk held an assortment of dress lengths in prints of her own designing, but those bizarres— so worldly, so knowing—seemed unsuitable for an infant of seven months. Hadn't she saved an outworn shirt of Hugh's that might be cut up and remade for Livia? She plunged her hand blindly into the depths of the trunk Her fingertips sought the feel of old much-washed linen, but touched instead upon something hard, sharp-cornered: a small book. She drew it out—and recognised the volume she had impulsively bought at Newcastle for five shillings:

EXPLANATIONS:
A Sequel to
"Vestiges of the Natural History of Creation."
BY THE AUTHOR OF THAT WORK.

She had forgotten all about it.

Still kneeling beside the trunk, Constantia opened the book at random, and by some chance her eye alighted upon this, on page 55: "Now, I cannot tell what good naturalists may say . . . but I feel, for my own part . . ."

She turned over a few pages more, to page 63, where her eye seized upon: "How a good geologist can have allowed himself to speak in this manner . . . I am quite at a loss to understand . . ."

How odd, that the style of these phrases should be so familiar! Was it not very odd?

For once, Livia in her dresser drawer slept on, her fingers in her mouth.

Constantia got off her knees and into the chair under the window; then turned back to begin again properly at the beginning: " . . . public favour and disfavour were alike beyond the regard of an author who bore no bodily shape in the eyes of his fellow-countrymen, and was likely to remain for ever unknown . . ."

It was not mere phrases that were familiar—but entire ideas, images, paragraphs. It was the author's mind that was familiar. But, she reminded herself, she had closely read *Vestiges*, so was it not reasonable that this production, from the same author, should seem familiar?

And might not many of these familiar phrases be in general use? More ordinary and more widespread than she had realised? Such as: "A trifling objection." And "babies are a mere fancy." And "the great and amazing fact." And "a scanty and most defective development of life." Commonplace, these expressions, weren't they? Not peculiar to the Chambers family? Proof of nothing?

But when she read this Unknown's explanation of how rotation must have commenced in the celestial bodies, her scalp tingled and her hair rose. She could not help but remember crossing the Roman bridge at Musselburgh one afternoon with the Chambers children and their mother. Mrs Chambers had called her children's attention to the eddies, dimples, and little whirlpools in the River Esk below; and hadn't she cited some professor on that occasion? Hadn't she cited, Constantia thought, the very extract that appeared here, in this book?

And then Constantia found this: "It is humiliating to have to answer an objection so mean. There is no statement that the animals came in this order. I have only put the words into this arrangement, in accordance with the custom now commonly followed of observing the ascending grades of the animal kingdom."

Constantia shut the book, and then shut her eyes, the better to see in her mind's eye just where she had read this before . . . one night when she had been fatigued beyond sleep. The *Edinburgh Review* had slipped to the floor. She had picked it up; opened it. In her mind's eye she could still see the handwriting in the margins, small and neat, and unknown to her. Whose handwriting was that: "humiliating to answer an objection so mean"? Whose, the indignant commentary which filled the margins of that sneering review of *Vestiges?*

Well, whose?

Livia awakened, fretful, and Constantia had to put down her book—for babies are no mere fancy.

What plausible explanations were there for this remarkable coincidence? Could even this result from mere chance?

As soon as Livia was content once more at her breast, Constantia took up the book again, awkwardly in her free hand, and read on. It was as though she were hearing Mrs Chambers's cheerful and lively voice; as though Mrs Chambers were in the room, just across the table and chatting comfortably over the tuneful teacups and gingerbread.

Constantia laid down her book and gazed out at the stormy sky, thinking, unseeing. But how astounding! Could it be? How could it be? Was Mrs Chambers the author not only of these *Explanations*, but also of the fascinating and provocative *Vestiges* which had preceded it; the publishing sensation of the age? Mrs Chambers, who shut herself into the library each morning, not to emerge until tea-time (her ink-stained fingers then taking up the particular teacup which chimed perfect A)? Mrs Chambers, whose "extensive correspondence" prevented her nursing her own baby? Was Mrs Chambers, then, the Great Unknown, the disembodied author? The Incognita?

So it seemed!

So it seemed. What degree of certainty could be assigned to this new idea, this theory, this possibility? What shadow of doubt? The more Constantia thought of it, the more certain she felt. A truth is true even before it can be proven; even before sober proofs can be brought forth; even though it has been only guessed-at, leapt-to; when it is mere hypothesis. A truth is true even if it can never be proven; even if it has left no traces, no evidence amounting to proof.

Some critics had hazarded an opinion that the author was a woman; had even nominated candidates: Ada Lovelace, Harriet Martineau, Catherine Crowe. But if Constantia was right, the Incognita was not one of London's celebrated bluestockings. No, she was Nobody: the unregarded Mrs Robert Chambers—Anne Kirkwood Chambers—daughter of a provincial clockmaker, wife of a scribbling journalist, mother of a large family.

Mrs Chambers! Of no credentials; of no reputation; of no authority. No wonder, then, that those sensational books, *Vestiges* and *Explanations*—of unprecedented scope and boldness—had been published anonymously; launched upon the sea of public notice unburdened by any association with their unesteemed author, who bore no bodily shape in the eyes of her fellow-countrymen.

Chambers. Camera obscura, Constantia now remembered; Mr Chambers had called his wife that. Now she saw into their private joke. For them, the term referred neither to the tourist attraction atop Edinburgh's Calton Hill, nor to the camera used at Mr Hill and Mr Adamson's calotype studio. For Mr and Mrs Chambers, the term meant—literally—the "obscure Chamber": the unknown—the hidden—authoress herself, Mrs Chambers.

The Maker leaves the marks of His fingers upon His Creation (her fingers; her creation). In its language, its ideas, its arguments, this book bore Mrs Chambers's inky finger-prints throughout.

Constantia felt herself bursting with sudden revelation. It was not precisely knowledge; it was instead enormous conviction, something akin to religious faith. Her conviction about the parentage of this book was like her conviction about her own parentage.

At first she felt she must tell someone. Tell Hugh! Tell Miss Grant and Miss Buckley! But Hugh was away, in the south. Miss Grant and Miss Buckley were at their Muséum workroom. The urge to tell someone soon passed away, and was replaced by a resolve, born of delicacy, loyalty, and discretion, to keep her discovery to herself.

By the middle of March, Constantia and Hugh were nearly certain that their Useless Rubble was of incalculable value. One Sunday morning when the spring light was good, they invited Miss Grant and Miss Buckley to the garden shed, for its unveiling. "I fear it is always chilly in here," admitted Constantia as they all sidled into the narrow margins left around the large draped work table, "but Mme Mouchy has promised to bring out our tea very soon, to warm us, and Livia simply must wear her mittens, whether she likes them or not."

"I'd no idea of its being so large as this," said Miss Grant.

"There remains yet more work to be done," said Hugh, "but we desire that you should see it, and give us your opinion of the state of preparation we have achieved thus far—and perhaps help us to arrive at some estimate of its value to the world, too." With a flourish Hugh drew off the canvas drape.

"Oh!" cried Miss Grant.

"Ah!" cried Miss Buckley.

"But it's—surely—"

"Isn't it a—"

"The astounding length of the neck—"

"And the smallness and narrowness of the head—"

"The abundance of the digits in its four paddles, each still in its proper place—"

"Well?" said Hugh.

"A plesiosaur, surely," said Miss Grant. "A very fine specimen, and beautifully cleaned, too."

"It certainly has a most plesiosaur-like appearance," said Miss Buckley, "though I should wish to examine the vertebrae for the characteristic fossets before pronouncing with certainty—"

"Have we Baron Cuvier's *Le Règne Animal*? There is an excellent plate which—"

"Yes, we have it here, in Mr Pidgeon's translation: *The Animal Kingdom*—with the very plate. Listen," said Hugh, and read aloud: "'The magnificent specimen from Lyme is composed of many stones, which fit well to each other. The only doubt that can possibly be attached to them relates to the narrowest part near the base of the neck.' For quite some time, you see, it was doubted that the neck and the body could belong to one another, for the neck was so preposterously long, so unlike any other creature whatsoever—at least half neck—and totaling some forty cervical vertebrae—"

"Yes, yes, we know," interrupted Miss Grant. "But with your magnificent specimen, there can be no doubt whatever as to the relation of neck and body: One sees them together here, perfectly preserved, in the same unbroken stone matrix."

"Ah! And here," said Miss Buckley, "we may easily see those small oval fossets by which the plesiosaur is recognised."

"Yes," said Hugh. "And my beast, too, like the Lyme specimen, lies on its belly, its ribs nearly in their places, the sternal apparatus apparent beneath."

"Now do look at this, Julia," said Miss Buckley. "Here are the belly ribs, and there, the pelvic structure. What puzzle, though, lies here? The bones repose intact, complete, in an entirely convincing relation to each other, undisturbed, it would seem. Yet what have we here? A pile of rounded pebbles, all tumbled about and mixed with—with fragments of bone, I think."

"Hollow bones—pterodactyl bones, surely," said Miss Grant.

"Yes, it was those which first attracted my notice," said Hugh.

"You don't suppose it might have swallowed these pebbles by mistake—while feeding along a muddy sea floor, for instance?"

"No. That is preposterous," said Miss Buckley. "How is one to believe in any creature which fails to distinguish rocks from food? Livia, your mitten."

"Deliberately swallowed, then?"

"Plesiosaurus could tear—but not chew, not with those teeth," said Hugh. "Like birds of prey. How do birds chew their food? Pigeons, for instance?"

"They don't, of course," said Miss Grant. "They swallow sharp bits of gravel, which remains in their crops to break up their food before it passes into their stomachs."

"Aha! . . . and hence, these pebbles," said Miss Buckley.

"I daresay you may be right, Harriet," said Miss Grant seriously. "These pebbles may be gastroliths, though I have never heard it proposed before this. And there, resting within the pelvis, a—well, what is that, then?" Removing her tinted spectacles, Miss Grant bent to look more closely.

"Another creature, a small huddled-up skeleton, quite complete, long-necked—"

"Very long of neck. And so tidily curled up, as though for a nap."

"Is it undigested prey?" suggested Miss Buckley. "Might the plesiosaur have swallowed this smaller creature entire—and then met its own end, while its last meal remained undigested?"

"But here, up here, are the stomach contents: all hashed up, mere fragments, those pterodactyl bones, and mixed in with these rounded pebbles. They are higher in the pelvis, not lower. The intact creature is lower in the pelvis."

"Why is it intact? How could it have been swallowed whole?"

"Perhaps the intact creature lies under the plesiosaur—not within its pelvis, but beneath it?"

"No, look. It huddles within the bones of the pelvis—within the pelvic cradle. That is undoubtedly the case."

To Constantia, the curled intact creature resembled those embryonic ducklings—unhatched, but fully formed, even faintly feathered—which in China are cooked in the shell and eaten, savoured as delicacies.

"What will you think when I tell you that the small creature, too, has forty cervical vertebrae?" said Hugh.

"Has it indeed?"

"It is an unborn plesiosaur, to be sure," said Miss Buckley.

"There is no sign of a shell in development," said Miss Grant.

"Nothing like a shell," agreed Miss Buckley.

"Did they not lay eggs, then, these plesiosaurs?" said Miss Grant.

"Unknown—until now," said Hugh. "This fossil is proof that they brought forth their young alive."

"Proof!"

"Evidence, at the very least," he said. "Convincing evidence."

Said Miss Buckley, "There is only the one embryo—not a clutch of them, not a litter of them. But only the one—and rather larger than might have been expected. To be brought forth shell-less; alive. I confess I feel differently about the creature now—now that it more nearly resembles a mammifer—resembles our own kind!—in this respect. Oh; Livia has succeeded in shedding a mitten after all—but only one of them. Here it is."

"How utterly remarkable this is, Mr Stevenson."

"Stunning."

"I should think it ought to prove of inestimable value to the Muséum."

Mme Mouchy appeared at the door, carrying the tea-tray. Constantia, holding Livia on her hip, hastened to clear a space for it on a tool-shelf at the front of the shed. The landlady did not turn around until she had safely deposited the tray; and then she started, or pretended to, at the sight of the fossil bones disposed across the work-table. "Oh! Mais c'est laide, ça!" she exclaimed, laying dimpled hand to fat bosom. "Frightening! Who wishes to carve such a monster as that? What a pity, to lavish skill and patience upon making so ugly, so monstrous a carving as this! A great waste of time and effort, Mme Stevenson, when something beautiful might have been made, just as easily." And, grimacing her disapproval, out she went.

What was the value of this discovery? Having undertaken to investigate this question, Miss Grant and Miss Buckley invited the Stevensons one evening, a week later, to their private sitting room to hear their findings.

"Feckless stuff," said Miss Buckley as she poured out a cup of Mme Mouchy's pale after-dinner tea for Constantia, and another for Hugh. "She imagines that we do not know."

"It is provoking," agreed Constantia, moving her cup out of Livia's eager reach, "but then, French coffee is only too feckful."

"Shall we commence?" said Miss Grant, consulting her notes. "Yes. We have directed our attention to the past twenty five years, and although a great many transactions must have been concluded between individuals in private, we did succeed in finding several public reports of the sales of certain important fossils, beginning with the year 1820, when an ichthyosaur, one of the very earliest to be found, fetched a hundred pounds at an auction organised by Colonel Birch at Bullock's Museum."

"That will have been the benefit auction, however," said Miss Buckley.

"Yes, it was," said Miss Grant, and explained: "Colonel Birch organised that auction to sell his own collection—much of which he had bought originally from the Annings, frère et soeur—as a benefit for them when they had fallen on very hard times."

"And one ought to consider," said Miss Buckley, "that prices realised at charity auctions do not always indicate the true state of the market. Prices may be somewhat—inflamed, let us say—by a rare uncontrolled spasm of generosity on the part of bidders—in the public view!—for a good cause."

"So cynical, my dear Harriet!" said Miss Grant. "But never mind; let us go on. The next figure I have to report is from 1830, when Miss Anning sold her famous plesiosaur to Lord Cole, the Irish MP, for, let me see . . . two hundred guineas."

"Two hundred ten pounds," said Hugh. "That was a very important plesiosaur, as I believe. The first *Plesiosaurus macrocephalus.*"

"So it was," said Miss Grant. "Does anything remain in that teapot, Harriet?"

"The merest drop," said Miss Buckley, demonstrating over Miss Grant's cup. "But I have already rung for more."

"Then, in 1834," continued Miss Grant, "we know of the British Museum's acquisition of Mr Thomas Hawkins's entire collection—twenty tons, or so, of saurian fossils—for the sum of twelve hundred fifty pounds."

"Now, there is a figure to chime sweetly in one's ears!" said Hugh.

"I daresay it did not chime quite so sweetly in Mr Hawkins's, however; for he had at first asked four thousand pounds for them; but agreed that they should be valued by two experts. And the experts—Dr Buckland and Dr Mantell—independently of one another, both arrived at a figure of twelve hundred fifty pounds."

"Independently! Give me leave to doubt that," said Hugh.

"Even so, when the museum's curator finally got a look at the fossils, he cried foul, upon discovering how much of the collection was made up of imaginative plaster 'restorations,' not actual fossil bones," said Miss Buckley.

"Oh, but that came to nothing," said Miss Grant. "Mr Hawkins had never made any secret about it, and Dr Buckland assured the trustees that his valuation had accounted for the plaster reconstructions. No, it was money well spent, that twelve hundred fifty pounds."

The maid entered, bearing a kettle of steaming water. "That will never do," said Miss Buckley to her. "These leaves have given their utmost; it would be injustice to ask any further effort—or effect— from them. We don't want hot water; you may tell Mme Mouchy that we want tea itself, a fresh pot of it. I beg your pardon, Julia; do go on."

"But by 1835, it seems, the general depression was weighing upon the market for fossils, too. In that year, Miss Anning parted with a perfect ichthyosaur, four feet and a half in length, to Dr Adam Sedgwick for a mere fifty pounds."

"Oh, Dr Sedgwick!" exclaimed Constantia. "I cannot help but dislike even the arrogant and sarcastic sound of his name; and I daresay that poor Miss Anning's fossil must have been worth considerably more."

"I had no idea that you had so little opinion of Dr Sedgwick! Do you know him?" asked Miss Buckley.

"Oh—no; but I have reason to believe that he has treated a friend of mine—an acquaintance—ungenerously, and unjustly," explained Constantia, in some confusion.

"And, most recently of all," continued Miss Grant, "we have seen a price list of Miss Anning's from just two years ago—1844—when she was offering an excellent ichthyosaur, six feet in length, in a matrix of black clay, for fifteen pounds. For all I know, it may still be on her hands."

"Unsold, at fifteen pounds!" said Hugh. "That is discouraging."

It was Mme Mouchy herself who brought in another pot of tea. Miss Buckley promptly poured an inch of this fresh tea into her cup. The tea was nearly colourless; a pale watery tan. "Regardez, madame, s'il vous plaît," said Miss Buckley, indicating the sorry stuff to the landlady.

Mme Mouchy retorted, "Tiens, mademoiselle must exercise patience a little, and allow the pot to steep some moments longer. Voyons, there is an abundance of tea leaves in the pot, leaves of excellent quality." She lifted the lid of the pot to show that it was indeed swimming in leaves; choked by leaves. "It is the most choice of teas, un thé du soir, a tea most raffiné, a tea which can be appreciated only by those of the most advanced taste, not a coarse brackish tea such as satisfies the low tastes of the English shopkeepers, no indeed! But a tea for cultivated persons. However, if mademoiselle is unable to appreciate . . ."

Here Mme Mouchy swooped, as if to remove the teapot—but Miss Grant intervened, saying, "You may leave it with us, madame. Yes, thank you. Good evening!" she added, and closed the door firmly behind the landlady. "You know very well it is no use arguing with her, Harriet," she added, returning.

English guests were not particularly welcome in some boarding-houses, because they drank tea, expensive tea, in such ruinous quantities. But thrifty Mme Mouchy had overcome this difficulty with a little stratagem of her own. Each morning after breakfast, she removed from the sideboard her large square gilded white porcelain teapot—drained now of tea—and carried it downstairs in her own hands to the kitchen. There she would shake out the spent leaves carefully onto a pan, spread them, and place them into the oven to dry. She had learned even to toast them judiciously, for better colour. These toasted leaves then performed again that same evening, in the silver-plated after-dinner teapot. Her cook was in on the secret, but Mme Mouchy imagined that her guests had no inkling; supposed that they, being English, were devoid of palate. In fact, they knew very well; it was notorious that tea taken after dinner chez Mme Mouchy had no power to revive. Those who looked forward to a good night's sleep partook safely of Madame's thé du soir; but those who wanted stimulation—for study, for conviviality, for amour—knew to take their after-dinner tea elsewhere, or ask for coffee instead.

"It amuses me, though, to provoke her," said Miss Buckley.

"The fact is, you are insulted by her supposition that we are too stupid to detect her fraud. And, worse still, you don't like to be referred to as 'mademoiselle' in that particular way of hers," said Miss Grant. "Do you imagine that she will change?"

"Certainly not; no one ever does. Humankind may change, may

indeed progress! But individuals cannot," said Miss Buckley. "That is why we all must die: to make way for the new and improved individuals who are coming along behind us—such as our splendid Livia; such promise! Now, Julia, you may quarrel with me later if you like, in private; but let us not quarrel before friends. I shall now change the subject. Mr Stevenson, you must insist, as a condition of the sale to Professor de Blainville, upon its being called 'the Stevenson plesiosaur,' not 'the de Blainville plesiosaur'! It is inexpressibly provoking to hear those exquisite marbles removed from the Parthenon referred to as 'the Elgin marbles'—as though that plunderer Lord Elgin had brought them into existence!"

"But despite what Mme Mouchy may suppose, we did not make this plesiosaur, Miss Buckley; we only found it. We can take no more credit for its existence than Lord Elgin can take for the existence of 'his' marbles."

"No, but it was you who found it, and unearthed it, where no one else had; and it is high time that the humble finders of fossils— miners, quarrymen, ditchdiggers, farmers—received due credit for what they unearth. It can only be a careless, presumptuous, contemptuous disregard for an undistinguished female which prevents the savants from openly and publicly naming Miss Anning as the finder of so many of the most astonishing fossils of the last thirty years."

"May it not be a respectful reticence? A tender regard for the delicate sensibilities of the fair sex?" suggested Constantia. "What respectable woman likes for her name to be bandied about in public?"

"Let us dismiss such misplaced modesty as that! I am not so foolishly modest!" said Miss Buckley.

"No, indeed, Harriet; no one would accuse you of modesty. But others may differ," said Miss Grant. "It is conceivable, at least, that the savants respectfully assume—"

"Or pretend to assume—" interrupted Miss Buckley.

" . . . that Miss Anning is sufficiently modest to shun notoriety!" finished Miss Grant loudly.

"Or they wish to imply that she ought to be!" declared Miss Buckley, more loudly still. "But you, Mr Stevenson, need not conceal your name."

"Not while I remain in France, at any rate."

Constantia let herself spend a day in pleasant dreams of riches, successes, good fortune. She dreamt not a castle in the air, but quite the opposite: a pit in the earth. Oh, that quarry in the Cévennes! If ever a capital sum were to fall into their hands, she and Hugh would not hesitate for an instant; they would buy that quarry. Hugh often lay awake nights, thinking, calculating, planning how best to work it, if it were his. And why? Because (he had explained to Constantia) every printer and publisher in Europe and America was laying out substantial sums for lithographic stone: those slabs of exquisitely fine-grained limestone on which illustrations were drawn and inked, for printing. It was true that the slabs could be re-used many times (by grinding and sanding, to erase previous images, thus preparing the stone to receive new ones)—but still the world's appetite for printed images, and for the stone from which to print them, continued to grow, insatiable.

At present, every block of this prodigiously fine limestone originated from the quarries of Solnhofen, in Bavaria. The supply was small; the demand was vast and still increasing; the owners of those Bavarian quarries had become very rich indeed. French self-regard demanded a similar resource within its own borders. Hugh, after quitting the employ of Brassey & Mackenzie, had gone out to investigate quarries throughout France. He had identified one particular pit in the southern mountains—now little-worked, because the two elderly brothers who owned it were in failing health—as holding extraordinary promise. He was certain that this particular Cévennes quarry could, under careful working, produce satiny, lithographic-quality limestone. The two elderly brothers were willing to part with their holdings for a sum which did not seem impossible; and had executed an agreement to sell the quarry to no one but him, if he could raise sufficient capital to exercise his option by the end of the year. This year: 1846.

The Useless Rubble—now the Precious Trove—was moved once more: packed, laden onto a carrier's wagon, and hauled to the Muséum—to Miss Grant and Miss Buckley's well-lit workroom; there to be laid out to best advantage, and offered for sale to the holder of the Muséum's chair of comparative anatomy, Professor Henri-Marie Ducrotay de Blainville.

But from Hugh's manner of coming in, on the evening after his meeting with Professor de Blainville, Constantia perceived immediately that their hopes were to be dashed.

"He is not eager to buy," said Hugh, throwing himself into the only chair.

"He hopes to induce you to part with it for less than it is worth," said Constantia.

"He says it is of very little value."

"What preposterous nonsense!"

"He declares that the market has been sinking for several years now—but the truth is that the funds for acquisitions have been sadly depleted by his recent frenzied purchases of mastodons and mammoths from the Americas. Mastodons, I tell you! And mammoths!"

"Does he make any offer at all? Does he name a sum?"

"He . . . suggests that I might like to donate our trove to the Muséum, for the benefit of science."

"Donate! How dare he? You to donate these hard-won fruits of your own labour, your own enterprise? A year of your own labour, and the expenses you have incurred—not to mention the risks you have run! Does he forget that some unfortunates among us must work for our bread? Were we all of us born with silver spoons to our mouths? What can he imagine, this Henri-Marie Ducrotay de Blainville? He mistakes you, perhaps, for Sir Hugh DuStevenson de Coquet?"

By morning, Constantia's indignation had spawned a practical suggestion. "Supposing we were to publish its description ourselves?" she said, as soon as Hugh stirred beside her in their bed. "In time for the conference? Meticulously described, exquisitely illustrated—and offered for sale. There it is already, in Miss Grant and Miss Buckley's workroom, under their very camera. No one could engrave more exquisite plates of it than Miss Buckley. And you must write its description."

"Me? I am no one. No one at all. A stone-mason."

"And William Smith—'Strata' Smith, I mean—was only a surveyor; but his geological maps of England have won the highest esteem. Deservedly."

"Oh, esteem, aye! So highly esteemed was his map that a pack of unscrupulous printers instantly copied it, and republished it, without paying him a penny! Esteem for his map did not save him from debtor's prison. What use is posthumous acclaim?"

Presently, Constantia said, "Supposing it were published anonymously?"

"Oh, well . . . Anonymously."

"A newly-unearthed fossil of surpassing interest—text and plates of the highest caliber—the seller anonymous—all inquiries to be directed to you. I daresay the savants, when they gather here next month, would find it irresistible."

17

I N 1827, Muhammed Ali of Egypt had presented to Charles X
of France a young female giraffe. Delivered by ship to Marseille,
this docile giraffe had then been led the 900 kilometers to Paris
on her own four feet, accompanied every step of the way by the
elderly naturalist Étienne Geoffroy Saint-Hilaire, on his own (two)
feet. She had caused a sensation in every town she passed. In Paris
she took up residence at the menagerie, where Parisians in their tens
of thousands—tout le monde—came to gaze at her. She was called
Zarafa ("giraffe" in Arabic, so clever); and was widely admired for her
grace and beauty. Alas, in January 1845 the lovely Zarafa died, at the
age of twenty. But the taxidermists of Paris did their best, and before
long, a well-preserved Zarafa appeared again in public, now to grace
the lofty entrance hall of the Muséum, as celebrated in death as she
had been in life.

Constantia was carrying Livia through this busy echoing hall one
wet day in April—having just delivered a letter from Cévennes to
Hugh, who was assisting the Misses Grant and Buckley in their
Muséum workroom— when she was brought to a standstill by a piping vibrant young voice piercing through the hubbub. Utterly famil-

iar, in a Scotch-inflected English that soared above the murmuring of the French, the voice said, "But why such a very long neck, Mamma, when it might have accomplished the same end by growing very long legs instead?"

At once Constantia turned, scanning the crowd gathered around the far side of Zarafa's plinth, and—beneath the giraffe's belly—found the speaker: Tuckie. Of course.

With her mother—whose eyes met Constantia's, at that very moment.

Delight bloomed simultaneously across these three faces.

Exclamations of astonishment and joyful embraces were followed by explanations. For a treat, Mr Chambers had brought the two of them with him to Paris, where he was celebrating his forty-fourth birthday (two months early, it must be admitted) by attending the international conference at the Muséum. While he reveled, day after day, in hearing the world's savants read aloud their learned papers in geology and paleontology, Tuckie and Mrs Chambers were walking Paris's avenues and boulevards, regaling themselves with novelties and delights, for the eye and for the palate.

"Mrs MacAdam, did you notice?" said Tuckie, turning her head from side to side, to show her profile. "It is the very first bonnet I've ever had from a shop, new just for me, not handed down from my sisters! A Paris bonnet!"

"Exceedingly elegant, and suits you admirably," said Constantia. "What will your sisters say, poor dears?"

"We have bought rabbit muffs for them," said Tuckie. "Or Daddy did, rather."

"A pity about the rain," said Constantia. "You cannot think how often I have blessed you, Mrs Chambers, for this handsome cloak, during this coldest and wettest of springs—but it is unfortunate that the weather is so unpleasant for your visit. The charms of Paris are not so evident from under an umbrella, whilst one's stockings are being splashed."

"Oh, but damp stockings are nothing to us," Tuckie assured her.

"We're hardier than that, Mamma and I—indeed, it was snowing the day we left Edinburgh. Paris feels quite like the tropics, by comparison; and this warm rain like the monsoon, as I suppose. It was you who told us of the monsoon, Mrs MacAdam. How we have missed you, ever since you went away! And to think of finding you and Livie here! Livie, Livie, such a big plump girl now—look at you! Do you remember me, Livie? Of course she does! See her smile! What pretty teeth she has got, too!"

"We have acquired a great stock of presents to carry home, quite a merchant's cargo," Mrs Chambers was saying, "but in all of Paris, I have not been able to find a suitable present for my husband. He tells me he wants nothing but a new surtout, to replace his old one, now too much worn to be presentable. Of course I have ordered one for him, but I do desire to give him something handsome and impractical as well."

"I understand: no quotidian necessity, but glorious superfluity," said Constantia.

"And, as it happens, a modest legacy has just fallen to me, my own to use as I like; entirely unexpected, left me by an acquaintance who recently passed away. Oh! but you knew her yourself, now that I think of it—for you must remember Lady Janet!—who was taken to her heavenly rest most unexpectedly, soon after the New Year."

Constantia doubted that Lady Janet was constitutionally capable of heavenly rest; it was far easier to imagine her setting an example of virtuous industry for the angels there—if there she was.

"You may imagine our astonishment at learning not only that poor Lady Janet had anything to leave—but that Nina and I were among her legatees!" Mrs Chambers was saying. "To Nina she bequeathed her japanned cabinet—not yet finished inside one of the door panels, however—and with a moderate sum, on the condition that Nina should finish its decoration. After consideration, Nina has accepted the bequest, and is inking the final panel with meticulous care—but with a design which Lady Janet would never have approved, for it is an anatomical rendering of the human hand—holding sprigs of opium poppy, in bud, bloom, and seed. Aye, it is rather grotesque, but inside the cabinet door, you know, it will seldom be seen. The bequest left to me, however, is without strings, and is just that ideal sum which is too great to be squandered, yet too small to be responsibly invested. It is just such a sum as will enable me to surprise my frugal husband with the present he deserves, but never expects, and never seeks for himself—if only I could find precisely the right article."

"You are in the right city for marvelous presents, to be sure."

"We have been astonished by the opulence of the shops in the rue St Honoré and rue de Rivoli. We have inspected every gold watch and chain in the city; and the most remarkable top-hats, which would be the wonder of Edinburgh. I was tempted for one entire day by an antique Etruscan jug; and another day by a curious Egyptian alabaster figure with a dog's head. I considered an orrery, but I was not certain of its accuracy. Tuckie was enchanted by the stuffed baby zebra we saw at Deyrolle's. I nearly made up my mind to have a handsome old set of Napier's bones—for making calculations, you know—which were said to have belonged to Voltaire. But I held back, for none of these struck me as the Very Thing, and I was beginning to despair when, last evening, Mr Chambers came in with this little handbill which he had picked up here, at the conference." From inside her muff she drew out a leaflet and unfolded it.

Constantia, who knew it instantly, felt a thrill run through her.

"Handsomely illustrated, too," Mrs Chambers was saying. "It describes an extraordinary fossil, only just discovered, rather like a Chinese puzzle, it seems: one creature preserved inside another—if I understand the French correctly, which is far from certain. It was plain that he was utterly smitten, though he never thinks of spending anything on his own pleasures. How could I have been so slow to think of it? Not Napier's bones, no; but bones of quite another sort! It is offered at a price very near what I am able to pay; and inquiries, it says here, are to be directed to a M. Stevenson, to be heard of at this Muséum. I daresay that with a name like Stevenson, this monsieur may even speak English. If only I could make the porter understand me, and direct me! But no; he refuses to understand my French; apparently I am no more intelligible than an orangutan, although Mam'selle has always assured me that my pronunciation is no worse than that of other Scots ladies. Perhaps he would be obliged to understand you, Mrs MacAdam?"

"Let us dispense with the porter entirely," said Constantia. "I know just where Mr Stevenson is to be found. I assure you that he speaks English perfectly, and nothing could better please me than to introduce him to you. No, it is no trouble at all; come this way, pray," she said, leading Mrs Chambers and Tuckie out of the high echoing hall, around a corner, and behind a screen, to a jib door which opened into a low passage. "Yes, I know Mr Stevenson—rather well. As a matter of fact," said Constantia, shutting the door behind them, "he is my husband."

Mrs Chambers was not the first to approach Mr Stevenson wishing to see his spectacular fossil. There had been more or less frank interest on the part of at least three others. The first of these had promptly tendered a rather low offer, hoping to snap it up at a bargain price in early-bird style. The second, known to represent a minor European royal personage possessed of- -or by—a burgeoning collection of fossils, had sent an enthusiastic account to his principal, and was now anxiously awaiting instructions. The third had made several disparaging remarks as to the preparation and cleaning of the fossil; then offered Mr Stevenson a small sum to withdraw it from the open market for a fortnight, an inducement which Mr Stevenson had declined.

Mrs Chambers was another sort of buyer altogether. She saw everything to praise and nothing at all to criticise in the fossil itself: its beauty! its importance! the excellence of its preparation! She must have it; her husband certainly ought not to have to live another day without it. There followed indeed some quibblings over price. Mrs Chambers insisted that it was worth rather more than Mr Stevenson asked; she would never forgive herself if they would not accept a premium above his asking price. Mr Stevenson, however, declared himself unable—really not within his power—to accept from the friend and benefactress of his wife and child, even so much as his original asking price; the price for so kind a friend was of course rather less. Mrs Chambers argued that it was not herself but Mrs MacAdam—ah, Stevenson!—who had acted the part of friend and benefactress; a debt that never could be repaid . . . and so on.

But with the encouragement and aid of Misses Grant and Buckley they came eventually to a compromise, settling upon the original asking price; and the Stevensons—and the Misses Grant and Buckley too—agreed to come as guests to Mr Chambers's celebratory dinner some evenings hence, at the restaurant called Les Trois Frères, at the Palais Royale.

On their way out of the Muséum, Constantia offered to lead Mrs Chambers to the assembly rooms where the conference was under way, saying, "I daresay that you in particular, at least as much as your husband, would like to hear the learned papers read; Tuckie and I might amuse ourselves meanwhile by inspecting the displays in the exhibit hall. There are some marvels to be seen."

Mrs Chambers only smiled faintly, and shook her head.

Constantia tried again: "Indeed, I am surprised, Mrs Chambers, that you do not take your place by his side. You have, after all, a far more than ordinary interest, and expertise, in these matters."

"Oh, not I. One can hear enough of that sort of thing," declared Mrs Chambers. "My husband comes in each evening eager to tell the news; overflowing with it. A few years ago, it was the titanic clash between the diluvialists and the fluvialists; and then there was the Great Devonian Controversy, satisfactorily settled at last. But the great revelations of this conference, I gather, are furnished by Mr Agassiz and his party, with their mounting evidences of glaciers practically everywhere; my husband is beside himself with joy about the deeply scratched bedrock atop our very own Corstorphine Hill, just outside of Edinburgh, and vows to go inspect these telling glacial gouges for himself, just so soon as we shall have returned home."

Was this not a decided—if tactful—rebuff? But as Mrs Chambers had never demanded to know Constantia's secrets, Constantia felt bound to accord her an equivalent deference. In any case, Mr Chambers was apparently reporting the proceedings to her, in some detail.

The Stevensons, having accepted Mrs Chambers's (formerly Lady Janet's) good money for the Precious Trove, packed the fossil stones once more into their crates; gave notice to Mme Mouchy; and, trying to subdue a giddy and premature sense of triumph, set an appointment for a day early in May to meet the sellers of that Cévennes quarry in the presence of notaire and avocat, for purposes of conveyance.

It was quick work to sort through their scanty personal goods. Of her remaining dress lengths of bizarres, Constantia set aside one—a reciprocal stripe based upon planaria, in gold and mauve—as a present for Miss Buckley, who had particularly admired it. The remainder could be sold to one of the maisons de confection, which proffered ready-made clothes to the middling classes. Those of Hugh's old shirts worn beyond repair would go to ragpickers. Wrapped in the oldest of these, at the back of a drawer, was a book she had never come across before. "What is this book, my dear?" she asked Hugh who, seated beneath the window, was reckoning yields in his works-plan for the new quarry. She read aloud the imprint on the spine: "MATTHEW ON NAVAL TIMBER AND ARBORICULTURE. Do you take an interest in such subjects?"

"Oh, that!" said he ruefully, as she passed it to him. "I had nearly succeeded in forgetting all about it. Indeed, the very sight of it is a reproach to me—for it does not belong to me. No, it must have been lent me at the time I was taking my leave from Scotland in 'forty-two . . . but my departure, you know, was so exceedingly hasty and fraught—so near a thing, with so many nocturnal flittings between hiding places arranged by Chartist friends who preferred, for their safety and mine, to remain anonymous—that, while I am convinced it came into my hands at that time, I do not know who lent it—and I have been unable to return it to its owner. As neither timber nor arboriculture holds for me any charm, I cannot fathom why it should have been bestowed on me. But here is a bookmark, still . . . Well! How very odd! Do you know, my dear, I was thinking not long ago of these very phrases, these very words—though I could not remember where I had read them. Listen: 'As the field of existence is limited and pre-occupied, it is only the hardier, more robust, better suited to circumstance individuals, who are able to struggle forward to maturity, these inhabiting only the situations to which they have superior adaptation and greater power of occupancy than any other kind; the weaker, less circumstance-suited, being prematurely destroyed.' How unruly a servant is memory! Mine is, to be sure. Presumably the owner wanted his property returned to him, for he has written his name here, on the fly-leaf—but I do not remember ever meeting him, nor have I ever heard of Spring Gardens."

Constantia took the book back again. On the fly-leaf was written, in a large bold hand:

J. Gunn. his Book.
Spring Gardens.

"But," said Constantia, after an electric moment, "I know Spring Gardens. I know Mr Gunn, too. And furthermore, I know who will be so good as to carry his book back to Scotland, and return it to him."

(Could this, too, happen by chance? Could it?

It could. And here is the proof: It did happen.)

Meanwhile, there was a dinner to be eaten, at Les Trois Frères. Constantia's best gown of plain indigo silk broadcloth was just good enough, although she knew that she looked as sober as a Quakeress in it, and not at all Parisian. Hugh's best coat, perhaps no longer quite impeccable by daylight, could still pass muster by evening's gaslight and candlelight; and his hat was above reproach. Leaving Livia for the first time in the charge of Mme Mouchy, they splurged on a fiacre to deliver them unspattered to the Palais Royale—unspattered, though slightly crushed, for Miss Grant and Miss Buckley crowded into the fiacre with them. Constantia carried Mr Gunn's book, wrapped in paper and tied with twine, to pass to Mrs Chambers.

Behind a sort of lectern at the entrance to the splendid dining salon there presided a glossy and ceremonious maître d'hôtel—connoisseur of every nuance of dress and deportment—who received them in English even before they spoke, and bowed them to a table near the gilded boiscrie where Mr and Mrs Chambers were already seated. The white napery was luminous damask; the faceted wine and water glasses glittered in the light of massy ormolu gasoliers; the silver forks and spoons gleamed. At a signal from Mr Chambers, a waiter poured iced champagne into each glass, and then Mr Chambers raised his glass, saying: "By rights, of course, we ought to be drinking wormwood and gall tonight, not champagne—for this, you will surely have remembered, is the centennial of the catastrophe at Culloden. Aye, but it is: the sixteenth of April, the year 'forty-six. But let us not dwell tonight upon strife and sorrow; although every human endeavour must meet the same end, there may be numerous occasions for rejoicing meanwhile— and this is most certainly one of them. A friend rediscovered and a mystery elucidated—" (he bowed toward Constantia), "valuable new acquaintances gained—" (toward Hugh and the Misses Grant and Buckley), "and a most remarkable vestige of former worlds, newly brought to light—" (Hugh, again), "and, astonishingly, into my own possession!" (toward his wife). "My wonder at these unlooked-for events is exceeded only by my delight in them. I beg you all will drink a glass with me, in honour of remarkable coincidences, and accidental discoveries!"

The room was high, luxuriously warm, extravagantly illuminated;

and sounded of very civilized revelry: of the tinkling laughter and flutey voices of French ladies; of their fans, their bracelets; a general rustling and preening and striking of becoming attitudes, which might be demure or coquettish; arch or artless; resisting or yielding. Frenchmen were always far more attentive to their ladies than were Englishmen to theirs, because Frenchmen never felt abashed or shy or awkward in feminine company. They knew themselves to be the most dashing, fascinating, admirable, clever, brave, handsome beings in the world; hadn't their mothers and aunts and even their sisters convinced them of this, each and every garçon of them, since their earliest boyhoods? With plenty to say, they bent toward their companions, unfrightened by those rosy plump arms and shoulders and necks.

But not all the voices were French. For Englishmen abroad, a dinner at Les Trois Frères was all but obligatory; one could scarcely claim to have been at Paris at all, unless one had dined at Les Trois Frères; or else the Café de Paris; or, preferably, both. In the bustle of meeting, greeting, and seating, Constantia had had no attention to spare for the party seated at the next table further along, behind her chair; now, however, she could hear them from time to time: a mixed party of Englishmen and Englishwomen. "By dint of triple shifts, and unrelenting push . . ." a man's voice was saying behind her, in English.

Constantia applied herself to the carte de menu before her. Mr or Mrs Chambers had ordered the dinner in advance, so there were no decisions to be made, but only the pleasures of anticipation and enjoyment. Soup appeared: potage à la reine. Mr Chambers was saying to Hugh, "It would be impossible, Mr Stevenson, for you to sate my appetite or satisfy my curiosity as to the details of your discovery and your excavations. I crave to hear even the most minute particulars; and do now beg the pardon, in advance, of anyone present who may not share my enthusiasm. Tell me, sir: when, and where, and how did you first come across it?"

Hugh plunged deeply into this riveting subject, while Mr Chambers penciled notes into the dog-eared notebook drawn from his waistcoat pocket. Miss Grant and Miss Buckley and Mrs Chambers

were all equally fascinated, not only during the soup but also throughout the turbot in hollandaise sauce which in good time succeeded it.
Constantia's thoughts strayed eventually to Livia: How did she and
old Mme Mouchy like each other?

"Well, yes; I have been contemplating writing it up—while
redacting, of course, the precise location," Mr Chambers was saying,
as tiny lamb cutlets in a chestnut purée presently replaced the turbot.
"To send to the journals for publication; perhaps to the *Edinburgh
Philosophical Journal* or, better still, to one of the London quarterlies.
I cannot claim any particular qualification, of course; mine is merely
the ardent interest of the amateur; but what a coup! Oh no, sir; this
is not at all the sort of thing my brother and I ought to publish; there
are better places for such a subject than *Chambers's Edinburgh Journal*.
Not to say, pearls before swine, exactly; but thistles before Scotsmen,
perhaps. As for illustration, your very fine lithographs, Miss Grant
and Miss Buckley, could scarcely be bettered; and I should be most
obliged to you for permission to republish them."

"You shall have the very stones themselves, to carry off to Scotland," promised Miss Grant. "Their additional weight will be nothing, among Mr Stevenson's stones."

"I should like to stipulate, however, that the line 'J. Grant et H.
Buckley, grav.' ought to appear with them," said Miss Buckley.

"We are not bashful as to fame, you must understand," said Miss
Grant. "As some ladies are."

"And some gentlemen, too," said Mr Chambers.

Lobster in mayonnaise now appeared before them, and for a long
moment these exquisite morsels so gratified their palates that silence
fell. Too well-bred, however, to comment on food, they soon succeeded in bringing forth words once more. "What an unnecessary
deal of trouble it has turned out," said Hugh, "all this hauling, of all
this stone! Over leagues of ocean! Up miles of river! If only it had
been possible to forsee that my ancient beasts were destined to return
to Edinburgh—so near their place of origin—I might have saved
myself, and you, sir, a quantity of trouble and expense."

"It was far from destined, however," said Miss Grant. "Matters might have turned out very differently. How disappointed he was, the envoy from—"

"Ahem!" interrupted Miss Buckley, in a fit of discretion.

"—to learn that he had not been quick enough! that, while awaiting instructions, he had lost his opportunity! Yes, I saw him," continued Miss Grant; "something very like tears welling up in his eyes; I nearly pitied him. At this very moment, Mr Stevenson, your creatures might very well have been on their way to—"

"Ahem!"

"Prague!" cried Miss Grant triumphantly.

"Prague; so they might," said Hugh. "Well, I am glad they are not; glad that my creatures are to return to their native shore after all. Not all of us can do that," he added softly.

"Not yet. The time will come, however," said Mrs Chambers, "and before long, I trust. When the Six Points have been gained at last, and the franchise extended to all—as it inevitably must—then you champions of the newly-enfranchised, returning at last from honourable exile, then you will be welcomed and fêted and—and revered!—as the heroes you are, and always were!"

"Hear, hear! To the inevitable day! To our champions! Our heroes!" said Miss Buckley, for her glass was newly refilled, now with Chambertin.

"To the Six Points, Mr Stevenson," said Mrs Chambers, raising her glass to Hugh.

"Oh well! To the Six Points," he said, and drank with her, flushed but pleased. "You are an optimist, then, Mrs Chambers; a believer in progress."

"In development, rather," said Mrs Chambers. "Which is not quite the same thing, is it?" The wreck of the lobsters was taken away, to be replaced by cardoons almondine.

The party of English people at the table behind Constantia was getting noisier. "You had some colossal luck there, Mackenzie," declared one of them, too loudly.

The retort, behind Constantia, was forceful, devoid of any Scottish accent: "Luck be damned; nothing at all to do with luck. Hard work—experience—foresight—diligence!"

"Oh aye, all that, I grant you . . . and confounded lucky besides. If anyone had been killed—"

"Never any likelihood of that."

"Nonsense. Matters might have turned out very differently. I say it was luck."

"Oh, do get down from your high horses, you two," said an Englishwoman's voice. "This is not the moment for it. Anyone would suppose that you had been born and bred in America," she berated them, before her voice dropped to a murmur.

When Constantia glanced again at Hugh, she saw that he had changed. Whereas he had been happy, proud, and expansive—now, suddenly, he was not. His gaze seemed to be fixed upon Mrs Chambers, but she saw a muscle working in his jaw, just in front of his ear. "I cannot say what celebrated tombs a good tourist might visit when in Paris," Mrs Chambers was now saying, "but I, for my part, should very much like to contemplate the final resting place of Napoleon Bonaparte . . ."

Presently Hugh ventured a glance in Constantia's direction, but it was to look past her. In that moment Constantia guessed—no, knew to a certainty—that at the next table, behind her back, was the very man Hugh had been aching and dreading to meet once more: Mr William Mackenzie, the great railway contractor. This was the man who would not be told; the man whose obduracy and wilful arrogance and greedy haste had brought down the Barentin viaduct. Constantia willed the English party to rise, to leave: Go! Now! Or, at the very least—if you must talk loudly—talk of something else!

" . . . at Les Invalides?" asked Mrs Chambers—and into the moment's pause following her question, Mackenzie's loud voice rang out: " . . . a warrant for his arrest in Edinburgh, as it turns out, for criminal conspiracy! And, as quarryman, incompetent from first to last. Insolent, and insubordinate."

Instantly, Hugh had risen from his chair and placed both palms flat on the damasked table behind Constantia. He leaned down into Mackenzie's astonished red face and said in a hoarse furious voice, "Insolent, was it, to contradict the great Mackenzie regarding the sufficiency of that indurated chalk? Insubordinate, to refuse to quarry any more of it for use as footings? How dare you, Mackenzie! How dare you!"

"You!" exclaimed Mr Mackenzie—when at length he found his tongue. "And here, of all places! You had better get out. This is no place for blackguards!"

Hugh seized the under-edge of their table and braced his shoulders as though to overturn it—but then, though he trembled with rage, stayed his hand; only retorting hoarsely through clenched teeth, "I quite agree; no place for blackguards. Hadn't you better go away, then, instantly? Before you are removed—by some better man than yourself?"

Several waiters loomed up nearby; the maître d'hôtel approached smoothly, followed by a large footman. Silence had fallen over every table in the salon; all faces turned their way, all faces astonished, or delighted: pale oval French faces, open mouths, round eyes. How badly they behaved, these English! What barbarians they remained, each one! They were sometimes amusing to watch, however; like curs fighting in the street, n'est-ce pas? No, like bulls. Comme les John Bulls.

"Who in the world might this be?" said the other man at Mackenzie's table.

"This," said Mr Mackenzie, "is the quarryman I was just telling you of. The man I sacked."

"That you never did," retorted Hugh. "That is a lie. It was I who quit your employ, when you refused to credit my warnings. When you refused to hear the sober truth—when you presumed to threaten and insult me. Stand up, Mackenzie!"

"Give me the lie, will you? Insolent rascal! Do you dare?" cried the contractor, and rose, unsteadily.

It ended quickly, in an avalanche of broken porcelain, shattered glass, overturned chairs and tables, and a surprising quantity of blood, all from Mr Mackenzie's nose. The Parisians found it vastly entertaining.

(The parcel containing *On Naval Timber and Arboriculture*, which Constantia had set on the floor under her chair, was left in the wreckage beneath an overturned table. Constantia never thought of it again. Mrs Chambers and Mr Chambers never knew of its existence. Upon finding the book, the cleaners at Les Trois Frères would dispose of it to a second-hand bookseller on the Left Bank—on whose premises it would remain, foxing and mouldering, unwanted, unopened, unread, until destroyed by fire during the riots of 1871. Such would be the end of that particular copy—one of the two hundred copies printed, in 1831—of Mr Patrick Matthew's prodigious, motley, and peculiar book. It fell upon stony ground.)

"The truth is, they cannot help themselves, the callants, the darlings," said Mrs Chambers to Constantia the next morning. "You and I may deplore the necessity, but necessity it remains— to them. I confess that my husband approved, heartily! 'What else was to be done under the circumstances?' is what he said."

"Quite the Culloden, after all," said Constantia.

"Ah! but on this anniversary of that bloody disaster, righteousness and virtue prevailed, at last."

"Will you be admitted ever again to Les Trois Frères?"

"Never mind that; the Café de Paris will have us."

Sunshine streamed; it was the first fine day in weeks. Constantia, with Livia on her hip, had met Mrs Chambers and Tuckie at the entrance to the House for Fierce Animals at the Jardin des Plantes— for Tuckie longed to see the tigers.

"Such an odd notion, though, this 'honour,'" said Constantia, as they went inside.

"*Homo inflatus*," agreed Mrs Chambers. "The puffed-up earthling."

"And yet . . ." said Constantia, who felt somewhat ashamed of feeling a little pleased by Hugh's righteous anger, and by his virile prowess upon the occasion. "On the whole . . . well. It is confusing."

"Oh aye, it is," agreed Mrs Chambers comfortably.

There were two tigers in a large cage, both flat on their sides; only the tips of their tails moved: up; down; up; down; as regular as the pendulum of a clock. Constantia still felt her breath come short at the sight of these creatures, these wicked, cruel, devious, dangerous creatures, not nearly as somnolent as they pretended—for their furious flicking tails gave them away. Unwittingly she fingered the flat-backed pearl at the hollow of her collarbone. "Have you been to the Labyrinthe yet?" she asked, when she could bear no more. "No? Let us go there. Tuckie, you shall find the way up through the maze; you shall lead us all the way to the top of the mount. It is worth the climb, I promise you: my favourite place in all the garden."

After so much rain, the yew maze which coiled upward around the mount in the southwest corner of the Jardin des Plantes was at its best and cleanest, its tall dense needly walls a deep-shadowed vigorous black-green, shining. For once, no one else was there. The ascent was steep, and they promptly lost Tuckie, who ran ahead. Mrs Chambers had to stop very soon, to catch her breath. At Constantia's frown of concern, she winked, and confessed: "Another baby: I am only seven weeks gone, but already breathless, as you see; and must confess myself drained of any ambition."

"Let us go slowly and comfortably then," said Constantia. "That is marvelously good news!" Certainly the Chamberses had always been wonderfully punctual at producing babies. "I congratulate you. But I daresay that even a new baby will scarcely slow you down. I don't know how you manage to accomplish so much important and valuable work—in every sphere of life, too."

"Oh, but I accomplish so very little, it seems to me, and that only in the narrowest domestic sphere," panted Mrs Chambers. "And for even that little, I rely upon the good hearts and diligent hands of so many others. If not for Mam'selle and Hopey, we should be lost. Nina, too, has been increasingly valuable to me of late; she has quite taken over the household accounts. I tell her it is very good practise for anything her future may hold. My correspondence, I am glad to say, is less burdensome than it was at Spring Gardens, now that we have returned to Edinburgh. How should I ever have managed there, if not for you? You, who came so selflessly to our rescue, when I did not know where else to turn."

The resolutely self-effacing modesty of this reply struck Constantia as excessive, disingenuous and unnecessarily deceptive. Offended, she set off again, leading the way up between the spiraling green walls in silence. Presently, though, having mustered her resolve, she halted and turned to say, "With me at least, Mrs Chambers, you need not turn away all praise; you need not deflect all credit. You need not fear that I will ever disclose your secret to anyone, unless with your consent. But I do think that, between us—after all we have been to one another, and done for one another—you might drop your guard, just for a moment, in private, and hear me, at least, in a spirit of frankness. You need not reply."

"Whatever do you mean?" gasped Mrs Chambers, breathless again already. "I do not understand you! Ought I to beg your pardon?" she asked, looking as sincerely perplexed as anyone could.

"What I mean, of course, is that 'burdensome correspondence'— as you so modestly refer to it. 'Correspondence' indeed! No, Mrs Chambers, I know very well that it is not mere long letters that have engaged— nay, engrossed—your energies! But rather, your two remarkable books! Your extraordinary books!"

"Books! What books?"

"Oh, do stop it! Yes, books! Of course, books: *Vestiges*, and *Explanations*! Books which have limned the shape of all Creation, for so many readers! You need not look like that, dear Mrs Chambers! Of course I have said nothing to anyone—not even to my husband— but I guessed the identity of their author some time ago. When one inhabits the same house—when one borrows the same books—

enjoys the companionship and the conversation, early and late—well, I should have been very dull indeed, Mrs Chambers, if I had failed to understand at last, that you are that anonymous author! You are that Great Unknown! Never fear; your secret is entirely safe with me. If you do not want it known, I will not let it be known; nothing could induce me to say a word to anyone. But the evidence, to one who has dwelt on the most intimate terms within your household for weeks and months, is unmistakable; irrefutable."

"Unmistakable! Yet you are quite mistaken!" Mrs Chambers let herself slump against the wall of yew, and laughed as though thoroughly enjoying a joke. But then she said, "Oh, my dear—do forgive me! But what evidence could you possibly have?"

Constantia summarized: the handwritten notes in that furiously annotated copy of the *Edinburgh Review*; those notes subsequently polished and published as *Explanations*; the distinctive expressions and phrases found in both *Vestiges* and *Explanations*, so characteristic of the Chambers family; Mrs Chamber's long ink-stained mornings spent sequestered in the library attending to her "heavy burden of correspondence"; and all the rest.

"Well; well!" said Mrs Chambers at last. "I do see how, and why, you have arrived at this conclusion. And yet I assure you, dear Mrs Stevenson, you are quite, quite, entirely mistaken."

Tuckie reappeared, running headlong. "Wrong way!" she cried—and disappeared again, up another path.

"Of course I have no right to ask you; to charge you with any Fitz-books," said Constantia, setting off again up the slope. "Indeed, I do not ask you. I only tell you that I do know. My conviction is unshaken, though you may feel yourself bound to deny it."

Panting, they attained at last the peak of the mount, the center of the spiral maze like the trailing arms of a galaxy—the graduated chambers of a nautilus—a whirlpool in the Esk at Musselburgh—an attentive listening pink ear.

The small high knoll was crowned by a gazebo, a wrought-iron confection set at top dead center: a wrought-iron nipple. Here they threw themselves gratefully onto the seat under the gazebo's open dome. From this lordly height there were fine views over much of the Jardin, northward toward the Seine. Tuckie, exulting, was swinging like an orangutan from one of the arches of the gazebo; and Livia, inspired, stood bobbing and bouncing ambitiously on her own two feet at Constantia's knees.

When Mrs Chambers had regained her breath, she said, "I solemnly declare to you, dear friend, that I am not the author of those books—deeply flattered though I am by your suspicion. I am not the mind behind them; I am only the hand, the amanuensis, the scribe. I think I may tell you so much as that."

"Do you mean that you took down the texts as heard by you?"

"That I heard a voice from on high? And transcribed it, Moseslike? No; I mean only that I copied out the entire manuscript so that the author's own handwriting might not be recognized and identified—by publishers, or typesetters, and so forth. And my same weary hand copied out all the correspondence relating to those books too, for the same reason: the corrections, the notes, the changes, the typesetting, the proofreading, the directions as to binding and distribution. It has indeed been a very heavy burden of correspondence, dear Mrs Stevenson; I make no evasion as to that."

To Constantia, this had the ring of truth. She said, "Must I relinquish, then, my fixed conviction?"

Mrs Chambers replied with a familiar phrase: "'The human faculties lead unavoidably to occasional error.'"

Constantia smiled, but said nothing. Side by side, the two of them surveyed the orderly green expanses and tidy hedged compartments of the Jardin. A breeze ruffled the treetops below, and flights of pigeons wheeled and turned against pale blue sky.

If Mrs Chambers was not the author of *Vestiges* and *Explanations*, who was?

Presently a quantity of small figures spilled out of the distant Muséum's monumental doorway onto the sun-warmed stone pavement in front of it. The last session of the conference concluded, the savants were emerging into the open spring afternoon. They looked like insects hatching out of some vast classical egg-case.

"There's Daddy!" cried Tuckie. "I see him! And there's Mr Stevenson, too!" Even at this distance, Constantia recognised Mr Chambers's characteristic gait—for his feet always hurt. Beside him, Hugh's stone-mason shoulders and arms were equally unmistakable.

"Dad! Daddy!" cried Tucky, waving madly, to no avail; her tiny piping voice floated up and away in the rising spring air, like that soaring balloon-boat in Lucknow, so long ago.

Constantia turned to Mrs Chambers and, saying nothing, only looked her question: He?

Saying nothing, Mrs Chambers only smiled her answer: a tiny smile; meaning, aye. Aye, my dear friend; just so!

Mr Gunn lay on his back, on the dirt floor of the doocot. He had crawled there upon regaining consciousness, to be out of the wind. Outside, that April wind blowing off the Forth battered at the eaves of the doocot. Inside, all was still but for the taffeta rustlings, the honey murmurings of the pigeons. Their bright round eyes peered down at him from their perches and nests which lined the rising circular walls, all above, all around. He was inside the Tower of Babel, looking up from the very bottom; and try as he might, he could not understand their murmurings. In through the pigeon-portals just under the roof there streamed tangible rays of sunshine. These rays illuminated a dung-spattered nest, empty; a lost feather, moving faintly as though it breathed; a bird's vivid pink foot, clutching; and, most fascinating of all, gorgeous glimmers of dust which circulated in the rise and the fall of the air.

That air. He could still breathe it. He breathed the superb odour of pigeon dung.

All of it—all—was so heartbreakingly beautiful. Therefore was his heart now breaking; and he could feel it happening. The crushing pain of it was beneath his notice.

Beauty, beauty. But why?

Am I not a Man? Have I not, therefore—in service to Beauty—laboured in this Garden all my life? And why? Did this distinguishing Sense render me better suited to circumstance? Did Beauty arm me for my strict ordeal?

Other words came, on familiar melody: Necessary to suppose; a part of a whole; a state in a Great Progress.

He could not suppose that. Of Redress there is none. Nothing lies in reserve.

Am I not a Man? Did I not, therefore, originate both Beauty and Justice? Worthy errors, both!

Outside the stone tower the wind suddenly rose, a magnificent blast like the beating of colossal wings; inside the stone tower the pigeons all at once opened their wings and took flight.

Amid this great rustling of wings, Gunn's mortal heart broke, all the way through.

The strict ordeal is finished.

Gravity relented, and off the Earth he fell; upward.

Afterword

I T IS ALMOST IMPOSSIBLE now to conceive how the world—the
cosmos—felt in 1845, when the anonymous *Vestiges of the Natural
History of Creation* burst upon the reading public. Patrick Matthew's *On Naval Timber and Arboriculture* of 1831, with its brilliant
little appendix, had escaped everyone's notice. Charles Darwin's mag-
isterial *On the Origin of Species* did not yet exist. It was a time previous
to knowing.

Try to remember being unable to read; that time just before you
got the knack of it. Here is the book, open on your knees. Here are
pictures, which are your friends, because they are quite intelligible. And here too are mysterious designs and signs called "letters,"
arranged according to some elusive protocol. Not random: they have
meaning; but how is that meaning to be unraveled? The world was
awash in magic, then; indeed, magic drenched everything, explained
everything. Then suddenly you learned to read, and the tide of magic
began its ebb; it has been subsiding ever since.

Try to remember when you apprehended for the first time that
the dirt beneath your feet is—contrary to all appearances—a spher-
ical planet called Earth. What did you make of that? What cosmos
did you construct in your mind? (Told that the Earth was round, like
a ball, I supposed it hollow, and concluded that we inhabit its safe

and enclosed interior surface; the luminous dome of sky overhead was evidently the far side. I remember still the wrenching difficulty of revising my cosmic views, at the age of four or five, when assured that we inhabit instead its exposed and vulnerable exterior surface. Could this be true? Such an inferior arrangement!)

Once a thing is known, there is no going back; no un-knowing it again.

In 1845, when he read *Vestiges*, Mr Darwin was unimpressed. But eventually he acknowledged its usefulness in preparing the public mind for the 1859 publication of his own great book. "In my opinion," he wrote, "it has done excellent service in this country in calling attention to the subject, in removing prejudice, and in thus preparing the ground for the reception of analogous views."

Mr Matthew's peculiar mongrel of a book *On Naval Timber and Arboriculture* escaped Mr Darwin's notice until 1860, when Mr Matthew drew it to his attention. Mr Darwin then inserted in the third and all subsequent editions of *On the Origin of Species* this statement: "I freely acknowledge that Mr Matthew has anticipated by many years the explanation which I have offered of the origin of species, under the name of natural selection."

Mr Matthew later wrote, "To me the conception of this law of Nature came intuitively as a self-evident fact, almost without an effort of concentrated thought. Mr Darwin here seems to have more merit in the discovery than I have had; to me it did not appear a discovery. He seems to have worked it out by inductive reason, slowly and with due caution to have made his way synthetically from fact to fact onwards; while with me it was by a general glance at the scheme of Nature that I estimated this select production of species as an a priori recognisable fact—an axiom requiring only to be pointed out to be admitted by unprejudiced minds of sufficient grasp."

Mr Robert Chambers's authorship of the sensational best-selling *Vestiges of the Natural History of Creation* and its sequel, *Explanations*, remained secret until after his death in 1871.